When Southern Girls Grow Old

ELIZABETH DOAK SHERMAN

WHEN SOUTHERN GIRLS GROW OLD
THREE HOMECOMINGS

2008

When Southern Girls Grow Old

ACKNOWLEDGEMENTS

Special thanks to Nancy Z. Lively for editorial services, to Brian Triesler for computer expertise, to Judy Caldwell for marketing management, and to all three for the TLC and patience they show the author.

Author photo: Brian Triesler

For All Wise Women Who Grow Younger As They Age,
Especially For "Group," Janey, And Jerri

PROLOGUE

This volume follows the Horton girls—Mavis, Sammie Jo, and Elmira—as they move into old age. Despite differences in circumstance and temperament, they face the common challenge of becoming more truly and fully their best selves as the grow older. Their stories are about retirement and friendship, hurting and healing, aging and coming to grips, being old and being young, who's sane and who's crazy and who's just excited, and getting and giving love and having enough left over to forgive, if not forget.

Mavis's story previously appeared in a single volume entitled *Birds of a Feather*.

BIRDS OF A FEATHER

BOOK ONE

*"Keep a green bough in your heart,
and a singing bird will come."*

—-Old Confucian saying

PART ONE
Autumn

"The Gooses Are Honking!"

CHAPTER ONE

When Mavis retired, Annabelle came to visit, and that was something of a surprise. Mavis hadn't seen her in ages. Not since she herself had left Piney fifty odd years ago. Of course, she had heard from her, twice, both times when Mavis herself was in the hospital. Annabelle had been real thoughtful of her then, but Mavis had brushed her off. Told her there was no need for her to come. Later, when she was confined to the house recovering, she'd wished she had Annabelle for company, but she didn't call her. Kept a stiff upper lip instead. A few gallstones and stomach ulcers, perforated or not, were no reason to be a baby.

So Annabelle didn't come either time, and now, all of a sudden, here she was. The morning after Mavis's retirement dinner. Not that Mavis had called and told her she was retiring and invited her to the dinner. Oh, no, nothing like that. It wasn't the sort of thing at all to which she would have invited Annabelle, had she thought to do so, which, of course, she hadn't. The dinner was a dress-up affair at The Club, which sits atop Red Mountain and overlooks downtown Birmingham. It was hosted by Harrison P. Clarke II, Mavis's boss and owner of Harrison P. Clarke & Son Fine Jewelry, Inc., and his wife, Bitsy, not that Bitsy had anything to do with it besides ordering flowers and writing out place cards. Harrison saw to the arrangements and did his best to make an occasion of it. Made a speech, a toast really, and presented Mavis with an engraved watch, a Movado, quite nice actually, and the guests all applauded. Well, the staff did. They were the guests. The four employees besides Mavis, three clerks and Joseph, the custodian. Mavis was—had been—combination clerk and bookkeeper herself for forty years. Second in command, manager when Harrison wasn't there, although he'd never officially given her a title.

Anyway, that had been the farewell party, followed by a lonesome drive to her dark house in Homewood, all the time trying to keep an unwieldy arrangement of gladioli and carnations from turning over on the floorboard of the car. Mavis hadn't wanted the flowers to start with, but Bitsy wouldn't have it but that she take the damn centerpiece home with her. Tried to give her the leftover cake too, but here Mavis drew the line. Bitsy could damn well take the cake home herself and feed it to Harrison. She didn't have to act like Lady Bountiful feeding the poor and foist it off on Mavis.

So retirement was here. Work was over and done with. No looking back. No regrets, no second thoughts. No longer was Mavis a fixture, a reliable source of advice and assistance to customers and the boss's right hand, at Harrison Clarke Fine Jewelry. She was just Mavis Horton, retiree. She'd learn to live with it.

Then, the very next morning, Annabelle appeared. Out of the blue. Not that she wasn't welcome. Of course, she was. Maybe. Actually, Mavis didn't know whether she was welcome or not. She didn't have a chance to think about it. She'd never expected to see her again. Never thought about seeing her again. Who would, after all these years? And suddenly there she was. Standing on the porch with her suitcase.

Mavis opened the screen door. "Annabelle? What are you doing here?"

Mavis would have known her anywhere. Annabelle was sixty-five now, about to turn sixty-six, as was Mavis herself. Still she knew her. They looked enough alike to be twins, except Annabelle was, and always had been, pretty. Mavis didn't consider herself pretty, and never had. Plus Annabelle had always known how to make the most of what she had, even when they were pre-schoolers, playing dress up in the clothes Mavis's mother had left behind. Mavis chose the more sedate outfits, ones her mother might have worn to church had she gone, but Annabelle always jumped right in and picked the bright print dresses and high heels with ankle straps. Ankle-strap shoes had been the very thing in the 1940s.

Now Annabelle was standing on the porch in a bright red coat and high-heeled black boots. In spite of a few wrinkles, she looked much the same. She still had fluffy blond hair, an impish smile, and those blue eyes that could look right through Mavis, which is what they were doing now.

There was no need to say much. Mavis set Annabelle's suitcase in the house, put on her own coat, and they went on a walk around the block, just as they had when they were little girls. They would take walks together all over town. Piney was a little town, not even a county seat, and, in those days, nobody worried about strangers or traffic or terrorists' attacks. Children were turned loose, and everybody looked after them and told them when it was time to go home to supper. Sometimes when Grandma Horton would call out the kitchen door, "Mavis, come in and set the table," Annabelle would answer. "Mavis isn't here right now," she'd say, and Grandma would say, "All right, Annabelle, then you come in and set the table," and Annabelle would. She knew how Mavis hated setting the table. Then often Annabelle would set a place for herself and stay for supper.

So now they walked around the block as if nothing had happened and half a century hadn't gone by.

"Nice neighborhood," Annabelle said.

"You think so?" Mavis seemed uncertain.

"Sure. You going to stay here?"

"I don't know. I don't know my neighbors."

"How come?"

"Too busy. Working, you know. Five, sometimes six days a week. I mean I know the couple next door to speak to. Well, their little boy anyway. And others up and down the street wave."

"I like it here," Annabelle announced.

"You do?"

"Nice trees, pretty houses, not too big. Fenced backyards. Close to the grocery store."

"Well, yes," Mavis agreed.

"You could live a life here."

"I suppose." Mavis looked around as if, in the dozen years she had lived here, she had never seen the street before.

"I like it better than that apartment you used to have on Southside."

"You never came to see me in the apartment."

"I know. It was too crowded. Here you've got plenty of room. You could get a dog." Annabelle gave her a sideways look. "You've got a place for one."

"A dog? Really, Annie, I don't think so. I've never had a dog. I don't think I like them. All that barking, and getting up to let them in and out all the time. And that jumping up and down. No, no, a dog is definitely out."

"Look at it this way," Annabelle said. "We could take turns letting it in and out. And, when we take walks, we'd have an excuse. And people wouldn't think we were talking to ourselves. Besides, you've always wanted a dog and you know it."

"I have not."

"Yes, you have. You most certainly have. You are just too scared to admit it."

"Scared? Now why would I be scared?"

"Because of that stray puppy that bit you when we were four years old. We were playing in the side yard, remember? House. You were the mommy and I was the daddy, and you tried to pick up this dirty little dog and put him in the baby carriage. You dropped him, and he bit you on the foot."

"Oh yes."

"You still have the scar on your big toe."

"True." Mavis thought this over.

They walked in silence to the corner.

As they neared the house, Annabelle said, "Do you remember the day we met?"

"No," Mavis answered abruptly. "We've always known each other."

"No, we haven't."

"Well, I don't remember when we met."

"I do." Annabelle smiled.

"Well, aren't you Miss Know-It-All!"

Mavis walked so fast the rest of the way home Annabelle had to hurry to keep up with her. When she reached the house, Mavis stopped on the front steps and looked over her shoulder.

"What do you call them? Those little fluffy white dogs that jump up and down when they're happy?"

"Bichons. Bichon Frises."

"That's it. One won that dog show on TV a few years back. Cutest thing I ever saw."

"See, I told you you wanted a dog," Annabelle said.

"Don't be a smart aleck," Mavis said and unlocked the door. "Well, don't just stand there. Come on in. We're going to have some coffee."

CHAPTER TWO

Now that Annabelle had worked her way back into Mavis's life, she didn't let up. Everyday it was something. First, it was the draperies.

"Don't you think this house is awfully dark?" she said.

"I hadn't noticed." Mavis looked around the living room. "I suppose so."

"How could you not notice?"

"I've been busy."

Annabelle gave her an incredulous look.

"Working."

Annabelle raised an eyebrow.

"W-O-R-K-I-N-G," Mavis spelled it out. "You know, making a living. Paying the bills. Keeping my head above water."

"You've been busy keeping your head in the sand."

Mavis drank her coffee. "That too," she said.

That afternoon they took the draperies down.

"What about the cornices?" Annabelle said.

"What about them?"

"Don't you think they look sort of dated? Old-fashioned?"

"Annie, why don't you just spit it out? Do you want the cornices down too?"

"Might as well, don't you think?" Annabelle climbed on a step stool and inspected the brackets holding the cornices. "They're just up here with a couple of screws."

They carried the dusty draperies and cornices out to the front porch.

"We'll call the Salvation Army to pick them up."

"Okay," Mavis agreed.

They sat on the front steps to catch their breath. The telephone rang. Without hesitating, Annabelle went to answer it. Mavis could hear through the open door.

"No, she isn't here. Can I take a message?...Yes, people tell us that all the time. I'm her sister, Annabelle.... Oh, you didn't?...I'm from Piney where we grew up.... Yes, just visiting.... Oh, I don't know. As long as she needs me.... Okay, I'll tell her."

Annabelle came back out and sat down. "That was Charlotte Warren from the altar guild."

"Oh?"

"Now that you've retired, she wonders if you'd like to become an active member and come to a meeting next week."

"Why'd you tell her you're my sister?"

"She said we sound just alike."

"Oh."

They sat and watched the sun get low in the sky. When it was almost dark, they went in to watch the evening news.

"You're fat."

"Don't hold back, Annie. Just say what's on your mind."

They were in the kitchen fixing supper. Mavis was serving up trays for them to take into the living room. They would eat while they watched Jeopardy.

"You know what Dolly Parton does, don't you?"

"No, Annie. What does Dolly Parton do?"

"Some years back Dolly was putting on the pounds. I mean more than just in the bosom. So she began dividing everything on her plate in two and eating only half and giving the other half to somebody else."

"Who?"

"DOLLY."

"No, who did she give it to?"

"I don't know. Maybe she just pretended to give it to somebody. To an imaginary friend maybe. Or to her husband. Or her hairdresser. I don't know. What difference does it make who she gave it to?"

"Well," Mavis said, slapping a spoonful of mashed potatoes on a plate, "I think it would make a lot of difference whether she *pretended* to give it to somebody else or whether she really did. If she just pretended, I bet she also just pretended not to eat it herself."

Mavis had built up a head of steam. Slamming a heaping plate onto a tray, she added, "Besides, Dolly is a busy woman. What with her singing and Dollywood and all. And I read she's even got another park kind of place down in Florida now. I bet she eats out a lot and with a lot of different people. I read that her husband stays home in Nashville while she travels. He's got a driveway paving business or some such. And you know she doesn't keep a hairdresser with her all the time because she wears wigs. What's she going to do with a hairdresser?"

Annabelle sighed and shrugged. For a minute, Mavis thought she'd won the argument. "So," she added, driving her point home, "who's she got to eat the other half?"

"I don't know about Dolly," Annabelle said, "but you've got me."

The next day Mavis found Annabelle on the computer checking out Bichon Frises.

"Annabelle, I am not getting a dog."

"I know. I know. I just thought we'd go visit them. No harm in that, is there?"

Annabelle continued punching keys. With her back to Mavis, she said, "Oh, by the way, you had an e-mail from your old boss."

"Oh? What did he say?"

"He said the new bookkeeper can't work the combination to the store safe."

"Oh, for crying out loud. If that woman hadn't been so eager to get me out of the way, she might have had the time to listen to a thing or two I tried to tell her. Did Harrison say he wants me to call him? I swan, the man is helpless without me and always has been."

"No need," Annabelle said, her back still to Mavis. "I handled it."

"What do you mean, *you* handled it?"

"Don't get your feathers ruffled, Mavis. I just e-mailed him back."

"What did you say?"

Annabelle called up her reply. On the screen, Mavis read: SORRY TO DISAPPOINT YOU, BUT MAVIS HAS LEFT THE BUILDING.

Mavis was speechless. She sank to a chair as if the wind had been knocked out of her. Behind hands pressed over her face, she muttered, "Annabelle. Annabelle...."

At first, Mavis appeared to be crying. Mavis herself thought she might be. Then she was laughing and crying at the same time, rocking herself in a helpless fashion until it looked as if she might fall out of the chair.

"I didn't think it was that funny."

"Oh, Annie, look what you've done. You've come in here, unexpected and uninvited, and started going through my life like...like a crazed gardener, pulling up things by the roots and tossing them aside."

Annabelle reached out a hand toward Mavis. "But only the weeds, right? Not the flowers?"

"The weeds? If Harrison Clarke could hear himself being referred to as a weed, he'd have a conniption."

"He's not your boss anymore."

"I know. But Harrison and that store of his have been my whole life until now. For forty years."

"And what do you have to show for it?" Annabelle said softly. "A social security check and a broken heart."

"And a watch. With engraving on it."

"Well, hot stuff, Mavis! You don't even have a decent pension."

"Now Annabelle, don't be that way. I've had a good job all these years, and Harrison never broke my heart. I understood. He was married. He had the family business, the family name, to carry on. He needed me. I needed him. And I needed my job. Let's not blame Harrison for the way things were."

"Oh, bullshit, Mavis!" Annabelle jumped up and threw her hands in the air. "For years, he's taken advantage of you and the situation, and you know it. I say let's blame him. Why not? I'm sick of you making excuses for him. You've been doing that for years."

Mavis stared at her for a long moment. So long that Annabelle sat back down. Perhaps this time she had gone too far, barged in where angels fear to tread.

Finally Mavis stood and walked across the room to the closet. "Look in here," she said, opening the door. "There's nothing here but dark suits. I've worn these and some just like them to work five, six days a week for decades, and then on Sundays I've worn them to church. First, I wore them to the downtown store on Twentieth Street, then to the Five Points store on Southside, and then to the Galleria when Harrison moved us out there. No telling over the years how many suits I've bought at Parisian to wear, day after day, to Harrison P. Clarke's store. I'm worn out with them."

"Is that why you retired?" Annabelle asked. "You were tired of wearing suits?"

"No, the real reason I retired was Harrison didn't want me there anymore."

"Oh?"

"When he announced he was moving the store out to The Summit—that's the new up-scale shopping center—very up-scale, he kept saying—I complained about the traffic. It's bumper-to-bumper out two-eighty. Getting to and from work was going to be a nightmare.

"Well, Annie, he jumped on it. On my reluctance about the move. Said maybe it was time I retired. Said there was no reason why I had to get up every morning and face all those cars. Said I'd earned the right to take it easy. Tried to make retirement sound like my idea.

"I hadn't given retirement a thought, even if I have turned sixty-five. He hurt my feelings. So, I guess I cut my nose off to spite my face. I quit.

"Come to find out, he'd already found my replacement. A young woman with a marketing degree and not a lick of retail experience. And he's paying her twenty thousand a year starting salary more than he was paying me! Plus, now listen to this, he gave her a title! Calls her a vice president! Vice president!

"I thought, well, if that's what he wants, let him have her. And that was that."

She sighed and looked at Annabelle. "So? You want to help me get rid of these suits?"

Annabelle walked to the closet. "We'll take them to the Y. They've got a program where they re-cycle business clothes to women on welfare. You know, to get them ready to go out on job interviews. They'll make good use of them. Then we'll go shopping. Get you something pretty to wear. I'll get the car."

CHAPTER THREE

Y ou do know, don't you, that the next big event in our lives will be death?"

Mavis and Annabelle were sitting at the breakfast table in matching bathrobes, pink chenille with big blue and lilac butterflies on them. They were eating waffles. Or rather Mavis was eating her half and Annabelle was eating the other half.

"Mavis, why did you have to go say that?" Annabelle licked syrup off her fork. "I swear you have an uncanny penchant for the mundane and the morbid."

"Well, it's the truth. There's no sense in being in denial about it."

"I'm not the one who lives in denial."

Mavis laid her fork on her plate, then adjusted it carefully so it pointed straight across from the three to the nine o'clock position. She was considering packing Annabelle's bag and throwing her out.

Annabelle continued eating with the pleasure and focus of a child. Concentrating on each bite, licking both sides of her fork.

Watching her, Mavis relented. She didn't want Annabelle to leave. It was just that living with her required so much readjustment, and Mavis had lived a long time by herself.

"It's our job in life," Annabelle said, pausing to lick her fork again, "to show some enthusiasm. If you can't be enthusiastic about your life, then I say get a new one."

"Like trading cars?"

Annabelle stopped her licking. "Bingo," she said and laughed.

Mavis laughed too. She couldn't resist. Annabelle was so outrageous.

"Speaking of which...," Annabelle said, taking up licking again.

"You want me to trade cars?"

"Yep."

"The Camry is perfectly serviceable."

"Boring. B-o-r-i-n-g."

"Oh." Mavis folded her napkin and laid it beside her plate. "Thank goodness you like my house or we'd be putting a for-sale sign in the front yard."

"I was thinking of one of those new Beetles. A red one."

Mavis carried her dishes to the sink, rinsed and put them in the dishwasher. "Well, don't just sit there. Let's get dressed."

Mavis walked around the brand new red Beetle parked in her driveway. It stood out and was really noticeable, like a bright cartoon character inserted into a black-and-white movie. She didn't know what to make of it.

The little boy next door came over and looked at it with her. He was probably four, still had his baby fat and a mass of dark curls. He was wearing black rubber boots, a black cape, and a black mask. He punched Mavis on the thigh and said, "Doodlebug."

"Doodlebug yourself," she answered, rubbing her leg.

"Is that your car?"

"Yes."

"Are you going to take me for a ride?"

"Now?"

"Yes."

"Well, maybe another time, Johnny. Right now I...."

"Jonathan."

"Jonathan. Right. Well, right now I have company."

"Who?"

"My friend Annabelle."

"Where is she?"

Mavis looked around. "I don't know. I guess she went in the house."

"Why?"

"I don't know. Maybe to have a cup of coffee."

"Can I have a cup of coffee?"

"No."

"When can I go riding in your car?"

"I don't know. Maybe tomorrow. We'll have to ask your mother."

"I'll go ask her now."

"Wait a minute." But he was gone, his short legs pumping up and down in his boots.

Annabelle came out on the porch. "You coming in?"

"In a minute."

"You want a coffee milk shake? We've got ice cream. I'll drink my half."

"Maybe. Wait until I come in. The little boy next door wants a ride in the Beetle."

"Who're you talking to?"

Mavis jumped. Jonathan was standing beside her.

"Annabelle. My friend."

Jonathan looked toward the house and then back at Mavis. He regarded her solemnly from behind his mask. "We can go now," he said at last. "I have to sit in the back seat and wear a seat belt."

"Okay."

"Do you know how to drive?"

"Yes."

"A Beetle?"

"Yes."

"I can only go around the block."

"Okay."

Mavis and Annabelle were getting ready for bed. They were wearing new pajamas. Annabelle's had scenes from "I Love Lucy" on them, and Mavis's had "A Thin Man" motif with Nick and Nora and Asta scampering about. Annabelle sat cross-legged on the bed playing solitaire. Mavis was propped up against a pillow rubbing cream into her face.

"Once," she said, "years ago, I went to a workshop. I've forgotten what they called it. Some sort of a getting-to-know-yourself kind of thing. The church sponsored it and they wanted everybody to go. Somebody talked me into it.

"Anyway, this clergyman, who was also a psychiatrist...no, a psychologist, I guess...anyway, he was in charge. He had us doing all sorts of things. Falling back into one another's arms to let the others catch us. All kinds of things. That was a trust exercise, he said. I never could do it. I kept thinking what if they drop me.

"Anyway, at one point, he had us all sitting on the floor with our eyes closed and we were to envision an escalator ride. We kept our eyes closed for a long time, and he talked in this soothing voice and told us just to get on the escalator and go with the flow and notice where it took us and anything we saw along the way.

"Annabelle, the oddest thing happened. I just kept going down and down into this black hole, faster and faster, until I was whirling around. I didn't know how dizzy I was until he told us to open our eyes. I had to put both hands on the floor to stay upright.

"I must have looked...I don't know how I looked, but he saw I was upset, and first thing, he says, 'Mavis, your escalator went down, didn't it?'

"I nodded. It hadn't occurred to me that anybody's would go any other way, but they had. Everybody else's but mine had gone up. This seemed so sad. I was embarrassed and then.... Oh, Annabelle, this is the awful part. I began to cry. And the more everybody said that was okay, the more I knew it wasn't.

"The leader...his name was Bill something. I don't remember. He came and sat beside me and put his arm around me and tried to console me, and I couldn't stop crying. Finally, I just left. Got up and walked out. Got in my car and came home."

"Why?" Annabelle laid one card on another.

"Why? Why do you think? It was the most humiliating experience imaginable."

"He was just trying to be helpful."

"Strange way to go about it. Making people cry in public."

"Obviously you were depressed. He must have been worried."

"Depressed? What did I have to be depressed about?"

"You tell me." Annabelle laid another card down.

Mavis kicked the cards off the bed.

"Hey!"

"You act that way and I'll send you to the guest room."

"Now, Mavis, why would you do that when we have such interesting conversations?"

"Interesting indeed!" Mavis scooted down in the bed and pulled the cover under her chin.

Annabelle switched off the bedside lamp and snuggled down. "Do you want me to leave?"

"Yes."

"No you don't."

A few days later the doorbell rang. Mavis answered it to find Harrison P. Clarke standing on the porch. He was looking at the Beetle parked in the driveway.

"Who's car is that?" he said.

"Hello Harrison. How are you?"

"I'm fine. It's you I'm worried about."

"Me?"

"Mavis, may I come in?"

"Now? No, Harrison, I'm sorry. This is not a good time. You should have called first."

"I did call. I've been calling every day for the past two weeks."

"Oh?"

"I must have left a half dozen messages on your machine. Why haven't you returned my calls?"

"I've been busy."

"Busy? You're retired, for God's sake. How could you be busy?"

Mavis didn't reply. She stepped out on the porch and closed the door behind her. She was wearing her pink chenille robe with the butterflies on it.

"Look at you," Harrison said. "It's two o'clock in the afternoon. Why aren't you dressed?"

"I like wearing my robe. It's new. Isn't it pretty?"

He gave her a keen look. "You're not sick, are you?"

"No. I feel fine."

"Why did you put that new message on the phone? Saying you've gone on a cruise. On a slow boat to China!"

"Is that what it says?"

"You know damn well it is."

"Annabelle must have put it on there."

"Who's Annabelle?"

"My friend. Annabelle Lee Jones. She's visiting from Piney."

"Piney?"

"Where I grew up, Harrison."

"Oh. I'd a sworn it was your voice."

"We sound a lot alike."

"I've never heard you mention her before."

"We'd lost touch."

"I suppose that's her car?"

"Why, yes. Yes, as a matter of fact, it is."

"Where's yours?"

"Mine?"

"Your Camry, Mavis. Remember? I bought it for you. Two years ago."

"It's at the dealership for a tune-up."

"I'd like to meet this Annabelle. Why don't you invite me in?"

"It's not a good time, Harrison. I told you that."

"Why not?"

"Annabelle's taking a bath."

"Unhuh. I see."

Harrison folded his arms and appeared to chew on the inside of his jaw. He was making up his mind about something.

"All right. If that's the way you want it, Mavis. But don't come running back to me when this Annabelle character is gone."

He turned and went down the steps. He was getting in his car when Mavis called after him. "You didn't buy the Camry for me. It was a company car you signed over to me when you were finished with it."

She went back in the house and closed the door.

CHAPTER FOUR

Jonathan had on blue tights, a blue shirt with a red *S* emblazoned across the front, red bedroom slippers, a towel pinned cape-fashion around his neck, and his black mask. He was waiting beside the driveway.

Mavis was coming out the front door, shouting over her shoulder. "I tell you, Annabelle, enough is enough. I am not wearing a purple dress and a red hat!"

"You might want to try it. A lot of people are doing it. It's kind of like a club or something."

"A club?"

"Yes. I think so."

"Sounds more like a cult to me. A cult of people desperate for attention."

"Now, Mavis, you don't know a thing about them."

"I know I'm not joining them."

"Okay, be that way. But you'll miss out on a lot of fun."

"Oh, for heaven sakes, Annabelle! I give up!"

Mavis had the car keys in her hand. She was on her way to the post office to buy stamps.

"Hi," Jonathan said.

"Jonathan."

"Were you and your friend Annabelle fighting?"

"No. Just arguing."

"Why don't you invite her to go for a ride with us?"

"Are we going for a ride?"

"I'm ready. I've already asked my mother."

"I see. I'm going all the way to the post office this time."

"How far is that?"

"Maybe a mile."

"I'll go ask again."

"Okay. I'll wait."

When Jonathan came back, he climbed in the back seat and waited patiently while Mavis buckled his seat belt. They had gone a couple of blocks when he said, "Is Annabelle mad at you?"

"No, I don't think so." Mavis looked at him in the rearview mirror. Superman with curls and chubby little legs. "Sometimes she's just very opinionated."

"What's that?"

"Oh, bossy, I guess."

"Rotten Eddie's very o-pin-u-headed too."

"Who's Rotten Eddie?"

"My friend."

"Oh?"

"Sometimes I just give up on him too."

"I see."

"Yesterday he threw a truck into my baby sister's bed."

"You have a baby at your house?"

"Yes. Everybody knows that."

"How old is she?"

"She's not old. She's a baby."

"I see."

"She was in her bed, too, when Rotten Eddie threw the truck in it. He had to have time out in his room for a long time. Nearly e-leb-ba-teen hours. I told him not to do it."

They rode in silence the rest of the way to the post office.

"I like your hair that color," Mavis told Annabelle, who was sitting on the dresser bench brushing her blond curls. "It's the same color mine used to be before it went gray."

"Oh well, mine would be as gray as yours without the Clairol."

"Oh." Mavis looked surprised.

"Just holding on to what I used to have, Missy, and what is still rightfully mine," Annabelle said. "You could too."

"Oh?"

"Sure. Why don't we go to the beauty parlor and have them wash away your gray?"

Mavis smiled. "Sort of like in 'South Pacific' when Mary Martin 'washed that man right out of her hair'?"

"Sure. Him too."

"I'm not talking about Harrison."

"Why not?"

"I'm talking about my gray hair."

"Same thing."

"How do you figure?"

"They're both dragging you down. Making you old before your time."

"What are you talking about?"

"Oh, Mavis, Harrison wants you to believe you're old. That you've run out of choices. He always has. He's always wanted you to believe the jewelry store and the little he was willing to offer, both as a man and a boss, was the best you could do. That that was your only option. That he was your only option."

"What's that got to do with growing old?"

"That's what growing old is: thinking you've run out of options. That you've already made all your choices in life. That you can no longer make changes or be changed. That you're done. And done in."

"I am done."

"No, damn it, girl friend, you're not. In some ways, you're just now getting started."

"What's that supposed to mean?"

"It means retirement gives you the chance to go back to your most authentic self. The self you left behind as a child in order to make your way in the world. The self you used to be with me when we were kids and no one else was around. When we were two peas in a pod and did everything together. Before you had any armament, any thick protective layers. Before you knew you needed to defend yourself from invasion and attack."

"You make life sound like a war. I don't want to fight."

"Then stop!" Annabelle was agitated. She slammed the brush down on the dresser, stood and took Mavis by the shoulders. "Look at yourself. You're a beautiful woman. Don't fight who you are. Don't limit yourself. Let yourself be."

"Only change. Dye my hair. Buy new clothes, new car, new experiences."

"Well, yeah."

"Sounds like a contradiction of terms. Be yourself, only different."

"Don't make this harder than it is, Mavis."

"Well, it is hard."

"Yes. But it's not complicated. It's just experimental."

"I don't know what you're talking about."

"Yes, you do. It's not as if you've already tried life out to the fullest and you can truthfully say, 'I've already been there and done that.' Some folks can, but not you. Now is your time, Mavis. Now. What have you got to lose?"

"Everything. Life as I know it."

"Bingo! And what have you got to gain?"

"I don't know."

"Bingo again. Don't you want to find out?"

"What do you want me to do?"

"Every day, I want you to do something you've never done before."

"Oh, Annie. That's outrageous. That's too much. I can't possibly...."

"Today we'll do your hair. That's as good a place as any to start."

"I thought we'd already started. Clothes. Car. Diet. Now hair. Where's this going to end?"

"We're just getting started."

"Oh, Annie."

"One day at a time, Mavis. One change at a time. One adventure at a time."

"I'm scared."

"No, you're not. You're just excited."

"I can't tell the difference."

"Well, you're about to learn. Now let's go get your hair tinted."

CHAPTER FIVE

J onathan was wearing a fringed shirt, a cowboy hat, cowboy boots, and his black mask. Mavis was wearing pink overalls and raking the leaves. He was waiting for her to get them in a big enough pile to jump in.

"Are you married?" he said.

"No. Are you?"

Jonathan sat down and giggled. "No," he said, rolling over and over.

"How come?" Mavis pulled leaves loose from the tines of the rake.

"I'm a little boy."

"You're the Lone Ranger."

"Oh yeah. I forgot."

"Hi-ho Silver." Mavis sprinkled leaves on him.

"And away," he crowed, rolling into the pile.

Annabelle said, "How come you never married?"

She was perched on the step stool watching Mavis make lunch.

"Married? Is that all anybody talks about anymore?"

"Well, how come?"

Mavis spread mayonnaise on a piece of whole wheat bread. "Harrison was taken. There wasn't anybody else."

"Nobody?"

"Oh, there was a fellow named Raymond who used to come in the store. That's when we were on Southside, there in Five Points, but I knew it would be awkward if I let anything come of it."

"Awkward? For who?"

"Whom."

"Whomever then." Annabelle pinned her with a look.

"Oh, you know," Mavis said, scraping the jar with more energy than necessary. "Raymond was a customer. Harrison always expected me to maintain very business-like relationships with customers."

"He did, did he? Isn't that how he met Bitsy?"

"Bitsy?"

"His wife, Mavis. Wasn't she a customer at the store when he started dating her?"

"Well, I guess that's right. She was, wasn't she, although they'd known each other as children."

"Mavis, you do beat all."

"I do, don't I?" She turned toward Annabelle, knife poised in the air as if she'd been caught red-handed.

That night Mavis was propped up in bed filing her nails. Annabelle was doing yoga exercises on a mat on the floor.

"So," Annabelle said, rolling herself up like a cinnamon bun with her head stuck in the middle like a raisin, "how come you took up with Harrison in the first place?"

"Annabelle, you make it sound like he was somebody I met on the street."

"He was, wasn't he?"

"Well, technically, yes. I suppose he was. But we had been introduced."

"Ah yes. Mavis, ever a stickler for decorum."

"I'd come to Birmingham to take business courses at night school. You know that. He came to speak to the class, so I knew who he was. I mean, we hadn't been formally introduced, but I knew who he was and he had seen me in the class."

"So when he picked you up on the corner afterwards, it wasn't really a pick-up but more the continuation of a proper friendship?"

Mavis threw a pillow at Annabelle, who slowly unrolled herself and lay flat on the floor. Exhaling and raising her legs in the air, she assumed a shoulder stand before she said, "Admit it. You thought he liked you."

"He did like me. In his own way. I mean, Annabelle, really, we've had a very special relationship. Harrison has always said nobody understands him like I do. Why, I can practically read his mind. I knew exactly what he was thinking at the store. I knew what to do and when to do it, what to say and when to say it, how to be his right hand without ever getting in the way."

"Well, hoop-de-do."

"What does that mean?"

"So you got to be the office wife but never the bride. Never Mrs. Harrison P. Clarke."

"Well, no, but that wasn't in the cards."

"Why not? Isn't that what you wanted?"

"Now, Annabelle, it wasn't that kind of relationship. Still, in his own way, I've always known Harrison loves me."

"Loves you?" Annabelle thumped to the floor and, sitting up, stared at Mavis.

"When somebody loves you, Missy, they put your well-being first. They don't ignore your needs and desires. They honor them and try to fulfill them."

"How do you know that, Miss Smarty Pants? Did you read it somewhere in a book?"

Neither spoke for a minute.

Then Annabelle said, "I know it's true because that's the way I feel about you. I want you to be happy. I care about you. I want you to shine, to be the most you can be. Admit it, that's what love is. You know because that's the way you've always felt about him."

"I suppose."

"Of course, it is, Mavis. Why else did you stay there in that store with him all those years? Because you were in love with the business? Because you had something at stake in making a success of it? No, it wasn't your business. You had nothing at stake there except making a living. And you could have done that lots of places. Instead, you stayed. And you stayed. And you stayed."

"Because he needed me."

"Bingo."

"I wish you wouldn't say that."

Neither spoke for a minute.

"And," Mavis added, staring at the ceiling, "because I loved him."

"Bing…."

"Don't say it."

"And you kept hoping that someday he'd love you back the way you loved him."

"I kept thinking he already did. You know? I kept thinking he already did and someday he'd realize it."

"In spite of all the evidence to the contrary." Annabelle shook her head. "Mavis, you'll forgive somebody almost anything."

Mavis shrugged. "Maybe. Not bad manners and poor taste though."

"And Harrison was never guilty of those."

"No. You know, Annie, he would come to me over the years, first to the apartment on Southside and then here to the house, so distraught and upset sometimes. He and Bitsy have never been happily married. He would be beside himself. Say he had no one to turn to but me. Say he didn't know what he would do without me."

"Ah, the wife who doesn't understand him." Annabelle folded her mat, turned off the light, and climbed into bed.

In the dark, Mavis said, "You make it sound so trite."

"I don't mean to. He was the love of your life."

Mavis began to cry. "Yes, but I wasn't his."

She heard Annabelle take a deep breath.

"Don't even think about saying it," Mavis said, laughing and crying at the same time.

"I won't."

They held hands and stared at the ceiling in the darkness.

"I'm really tired of Harrison," Mavis said.

"Me too," Annabelle agreed.

"I always thought he was wonderful, handsome, special. Sometimes he made me feel special too, but then he'd...I don't know...withdraw, I guess, and I'd end up feeling...."

"Unworthy?"

"Yes. Not good enough somehow. Not like Bitsy. I was never in her class. She grew up in Mountain Brook and came from a wealthy family and went to a snooty girls' school in Virginia and...."

"And now," Annabelle said, "just think, she's stuck with him."

Mavis giggled. "Oh, Annabelle."

"I love you, Missy. Now let's go to sleep."

And they did.

CHAPTER SIX

I had an odd dream last night," Mavis said. They were at the breakfast table.

"Tell me."

"I dreamed a couple gave me a baby. They liked the baby and were sad to see her leave, but they thought she belonged to me."

"Did she?"

"I think so. At least, she reached her arms out to me. She was beautiful.

"We drove along a country road, and she seemed to get older. Maybe two or three. I pointed out the pretty sights to her. Barns and fields and animals. I told her we had two houses, one in the country that was small and one in the city that was big. I told her we were going to the one in the country and later we would go to the one in the city.

"Then it got dark, and I slowed down because I was having trouble finding my way. I saw someone walking along the road ahead of us. This person was going the same direction we were, and I tried to pass her but, even though we were in a car and she was on foot, I couldn't catch up to her.

"I never saw her face and didn't know who she was. She was wearing a coat that made a light like a red glow leading the way. I knew then that I didn't have to worry about getting lost. All I had to do was follow the red glow."

They ate their toast, each her half piece, in silence and sipped their coffee. When they were done, Mavis said, "Shall we take a walk?"

"Yes. Let's," Annabelle said. "I'll get my coat."

Not until then did Mavis remember the color of Annabelle's coat.

One morning, while they were sitting in the sunshine on the back steps, Mavis said, "I remembered when you came."

"I would hope so. It wasn't all that long ago. A few weeks. The morning after your retirement dinner."

"No. I mean the first time. Originally."

"Oh."

"It came to me this morning when I first woke up. Funny, isn't it, what comes to you then when you no longer have to jump out of bed and rush off to work but can lie there and listen to yourself? To your dreams, to your sub-conscious."

"Yes," Annabelle agreed. "It's almost like listening to the right side of your brain talk to the left side. If the right side could talk."

"That's weird."

"I know."

"Anyway, you first came to me when my mama died, didn't you?"

Annabelle hesitated before answering. "Once she was gone, you needed me. Someone just to be with you."

"That was you," Mavis said, "always there. Like a shadow.

"No," she interrupted herself, "not like a shadow. Like a friend. My best friend. My only friend, I guess."

"Well, yes," Annabelle agreed. "No one else knew what to do with you. No one else had any idea even how to talk to you. They called you a poor little orphan."

"Oh Annabelle. That's what I was—a poor little orphan."

"No, not really. You know that, Mavis. You were just yourself, and that was hard enough. It's hard, maybe impossible, to be your true self except up against another true self. Otherwise, you don't know where you end and somebody else starts."

"That's really weird."

"I know."

"Annie?" She reached for her hand.

"Yes."

"You're still my best friend."

"That's what I'm here for."

That afternoon Mavis was sitting in the window seat in the living room so she could catch the fading light on the needlepoint piece she was stitching. Annabelle was sitting in a chair nearby with a pad and pencil sketching Mavis, trying to capture the patterns of light from the window that fell on her face and shoulders.

Not looking up from her work, Mavis said, "The first time I saw you you were under the steps."

"I was?"

"Yes. The back steps. You said, 'Sh-h-h-h,' so I looked around to make sure no one saw, and I climbed under there with you. It was the day after the funeral."

"Mavis, there was no funeral."

"Why, of course, there was. They wouldn't let me go. I was too little to understand, and they didn't want to upset me, but they had a funeral at the Baptist church. Grandma and Grandpa were Baptists. They told me everybody in town came and there were lots and lots of flowers."

"Mavis, listen to me for...."

Mavis held up her needlepoint. "Do you think I should do the center of these flowers in green or yellow?"

"Mavis."

"Or maybe blue. That would be unusual. Not true to life but different. I don't think any flowers, least of all daisies, have blue centers, do you?"

"Mavis, look at me. What are you doing?"

"My daisies."

"Mavis."

"I'm doing what you said, Annie. Something new every day that I've never done before. One day at a time. Today I'm making the centers of my daisies blue. I've never done that before."

"That's not what I mean, and you know it." Annabelle put her pad and pencil down.

"I know no such thing."

"Oh, for crying out loud!" Annabelle jumped up now and threw her hands in the air. "It's been more than sixty years ago! Let's deal with it!"

"Don't shout, Annie. If I could do any better—or more—I would. Today this is the best—and the most—I can do. Enough is enough. For now."

"Oh, Missy, sometimes you frustrate me so."

"I know I do. And sometimes, quite frankly, you aggravate the hell out of me. Excuse the language. But right now I'm working on my daisies. We'll save further work on my psyche for another day."

And with that, she went back to her needlepoint, and Annabelle stomped out of the room.

The next day Mavis was leaving for the grocery store when Jonathan appeared in a Spiderman suit and black mask. He leaned in the car window.

"Where you going?"

"To the Piggly Wiggly."

"Can I go?"

"Go ask your momma."

He ran into his house and, a few minutes later, ran back out. "It's okay," he said, "only Rotten Eddie has to come too."

"Oh? How come?"

"Because my momma's really mad at him."

"Why?"

"He pinched The Baby."

"Oh my."

"Open the trunk so he can get in."

"He's going to ride in the trunk?"

"Yes. That way nobody will be looking at him."

"He doesn't want anybody to look at him?"

"Nope."

"How come?"

Jonathan gave Mavis an exasperated look. *"Because* he pinched The Baby."

"I see."

She popped the trunk and heard Jonathan tell Rotten Eddie to get in. Then he slammed it shut. When he'd climbed into the back seat, she said, "Will he be okay back there?"

"Sure."

"What if he suffocates?"

"What's that?"

"Can't breathe."

"Rotten Eddie can always breathe. And he likes small dark places best."

"Okay."

On the way back from the store, Jonathan said, "When we get home, can I meet Annabelle?"

"Not today."

"Why not?"

"She's having a time out."

"Was she bad?"

"Yes. Really annoying."

A few days later Mavis and Annabelle were in the Beetle on their way to the library. "You know, Mavis," Annabelle said, "there is more than one radio station. We don't always have to listen to NPR."

"I suppose," Mavis agreed with a sigh, "but...."

Annabelle punched the 'seek' button.

"One day," a big bass voice boomed out of the dashboard, "GOD will sink yore little boat and ask you to E-X-P-L-A-I-N yore self."

Annabelle began to laugh.

"What'd I tell you?" Mavis said, switching the radio off.

"Oh Lordy, Lordy," Annabelle whizzed between giggles.

Mavis gave her a look. "Is that what you're trying to get me to do, Annie? EXPLAIN myself?"

"Lord, no. What I'm trying to get you to do is stop explaining yourself, even to yourself. And just be."

"And what is this philosophy of yours? Buddhism? Hinduism?"

Annabelle didn't answer.

"And how'd you get to be so smart? You're a hick from Piney, same as me."

"Yeah, but all these years while you've been resisting and defending yourself against...I don't know...whatever you're afraid of, I've been listening."

"To what? To whom?"

Annabelle didn't answer.

"If you say God, so help me, Annabelle Lee Jones, I'm stopping this car and kicking you out."

Annabelle looked out her side window.

"It's not as if you have a direct pipeline, you know," Mavis continued.

She ran a stop sign and kept going.

"It's not as if you know something the rest of us can't figure out."

She hit a pothole and didn't seem to notice.

"I'm not some dumb, lost soul who can't find her way. I don't need to be lectured to."

She sped past the library without slowing down.

"I've lived a long time. Fairly long anyway. I've learned a thing or two myself. I know what I'm doing. Know where I'm going. Know how to get from A to Z."

She turned several corners and careened into a parking place, not stopping until she had jumped the curb and was halfway up on the sidewalk. Then she looked at Annabelle and announced, "This is not the library. This is Savage's Bakery."

"So it is."

"Well, don't just sit there. Let's go in and buy some cookies."

"Might as well," Annabelle agreed. "Seeing as how we're here."

"How many dimes in a dozen?" Jonathan asked.

"A dozen what?"

"A dozen pieces of bubble gum."

"Probably one plus two pennies," Mavis said, "unless inflation has gotten into it."

"What's in-de-lation?"

"A government program."

"Do you have two pennies?"

"Yes."

"I have a dime." He opened his fist to reveal the evidence. "Are we going to the Piggly Wiggly?"

"I don't know. Are we?"

"I'll run ask."

When he came back, Mavis said, "Why are you wearing your mask with a fire chief's hat? Firemen don't wear masks."

"I'm hiding from Rotten Eddie."

"How come?"

"So he won't get me in trouble."

"Oh."

On their way to the store, Jonathan gave a big sigh from the back seat. "Mabis?"

"Yes?"

"Sometimes I just don't know."

"Me either."

CHAPTER SEVEN

I think we should go get the dog today," Annabelle said. They were sitting at the breakfast table in their matching robes. Mavis cut a piece of toast in two and began eating her half.

"Why are you so intent on my having a dog?"

"You shouldn't be living alone."

"I'm not living alone. I'm living with you."

"What about when I'm gone?"

"Are you going somewhere?"

"I can't stay here forever."

"Why not?"

"I just can't, that's all."

"You stayed with me for fifteen years when we were growing up."

"Correction. For twelve years. From the time we were three until we were fifteen. And I didn't leave then. You did."

"They sent me away to school. I didn't have a choice."

"True," Annabelle said, pushing the plate back and putting her elbows on the table. "They sent you away because they thought you needed more friends than just me. And you do now too. I think a dog's a good start."

"Let's not rush things."

"I'm in no rush."

"Good."

"I just think…."

"I know. I heard you, Annie." Mavis stirred her coffee. "Do I have to give you half my coffee too?"

"No, dear," Annabelle said with exaggerated patience.

They were quiet for a few minutes.

"Annie," Mavis said, staring out the window, "why did you come?"

"I couldn't stand the idea of you alone in this house with nothing to do."

"No, I mean the first time. When we were three." She looked at her now.

"Oh, well then." Annabelle smiled. "After finding me under the steps that first day, what do you remember?"

"I remember you being in the sandbox with me. We talked. Grandma and Grandpa had been trying to get me to talk to them in the house, and I wouldn't, and I went outside and sat down in the sandbox, and there you were again. And we talked. And talked."

"It was a fall day, and the wind was blowing leaves all around us," Annabelle said.

"Yes. You had a pretty blue dress and naturally curly blond hair. You were so pretty and friendly and just my age and size."

Neither spoke for a minute.

So," Mavis said. "How'd you know I needed you? How'd you know to come?"

"Your mama was gone."

"She was sick. In the hospital until the day she died. Months later. A year later, I guess. She never came home. I kept waiting for her."

"She was gone, Mavis, from the outset. There was no way she was ever coming back."

"I guess not. Back then they didn't have the medicines they have now."

"She didn't die, Mavis. She left. And when she left, you stopped talking. That's when I came, and you talked to me. For years, you didn't talk to anybody but me."

"She left?"

"You know that."

"They said she died. Grandma and Grandpa Horton."

"They didn't want you waiting for her to come home any longer. She wasn't coming back, and they knew it."

"Where'd she go?"

"I don't know."

"Did they?"

"Probably not. She ran off with a salesman she met downtown."

"How do you know?"

"Everybody in town knew but you. I heard people talk."

"That's not so. My daddy got killed in the war, and my mama died of a broken heart in the hospital."

Annabelle began clearing the table and putting dishes in the dishwasher. "People don't die of broken hearts, Mavis. But they do stop talking."

Mavis and Jonathan were on their way to the post office when Jonathan spotted the Vulcan statue atop Red Mountain.

"Who's that?" he asked from the back seat.

"Where?"

"There. Up high against the sky."

Mavis slowed, looked to where he was pointing.

"Oh. That's Vulcan. He's the symbol of Birmingham's steel industry. They put him up there on the mountain back when there were a lot of steel mills here."

"Bul-cane who?"

"Just Vulcan. He doesn't have a last name."

With exaggerated patience, Jonathan said, "Everybody has a last name, Mabis."

"Oh? Well then, his must be Jones. Vulcan Jones."

"Jones? Like Annabelle?" Jonathan was excited at the possibility.

"Well, yes. I guess so."

"Is he Annabelle's brother? Brothers and sisters have the same last name."

Mavis was in over her head now. "I don't think they're kin, Jonathan."

"Sure they are. That's Annabelle's brother. Can we go up there and see him? Pay him a visit?"

"Now?"

"Yes."

"Well, okay."

It was a short distance, just a few blocks beyond the post office. Mavis drove up the winding drive, parked in the visitors' lot, released Jonathan from his seat belt and let him out. He stood looking up, too awed to speak.

Finally, in a whisper, he said, "Mabis, he's not wearing pants. He's showing his bottom."

"He is, isn't he?"

"Momma says not to show your bottom. She says it's not polite."

"H-m-m," Mavis said. How had she gotten into this? All she'd meant to do was mail a jacket that was too big back to L. L. Bean. Now here she was discussing the indecent exposure of a pagan god's tush.

"Well, maybe Vulcan didn't have a momma to teach him how to behave," she offered.

"No momma? But he looks like a baby. A BIG baby with whiskers. All babies have mommas. They have to have mommas to born 'em."

"That's true, Jonathan, but some babies lose their mommas."

"Lose 'em? How?"

Mavis had painted herself into a corner. "I don't know," she said crossly, "but clearly Vulcan lost his mother or she would have told him not to show his tushie."

"His tushie! His tushie!" Jonathan giggled. He thought this was very funny.

On their way home, he was quiet, thinking things over. Then he said, "Mabis, did Annabelle lose her momma? When she was a baby?"

Startled, Mavis said, "Why do you ask?"

"Well, if Bul-can Jones lost his momma and he's Annabelle's brother, then Annabelle lost her momma too."

"Jonathan, I don't think Vulcan and Annabelle are brother and sister. They just happen to have the same last name."

"Did her momma teach her not to show her tushie?"

"Well, obviously somebody did."

"Who taught you, Mabis?"

"Not to show my tush?"

"Unhuh."

"Annabelle."

"She's not your momma."

"Tell her that."

"You do have cousins, you know." Annabelle peered at Mavis over the newspaper.

"Yes. I know." Mavis ducked her head over the crossword. "So? Why are you bringing up The Cousins?"

"Well...?" Annabelle shrugged.

"Yes?"

"You seem lonely. You don't seem to have any friends."

"Oh, for crying out loud, Annabelle. I have lots of friends."

"Where are they?"

"They were at work."

"You mean customers?"

"Of course, I mean customers."

"I thought you said Mr. Too-Big-for-His-Britches Harrison said you couldn't be friends with the customers."

"You're deliberately twisting my words, Annabelle. What I said was he didn't approve of my 'seeing' customers, as in dating them."

"Oh?"

"Oh?"

"So, now when you need them, where are these so-called friends?"

"Oh, for heaven sakes! They don't know where I live. They're not the kind of friends who come to see you."

"Or ever call to see how you are?"

"No, I suppose not." Mavis looked thoughtful. This hadn't occurred to her before.

They were both quiet for a few minutes.

"Don't tell me you think I ought to return Charlotte Warren's call and join the altar guild?"

"Who's talking about the altar guild? You're changing the subject. We're talking cousins here, not the altar guild."

"Why are you bringing up The Cousins? Now after all these years? They hate me. Always have, always will."

"They don't hate you, Mavis. They just think you're peculiar. Lord knows, they got that right. I think you should invite them for Thanksgiving."

"Invite them for Thanksgiving!" Mavis sprang out of her chair. "Have you lost your mind? Why in the world would I do such a thing?"

"To find out about your mother."

"What about my mother?"

"They're older than you are, Mavis. They know things about her you don't know. You barely remember her."

"Stirring up what's past. Picking at old bones. Why do you do that, Annabelle? Why can't you just let things be?"

"You know why."

"No, I don't. I think you do it just to aggravate me. You're the most aggravating person I've ever known."

Mavis stomped out of the room and went upstairs to dress. When she came down, she was wearing the single business suit they'd saved from her work wardrobe.

"You look like you're going to a funeral," Annabelle said.

"I am. Yours."

Mavis walked out of the house, slamming the front door behind her.

"Where you going?" It was Jonathan, standing on the porch. He was crying.

"To work."

"At the jewel store?"

"Yes."

"Why?"

"Because I'm sick and tired of staying home listening to Annabelle harangue me all the time."

"You were fighting. I could hear you yelling."

"Why are you crying?"

"Me and Rotten Eddie had a fight."

"What was that about?"

"He said he wasn't going to be my friend anymore if I keep blaming him for everything. Somebody hid all The Baby's toys, and I told Momma it was Rotten Eddie, and she said if Rotten Eddie couldn't behave his self, I couldn't play with him anymore. When I told Rotten Eddie what she said, he pushed me down and hurt my arm."

"Let's see. H-m-m. It's kind of red. No blood though."

"Can I go with you? To the jewel store?"

"No."

Mavis sat down on the steps. Jonathan did too. She was aware she was getting her suit dirty. And now, too, Jonathan had a grubby hand on her jacket sleeve.

She sighed. So did Jonathan. She put her arm around him. He leaned his head against her.

"We could go shopping," she said at last.

"What for?"

"A turkey, I guess."

"For Thanksgiving?"

"Yes."

"Not go to the jewel store?"

"No. It's too boring. Besides I've retired."

"Can we get some ice cream too?"

"Sure. Go ask your momma."

When he came back, Mavis was standing in the driveway, shielding her eyes with her hand as she looked at the sky.

"What are you looking at, Mabis?"

"Canada geese. See them?" She pointed at a V of twelve or fourteen geese.

Jonathan squinted in the direction she pointed. "I see them," he said. "Where are they going?"

"South."

"Why?"

"For the winter. Listen! Can you hear them?"

"The gooses are honking!"

"Yes."

"Why?"

"I guess they're happy. Glad to be on their way."

CHAPTER EIGHT

I can't believe you got me into this and now you refuse to come out of the kitchen." Hands on her hips, Mavis glared at Annabelle.

"I don't like turkey."

"Don't be ridiculous. You love turkey." Mavis threw the dishrag in the sink.

"Mavis, The Cousins don't like me. Never have, never will. You refused to talk to them when we were children. Remember? You'd only talk to me, and that hurt their feelings and made them mad.

"Remember that time you insisted I come along to the circus? Grandpa Horton brought us all to Birmingham to the circus, and you just had to have me sit beside you, and it crowded everybody up, and they complained. You got so nervous you wet your pants, and we all had to leave before the trapeze act, and poor Grandpa didn't know how to calm everybody down."

"I remember, but I guarantee you today I will not wet my pants if you'll just come out to the living room."

"No can do."

"Oh, Annie, you got me into this. Why did you get me to invite them if you had no intention of supporting me through this?"

"Number one, you don't need me. You just think you do. And, number two, you're the one, not me, who needs to ask them about your mother."

"I do, huh?"

"You do."

The Cousins arrived together. Elmira sitting in the back seat, Sammie Jo up front with her husband, Claude. Mavis met them on the front steps. There were polite, stiff-armed hugs, air kisses. Claude stood back and watched the three women as if they'd lost their minds. He may have been the driver, but clearly he was only along for the ride.

Sammie Jo pretended to wipe lipstick off Mavis's cheek. "You're so sweet to invite us. After all these years."

Sammie Jo wore a mink jacket, perfume, and a false smile.

Elmira said, "Indeed." She wore a plain wool coat, Vick's Vapor Rub, and no pretenses. Elmira, Mavis noted, still had not developed a capacity for insincerity.

Somehow, with Claude bringing up the rear, they managed to get up the steps and into the house. Mavis took their coats, and they looked about the living room. Sammie Jo carried on about every little thing as if rooms with furniture in them were a novelty. Elmira took silent inventory as if she were a health inspector. Claude, for his part, tried not to get in the way.

Mavis went into the kitchen and whispered, "Now what am I supposed to do?"

"Offer them some sherry. Get them to sit down, and, for goodness sake, don't let them come back here." Annabelle smiled sweetly and pushed Mavis back through the swinging door.

"I wish you'd look," Elmira was saying. "Some things never change."

Mavis couldn't imagine what Elmira was talking about. It seemed to her as if almost everything had changed recently, herself most of all.

Elmira stood looking at the sketch Annabelle had done recently of Mavis sitting in the window seat. Mavis had propped it in a cubbyhole of the desk where she kept unpaid bills. It had not been on display. Not been on display at all.

Mavis was immediately reminded of how The Cousins were as little girls. The Busy Bees she and Annabelle had called them. They would come into her room to play and in no time would be reading the letters she kept hidden under her bed. Letters she printed in block letters to her mother. Letters that began, "Deer Mama. Wish you were hear." Or they'd find the pictures Annabelle drew of Mavis's mother. Annabelle had drawn them for her for years, childish portraits of faces with big blue eyes and long blond hair and smiling red lips. Mavis always kept them hidden in the back of the closet.

Now here was Elmira holding up this latest drawing by Annabelle. Some things didn't change, indeed.

"Still drawing pictures, I see." Elmira said.

"No," Mavis said. "Not still. I don't recall that I was ever much of an artist."

"Oh, that's right," Elmira said. "You had a *friend* who was the artist."

"Yes," Mavis said.

"Oh my," Sammie Jo said, looking over Elmira's shoulder. Mavis's knees went weak as she saw what Sammie Jo saw— Annabelle's signature in the corner of the picture.

So the cat was out of the bag. Annabelle was back, and they knew it.

"How have you been?" Elmira asked, as she put the picture back where she had found it. This didn't sound like an idle question. "Has retirement been a big adjustment?"

Mavis didn't like the tone of this. "Oh, no," she said airily. "I have so much to do I really don't know how I ever had time to work."

"Is that right?" Elmira gave her a knowing look. "What keeps you so busy?"

Mavis was stuck. "Oh this and that. You know. The altar guild. My club work. Volunteering."

Goodness gracious. Where were these lies coming from? She hated herself when she lied.

"Excuse me," she said. "I need to check on the turkey."

As she entered the kitchen, Annabelle thrust the turkey on a platter at her and said, "Don't even slow down. You're doing fine. Now get back in there."

Sammie Jo, to her credit, got them through dinner and dessert. She talked non-stop about her grandchildren. How many teeth they had, how tall they were, which ones loved her the most, which ones played soccer, which ones played musical instruments, which musical instruments they played.

Claude, for his part, watched her across the table as if he'd never laid eyes on his wife before. Every now and then she would prompt him to agree with her by asking, "Isn't that right, Claude?" and he would reply, "Yes, Sammie Jo, that's right. Right as rain."

After dinner when it came time for coffee in the living room, he excused himself and went outside to smoke. Mavis went to the kitchen to get the coffee pot.

"It's now or never," Annabelle hissed. "Get on with it. Ask them."

"All right a-ready. I'm getting there."

In the living room, Mavis poured each cousin a cup and one for herself, took a deep breath with her eyes closed, and said, "I want you to tell me about My Mother."

"Oh my," Sammie Jo said. Now, for the first time, at a loss for words, she looked at her sister.

Elmira set her cup down, wiped her mouth with a napkin, and cleared her throat. "What is it you want to know, Mavis?"

Mavis eyes filled with tears, which made her hate herself. "Is she still alive?"

"I don't know," Elmira said.

"You know Grandma and Grandpa told me she died of a broken heart when she heard my daddy was killed in action."

"I always thought you just made that up yourself," Sammie Jo said.

"No, that's what they said."

"They shouldn't have told you that," Elmira said.

"No," Mavis agreed. "Why did they say such a thing? Tell a child her mother was dead when she wasn't?"

"So you'd stop crying, I imagine," Sammie Jo said. "You were just a toddler and you wouldn't stop crying for her. My guess is they wanted to make you understand she wasn't coming back."

"Why didn't she come back? Where did she go? What happened to her? Didn't she love me? Didn't she want me?"

Somewhere inside Mavis a dam had broke, and, to her humiliation, she now began to sob. She got up and fled to the kitchen, the door swinging shut behind her.

"Now look what you've done," she hissed at Annabelle. "Why are you such a busy body? Always sticking your nose into other people's business. My business. I was doing just fine, but would you leave well enough alone? Oh, no. Invite The Cousins, you said. Clear the air. Find out what really happened."

"Mavis, honey, it's okay. All you did was cry a little. What's so bad about that? Now you just pull yourself together and go back in there as though nothing happened."

Mavis began to shake and cry harder. "I can't," she said. She threw herself into Annabelle's arms. "I can't. You go."

"No. This is something you have to do yourself. I can't do it for you."

"Please. I'll give you the left over pumpkin pie. No halvers. You can have it all."

"Mavis, get a hold of yourself. Here, wipe your face." She handed her a tea towel. "Now go back in there and find out about your mama and listen to every bit of it. No hiding from it. And tonight, after they're gone, we'll talk about it and sort it out."

"Promise?"

"Promise. Now go." She swatted Mavis's fanny and pushed her through the door.

"Excuse me," Mavis said to The Cousins. "I had a frog in my throat. A little allergy problem."

Elmira raised an eyebrow and took a sip of coffee. Sammie Jo said, "Oh my," and fanned her face with her hand.

"Now where were we?" Mavis asked as if trying to recall whose bid it was at the bridge table. "Oh yes, I believe you were going to tell me what happened to...My Mother. You were old enough to remember, you see, and I wasn't. Right?"

"Well, yes, that's right," Elmira agreed. "When she left, I must have been ten, and that would have made Sammie Jo eight. We were old enough to, uh, remember and to be told... The Truth."

"Yes, yes, The Truth," Mavis said.

"Your mother ran away," Elmira said, no sugar-coating there. "With a salesman she met downtown."

"At the five and dime," Sammie Jo said. "Remember? It had a soda fountain."

"They left that afternoon on the train," Elmira continued.

"Where'd they go?"

"To Texas. Dallas, I think it was. Grandpa went after them, but she wouldn't come back."

"Did anybody ever hear from her again?"

"Oh yes. Sometimes Grandma Horton got postcards," Elmira answered. "For a while the cards came from California. Aunt Tootsie—that's what we called her—always said she was all right. She never mentioned the salesman. Said she'd gotten a job in a factory. Something to do with the war effort."

"One of the postcards had a picture of Rosie the Riveter on it," Sammie Jo said. "Remember Rosie the Riveter?"

"Grandma hid the postcards from Grandpa, but she showed them to us," Elmira explained.

"One had a picture of the Pacific Ocean on it," Sammie Jo chimed in. "To this day, I've never seen the Pacific Ocean."

"Later," Elmira went on, "after the war, she sent Christmas cards from Chicago where she was living."

"And no one ever told me? No one ever showed me the cards?"

"The Christmas cards were always snow scenes," Sammie Jo offered. "I remember because we never had snow in Piney."

"Grandma knew better than to share the cards with Grandpa," Elmira said. "He wouldn't even let anybody say her name in his house. He said as far as he was concerned Althea was dead. No daughter of his would get pregnant by one man and then up and run off with another, and both of them strangers."

This was followed by a silence.

Then, remembering, Mavis said, "Althea, that was her name."

"We called her Aunt Tootsie though," Sammie Jo said, "when she was there. I mean before she left."

"Did you ever see her again?"

"No."

"Why did she leave me?" Mavis asked. "Didn't she love me?"

"She couldn't do anything right," Sammie Jo said.

Elmira gave her sister a warning look.

"Well," Sammie Jo said, "that's what Grandpa always said. I mean even before she left. Before he stopped mentioning her at all. 'Althea doesn't have the sense God gave a goose.' That's what he said. I heard him myself."

"Your mother may have had mental problems," Elmira said more kindly. "Even before she left. All her life, I reckon. Grandma always spoke of her as a bit out of touch."

"I guess so," Mavis said, "if she couldn't even send her own daughter a postcard."

"Everybody had hopes for Aunt Tootsie for awhile," Sammie Jo said. "She was the prettiest thing you ever saw. The prettiest girl in Piney, barring none. Always wild though. From the get-go. She was still in high school when she met your daddy at a dance in Mobile. It wasn't until after he got shipped overseas that it became obvious she was pregnant. That was terribly hard on Grandpa and Grandma. I'll say this for them though, embarrassed as they were, they put the best face on things they could. Don't you think so, Elmira?"

Elmira gave a slight shrug as if she didn't have an opinion about that.

"Well, they did," Sammie Jo insisted. "They made her write and tell him she was pregnant and that she expected him to marry her when the war was over. Of course, his plane got shot down, and nobody ever heard from him again. Aunt

Tootsie went out of her head after that. It wasn't long before she just up and ran off."

"She and my daddy were never even married?"

"No. Why'd you think your last name was Horton?"

Mavis shook her head sadly. She'd always thought her last name was Horton just because her grandparents raised her. Not because she was illegitimate.

"Out of touch all those years," she said to herself, "and not once could she even send me, her own daughter, a postcard."

"Oh, there was no point in that," Sammie Jo assured her. "Grandpa wouldn't stand for it. He acted as if Aunt Tootsie never even existed. Except for you, he would have forgot all about her. You served as a reminder, I reckon, and that made things worse."

"Sammie Jo!" Elmira said and raised part way out of her chair.

"I'm just saying Mavis looked so much like her and acted so much like her that she was bound to have put him and Grandma in mind of Aunt Tootsie herself every single day. That wasn't Mavis's fault. That's just the way it was."

"I looked like her?"

"Oh my, yes. Everybody thought so."

"And nobody even knows what became of her?" Mavis asked. "She just disappeared like she never existed? Except for me?"

"Well, not exactly," Sammie Jo said nervously. She looked at Elmira.

"When Grandpa died, Grandma got in touch with her," Elmira said. She seemed to be choosing her words carefully. "That was thirty, thirty-two years ago now. Aunt Tootsie, Althea, was still living in Chicago. She was married to a man named Philpot, I think it was. Grandma told her to come home, that Grandpa was gone and it was time to let bygones be bygones. She said she would."

Mavis was sitting so stiff and tense on the edge of her chair she seemed about to break in two. Instead, the handle of her coffee cup snapped off in her fingers. The cup rattled back into the saucer she held beneath it. She scarcely noticed and set the broken china on the end table beside her chair.

"She came home?" she whispered.

"No," Elmira answered. "She said she would but she didn't. Never did. Not to this day. Grandma continued to call her. Called her over and over. Althea always said she'd come, but she never did."

"Did she ask about me?" Mavis asked, her voice breaking.

"Oh honey," Sammie Jo said.

"I think it was more than Grandma could stand," Elmira went on, not answering Mavis. "Grandma died. What was it? Four, five months later?"

"Five, I think," Sammie Jo answered. "She passed away on Palm Sunday. I remember because the church was still decorated with palms when we had the funeral two days later. Remember all those pots of palms around the casket?"

"And she still didn't come," Mavis said, talking to herself now.

"Well, I guess there wasn't any point in it by then," Sammie Jo said.

"No point?" Mavis said, her voice rising with a note of hysteria.

"Oh my!" Sammie Jo's hand flew to her mouth. "I didn't mean anything about you, Mavis. I only meant…."

"Hush, Sammie Jo." Elmira cut her sister off. "When Grandma died, the lawyer said we had to make a good faith effort to inform all the heirs. Not, as we all remember, that there was much of an estate, just what was left from selling the old home place after we paid the doctor bills."

"Did you talk to her?" Mavis asked.

"No," Elmira said. "I was the executor of the estate but, to be perfectly frank, Mavis, I didn't have much use for your mama myself by then. I had the attorney call her."

"What happened?"

"You were there. You know she didn't come to the funeral."

"Yes, but what did she say?"

"She told the lawyer to send her a check for anything she had coming to her." Elmira sighed. "Which, of course, wasn't much but, as far as I was concerned, shouldn't have been anything. And, if Grandpa had still been alive, wouldn't have been a single dime. Grandma, of course, always had a forgiving heart, and I think she thought if she remembered Althea in her will, her daughter might come home. Finally. Make amends if amends could be made."

"How come you never told me? How come Grandma never told me after Grandpa died?"

Elmira drew herself up. "Told you? Me? It wasn't my place to tell you. As for Grandma, she couldn't see any point in breaking your heart all over again. You'd already lost your mama when you were a child, practically still a baby. Why go through it all again when you'd been satisfied all those years that she was dead?"

"Satisfied?" Mavis jumped up. "Satisfied? Believe me, there was no satisfaction in thinking my mother was dead."

"Now Mavis, that's not what I meant. I just meant maybe it was better that way."

"Lord, yes," Sammie Jo said. "It was better than learning the truth, that she'd just run off and left you."

"Sammie Jo, for heaven's sake!" Elmira said.

Mavis stood up carefully and walked blindly out of the room. "Please excuse me," she said.

When she got to the kitchen, her eyes were filled with tears. "I don't think she loved me at all," she said and sank to the floor beside the pantry door.

"She was just a girl, Mavis. She would have loved you if she could. She just didn't know how." Annabelle slid down the doorframe to the floor beside her friend and put her arms around her.

"Mavis, listen to me. She would have loved you if she could. You were the most lovable little girl in the world. And now you're a lovable big girl."

"You mean a lovable old lady."

"That too."

"What are we going to do?"

"I don't know. Let all this settle in our minds for awhile, I guess."

Neither spoke for a moment.

"Wanna go for a ride?" Annabelle suggested.

"Now?"

"Yes."

"You mean leave? Just get in the car and drive away?"

"Yes. We can go out the back door."

"Annie, you're crazy. We've got company in the living room. Company we invited."

"So? What's your point?"

Through her tears, Mavis gave a sheepish grin. "Just leave, huh?"

"Have you got a set of car keys handy?" Mavis stood and retrieved them from a pegboard beside the back door.

"Maybe I should say something to them first."

"Okay."

"Only I can't go back out there. I just can't."

"Okay." Annabelle waited for her to decide, one way or the other.

Mavis cracked the swinging door and called through the dining room into the living room. "Please excuse me. Something's come up, and I have to leave now. Thank you so much for coming."

She turned around, grabbed Annabelle by the wrist, and said, "Come on. Let's get out of here."

They ran out the back door and jumped in the Beetle. Claude's car was blocking the driveway. Mavis drove around it, through a flowerbed, across the front yard, over the curb, and into the street. Claude stood up from his seat on the porch and, looking mildly puzzled, gave them a little wave as he watched them drive away.

PART TWO
Winter

Swarming Blackbirds

CHAPTER NINE

After Thanksgiving, Mavis went to bed and stayed for ten days. She wasn't sick, and she knew it. She just didn't want to get up, and there wasn't anything she wanted to do or anybody she wanted to see. And she didn't have anything to say. To anybody.

Annabelle fed her toast and peanut butter and did not leave her. She crooned little songs and held her. When Mavis cried, she said, "There, there," and patted her and brought cold washcloths for her face.

On the second day while she was washing Mavis's face, she said, "I saved your letters."

"What letters?"

"You know. The ones from boarding school when they sent you away. And one from Pittsburgh when you ran away and no one knew where you were. And a few from your early years here in Birmingham when you hardly knew anyone and were so lonely.

"And the ones from when you first fell in love with Harrison and thought he was going to marry you."

"Those too, huh?"

"Yes."

"Where are they?"

"In my suitcase. Do you want to read them?"

"Yes."

"Aloud?"

"No. By myself. Here in bed. And don't ask me about them, okay, Annabelle? Don't rub salt in the wounds. You hear?"

"Yes, Mavis, I hear."

"Just get them and put them under the bed, and I'll read them when I want to."

"Okay."

Letter #1 from the Christian Children's Home and School (CCH&S) in Pensacola, Florida, Fall 1955:

Dear Annabelle,

Where are you? Why didn't you come with me? I don't know anybody here, not a soul, and I need you.

The first night in this dormertory (prison) I thought maybe you were hiding under the bed and I looked but you weren't there. I hate you!!

My roommate's name is Juanita Bloodsoe. Isn't that an awful name? (And I thought Mavis Horton was bad. Go figure.) JB is a real eyesore and a real Eyore to. Always crying. Sniff, sniff, sniff, all nite in her bed. I hate her. In the morning her nose is all read like Rudoff's and she has pimples. Ugh! Terrible zits. I call her Juanita Bleeding-sore, or would if I talked to her. Which I don't.

I'm not ever going to like this school, and I hate Grandpa for sending me here just because I wouldn't answer him when he asked where I'd been. He said I'd been in the Hofstetter's barn with Jimmy Hofstetter, and I had to, but we weren't doing nothing. Grandpa said I was turning out just like my mother and he wasn't going to stand for it.

Why did he say that, Annie? That's the only thing he ever said to me about her since he told me she was dead. Did he mean I am going to die to?

Maybe I am sick and don't know it and they aren't telling me. Is that why they sent me here? I threw up twice today. The food here does not agree with me.

Jimmy H showed me his you-know-what. I thought it would be skin-colored but it was red and looked sore. I told him I was sorry. It was the only thing I ever said to him, and it made him mad. Go figure, huh?

That's what I say now. Everybody says I have to talk, so that's what I say. Go figure.

If you will come I will give you ½ the brownies Grandma sent me.

XXXXXOOO, Still your friend (Go figure), Mavis

Letter #2 from Pittsburgh, Pennsylvania, train station, Spring, 1957:

Dear Annabelle,

Why aren't you here? I am looking ever where for you. I thought you would be here waiting for me. That's why I came. I have been riding trains for a nite and a day and part of another nite, plus 45 min. sitting here in this depot. (Why don't they spell it deep hole?)

I left CCH&S in the middle of the nite so I would not have to get up and face another day there. I did not have my algebra homework. Not once have I ever had my algebra homework. I was going to detention for sure. I hate detention.

I like a boy. His name is Edward. I asked him to run away with me but he wouldn't. I said why not and he said because he can't run. (It's a joke, see, on account of he got polio and has a brace and crotches.) (sp?)

On the train was a soldier. A sargant, he told me, 34-yrs-old. He was drinking out of a bottle in a paper sack. He tried to get me to. I said no. Otherwise I did not talk but he did all nite until he went to sleep on my shoulder. He said things he shouldn't (the F word) and called me honey and kissed my neck. At 1ˢᵗ I didn't like it and then I did. It was warm and cozy and the lights were low in the coach car. He put his hand under my fanny and breathed on my neck. We rode like that all nite til I got off and changed trains.

I know your not supposed to let strangers kiss your neck and touch your fanny, and I don't know why I did. You cannot tell anybody EVER.

DO YOU HEAR ME, ANNABELLE? I am homesick but I don't know for where. I am homesick for you, Annie. How can you forsake me?

I don't have anyone but you and now I am forsaken by you to. I'm not ever going to speak to you again. I am going to forsake you like you forsaked me.

FOR SAKE. FOR (my) SAKE, come back. (Change a letter and you have FOR SALE. I feel like I am for sale and nobody is buying.)

Your former friend, Mavis Horton

Letter #3 from CCH&S, Winter, 1958:
NOTICE
TO: Annabelle Lee Jones
FROM: Mavis Horton
This Notice is a Warning. BEWARE! If I do not hear from you soon, I am going to become a SLUT. That is a girl with a bad reputation. This is what my house mother has told me, and she quotes chapter and verse on the topic.

The way you can tell if you are becoming a slut or not is if you miss bells. I am missing bells, Annabelle. I am telling you! Do you hear??? I AM MISSING BELLS.

(And marbles too. Do you know what I mean?)

I stayed out with HNC (that stands for Horny Nut Case) until 12:30 last nite and that is a ½ hr past midnite and 3 ½ hrs past bells on a school nite and 2 hrs on a wkend, but it was a school nite. I got caught and they had a faculty meeting about me and assigned Mrs. Snoopy Head (house mother) to speak to me. She said one more time missing bells and it will be official: Mavis Horton is a slut.

Horny Nut Case is not his real name. (Do tell.) It is Horace Neal Calloway but I call him Horny Nut Case because he is horny and crazy. He will do anything and not care a whit. (What is a whit? I dunno.) I am learning to be like him. Not give a whit, only he says a rat's ass. Okay, so I don't give a RA.

I don't like him or anything. You know. Still we sneak out and neck and smoke cigs. I told him next time I will go all the way. He's been all the way lots of times. Girls who go all the way can't ever come back. You know what I mean? Boys can start over ever time. Girls are never the same. I don't want to be the same, but I don't want to be a slut either. I want someone to hold me and talk to me. Not just talk about me afterwards. Sometimes Horace talks to me, mostly about how he hates his old man. That's what he calls his daddy. I wish I had a daddy. When I said that he laughed at me and said no, I didn't.

But I do, Annie. And I wish I still had you but this is no place for a friend like you. I don't blame you for not wanting to come here.

Letter #4 from CCH&S, Spring, 1959:
Dear Annabelle,
This is how things are going:
Algebra—D
English—B
Home Ec—D (I burned the muffins. Twice.)
Civics—C
Deportment—C (improved from a D- last time because of being a slut for 6 wks with HNC)
Art—A
An A in art!!!
Can you believe it? I can NOT. Do you know why? Its not because I can draw real good. Its because of Miss Arliss. That's her name. She is my teacher sent here to CCH&S 2 days a wk. She is really nice and kind and pretty and talanted. I wish I was her so I could be talanted to.

She says I am but I must learn and stop wasting myself on being a slut. So that's what I am doing. Rite now I am doing 2 things for her. 1) Drawing "in perspective" in class and 2) Painting what is in my heart like she says which she and I do on our own together on Sat.

Thus far, besides drawing "in perspective," I have painted 3 pictures of you, Annabelle, and one of my mama in her caskett. Tomorrow which is Sat. I am going to paint a picture of me in the sky flying around because that is how happy I feel when I paint with Miss Arliss.

XXXOOO luv from your friend and fellow artist, Mavis

P.S. Miss Arliss said I should not have run away that time to Pitsburg. She said it was childish and I scared Grandpa and that is why he was so mean to me when he and the superendent of CCH&S came to get me.

P.S.#2 Miss A also said HNC is a troubled boy and I should not sneak out with him. I did not tell her about going all the way, which I did only once and found it was a one-way ticket to no where from whence a girl cannot return. (I also did not tell her about the sargant on the train. Only you.)

Letter #5 from Birmingham, 1966:

My dear Annabelle,

I am a career girl now. All grown up and living comfortably in Birmingham, Alabama, on the Southside in a room I share with another career girl.

I graduated from that retched institution in Pensacola finally and hung around Piney where I could not stay on account of Grandpa Horton's sorrowful outlook on life and me in most particular. Grandma gave me start-up money because she says everyone needs a leg up to get started.

I am now started and will repay her as I can and as she sees fit. I have a paying job at the 10 cent store in 5 Points where I am Clerk and

ASST Cashier and I am taking Bus Math and Beginning Bookkeeping at nite school. I wanted to take art class but I am too intentional toward making a start on life not to be practical minded. This not only is in my own self interest but also on the advice of Miss Arliss with whom I correspond upon ocassion when I can find the time.

Your friend always, Mavis

P.S. You are invited to come see me and view my new circumstances.

Letter #6 from Birmingham, Spring 1968:

Dear Annabelle:

I am writing to inform you I have my own apartment now. All my own with two rooms and a bath (no tub), and you are most welcome to pay me a visit. I am learning to be a good hostess who can show guests all the comforts of home.

I have a regular and very good job at Harrison Clarke & Son Jewelry Store, thanks to Mr. Harrison Clarke himself (the son, not the father who is retired and in ill health). (Nearly dead, if truth be known.) Harrison (I call him by his first name when we are alone and Mr. Clarke in front of other employees and, of course, customers, as per his request) is a wonderful boss and knows his business. He is also a wonderful and handsome man who knows how to make the most of what has been given to him, which is quite a lot.

You see, we are not only boss and employee but dear, dear friends, though that is our private life and nobody's business but ours.

I am not a slut and he knows it but "a very attractive girl with lots of promise," according to Harrison himself. He is showing me the ropes of the jewelry business and how to have a gratifying private life that is no one else's business but our own.

Last night when he came here for a private dinner (we ate by candlelite) he brought me a portable hi-fi, so you can see he knows how to treat a girl like a lady.

Do come and see me sometime altho I should warn you I am very busy with my job and am still taking one course at nite (Bookkeeping II). Also, I do not expect to be in this apartment for long, but living in a big house in Mountain Brook. (Not that Harrison has popped the question yet, but I can tell it's just a matter of time. He's leading up to it.)

Love from your old friend, Mavis

Letter #7 from Birmingham, Summer, 1975:

Dear Annabelle:

This will be my last letter to you because I am grown up now and must put away childish things.

Old Mr. Clarke died a few months ago and his last death wish was that Harrison marry a suitable Mountain Brook sort of girl (which means high society in B'ham, which, after all, is what Harrison and all the Clarkes are themselves) which explains why Harrison is marrying Bitsy Parker this afternoon in Advent Cathedral with reception afterwards at the Birmingham Country Club and why I have to go and wish them well and put in an appearance and up a good front.

Bitsy had been away at a girls' school in Virginia and then in Washington for several years working for an Alabama congressman (family connections, you know). She came home last summer and dropped by the store one day. Harrison hadn't seen her since they were children. So he's been dating her ever since because, of course, he had to as that is what the family wanted—and then he promised his father too.

So it is time for me to be a big girl and happy for him, which, of course, I am, altho I very much doubt she is the girl for him.

You see, she doesn't understand him and I do, and he knows that and says he is so glad he still has me to rely on because otherwise what would he do. And I don't know because we both realize he can't get along without me.

Annabelle, I can hear you tsk-tsking as you read this. I know you do not approve and do not understand, but you are the friend of my childhood, not my adulthood, and so I am saying good-bye and thanks for the memories and I am all grown up now and can take it from here.

Your old friend now grown up, Mavis

CHAPTER TEN

During these days while Mavis was in seclusion, reading old letters and trying to figure out how she got to where she was, Jonathan sat on the front steps and waited. One day Annabelle came out and sat with him. He took her presence in stride as the natural course of things, and they waited together.

"What's the matter with her?" he asked.

"She's grieving."

"Is that like the earache?"

"I don't think so."

"The earache makes you cry and want your momma."

"Then I guess grieving *is* a lot like the earache."

"Here, give her this." He pulled a bedraggled stuffed elephant from under his sweater. "It's my Fantie. He always makes me feel better. Maybe he'll make her feel better too. But tell her I'll need him back when it's nap time."

"Okay. Thanks, Jonathan."

"You're welcome."

Another day when they were sitting there, Jonathan said, "You know, Annabelle, I didn't use to talk to you."

"No? Why was that?"

"I thought maybe you were pri-bate."

"You mean like I just belonged to Mavis?"

"Yes. Like me and Rotten Eddie. Nobody talks to him but me. Momma pretends to sometimes, but she doesn't really."

"I'll let you in on a little secret. Sometimes I talk to Rotten Eddie."

Jonathan's eyes got big. "You do?"

"Yep."

"What do you say?"

"I tell him to straighten up and fly right and to stop getting you in trouble."

"You do?" Jonathan was awed.

"Yes."

"Does he get mad?"

"No. He runs and hides."

"In the trunk?"

"Yes."

"He stays there a lot."

Neither spoke for a while.

"Annabelle?"

"Yes."

"Why won't Mabis come out?"

"She feels bad."

"Why?"

"It's complicated."

"Is she mad 'cause I'm talking to you?"

"No. Why would that make her mad?"

"B-e-c-a-u-s-e."

"Because why?"

"You know."

"No, I don't."

"B-e-c-a-u-s-e...." He held his hands as if releasing a bird. "Because now you're being pri-bate with me, not just with her."

"Oh."

Annabelle thought this over.

"Jonathan, I think Mavis would like my being private with you too. I can be private with her, and I can be private with you too."

"Okay."

"And we can all be private together. But let's not tell anybody else."

"No," he said solemnly, "let's not."

During this time, Mavis didn't answer the phone or the door and Annabelle didn't either. One day Harrison appeared on the front porch and, when Annabelle told Mavis he was there, Mavis got out of bed and went to the door. She stood looking at him through the screen.

He appeared stunned by her appearance—uncombed, unwashed hair, a faded old flannel robe, gym socks. At first, he couldn't seem to remember what he had come to say.

Mavis waited without a word.

Finally, he said, "Mavis, are you sick?"

She shook her head.

"You aren't answering the phone."

She shrugged.

There was an awkward silence. He jiggled the change in his pocket, cleared his throat, looked away.

Finally he said, "The thing is I'm in a jam. It's the Christmas rush, and I've got two sales people out with the flu."

She didn't reply.

"Florence and Gilbert. Both out sick."

Pause.

"Mavis."

Nothing.

"Look, honey, I know somehow, unintentionally, I've offended you. I don't know how I did it, but I'm sorry. I wouldn't deliberately hurt your feelings for the world. You know how I depend on you, count on you. Always have because you never let me down."

Still no response.

"Look, Mavis, I'm telling you, I don't know where else to turn. The next three weeks are the busiest of the year for us. You know that. Christmas makes us or breaks us. In a specialty store like ours, I can't bring in a bunch of temps during the holidays. People without any training or experience. I need someone like you who knows the business, knows the inventory, knows what needs to be done and how to do it."

Finally she said, "What about the new girl?"

"Oh, well. Shana's fine. Good. Real competent. But right now, Mavis…. Well, sweetheart, right now, I need you."

He gave a little shrug, a self-deprecating chuckle, a helpless shake of the head. "What else can I say? No one else will do."

With an impassive face, she stared at him for a long moment. The earth hesitated in its rotation while she made up her mind. The planets held their breath. The clock on the mantle strained so intently for her answer it failed to tick.

At last, she nodded. "In the morning," she said. "I'll be there in the morning."

She closed the door and, unable to face Annabelle, fled to her room.

Annabelle sank in defeat. She had exhausted her efforts. She considered leaving for good. Instead, after awhile, she withdrew to the guest room where, this time, she herself went to bed and pulled up the covers.

CHAPTER ELEVEN

E very morning for the next twenty days, Mavis got up early, put on her one remaining suit, drove down two-eighty in rush hour traffic to the new store at The Summit. It was, indeed, 'very upscale.'

At home, she and Annabelle avoided one another. Mavis ate breakfast alone each morning before she left and supper alone each evening when she returned. Annabelle stayed in the guest room. Mavis pretended she wasn't there.

During the day, Annabelle continued to sit on the front steps with Jonathan. Over and over, he said, "I miss her. When's she coming home?"

And over and over, Annabelle said, "I don't know. At Christmas, I reckon."

"Before or after Santa Claus?"

"Before I hope."

"I hate the waiting."

"Me too."

"Annabelle, are you trying to be good?"

"Yes. Are you?"

"Yes. I locked Rotten Eddie up until after Christmas."

"So he won't get you in trouble?"

"Yes. He's in the trunk of the Beetle. He rides around in there with Mabis, and she doesn't even know he's there."

"He's probably a bad influence on her."

Jonathan frowned. "What's that?"

"He might get her in trouble like he does you."

"Oh." He thinks this over. "Is Mabis in trouble?"

"I hope not."

"Me too."

The next day Annabelle and Jonathan stood in the backyard and tried to figure out what was going on. The air was cold and still, the sky dark and dreary. The bare trees were full of blackbirds, hundreds of them, maybe thousands, making a loud screeching noise.

Jonathan reached for Annabelle's hand. "What are they doing?" he whispered.

"They're swarming."

"Why?"

"It's winter time, and they don't know what to do with themselves."

"I wish they'd go away."

"Me too."

Then she said, "Watch." She raised her arms suddenly above her head and shouted, "Shoo-o-o-o!"

In unison, all at once, the birds rose above the trees, hovered for an instant, and then settled back onto the same stark limbs where they'd been roosting.

"Oh, Annabelle, chase them away. Make 'em get out of here."

"I can't. I can make them fly up, but I can't make them leave."

"I'm going to. I'm going to make these bad old birds fly away."

He began to jump up and down, clapping his hands and shouting, "Shoo. Shoo."

The birds flew up and hovered, and, at the ongoing racket below, moved to the trees in the yard across the street and settled there. Jonathan ran after them, pell-mell, flapping his arms, yelling, forgetting he wasn't allowed to cross the street.

Annabelle called after him, but he paid no attention.

Across the street, he jumped up and down under the trees there, shouting, "Shoo, shoo," and clapping. Again the birds rose up, hovered, and swarmed. This time, to his dismay, they flew back over his head and settled again in the trees in Mavis's yard.

Jonathan's momma was on her front porch now calling him. "Jonathan, what do you think you're doing? You know you're not supposed to cross the street. Wait. Wait. Don't come running back. Let me come and get you. You come on back in the house until you can remember what you are, and are not, allowed to do."

Jonathan ducked his head until she came to fetch him. As he followed her inside, he gave Annabelle a helpless shrug.

CHAPTER TWELVE

Mavis came home mid-afternoon on Christmas Eve. She was out of breath, carrying packages, and yelling when she reached the house.

"Annabelle, open the door. Hurry up!"

"For crying out loud, Mavis, what's gotten into you?"

"Have the police been here?"

"The police? No. Why in the world would the police be here?"

"Look!" Mavis dropped her packages on the sofa and turned to Annabelle, tilting her head first this way and then that. Her ears glittered like headlights on high beam.

"My God!" Annabelle cried. "Are they real?"

"Of course, they're real. One point five carats each. Excellent color and clarity. First-rate stones. In the neighborhood of fifteen thousand if you don't count the tax. Even with my employee discount, well over ten thousand. I don't know exactly how much. I took them out of the safe before they'd been priced."

"You borrowed them?"

"I stole them!"

"What?"

"Oh, and that's not all." She reached inside a large shopping bag and began tossing bundles of wrapped ten, twenty, fifty, and hundred dollar bills into the air. They landed on the sofa, the coffee table, and the floor.

"Dear God in Heaven," Annabelle said and sank among the cushions. "How much is that?"

"Don't know. I didn't take the time to count it. I just walked right out of the store with it, wearing my diamond earrings."

"Mavis, they are not your earrings!"

"Well, not technically. That's why I asked about the police."

"Mavis, listen to me. Have you lost your mind?"

Mavis cocked her head and stared at Annabelle as she appeared to consider this. "I don't know," she said finally, "but I'll tell you this—I'm very excited."

"What in the world possessed you?"

Collapsing like an empty moneybag herself, Mavis sank to the sofa amid the scattered bills. Ears twinkling but with somber eyes, she said, "He's sleeping with her. I had to do something."

"Who?"

"Harrison!"

"No, I mean who is he sleeping with?"

"Shana. You know, Wonder Woman. The girl who took my place. My successor. The one who can't open the safe."

"Shana?"

"Yes. Can you believe her name is Shana?"

"No."

"Me either."

"How do you know?"

"Know?"

"About her and Harrison."

"Oh, Annabelle." Mavis began to cry. "Because I've been there. Because I used to be her."

Annabelle sat down beside her and held her hand. "How long have you known?"

"I don't know. From my first day back on the job, I guess. I've been watching them. Couldn't help myself. It was like I was hypnotized."

She wiped her eyes with the back of her hand. "All the signs were there. The little glances. The private jokes. The intimate little chats in his office.

"I told myself I was imagining things. That I was jealous. Then this afternoon I came back from lunch early. We were so busy I didn't want to be gone long. I was hanging up my coat in the storeroom, and I saw her duck into his office and ask him something. As she turned to leave, he grasped her hand, pulled her to him, and, Annabelle, he kissed her! Right there in the office, before God and everybody, he kissed her! I couldn't stand it!"

"Oh Mavis." Annabelle sat shaking her head sadly. "Maybe it's not as bad as you think. Maybe he's just..., you know, fooling around with her. Maybe he's not...."

"No. No way. I'm telling you, Annabelle, I know this man."

"Okay. I guess you do at that."

"Anyway, when they left a few minutes later to go to lunch, I went into his office and opened the safe and took the diamonds and the money."

"Do you really think he'll call the police?"

"I don't know. Harrison doesn't like to be made a fool of."

"Do you want to take the stuff back?"

"No." She gave a helpless smile and a shake of her head. "I've felt angry and hurt for so long now, even when I've denied it to you. Now I'd rather have him feel bad for a change. It helps even the score."

"Yes." Annabelle gave a wry smile and squeezed her hand. "I suppose it does."

That evening after dark, the doorbell rang. Harrison was standing on the porch. Annabelle was relieved to note there was no policeman with him.

Mavis went to the door and opened it. She was still wearing the diamond studs.

Harrison came in. Mavis stood back. Annabelle took refuge out of sight where she could watch.

Like a bull who'd just entered the ring, Harrison glared at the bundles of cash still scattered on the sofa and the floor. Annabelle half-expected him to paw the ground and snort smoke.

"Mavis, what the hell's the matter with you?"

"I saw you with her."

"What?" Furious as he was, he looked at her as if she were speaking Greek. He shook his head. Maybe he thought it was Swahili.

"What in tarnation...?"

"Shana. I saw you with her. This afternoon in your office."

"Is that what this is about?" He was incredulous.

Mavis herself was paralyzed. She'd forgotten to breathe. But then maybe breathing was no longer necessary. She'd set something in motion here that was now carrying on without her.

"You left me without enough in the safe to make change for cash customers. On Christmas Eve afternoon. What the hell were you thinking?"

Mavis had turned to stone. She didn't answer.

"I've been worried about you, Mavis. Frankly, I think you've gone off the deep end. I had thought maybe getting back to the store for a few days would be good for you. Make you feel useful again. I was trying to help you out. Give you something to do. Let you get a little Christmas money together.

And then you go and pull a stunt like this. I don't know what to think. I'm at a loss as to what to do."

Turning to her as if for answers, he did, indeed, look bewildered. Fit to be tied. "Can you help me out here? Explain to me what's going on."

When she didn't answer, he said, "Look, Mavis, we've had a long run together. A good run. Why spoil it now?"

"I don't think I'm the one who's spoiling things."

"No? You've retired, Mavis. I've moved on. You need to move on too."

"You pushed me out the door so you could replace me with her."

"Now, Mavis, that's the sound of a jealous woman talking. Don't act that way. It doesn't become you."

Mavis heard Annabelle clear her throat in the hall. It caused her to prick up her ears, straighten her shoulders.

She wondered if Harrison heard Annabelle too. Apparently not. He began to move toward the scattered bundles of money, as if to collect them.

"I'll tell you what. Let's let bygones be bygones. Suppose I let you keep the diamond earrings. Although, I must say, they are some of the nicest stones we've had in the store in some time. But, let's call them a Christmas present. From me to you."

"Yes," she said. "A Christmas present. That's good."

She was beginning to get her wind back, but she knew him too well not to be braced for what was coming. She moved between him and the money.

"And," he continued, "I'll simply return this cash to the company safe and we won't say another word about it to anybody."

"No. I want to keep the money too."

"Mavis, do you realize how much that is?"

"No, I haven't counted it."

"There's some eighty-seven thousand dollars here."

"Oh. Well, that's all right. I guess that's enough."

"Enough?"

"I mean I think I'll settle for that."

"Settle?"

"Yes."

"Mavis, we're not negotiating here. These are company funds."

"I know."

"When you take company funds, that's called embezzlement."

Somehow the sound of the word jarred Mavis out of her trance. "Embezzlement?" she cried. "I didn't embezzle the money, Harrison. That implies something sneaky, undercover, behind your back. I walked right out the front door with it in broad daylight. Nothing sneaky about it. Nothing secretive. Unlike you, I don't go sneaking around. Deceiving people. Lying."

"Oh please! So you saw me kissing the help. So what?"

"We both know you're sleeping with her."

"Mavis, it's time you stopped living in the past and moved on."

"I think so too. That's what I'm going to do with the money. Stop living in the past. Move on."

"Now look here! If you think you can blackmail me...."

"Bitsy is not a forgiving woman."

"Mavis! I don't believe you."

"You'd better start."

"Bitsy would never listen to you. She'd think the same thing I do. That you're just jealous and can't bear to see someone else in your place at the store."

"Oh, Harrison, I'm really not talking about Shana. Not really. I think this is a crummy way for you to behave, but it's none of my business. At least, not anymore.

"What I'm talking about is you and me and forty years during which I made your happiness and well-being my first priority. I shouldn't have, but I did, and I think you owe me for that. Sure, I'm a grown woman. I had some choice in the matter. I know that. Still, over the years, you said a lot of things to me, Harrison. Things I believed. Things I hung my hopes on."

"I never promised you anything, Mavis."

"You didn't have to. I was willing to accept things the way they were. In hindsight, that seems sort of pitiful. Still, it never occurred to me that one day you'd just throw me over for a newer, better, more up-to-date model."

"Oh, for crying out loud!"

"What I don't understand is what took you so long? I've been getting older for decades now. Decades of building my life around you. Decades of keeping diaries, records, calendars of my relationship with you. That's what bookkeepers do, Harrison. Keep records. I even saved a few love letters over the years that you told me to throw away. All these mementos are filed away in a hope chest in my bedroom closet. A hope chest! Can you imagine? They date back to when I was young and pretty like Shana is now. Bitsy would be interested in those. But why hurt her unnecessarily, Harrison? I'd hate for her to see them, and I don't see any real reason why she has to."

"Bitsy'd never believe you."

"I think she would. And it would be very unpleasant for you."

"And for you, Mavis."

"For me? Oh, I hardly think so. I'm old, but I'm hardly used up. I think I might enjoy a reputation as a home wrecker.

As a woman to be reckoned with. People would be surprised, but they'd be interested. Give 'em something to talk about. I think I'd like the attention."

"Mavis, I hardly think...."

"What? You hardly think what?"

"That you'd want to bring gossip down on yourself."

"Then you don't know me as well as you think you do."

"Mavis, stop talking like this. We've meant too much to each other through the years for you to talk this way, for you to threaten me. There's no reason in the world for you to behave this way."

"Oh, Harrison, I think there's every reason in the world. I have a lifetime of reasons. I'm keeping the diamonds and the money, and that's all there is to it. I've earned the right to both. You can call it a severance package for the best and most loyal employee you've ever had or, are ever likely, to have. And I'll use the money to pay off my new car and to take a cruise. Not a slow boat to China, but a trip to the Bahamas. I've always wanted to do that. And I'll have a little cushion left over to fall back on."

Harrison stared at her for a long time. This was not a Mavis he knew. This Mavis alarmed him. Scared him actually. He wasn't sure just what she might be capable of. He wondered if she was dangerous, if perhaps something really had snapped.

"Mavis, be reasonable. You can't expect me just to give you eighty-seven thousand dollars out of the company safe. That's a good chunk of this Christmas season's profit. I can't afford that kind of loss."

"Of course you can! You forget I've kept your books all these years."

"And I'm supposed to just write it off?"

"I've been thinking about that," she said, falling back into the role she'd played for years of helping him solve his problems. "I don't think it's a good idea to show it on the company ledger. I think you should pay it back to the company out of personal funds."

"Good God, Mavis, you know I don't carry that much in my personal bank account. Besides, it's in Bitsy's name too. She'd have a fit."

"There's that," Mavis agreed, "and I suppose if you did it as a line of credit on the Mountain Brook house, she might find out about it.

"I know! Do it as a line of credit on the Destin condo. She'll never know, and you'll never miss the money. In no time, you'll have it paid back."

"Mavis, listen to yourself. You've gone around the bend. I'm not letting you keep the money."

Again he made a move toward the stacks of bills.

This time, with a raised hand and a sharp tone, she stopped him cold.

"Yes, Harrison, you are. If you can't admit it's the right thing to do, then rest assured it's the easy thing. I've got nothing to lose here, and you've got everything."

"Mavis, that's absurd."

"I know. It is absurd. And it's the God's truth."

They looked at each other for a long moment. Four decades between them were crystallized in that moment and, if understanding failed to emerge, resignation did. On both their parts.

"Mavis, I think I'll go now," he said at last.

And then, to save face, he added, "I can't tell you how disappointed I am in you. I never thought I'd see the day when you'd turn on me like this. When you've thought this through and come to your senses, you let me know. Until then," he paused for emphasis and gave a wry smile, "I'm going to leave you alone."

She knew to let him have the last word. It was the least she could do for him, and the most.

He left, and she closed the door behind him.

CHAPTER THIRTEEN

On Christmas morning, Mavis and Annabelle sat amid the bundles of cash still scattered about the living room and drank coffee. They were wearing their pink butterfly robes, and Mavis still had on the diamond earrings.

"Well now," Annabelle said, "I sure am proud of you."

"I'm right proud of myself," Mavis said. "And I haven't been much of my life."

"You've always had a lot to be proud of. You just didn't always know it."

"Maybe not."

Annabelle smiled. "You've earned your keep."

"Oh heavens, yes. And now I've rewarded myself. It's Christmas after all, which reminds me, I have Christmas presents for you. For you and for Jonathan, my two friends."

"Is that what these are?" Annabelle gestured toward the packages Mavis had arrived with yesterday which, amid the excitement about the money and the diamonds, had been overlooked.

"Yes." She fetched several bundles and handed them to Annabelle. "Here, these are yours. Open them."

They weren't gift-wrapped but in shopping bags from the Alabama Art Supply Store. They contained a portable easel, an array of paints, and a set of brushes.

"Mavis, honey, how wonderful! Thank you so much. I haven't painted since we were children together. We had such fun then."

"I know. Now you can paint with Jonathan. I got him a child's easel and a set of poster paints."

"Oh, that's perfect. You know, Jonathan and I became pals while you were working."

"I'm not surprised."

They sat in silence for a moment.

"Mavis?"

"Yes?"

"A package came for you yesterday."

"Oh? A Christmas present?"

"I don't know. It's from Elmira."

"Good Lord. We don't give each other presents."

"I know."

Annabelle fetched a package about the size of a book, wrapped in brown paper and tied with string. She placed it in Mavis's lap.

"What now?" Mavis said, holding her hands up as if afraid to touch it.

Annabelle pulled the string off for her and tore off the wrapping paper to reveal a yellow candy box, an old-fashioned Whitman's Sampler.

"She sent me chocolates?"

"I don't think so," Annabelle said. The box was not new but tattered and worn. "Here's a note. Read it." She handed a white envelope to Mavis.

Mavis flapped her hands and refused to take it. "You read it."

Annabelle gave Mavis a long, thoughtful look and carefully opened the envelope. Holding Mavis still with a firm hand on her thigh, she read:

Dear Mavis,

Grandma left this box in the bottom of her cedar chest. I found it the other day when I was looking for her boiled custard recipe. Thought you might like to have these few remaining mementoes of your mama (though I can't imagine why at this late date). Anyway, Merry Christmas.

Your cousin,

Elmira

P.S. You don't happen to have the custard recipe, do you?

Mavis lifted the lid cautiously as if she expected a jack-in-the-box to jump out at her. Inside were ten pieces of mail, four postcards and six Christmas cards. Besides the Pacific Ocean and Rosie the Riveter postcards Sammie Jo had mentioned, there was one with the famous Hollywood sign on it and another showing the corner of Hollywood and Vine. They were all addressed to Grandma. None were dated, and none carried return addresses. They were all postmarked Los Angeles during the last year of the war and were sent in the following order.

Pacific Ocean postcard:

Dear Mama,

How are you? I am fine. I am in the sunshine state. Or is that Fla.? Irregardless, it never rains in Calif. Not like rainy old Ala.

Your daughter,
Althea Horton

Rosie the Riveter postcard:

Dear Mama,

I am a career girl now. (See my photo on the other side. Ha ha!) I am luckie. I am on the day shift.

Your daughter,
Althea Horton

P.S. Tell my hateful daddy I have too amounted to something. He said I never would, so what does he know?

Hollywood & Vine postcard:
Dear Mama,
This is where the movie stars meet. I keep an eye out but have not seen one yet. Maybe tomorrow.
Your daughter,
Althea Horton

Hollywood sign postcard:
Dear Mama,
I saw Betty Grable! She is even more glamorous in daily life than on the silver screen. She was driving a convertable. I'm sure it was her.
Your daughter,
Althea Horton

The Christmas cards did, indeed, all have snow scenes as Sammie Jo had said. There were no messages on them, and they were all signed Althea and Wayne Philpot. They were all addressed to The Horton Family, which was as close as any of the mail came to acknowledging Mavis's existence.

Underneath the cards were a few snapshots that Grandma had saved, apparently hidden from Grandpa. They appeared to have been taken with the family box Kodak and torn out of an album. One was of a pretty blond toddler on a tricycle in front of the Piney house. At first, Mavis thought the child was herself. She had ridden the same tricycle. But it wasn't. On the back, in Grandma's handwriting, it said "Althea, age four." Another was of a long-legged girl of ten or so with a pet goat hitched to a two-wheel cart. And a third showed a teenager in a cheerleader's skirt and sweater and bobby socks, hands on her hips, trying to strike a provocative pose.

And finally, in the bottom of the box, Mavis found a picture of the same teenager in a winter coat, her head tied in a scarf, holding a baby wrapped in a bunting, its tiny face barely visible. The girl appeared impatient, the baby asleep.

"I can't stand it," Mavis said. "I simply can't stand it."

Annabelle hugged her and said nothing. After awhile, she went to the kitchen and returned with a tray of eggnog and fruitcake for breakfast.

"No halvers today. It's Christmas. Eat up."

"Shall we flavor the eggnog?" Mavis asked.

"You betcha. Where do you keep the bourbon?"

"On the third shelf in the pantry, behind the oatmeal."

And so they drank their spiked eggnog and ate their fruitcake. This was followed by a little toddy to cap it all off. Then, with gas logs burning in the fireplace, they took a long nap on the sofa.

CHAPTER FOURTEEN

A few days passed. Mavis worked on her needlepoint. Annabelle experimented with her new paints. They took turns playing with Jonathan. Santa Claus had brought him a football, helmet, and University of Alabama jersey, all just his size. They threw the ball to him, and he wove a circuitous path around the yard, shouting, "I'm running. I'm running. I'm falling down."

One pretty day he and Annabelle set up their easels in the backyard. He wore an apron of Mavis's over his football jersey and kept his helmet on while he painted, which he did enthusiastically.

On New Year's Day, Mavis and Annabelle watched the Rose Bowl Parade on television. With her eyes on the flowered floats and marching bands, Annabelle said, "I found your mama in Chicago. She's still alive."

Mavis jumped so high a wooden bowl flew out of her lap, causing popcorn to rain down on them like confetti.

"Good gracious, Annabelle! Now look what you've done."

Annabelle picked the popcorn up off the rug while Mavis sat dumbfounded and watched her. "She's still alive? She must be up in her eighties by now," she said. "How'd you find her?"

"I looked up the Chicago phone book on the internet. She wasn't listed, so I called all the Philpots until I found her stepson. Seventeen of them."

"There are seventeen Philpots in Chicago?"

"No. I don't know how many there are. I didn't count them. I found her stepson on the seventeenth call."

"Did you talk to her?"

"No. She's in a nursing home in Evanston."

"My God, Annabelle, what did you say to him?"

"I told him who I was and…."

"Who did you say you were?"

"Annabelle Lee Jones. Who did you think I would say?"

"I was afraid you told him you were me."

"Of course not. That would have been presumptuous."

"Well yeah. And we wouldn't want to be presumptuous, would we?"

"Mavis, just listen, okay? I just told him I had known her when she was a girl growing up in Piney, Alabama, and we'd been classmates, and our old high school is having a reunion. And, I said I'm on the committee to locate as many of us as are still around, still alive and kicking, and…."

"One lie after the other."

"Well, yes."

"So she's still alive? How old?"

"Eighty-one. She's been in the nursing home about five years now. Doesn't get out at all anymore."

"What about her husband?"

"He's been dead a long time, the son said. Nearly twenty years."

"Annabelle, you do beat all."

"Are you mad at me?"

"Yes. No. I don't know."

"I told him I'd like to send her an invitation to the reunion, even though she can't come, as a courtesy, you know. As a gesture."

"And did you?"

"Of course not, Mavis. There is no reunion. But I got her address. I would have gotten her phone number too, but he says she no longer talks on the phone."

Mavis said nothing.

"So...?" Annabelle said.

"So?"

"So, I thought we'd go see her."

"To Chicago?"

"To Evanston. That's where the nursing home is. Evanston is just north of Chicago."

"I know where Evanston is!"

"I just thought...."

"Oh, for crying out loud!"

"Can I take that as a yes?"

"Annabelle, Annabelle. After all these years? What's the point?"

"It's unfinished business, Mavis."

"I can't possibly go up there by myself."

"You won't have to. I'll go with you."

"And keep your mouth shut and stay out of the way?"

"Yes. And you can talk to me whenever you need to, and I'll be right there."

On the airplane, Mavis made a list of actual memories she had of her mother. Not things, often untruths apparently, that she'd been told, but things that she felt certain were her very own memories. All she had of her mother that she felt she could trust.

MEMORIES OF MY MOTHER
1) Fluffy yellow hair
2) Falling off a stool at the soda fountain downtown in Piney and her laughing at me for losing my balance when she spun me around

3) A song about a pistol-packing mama she sang to me on the porch swing

4) Being fed red licorice to stop crying at the picture show when Bambi's mother died

5) Going to the beauty parlor with her and playing with the electric permanent curlers that hung on wires above my head

6) Being told I was a little doll and to sit still in the wing chair in the living room and not get dirty

7) Being spanked for getting dirty

8) Rolling down a grassy hill, the two of us, and laughing and a man watching us, a stranger, and her kissing him and, on the way home, her saying, if I told, she'd whip me (Mavis thought this may have been the same day she laughed at her for falling off the stool at the soda fountain.)

9) A pink sweater that I slept with after she left that smelled of Evening in Paris

10) And....

And, for the life of her, Mavis couldn't think of a tenth memory. She only remembered nine things about her mother.

"That's pitiful," she said to herself and blinked back tears.

"Hush now," she heard Annabelle whisper.

CHAPTER FIFTEEN

When they got to O'Hare, Mavis went to the rest room and locked the stall door. She and Annabelle held hands and counted to one hundred together. Then they went and found a taxicab.

They didn't have to wait long for a train to Evanston, and Mavis found this disconcerting. She would have liked a lengthy delay. At one point, she considered turning around and, instead of going on to Evanston, going back to O'Hare and getting on the next plane to Birmingham. Annabelle said, "Don't you dare," in her ear, and she didn't.

Then she didn't have a chance to think about turning back again because there was a rush to board the train and, rather quickly, they were in Evanston. She had to locate another cab and then, too quickly again, she found herself dumped on the sidewalk in front of a long, low brick building that was the nursing home.

When she leaned in to pay the driver, she started to tell him just to take her back to the train station, but she heard Annabelle say, "Don't even think it," so she didn't. Instead, she took a deep breath and went up the walk and entered the building.

It was not as awful as she expected. Nursing homes usually frightened her, and she tried to avoid any circumstances that caused her to have to enter one. This one was bright with fluorescent lights, white walls, long corridors, and smelled more like bleach and antiseptic than sickness and death.

Mavis had to sign in, and she used Annabelle's name. Might as well, she thought. Annabelle said she'd wait in the waiting room. Mavis called her a coward, but Annabelle pretended not to hear. When the receptionist, who was giving directions, looked at her strangely, Mavis pretended she was talking to herself.

She walked down three long, white corridors, past two nurses' stations surrounded by clusters of crumpled bodies in wheelchairs. Wrapped in bathrobes, these residents sat open-mouthed and rheumy-eyed, heads lolling atop sagging shoulders. Their white hair either stood up in electrified-looking tufts or hung down in discouraged-looking shreds. As Mavis hurried past them, their claw-like hands clutched at her skirt and, in voices like the cawing of crows, they called after her.

"I pray to God," she muttered, "that one of these creatures is not My Mother."

When she arrived at the room number she'd been given, she stopped, afraid a blackness inside her eyelids was enveloping her. She waited a few seconds and heard a voice say, "Are you okay?"

She opened her eyes and saw a plump woman in a flower-patterned uniform that resembled pajamas staring at her. Her nametag said Vicki.

"Yes," Mavis said. "Are you a nurse?"

"Nurse's aide."

"Is this Althea Philpot's room?"

"Unhuh. You come to visit her?"

"Yes."

Vicki immediately moved into action, all business. She knocked on the door, pushed it open, and called out "Miz Philpot, wake up, you got company," all at the same time. Mavis followed her into the darkened room. Standing just inside the door, she waited for her eyes to adjust. Vicki pulled a chord and draperies flew open, flooding the room with bright light. Mavis saw the hospital bed was empty.

Thank God, she thought. She's not here.

Then she saw her in a lounge chair in the corner. A tiny creature under an afghan with a wrinkled gnome face and tufts of white hair. She opened her eyes, blinking at the light, and raised her face. She held out a frail hand toward Mavis and smiled.

Vicki pulled a straight chair up beside the lounger, motioned for Mavis to sit, and said loudly, "Enjoy your visit now," and left the room.

The Old Woman continued to smile sweetly and expectantly at Mavis. She held onto Mavis's hand and waited as if she knew her and this was a ritual they had performed many times.

Mavis stared at her. What was she waiting for? What did she expect?

Finally, The Old Woman leaned forward and whispered conspiratorially, "Where is it?"

Involuntarily, Mavis jumped. "Where's what?"

The Old Woman cackled. "You know."

"No, I don't."

The Old Woman looked at her shrewdly and gripped her hand tighter. She was surprisingly strong.

"Do you have any idea who I am?" Mavis asked.

"You're the lady who brings the candy. Where is it?"

"I don't have any candy."

"Yes, you do."

"Do you remember where you lived when you were young? Do you remember where you grew up?"

"What's in there?" The Old Woman pointed at Mavis's purse.

"Does Piney, Alabama, mean anything to you?"

She snatched Mavis's purse from her lap and began going through the contents. "Where is it?" she demanded.

Mavis took the purse from her, found half a package of peppermint Life Savers and gave them to her. The Old Woman put them all in her mouth, four or five of them, and leaned her head back and closed her eyes, cheeks sucking, lips smacking.

Mavis watched, appalled. The Old Woman had curly white hairs growing out her chin. She didn't look anything like the girl in the pictures Elmira had sent. She didn't look anything like the mother Mavis had envisioned all these years either. And, certainly, Mavis consoled herself, she didn't look anything like Mavis herself. Or anything like Mavis would ever look. She hoped.

"I can't stand this," she said aloud.

She slapped The Old Woman's hand lightly. It was drawn and withered, covered with blue veins and purple splotches. The Old Woman moved it out of reach and slid it under the afghan.

Mavis said, "Listen to me. I've come a long way to see you. You have to talk to me. I want to get some things straight."

The Old Woman gulped loudly and appeared to choke. She made a strangling noise, followed by a spasm of coughing. Her eyes bulged open, and her body went rigid. She grasped the arms of her chair and appeared unable to breathe.

"Oh my God, I've killed her," Mavis cried.

She looked in The Old Woman's mouth, which had now opened into a huge circle. She couldn't see anything. There wasn't enough light. She poked her finger into the hole to see if she could dislodge a stuck Life Saver. The Old Woman immediately bit down as hard as she could.

"Ouch!" Mavis yelped.

She jerked her finger out to find tooth marks, saliva, and blood between the first and second knuckle. Her finger throbbed and dripped blood. Pulling a silk scarf from around her neck, Mavis wrapped it around the wound and ran out into the hall.

It was empty. She shouted, "Vicki! Vicki! Where are you? Help! Somebody help!"

Vicki appeared from a closed door three rooms down. "What is it?" she asked.

"The...the...." Mavis couldn't think what to call The Old Woman. What in the world was her name? "She...she's choking."

Vicki did not appear in the slightest alarmed. She flung a towel across her shoulder and walked briskly into The Old Woman's room. There she pounded her on the back and shouted, "Spit it out! Do you hear me, Miz Philpot? I said spit it out! Now!"

The Old Woman spit into the towel.

"There. That's better. How many times am I gonna have to tell you not to try to swallow candy whole. Chew it or suck it, but do NOT try to swallow it whole. Okay? Now remember that."

Vicki turned to Mavis. "She's okay. She does this all the time." As she left, she added, "You might want to get her a cup of water from the bathroom there."

Mavis found a plastic cup in the bathroom and filled it with water. She took it to The Old Woman and held it to her gummy lips. The Old Woman suddenly jumped with a loud hiccup, upsetting the cup and sending the water down the front of her dress.

"Owie!" she cried out and, with a sudden swat, knocked the cup out of Mavis's hand. It sailed across the room and bounced off the wall. She blinked twice and then, once again, closed her eyes. Rhythmically, she continued to hiccup.

Mavis stood. Was this the visit then? Having come all this way, was she now to leave knowing no more than when she'd arrived? After all these years, was this all there was?

Squeezing the scarf around her throbbing finger, she walked around the room. She examined a group of pictures on the dresser. One showed a couple, side-by-side, in a booth at what appeared to be a nightclub. Both held martini glasses and cigarettes. The woman had blond hair and a glamorous face and wore dark lipstick, and the man was heavyset with a pencil mustache and wore a pinstriped suit.

A second picture showed the same man and woman with a half-grown boy standing beside a two-toned car with big fenders.

Another picture was of the same boy, older and wearing a naval uniform.

And in a small frame pushed to the back, Mavis found a snapshot of a little blond-haired girl on a tricycle. At first glance, she thought it was the same picture Elmira had sent of her mother as a child, but on closer examination, she recognized the sun suit the child was wearing. Even though the picture was in black and white, she knew the sun suit was yellow with brown rickrack trim. Grandma had made it for her when she was three.

Mavis picked up the picture and went into the hall. She looked for Vicki but didn't see her. She went down the corridor to the nearest nurses' station surrounded by its Greek chorus of crones in wheelchairs and found a woman in a white pants suit looking at a stack of charts.

"Excuse me," Mavis said. "I'm visiting Mrs. Philpot down the hall, and I saw this picture on her dresser. I wonder if you can tell me who it is?"

The woman looked up from the charts, tried to smile patiently but couldn't quite manage the effort, and shook her head. "I wouldn't know. I'm the medical supervisor for this entire unit. That's forty-eight patients. You might ask Mrs. Cook. She's in the room next to Mrs. Philpot. One-fifty-three. They're great friends."

Mavis went back down the hall and knocked on one-fifty-three. An ebullient voice shouted, "Come in."

A fat lady was sitting in a wheelchair, holding a newspaper up to the light from the window and attempting to read it with a magnifying glass.

"Excuse me," Mavis said.

Mrs. Cook put the magnifier down and squinted at Mavis. "Who is it?" she asked.

"I'm Annabelle Lee Jones, here visiting Mrs. Philpot. I knew her years ago, but she doesn't seem to remember much. I was wondering if you could tell me about this photograph I found on her dresser."

Mrs. Cook beckoned Mavis closer and held out a hand. "Althea's getting worse and worse," she said. "Used to, all she talked about was California. Now it's food. I hope you brought her something good to eat. All she wants is sweets."

Mrs. Cook examined the picture with her glass. "Oh yes. She used to talk about this picture a lot. Carried it around with her and told anybody who'd listen that this was the baby girl she lost. Back during the war. First she lost her young man, 'her true love,' she always called him, though, if you ask me, that was right insulting to her husband, who looked after her and put up with her for forty some odd years. He'd died when Buddy, that's her stepson, moved her in here. I know for a fact Buddy got tired of hearing about her lost love. He told me so.

Last time he was here. He was fed up. Now his wife comes. Once a month. Brings her candy and pays the bills."

"But the little girl," Mavis asked, taking the picture back. "What happened to her?"

"Oh, she died. When she was a toddler. Just three years old. 'My precious baby,' Althea used to say, and then she'd cry over her like it was yesterday."

"What did she die of?" Mavis could barely form the words.

"I have no idea," Mrs. Cook said. "Althea never said. Frankly, I was like Buddy. I got tired of hearing about Althea's tragic life. It was a great relief to me when dementia set in and she forgot about it. Now nothing matters to her except food."

"Thank you, Mrs. Cook," Mavis said. "I'll be going now."

"All right. Nice to see you.

"By the way," she added as Mavis reached the door, "where you from?"

"Piney," Mavis said. "Piney, Alabama."

She closed the door and went back into the room next door. The Old Woman was asleep with sticky, sweet drool running down her chin onto her wet dress. Mavis leaned over her, got right up in her face, and shouted, "I'm leaving now, Mama. Do you hear me?"

The Old Woman jumped and opened her eyes, a crazed, frightened look on her face. She drew back from Mavis and gasped.

"I'm taking my picture," Mavis hissed into her face. "It's not yours to keep. It belongs to me."

The Old Woman's eyes took on a mean shine, and she said, "I don't know you."

"I don't know you either," Mavis said.

Mavis walked out of the room, down the long corridors, out the front door, down the sidewalk. She'd gone several blocks at a very brisk pace before Annabelle caught up with her.

"Let's go take a look at Lake Michigan," Mavis said, "and then let's go home."

PART THREE
Spring

Hitch-Hiking with Rosy Finches

CHAPTER SIXTEEN

I liked her better dead than alive," Mavis said.

They were back home, eating cereal, each her half bowl, at the breakfast table.

"At least, dead she couldn't bite you," Annabelle said.

"Oh Annie, that's so awful!"

"I know."

They both put their hands over their mouths and giggled.

Mavis sobered and, examining a bandage on her forefinger, said, "Apparently she liked me better dead too."

"Maybe that wasn't so unfortunate."

"I thought your name was Annabelle, not Pollyanna."

"I'm just saying things might have been worse if she'd stayed. What if she'd raised you?"

"Instead of Grandma and Grandpa?"

"Yes."

"I don't know. At least, then I'd of had somebody besides you to talk to."

"Yeah, but you might not have had me."

Mavis smiled at her friend. "I can't imagine me without you."

Annabelle smiled back. "Me neither."

"That doesn't mean I'd rather have had you than a mother."

"You shouldn't have had to make the choice."

"I deserved better, didn't I?"

"Of course, you did."

"I'm really pissed off." Mavis clamped her hand over her mouth, and tears sprang into her eyes.

"I think that's okay, honey."

"And I'm sad. I've mourned my mother's death all my life, and now I'm mourning her life. Why did she have to do that? Pretend I was dead? When she'd gone off and left me!"

Mavis threw her spoon down on the table. It bounced off onto the floor, and she kicked it across the room. "I can't even hate her. She's a pathetic old woman who's lost her marbles."

She covered her face with her hands and sobbed.

Annabelle put her arms around her.

"Why'd she do it, Annie? Why?"

"She was too young to have a baby. She didn't know how to be a mother."

"I don't mean why did she leave me. Why did she pretend I was dead? Why did she just erase me off the face of the earth as if I haven't existed for the past sixty-two years? It's like she just chose to turn me into a nonentity. A non-being."

"I know, honey. But she doesn't have the power to do that. Not unless you give it to her. And you're not going to do that."

"No, I suppose not."

"Think about it this way. She couldn't acknowledge your existence without acknowledging what she'd done and who she was. And she couldn't accept that. It wasn't you she was rejecting but herself."

"I suppose. But it felt like me. All these years I preferred to pretend she was dead rather than face what I knew, in my heart of hearts, which was that she left me."

"And she preferred to pretend you died rather than face what she knew, maybe still knows, which was that she deserted you. She couldn't face that and live with herself."

"So, you're saying, she couldn't live with the guilt?"

"That's right."

"And now I'm just supposed to live with the hurt?"

"Now you're strong enough, Mavis, to live with the truth. You don't have to lie to yourself anymore. She's not strong enough to do that. Never has been, and now it's too late for her, but it's not for you."

"Oh? Annie, I'm sixty-five years old, soon to be sixty-six. I'm too old for all this...this...unfinished business. I know everybody has to forgive their parents for something, but, my god, isn't that what your twenties are for? Or even your thirties?"

"Well, there's no time limit on grief. Or on forgiveness. And you had a bigger load of shit to forgive than most. Give yourself some leeway."

"Forty or fifty years?"

"Sure. Why not? Be as good and gentle with yourself as you are with other people."

"Maybe I'll burn the postcards and Christmas cards."

"Sure. If you want to."

"Or, better yet, I believe I'll just send them back to Elmira with a note and say thanks for letting me see these and I'm returning them to you to put back in Grandma's cedar chest. They belonged to her, not to me."

"Good idea."

"Get them out of the house. My house. Out of my life."

"Yes."

"Now let's get dressed and think up something to do today."

"Maybe go to the art museum. Look at some pretty pictures."

"Excellent idea. And while we're there," Mavis added, "let's visit the sculpture garden. You know that statue of the big, fat woman? The reclining nude?"

"Unhuh."

"I just love her. I always touch her big toe. You know, for luck."

"Mavis, you're a peculiar woman."

"I'm getting there."

Annabelle and Jonathan were sitting on the back steps. Jonathan was crying and hiccupping.

"Why don't you just punch him in the mouth?" Annabelle asked.

"He's my friend. My best friend." Jonathan hiccupped. "You don't supposed to punch friends in the mouth."

"I don't know about that."

"You don't? Momma says no hitting, period. When Rotten Eddie hits The Baby, Momma has a fit."

"Well, yes. But that's different."

"What's different about it?"

"Baby Sister can't defend herself. That's like pulling a puppy's tail."

"That's mean."

"Right."

"Rotten Eddie was mean to me. He tripped me coming down the stairs with my Legos, and I fell into The Baby's swing and knocked her over."

"Ouch," Annabelle said. "That was mean."

"Rotten Eddie's my friend, and I don't like him anymore."

"So, why don't you sock him in the mouth? Teach him a lesson."

"Does Mabis ever sock you in the mouth?"

"Well, no, she doesn't sock me, but she fusses at me. Tells me when I've gone too far."

"Too far where?"

"You know, hurt her feelings."

"Rotten Eddie doesn't hurt my feelings. He hurts my face. See."

He pointed to his forehead.

"Yes, you've got a bump, all right. I wouldn't let him get away with that."

"What would you do?"

"I'd punch him in the mouth, but that might be going too far. On the other hand, you could nail him with a good fast ball here in the yard."

"Yeah." Jonathan bared his teeth and clinched his fists.

"You know how to throw a fast ball?"

"Sure. You throw it fast."

"Here. Take this rubber ball and practice. Throw it against the garage wall until you've got your aim down good, then call Eddie out for a game of pitch and catch."

"Good idea," Jonathan said, standing and taking a deep breath. "I'll nail him with a good fast one."

"Mabis," Jonathan said, "are you home for good?"

"I reckon. For better or worse, anyway."

"Your ears are all sparkly."

"You like my earrings? I got them for Christmas. Annabelle gave them to me."

"She said you gave them to her."

"Well, we gave them to each other. Along with the easel and paints."

"That's weird."

"Is it?"

"You can't give the same present to each other."

"You can't?"

"No-o-o-o. That would be like I gave Iris a teddy bear and she gave it to me."

"Iris? Who's Iris?"

"The Baby."

"The Baby's name is Iris?"

"Of course. What did you think it was?"

"I didn't know. I thought it was Baby."

"Mabis, you're weird. You know that?"

"So I've been told."

Jonathan had a toy airplane in his hand.

"Did you get that for Christmas?"

"Yes."

"From Santa Claus?"

"No. Iris gave it to me."

"Oh. What did you give her?"

"I told you. A bear."

"Oh yes. You did, didn't you?"

"Mabis?"

"Yes."

"Sometimes you're weird."

"How many times are you going to say that?" She poked him in the ribs.

He giggled. "A hundred million. Mabis is weird. Mabis is weird. Mabis is weird. Mabis-is-weird. Mabis-is-weird. Mabis-is-weird-Mabis-is-weird-Mabis-is...."

"Let's go get ice cream."

"Yes!"

"Go ask."

He was gone.

CHAPTER SEVENTEEN

Mavis and Jonathan were on their way to rent "The Incredibles." He was wearing a Mr. Incredible suit and his mask.

"I have magic powers. I can blow up the world," he said from the back seat.

"Oh my. Can you now?" Mavis slowed at an intersection, looked both ways. "Does Rotten Eddie have magic powers too?"

"Don't be silly." Jonathan giggled.

"What's silly about that?"

"Rotten Eddie doesn't need magic powers. He's in-bis-able."

"So, isn't that a magic power? Making yourself invisible?"

"Mabis, you just don't understand."

"I don't?"

"No. Rotten Eddie doesn't *make* his self in-bis-able. He *is* in-bis-able."

"Oh." Mavis turned a corner, then sped up.

"Have you ever noticed how, as you get older, you become invisible?"

Mavis was flipping through a fashion magazine with big, glossy pages. Annabelle was painting her toenails a startling shade of fuchsia.

"How do you mean?"

"When you're young, it's like you're on parade and everybody's watching, and then one day you're just invisible. Everybody is calling you 'sugar' and 'darling' one minute and then the next you're 'ma'am' and 'that old lady down the street'."

"You don't want to be the old lady down the street? You still want to turn heads?"

"Oh, I don't know, Annie. It's not as if I want construction workers whistling at me and catcalling. I'd just like to know that I still could elicit a little admiration, a little acknowledgment from somebody upon occasion."

"You still could if you wanted."

"I don't think so."

"Sure. All you have to do is strut your stuff. You just don't use what you've got. Somewhere along the way you just decided to fold your tent."

"What tent? What in the world are you talking about?"

"Mavis, just look at yourself."

Mavis dropped the magazine and stood before the full-length mirror on the back of the closet door.

"So?" she demanded, as much of her reflection as of Annabelle. "What you see is what you get."

"I'm just saying you don't have to be such a sad sack. You're still the same person you've always been. At least, underneath there somewhere."

"Are you calling me fat again?"

"No, Mavis, I'm not. You've lost ten, maybe fifteen pounds. You don't need to lose any more weight. You're a very nice size." Annabelle sounded annoyed. She screwed the top on the nail polish and came and stood behind Mavis. "Just look. Really look."

"I'm looking. I'm looking already."

"No, you're not. All you're seeing are sags and wrinkles."

"Are you saying I'm old?"

"Of course, you're old, Mavis. At least, older. We all are, thank God."

"Annie, I can't help it that I'm not pretty like you. Never have been, never will be."

"Nonsense! Who's to say who's pretty? You're as pretty as you think you are."

"Grandma used to say 'pretty is as pretty does.' Now you're saying 'pretty is as pretty thinks.' I'd settle for 'pretty is as pretty looks'."

"Hm-m-m-m," Annabelle said. "Maybe all those things are true."

"How so?"

"If we change how you act and how you think, maybe it'll transform how you look. Have you ever thought of that?"

"No, and I don't want to." Mavis climbed into bed and turned her back. "Turn out the light and come to bed," she said grumpily.

"Maybe it's time to do something about your wrinkles," Annabelle said the next morning.

"My wrinkles?" Mavis did not like the sound of this.

"Yes. If we work on your wrinkles, maybe it'll help your self-esteem."

"My what?" Now she really had her back up.

"The ladies on The View don't advocate plastic surgery, although I personally suspect Barbara Walters has had work done."

"Had work done?" Mavis looked at Annabelle in amazement. "You're talking about this as if it's a normal, reasonable thing to do."

She got up from the breakfast table and marched around the kitchen. She wiped off counters, slammed cupboard doors. "Every morning it's something. We can't have breakfast without one of your outlandish proposals."

"All I said was...."

"I know what you said, Annabelle, and after gallstones and ulcers, I am never going to a hospital again unless they carry me there unconscious in an ambulance."

"They don't put you in the hospital, Mavis. Calm down. You can have it done at some kind of a...what do you call it? Some kind of spa. With pretty nurses and soft music and aroma therapy."

"Have you lost your mind? Voluntarily get cut up with knives to tunes by John Tesh while they seduce you into believing you're only taking time to smell the roses!"

Annabelle giggled. "Mavis, when you get riled up, you're funny."

Mavis ducked her head and smiled. People didn't usually find her funny. Annabelle, on the other hand, was often hilarious.

"Actually," Annabelle said, "I wasn't proposing plastic surgery. Something non-invasive, like dermabrasion."

"No way. That makes you look like a boiled onion soaked in red food coloring." Was that funny? Mavis hoped so.

This time Annabelle's smile was indulgent. "The ladies on The View have been talking about something called micro-dermabrasion and ultra-sound treatments with maybe a few Botox shots on the side."

"No needles. No way. What kind of fool would pay somebody to stick needles in their face? Needles filled with poison yet!"

Annabelle couldn't help but agree. "Okay then, let's go for the micro-dermabrasion and ultra sound."

"What's this 'let's-go-for-it' stuff? It's your big idea. You go. I'll stay here and read a book on growing old gracefully and accepting myself, wrinkles and all."

"Mavis, that's just throwing in the sponge."

"What sponge? I'm ready to be me. What does anybody care about how I look? Who? Tell me that, Annabelle! Who cares?"

"That's depression talking. I care. You care."

"Then you go."

"Okay, I will. And I'll look beautiful and you'll look like an old hag, so there!"

Annabelle stormed out and went to call for an appointment.

Mavis opened a cupboard door and slammed it, but it didn't stay shut. She looked at it with dissatisfaction and sighed.

A few days later when Annabelle came home from the spa, she was all rosy and excited. "You would love Clarice," she told Mavis. "We just talked and talked while she did it."

"Did what?"

"The treatment."

"I mean what is it? What does she do? Besides talk."

"She rubs creams into you and wipes them off. Then she vacuums you up."

"Vacuums you?"

"Your face. With this little suction instrument. And she blows all this steam on you and rubs this thing, like a metal disc, on you. And the spa is so pretty and has soft lights and...."

"And John Tesh on the sound system."

"No, Nora Jones, Smarty Pants."

"So what did you talk about?"

"Ourselves. Well, she talked about herself, and I talked about you. She has three grown children and a husband in the sporting goods business."

"You talked about me?"

"Well, sure. You didn't think I was going to talk about me, did you?"

"What did you say?"

"Oh, how you worked in the jewelry store all those years and just retired and how you hate the way you look and need help pulling yourself together and getting out of the dumps and how maybe you need a make-over."

"Annabelle! How dare you tell a perfect stranger things like that about me! Who gave you the right? The very idea!"

"Now Mavis, don't get your panties in a wad. I told her you were me. Or I was you. Whichever. Anyway, I used your name, so it wasn't as if I was talking about you behind your back."

"Oh, well, that makes it okay!" She threw a magazine across the room at Annabelle's head. She missed and knocked a table lamp to the floor with a crash. The shade came off, and the bulb broke and shattered.

Mavis burst into tears. She threw herself onto the sofa and cried. And cried some more. Big, body-shaking, nerve-wracking boo-hoos. Annabelle came and sat beside her and tried to comfort her, but when she touched her shoulder, Mavis shook her hand away and wailed even harder and harder.

"I'm behaving like an adolescent," she said between wails, "and I know it. I'm carrying on like a teenager."

"Well, it's about time," Annabelle said, kissing her cheek.

"What's that supposed to mean?"

"You're just going back, picking up some stitches that got dropped when you were growing up."

This made Mavis wail all the louder.

The following week when it was time for the skin treatment, Mavis went herself. She wanted to straighten things out. Let this Clarice person know she wasn't some pathetic sad sack.

Annabelle was right. Even if it was in a strip mall, the spa was a pretty place. When you went inside, it was luxurious and fancy. Lots of smoky mirrors and round tables with big dried flower arrangements and damask cloths that bunched up in pretty folds on the thick carpet and velvet chairs with leopard print pillows. Oh, it was pretty, all right.

And so was Clarice. She was, Mavis supposed, what's called 'a woman of a certain age,' unlike Mavis herself, who was just plain old. Clarice wore black trousers and high heels and a raspberry-colored sweater cut out at the neck with pushed-up sleeves. And earrings, gold ones that matched her necklace, and she had a real hair-do, not too big but not flat either and certainly not bed hair like Mavis's often was. And a lovely smile. Clarice, of course, had perfect make-up that didn't feather around the mouth or smear in creases around the eyes.

"Hello Mavis," she sang out when Mavis came in, as if they were old friends and well acquainted.

"Hello," Mavis said, and then, in spite of herself, she blurted, "You're so pretty."

"Why, thank you, darling. So are you."

"Now really. You don't have to...."

"Mavis, I mean it. You're a beauty. You just haven't reached your full potential yet, but you're getting there. You're already off to a good start. And, remember, where we start is with the skin, and we work from the skin out and from the skin in."

They went into the treatment room then. The lights were dim and the music soft, and Mavis lay down on a padded, arm-less lounge chair, closed her eyes and kicked off her shoes. Clarice touched her face with warm ointments and cool instruments and a soothing mist sprayed down on her skin, and Mavis knew she was growing more beautiful from the skin out, and from the skin in, and that she was beginning to fulfill her potential.

CHAPTER EIGHTEEN

Mavis and Jonathan were sitting on the back steps eating green grapes. The forsythia bushes along the back fence were beginning to bloom. Their bright yellow flowers reflected the sunshine of a beautiful spring day.

Between grapes, Jonathan said, "Look, Mabis, the bushes are doing a dance. See how they're moving."

And they were. Initially, Mavis couldn't see what was making the branches shake, first one and then another. Then she saw them—dozens of little brown birds darting in and out, first you see them and then you don't. Sparrows, she thought, but no, the coloring was different, richer, giving them a pinkish glow.

"Rosy finches," she exclaimed. "The rosy finches have come."

"Why?"

"To welcome the spring."

"What are they doing?"

"Celebrating, I think. Rejoicing in this beautiful day."

Jonathan looked at her closely. "You sound happy, Mabis. Are you glad they've come?"

"Yes, I am."

They ate some more grapes and watched the birds.

"Look! Lookie, Mabis! One of 'em's got on a coat of many colors! See him? See him?"

"Oh my, I wish you would look." Mavis caught her breath.

There amid the rosy finches in the bushes was a single flash of bright red, blue, and green. He was the same size and shape as the others but a patchwork of Technicolor.

"He's gotten out of a cage somewhere and joined his friends," she said. "He's a finch too, only not a rosy finch."

"Mabis, he is be-oo-ti-ful!" Jonathan whispered, awestruck.

"Yes," she agreed. "They're all beautiful, but he's special."

"Why's he with them?"

"He's hitchhiking a ride. He needs their company. This is his own coming-out party. He's escaped his cage to welcome the spring."

"Last night I dreamed we danced." Mavis was staring dreamily off into space over her coffee cup.

"You did?" Annabelle was eating her half of a piece of toast. "Was it fun?"

"Oh, Annie, it was wonderful! We were in college together. First we were taking a poetry class together, only the poetry was in Italian and I couldn't make heads or tails of it. But a group, including you, began to sing it, and it was beautiful. I wanted to be a part of the group and to sing it too. I was filled with a terrible yearning. Then you came and put your arms around me, and we danced away to the music of the singing.

"I could feel your arms around me and your legs against mine, and we moved to the wonderful Italian singing as if we were one person."

"Mavis, that's lovely. Maybe we should sign up for dancing lessons."

"I couldn't do it without you."

"You wouldn't have to. I would be right there, and we would be dancing as one."

"Mabis, what you doing?"

"Thinking about having a birthday party."

"Whose birthday is it?"

"Mine."

"Really? Aren't you too old to have a birthday party?"

"No. I'm just the right age."

"Can I come?"

Of course. It'll be you and me and Annabelle. Shall we invite Rotten Eddie?"

"No! Rotten Eddie would ruin a birthday party."

"What would he do?"

"He would smush the cake and steal the presents."

"Then let's not have him."

"Mabis?"

"Yes?"

"You know you're supposed to have a cake, don't you?"

"Is that right?"

"Yes. Do you know now to make a cake?"

"No. Do you?"

"No! I'm a little boy! Momma makes my cakes."

"Well, we'll go to Savages and get mine. They make good cakes."

"With candles?"

"We'll see. Go ask your momma."

They had the party in the backyard. Mavis set up a card table, covered it with a pretty embroidered cloth, and brought out three chairs from the kitchen. The cake was chocolate with yellow flowers and six yellow candles. Mavis said six was enough.

Annabelle and Jonathan sang "Happy Birthday" to her, and she made a wish and blew out the candles. She refused to tell what her wish was on the grounds that it was bad luck and then wouldn't come true.

Annabelle and Jonathan each gave Mavis a present wrapped in tissue paper and tied with yarn from her needlepoint basket. Both gifts were portraits of Mavis. Annabelle's depicted her dancing on clouds with flowers in her hair and pretty bluebirds pulling a banner across the sky that read "Happy Birthday, Mavis." Jonathan's showed a happy face with big diamond earrings. It was inscribed "HAPY BIRD DAE."

Mavis said these were the best birthday presents she'd ever had.

They were almost finished eating their cake when Jonathan suddenly shouted, "Look out! Here comes Rotten Eddie. Quick! Hide the cake! Don't let him smush it!"

They immediately went into action. Mavis hid the cake under a napkin, and Jonathan and Annabelle took off chasing Rotten Eddie around the backyard. Around trees, in and out of bushes, over flowerbeds.

Annabelle was shouting, "You rascal! You better run! I'm going to catch you!"

And Jonathan was squealing, "No cake for you, Rotten Eddie! No cake for you!"

When Annabelle pursued Rotten Eddie out of sight behind the garage, Jonathan came, exhausted, and sank back into a chair beside Mavis. He was laughing and gulping for air.

"Whew!" he panted. "That was a fun game."

"Shall I uncover the cake now?" Mavis asked.

"No, no. There they go again. Run, Annabelle! Run! Catch him Catch him."

"They sure are having fun," Mavis said.

"Oh, yeah!"

"How come they're having so much fun?"

"They don't know we're watching," Jonathan explained. "And they're not watching their own self. That's how you have fun, Mabis."

"You know, for a four-year-old, you're pretty smart."

"But not as smart as Rotten Eddie."

"Maybe not. But then I'm not as smart as Annabelle either."

"Mabis, you're not near as smart as Annabelle."

CHAPTER NINETEEN

I dreamed we collaborated on a book and, before we sent it off to a publisher, you said we had to proofread it, and I didn't want to."

Mavis lay in bed beside Annabelle. Every morning now, before she got up, she had taken to telling Annabelle her dreams.

"Why didn't you want to proofread it?"

"I was afraid my version wouldn't match your version."

"Oh. And whose version was right?"

"Yours. It was more complete. My version left out things so, in the end, the pages didn't add up right."

"Well, well." Annabelle looked smug and stretched her arms above her head.

Mavis hit her with a pillow. "Oh, don't be so pleased with yourself. One of these days I'll throw you out of here."

"One of these days," Annabelle told her, "you won't have to."

"Mabis."

"Yes."

"I need to tell you something."

"Okay."

"It's pri-bate."

"Okay."

"It's about Rotten Eddie."

"Okay."

"This morning somebody took all of Iris's applesauce out of the frig-gy-rator and dumped it in the garbage can. When it was time for her to eat it, it wasn't there and she cried and cried."

"Oh dear."

"I told Momma Rotten Eddie did it, but he didn't. I did."

"I see."

"You do?"

"Well…."

"Iris really yelled. Her face got all red, and she wouldn't stop screaming."

"How upsetting."

"It wasn't upsetting. It was loud."

"Did it make you feel bad?"

"It hurt my ears."

"What are you going to do?"

"Do?"

"About the applesauce."

"Mabis, I told you. The applesauce is gone."

"So, what are you going to do about Rotten Eddie?"

"I'm going to do what Annabelle said."

"What's that?"

"Sock him in the mouth."

"Why?"

"Because I'm mad at him for not throwing away the applesauce his own self."

"This morning, right before I woke up, I had the most beautiful dream," Mavis said.

"What was it about?"

"It was about Impressionism."

"Oh my."

"I was in a big, light room with a tall Palladian window that looked out on a lovely garden with many kinds of flowers. The panes in the window were that old-fashioned kind of glass. You know? The kind that's all wavy?"

"Yes."

"When I looked out the window, it distorted my view of the flowers so that, instead of looking like blossoms, they looked like a wild juxtaposition of colors forming breath-taking patterns. Like a beautiful kaleidoscope."

"How wonderful!"

"It was wonderful, Annie. I felt privileged, as if the Impressionists—Monet and Van Gogh and Renoir—had granted me a private, first-hand showing of what they saw when they painted. I got to see the world though their eyes."

"Oh, Mavis, that's quite a vision!"

"It is, isn't it? It reminded me of what I liked about the jewelry business. You once said I had nothing at stake there. Remember? That I spent my life working there just because I was in love with Harrison?"

"Yes. Maybe I overstated the case."

"Maybe. I don't know. But I loved the gemstones. I loved their facets and colors and patterns. Sometimes it made me want to paint them. You know? Paint what I saw when I looked at them up close through a loupe, so that their sparkle and splendor completely filled up the eye."

"You know, you can do that, Mavis. Paint what you see in your mind's eye. There's no reason why you can't."

"I think I'd like that."

"When do you want to give it a try?"

"Don't rush me, Annie. Sometimes you rush me. Push me too fast. Let me get used to the idea first."

"Okay. But don't put it off just because you'd be afraid."

"Afraid? Why would I be afraid?"

"Deciding to create something from nothing requires a certain courage, Mavis."

"I hadn't thought of it like that. I was just trying to decide whether it was something worth doing or not. Maybe it's a dumb idea."

"That's cowardice talking. Expressing our own inner vision is never a dumb idea. But only the brave take the risk."

"I'm not very brave then, Annie."

"Nonsense. You're plenty brave. You've just gotten out of the habit of taking risks."

"Until lately."

"Well, yes. I would say lately you've been taking a lot of risks."

Jonathan was painting at his easel in the backyard. He had painted what appeared to be a monster with a huge head, bright red eyes, a yellow tongue, and green hair.

"Tell me about your picture," Annabelle said. She had learned better than to ask him what a picture was. Once, when she'd put the question to him that way, he'd looked at her like she had lost her mind and replied, "It's paint, Annabelle. What did you think it was?"

"That," Jonathan said emphatically, "is Rotten Eddie. And this," he added, taking a big brush of black paint and covering the entire picture, "is how I feel about him."

"Oh, my," Annabelle said. "That's a pretty strong statement."

Jonathan was in the back seat. He and Mavis were on their way to the store to buy a kite. "Mabis," he said, staring out the window, "I know a secret."

"Oh? Are you going to tell me?"

"Maybe. Promise you won't get mad."

"Why would I get mad?"

"You might not like it."

"Why not?"

"It's about Annabelle and Rotten Eddie."

"What about them?"

"Sometimes they play together when we're not around."

"They do?"

"Yes."

"What do they play?"

"Let's pretend."

"Oh? What do they pretend?"

"That they're you and me."

"Wow. Really?"

"Yes."

"Why do they do that?"

"They pretend so they don't really have to be you and me."

"I see."

"Are you mad?"

"No, but I'm surprised."

"Me too. Sometimes we could surprise them back, and you and me could pretend to be them."

"Jonathan, this is getting way too complicated for me."

"Me too."

PART FOUR
Almost Summer

A Singing Bird

CHAPTER TWENTY

First there was a whizzing sound, then crashing noises, and, finally, a thud.

There were whirling tree limbs and tumbling leaves, a flash of bright light, and then blackness.

Jonathan was screaming, a high keening screech like a terrified animal. Then he was yelling and crying all mixed together.

"Mabis. Mabis-s-s-s. Mabis-s-s-s. Help! Help! Come quick! Come quick. Annabelle fell! All the way from the top of the tree. She'd gone to get my kite. It was stuck in the tree. Help! She won't get up. She isn't breathe-ing. She's dead. She's dead."

"Hush, Jonathan. Listen to me. Can you hear me? Run. Run to your house and tell your momma to call nine-one-one. Now. Now.

"Can you hear me? I'm talking to you, Jonathan. Stop screaming. Go. Go. Tell your momma to call nine-one-one. Can you hear me? Go now.

"That's a big boy. Go now. Do it for Annabelle. Do it for Mavis. That's good. You're a big boy now. Go. Go. Go."

When she woke up, she had a terrible headache. Light hurt her eyes. She couldn't turn her head, and she didn't know where she was.

She had cuts and scratches on her arms and legs, face and neck, bandages across her rib cage, and a cast on her wrist.

Very tired and unable to think straight, she closed her eyes and went back to sleep.

Annabelle was leaving. She had her bag packed and was standing in the foyer at the house waiting for a taxi. Mavis was pleading with her, and Annabelle was resolute.

"Don't go. Say you'll stay," Mavis was saying.

"No," Annabelle said. "It's time for me to go. You don't need me anymore."

"Oh, but Annie, I do. I'll always need you. I can't get along without you."

"You don't have to, Mavis. I'm always with you. In your heart, in your head. I'm always dancing with you. We're always singing the same song."

"Painting the same pictures?"

"Yes, we'll always be painting the same pictures together. Seeing the same visions."

"Annabelle, wait."

"No. My taxi's here. I have to go."

"Wait. Wait. WAIT."

Mavis sat straight up in bed, her eyes flew open. She couldn't fathom what she was seeing. A sea of white coats, a ring of faces, all staring at her.

Thump, thump, thump.

"Do you hear that?" she said.

"Do you hear something?" one of the white coats said.

"Thump, thump, thump."

"That's your head pounding. Can you tell me your name?"

"Is that a trick question?"

"Just answer."

She looked at him for a long moment. She seemed puzzled, as if she was sorting through a lot of information. She put her hand to her head and closed her eyes. Finally, she said, "I'm Mavis. Who are you?"

"Dr. Grogowski. Do you know where you are?"

"No."

"You're in University Hospital."

"Why?"

"You've suffered a concussion. You fell out of a tree."

"A tree? Not a taxi cab?"

"No. Can you tell me where you live?"

"Hm-m-m-m. You know that street in Homewood? The one with trees and houses?"

"Do you know what day it is?"

"No."

"Do you know what year it is?"

"Two-oh-oh-five. It used to be two-oh-oh-four, for a very long time. But it's not anymore."

"Do you know who's president?"

"Bush. Not the old one. The new one."

"Do you...?"

"Sh-h-h-h. Go away. My head hurts." She lay back down and closed her eyes.

Two days later when she arrived home in a taxi, Jonathan was waiting on her front steps. He ran down the walk and hugged her.

"Easy there," she said, trying to protect her sore ribs and not lose her balance.

"Does it hurt?" he asked, pointing at her cast.

"No, it itches. But I'm bruised and sore all over, and I need to sit down. Go ask your momma if you can come in and have some milk and cookies. We'll have a tea party."

"A tea party? You said we'd have milk and cookies. That's not a tea party."

"Just go ask, okay?"

Jonathan had a white mustache. He was dropping crumbs down his shirt front and onto the sofa. Mavis watched and let it go.

"So?" she said. "What's been going on while I was at the hospital?"

"Rotten Eddie told Momma it was his kite that got stuck in the tree."

"Oh?"

"He said Annabelle was trying to re-preve his kite when she fell."

"Retrieve."

"Retrieve."

"Oh?"

"But Mabis, that wasn't right. It was my kite. I told him so. He started crying like a baby and said it was so his kite."

Jonathan sighed as if some things can't be helped.

"So I beat him up."

"You beat him up?"

"Yes, walloped him good like Annabelle told me to. Punched him right in the mouth. I told him to go away, that he's not my friend anymore."

"He's gone?"

"Yep. Good rit-tance, Momma said."

"Where'd he go?"

"The garbage man picked him up. In his truck. He's gone all right. I told Kevin about him, and Kevin said he sounds like a snotty-nose kid. Do you think he was a snot nose?"

"Who's Kevin?"

"Kevin. He's my friend, my new friend at Mothers' Day Out. On Wednesdays at the Pest-a-terian church."

"Presbyterian."

"That's what I said."

Jonathan spilled some more crumbs. "Mabis?"

"Yes?"

"Do you think Rotten Eddie was a snot nose?"

"No, I think he was just Rotten Eddie. That was enough."

"Where's Annabelle?"

"She's gone too."

"With Rotten Eddie?"

"No. She left in a taxi cab."

"I liked Annabelle."

"Me too."

"She was kind of bossy though."

"Yes, she was."

"Can I have another cookie?"

"May I."

"Sure, you can. Can I?"

"Yes."

Several weeks later Mavis climbed out of the Beetle with a squirming mass of white fluff in her arms. Jonathan kicked a ball behind the shrubs and forgot to go get it.

"What is that?"

"It's a Bijon Frise."

"What's that?"

"A puppy."

"Is he yours?"

"She. Yes, she is."

"Can I hold her?"

"Yes."

"She's wiggly." He giggled. "She's licking me. Oh, Mabis, Mabis." He collapsed in the grass with the puppy jumping on him and smacking puppy kisses all over his face. "What's her name?"

"I don't know. What shall we call her?"

"Annabelle," he said, rolling over and over with her. "Oh, Mabis. Let's call her Annabelle. It's such a good name."

And so they did.

They spent that afternoon, and many thereafter, in the backyard playing with Annabelle. Jonathan kept falling down from laughing so hard, and Annabelle romped and jumped and tore around and round in circles. In the midst of shrieks and giggles and barks and yips, Jonathan rose up on his knees, cocked his head, and said, "Listen! Do you hear it, Mabis? That bird singing? Where is he? He's just singing his heart out."

"It's a mockingbird," Mavis answered. "There on the fence post. They sing all summer. They're the best of the songbirds. And you're right—he is singing his heart out."

"Is it summer, Mabis?"

"Almost, but it's coming. It's surely, surely coming."

EPILOGUE

Early that summer Mavis drove to Mobile and boarded a ship to the Bahamas. She stretched out on the deck in the sunshine. She saw beautiful scenery and took lots of pictures. She was thrilled by the tropical colors and the sparkling water. She met some nice people and played a little bingo and learned to dance the cha-cha. She had a good time. Clarice, the pretty lady at the spa, kept the puppy while she was away.

By the time she got home, her ribs and wrist had healed, and she signed up for a painting class and began volunteering at the Birmingham Museum of Art. Every Thursday she had lunch with Clarice and, afterwards, they worked on realizing their full potential. Sometimes they worked from the skin out and Mavis got a treatment, and sometimes they worked on their inner life, and talked about their hopes and their dreams. Mavis encouraged Clarice to expand her business and took over the bookkeeping for her, and Clarice admired Mavis's paintings so much she began exhibiting them at the spa.

Jonathan continued to go to Mother's Day Out once a week and make new friends. He turned five that summer and prepared to go to kindergarten in the fall. Rotten Eddie did not return, and The Baby, bit by bit, learned to walk and talk and, sometimes, even to make her big brother laugh.

So, if you're ever in Homewood, Alabama, keep an eye out and you might see a pretty woman of a certain age and a little boy walking a fluffy white dog named Annabelle. And, upon occasion, you might see them pushing a baby in a stroller. The Baby, you may remember, is named Iris.

WHEN SAMANTHA CAME HOME

BOOK TWO

"All who wander are not lost."

—Anonymous

PROLOGUE
Clipping from the Baldwin County Gazette

Memorial Day Celebration

*I*n true Wooten fashion, Doc and Sammie Jo Wooten celebrated
their 50th anniversary on Memorial Day with a gathering of
approximately 100 family and friends at their home near Piney.
*Distinguished guests included their four sons and their families: Horton
Wooten and his wife Ann and their twins, Oliver and Olivia, of Piney;
Garrett Wooten and his wife Cindy Lou and their children, B.B.,
Guthrie, and Emmy Lou, of Clarksdale, Miss.; Derwin Wooten and
his wife Darlene of Lake Norman, N.C., and his children, Tammy
and Kara of Talladega, Donnie of Daytona, and Brittany (Susie
Q) and her mother Sissy Winfrey of Piney; and everybody's buddy,
Buddy Wooten of Piney.*

*Other important guests in attendance were Sammie Jo's sister,
Elmira Horton of Piney, Sammie Jo's oldest and dearest friend,
Hopewell Jennings, formerly of Piney and now of Fairhope, many
of Doc's fellow golfers and their wives from the Piney Country Club,
Sammie Jo's "gang" from the Hoity-Toity Society, Derwin's pit crew
and fellow drivers and their wives and girlfriends from the NASCAR
circuit, as well as various Derwin fans, both local and out of town.*

*At music-lover's Garrett's invitation, the Mississippi Heritage
Band and other musicians from Clarksdale supplied the music. The
band set up in the carport with the paved area under the basketball goal
transformed into an outdoor ballroom and lined with tubs of gardenias,*

camellias and crepe myrtles, all graciously trucked in for the occasion by Buddy's long-time employer, Blooms Galore Garden Center.

Entertainment included skateboarding and trampolining for the youngsters and horseshoes and target practice for the adults, followed by an evening of dancing under the stars. Fortunately, the weather was beautiful.

During the afternoon, a cheerleading and baton-twirling exhibition was presented to enthusiastic applause. Organized and choreographed on the spot by Sissy, it featured Wooten granddaughters with Sammie Jo and other members of the Hoity-Toity Society joining in to show support.

Doc and his fellow Kiwanians were in charge of the barbecue, rising at dawn on the day of the party to begin grilling. Neighbors and the ladies of the Hoity-Toity Society supplied side dishes of potato salad, baked beans, cole slaw, bread-and-butter pickles, and sliced Vidalia onions and tomatoes. Beverages included sweet tea, lemonade, beer and champagne for toasting. Several bottles of the champagne were also put to good use for impromptu victory celebrations on the back-yard shooting range.

For dessert, a selection of gourmet confections from Jessie's Restaurant in Magnolia Springs was presented, along with an anniversary cake home-baked and decorated by Cindy Lou.

Watermelon was also served.

After dinner, Doc presented Sammie Jo with a lovely diamond anniversary ring. Her engagement ring (considerably smaller) had been his mother's and all he could afford at the time.

When Doc presented the new ring to her, Sammie Jo (and several others) cried.

Then, in a spontaneous and sentimental moment, she ran into the house and reappeared wearing her wedding veil over her T-shirt. Rising to the occasion, the band struck up "Stars Fell on Alabama" *and, to cheers and whistles, Doc danced her out of the carport, around the basketball court and down the driveway.*

The Wooten boys presented Doc with an all-expenses-paid trip to Orlando for a two-week golf clinic taught by famous professionals. They feted Sammie Jo with a brand-new aluminum walker with rubber tips to prevent slippage, which she, good-naturedly, threw at them before hiking up her skirt and performing a solo jitterbug.

Music and fireworks continued deep into the night, interrupted briefly when the sheriff's department arrived to see what the shooting had been about and to make sure nobody needed first aid.

A good time was had by all.

CHAPTER ONE
Tuesday, The Day After Memorial Day

The day after her fiftieth wedding anniversary, Sammie Jo Wooten changed her name. It wasn't all that hard: A trip from Piney up the road to Bay Minette where the Baldwin County courthouse was located. Two visits to the county clerk's office, first to pick up the form, then to take it back after she'd filled it out and had it notarized at a nearby bank. Eleven dollars and she was done. No questions asked.

Of course, being Sammie Jo, she explained anyway. To the woman who waited on her, whom she didn't know.

"I just don't want to be Sammie Jo anymore," she said. "I figure it's now or never. You know? I mean I never wanted to be Sammie Jo in the first place. Good ole Sammie Jo. And, you know something? I don't have to be. As my little granddaughter Susie Q says…that's what I call her. Her real name's Brittany. Anyway, Susie Q says, 'I am the boss of me.' Well, I am the boss of me.

"I think it's high time I had a proper name. Everybody else does. I was named for my Grandma Horton, Samantha Josephine Horton. Now there's a proper name for you! Seems to me I deserved as much. But, no, Mama had to go and name me plain ole Sammie Jo. Not a real name at all. A tacky ole, country-sounding nickname. I guess she thought two Samanthas in the same family would be confusing.

"Well, Mama's dead and gone now. And so is Grandma. So why not? I ask you, why not?"

By now, Sammie Jo was talking to a hippie-looking girl standing behind her. The woman behind the counter had stopped even pretending to listen and was seeking help from a co-worker to make the computer do what it was supposed to do. The hippie-looking girl seemed interested though.

"What about you?" Sammie Jo asked.

"Me? Oh well, my birth certificate says I'm Margaret, but I've always been Maggie, so I'm getting legalized. It was too much trouble in California. Lawyers and all. Lots easier here in Alabama. Now that I've moved here I thought I might as well update the record."

"So, not a big change for you."

"Nope. Not hardly."

"How do you like Alabama?"

"Fine. Everybody's friendly and helps you out. 'Course, in California, folks are nice too."

"Yes, I reckon so," Sammie Jo, said, though she had never been to California.

Why, she wondered, every place she went, did it take two people to operate the computer, one to punch the keys and another to determine which keys to punch. Sometimes it even took a whole committee. And yet, everybody was always telling her how much easier the computer made everything.

But now, at last, the computer produced the necessary papers. After she and the clerk had each signed them, the clerk gave her an embossed copy. Sammie Jo put the document in her purse, paid the eleven dollars, and turned to leave.

"Goodbye, Samantha. You have a good day now," the hippie girl said softly.

Sammie Jo felt her new name descend upon her like a blessing.

"Why thanks. Thanks a lot," she said.

She walked down the hallway, out the door, and into the afternoon light. Standing on the courthouse steps, she basked in the warmth of her new identity and felt she was on the brink of something. She didn't know what, but she was gearing up.

When she got home and told Doc she'd changed her name, he hardly knew what to say. She hadn't told him—or anybody else—she was even thinking about it.

She sat down on the couch in the den across from his recliner. "Doc," she said.

Even though his name was Claude, everybody in Baldwin County called her husband Doc. Sammie Jo herself only called him Claude when she was trying to get his goat. He'd get back at her then by responding to anything she said with "You're right, Sammie Jo, right as rain." They'd known each other forever.

They knew things about each other no one else knew. For instance, she knew he slept with a towel around his neck and a golf glove on his left hand and that he sometimes sang in his sleep and sometimes moaned, although he claimed not to dream.

He knew she wrote notes to God and kept them in an egg basket on top of the pie safe. He also knew she sometimes sent flowers to people she hardly knew with cards that said "from a secret admirer" and, when they were away on vacation, that she sent postcards home to herself that said "Wish you were here."

People started out calling him Little Doc. Back when he was a kid working behind the soda fountain at his father's drugstore. They called his dad Big Doc. Later, after Big Doc died and the store was his, people dropped the Little and just called him Doc, and Doc he'd been for nearly half a century now. He couldn't remember anybody except schoolteachers and his mother calling him Claude, and his mother had died when he was eight. He didn't have any brothers or sisters.

Nowadays, if anybody called him Claude, it was a sure sign they didn't know him. Well, except for Sammie Jo's cousin, Mavis, who lived in Birmingham. She called him Claude, but Mavis had always been a little strange.

Right now, Doc wasn't thinking about names, his or anybody else's. He was reading the newspaper.

"Listen to this," he said, chuckling. "A fella, Rob Lowe— he's a celebrity, I guess—anyway, he went out to Iowa to play in a pro-am tournament. He was making an approach shot to the fourth green and hit the state bird, a goldfinch, with his golf ball. The bird's just lying there on the green. Knocked silly. Lowe goes and looks him over. The paper says they reckon he got his birdie all right."

Doc shook his head and laughed.

"Doc."

"Uh-huh?"

"I need to tell you something."

Doc stayed hidden behind his paper for a count of five, maybe six. He needed the time to get his face expressionless. Wipe the dread off of it. No good could come of a conversation with Sammie Jo that started with 'I need to tell you something.' That and 'we need to talk' were the two worst possible ways for a woman to begin a conversation. It looked like they would learn that.

When he'd braced himself, he lowered the paper.

"What is it, Sammie Jo?" he said in the most neutral voice he could muster.

"I went to the courthouse today and changed my name," she said.

He didn't know what he expected—with Sammie Jo, he never knew what to expect—but it wasn't this. He was relieved. He thought maybe she'd wrecked the car again. Or gotten arrested. Sammie Jo was capable of that.

"Oh?" he said. That seemed safe enough.

"Yes." She bounced up and down a little on the couch cushion. She looked excited.

"Aren't you gonna ask me what I changed it to?"

"What did you change it to?"

"Samantha."

"Samantha, huh?"

"Yes. How do you like it?"

"Well, I don't guess I know. This has come at me out of the blue. It'll take some getting used to."

"Well, get used to it." She sounded a little offended, like he was supposed to have congratulated her or something.

"Samantha, huh? Like the girl on 'Bewitched?' You gonna wiggle your nose and make me disappear?" He was smiling.

"No, not like 'Bewitched,' Doc. Like a proper name. A real name. Not like some little girl who was never enough of a person in her own right to have a proper name."

She'd gone and gotten emotional on him. Doc could see that. Sammie Jo was prone to emotion. He was afraid she was going to cry. Since she'd finally gotten through The Change, there hadn't been many tears. He didn't want them to start up again.

"Well, okay. Okay then, if that's what you want. I'll try to get my mind around it."

He waited a minute to see if he could go back to his paper now.

"You don't object?" she asked.

"Why would I object? It's your name and your doing."

Then something struck him. He frowned and sucked in air. "You haven't changed your last name, have you? You're still Sammie Jo—Samantha, whatever—Wooten, aren't you?"

"Of course. And I'm still Mrs. Doc Wooten."

"Well, that's a relief." He picked up his paper again.

"Is that all you've got to say?"

He laid it down again and looked at her. There was a prolonged silence.

She couldn't tell by looking what he was thinking, but she suspected he was furious.

Actually, he was wondering how much longer this conversation was going to go on and if he'd have time to finish the paper and take a nap before supper. He'd just finished eighteen holes on the golf course and he was tired.

"You're not mad, are you?" she said finally.

"Course not. Does changing your name make you happy?"

"Yes."

"Then I'm happy. Can I finish the paper now?"

"Yes."

"Okay then."

CHAPTER TWO
Wednesday, Two Days After Memorial Day

What prompted you to do it?"

The question came from Hopewell Jennings, Sammie Jo's oldest and dearest friend. They were having lunch together. Often, on the days Doc played golf, Sammie Jo made pimento cheese sandwiches and drove over to Fairhope and ate with her. Fairhope was where Hopewell had her shop. It was a quaint sort of resort town, a few miles west of Piney on the Mobile Bay. It had galleries, specialty shops, and tourists and was not a regular town like Piney was.

Hopewell was Hopewell's real name and had been her mother's maiden name. You'd think everybody would have called her Hope, but they didn't. They'd say Hopewell with a southern drawl so that often it came out sounding more like Opal than Hopewell until some people thought Opal was her name. But Opal didn't suit Hopewell at all. To those who really knew her, she was Hopewell, always had been and always would be.

Now some of her customers had taken to calling her Hope. Trying to be chummy, Sammie Jo thought. And then, too, the name of her shop was The Hope Chest of Fine Linens, although she always added *Hopewell Jennings, Proprietor, Fairhope, Ala.,* to her business cards and Web page to be clear. Sammie Jo thought that sounded classy, but that wasn't anything Hopewell had to work at. She was classy. Some people were born that way, Sammie Joe figured, and had the name to go with it.

Today the shop didn't have many customers, and Sammie Jo and Hopewell could eat and talk without interruption. Not that The Hope Chest didn't do a good business. It did, but a lot of it was online. Buying and selling antique sheets and pillow cases, tablecloths and napkins, quilts and bedspreads, baby blankets and coverlets, even old counterpanes, all hand-made with fancy cross-stitching, crocheted borders, embroidered flowers, cut-work designs.

"Take off that T-shirt and let me get the wrinkles out of it," Hopewell said now. They were in the kitchen in the back, out of sight if a customer should come in but within earshot of the bell over the front door.

Sammie Jo struggled out of her shirt and handed it over. It said, "Pull up your big girl panties and DEAL with it." She sat in her bra and watched Hopewell iron. Hopewell was all the time ironing something.

"It was the anniversary that did it," Sammie Jo told her.

"Pushed you over the edge, huh?" Hopewell chuckled. "They'll do that to you."

Hopewell took a few more swipes at the T-shirt and handed it to Sammie Jo. It was warm to her skin when she put it back on.

"It just sort of sealed the deal," Sammie Jo said. "You know what I mean?"

"No, don't think I do. I thought it was a nice party, and I enjoyed it."

"Oh Hopewell, it wasn't a nice party. It was chaos."

"Well, yes, it was lively," Hopewell agreed. "Everybody had a lot fun."

"I suppose, but it looks like, just once in my life, I could have a party without the sheriff's office showing up."

"Ah, honey, they just wanted a reason to drop by and eat some barbecue."

"I reckon. At least, they didn't get on anybody about target practice in the back yard. And there wouldn't have been all that shooting if Derwin hadn't found his old twenty-two in the carport when they were clearing it out for the band to set up. The next thing I know half of NASCAR's fetched guns out of their cars and they're shooting bottles and tin cans off the back fence."

"Now sugar, that was okay. It added to the festivities."

"I guess I just expected a more dignified occasion."

Hopewell was a good friend, so she didn't point out that she'd recommended Sammie Jo have the anniversary party at the Grand Hotel over on the bay. That would have been a dignified setting, but Sammie Jo had said no, no, she wanted to have it at home. Hopewell also refrained from mentioning Sammie Jo's own behavior, which had in no way added to the dignity of the occasion. Her jitterbug, for instance, or the T-shirt saying "No Shirt, No Shoes, No Problem" that she'd worn with her bridal veil.

"A fiftieth anniversary is a milestone, don't you think?" Sammie Jo said now. Her voice sounded wistful.

"Sure, and something to be proud of," Hopewell agreed.

"Well, I don't know about that. It's not like it was any great achievement. It just sort of happened. But I thought I would feel different."

"Different how?"

"Like I had finally arrived. Like my life wouldn't be such a mess anymore. So disorganized, haphazard. Like I'd finally be somebody with dignity and self-esteem and recognized as such. Like I would be some grand dame, you know, not good ole Sammie Jo, but a real person. Somebody who knows how to have a party, for heaven sakes, without things getting out of hand.

"I didn't even know half the people who showed up. A whole parade of them followed Derwin into town, and local people fell in behind them when they saw who it was.

"Plus all those blues players from Mississippi. They were wonderful, but when Garrett said he'd supply some music, I hadn't expected half of Clarksdale.

"And then Doc went all over Piney inviting one and all. The whole day just turned into a free-for-all."

"Oh honey."

Sammie Jo tended to go on this way. Any time she'd had a lot of fun and let her hair down, she suffered remorse. She'd blame herself for not being more dignified, as if she should measure up to some ideal she'd set for herself. Hopewell had always hoped she'd outgrow this line of thinking, but she hadn't.

All her life, Sammie Jo had longed to be a serious person. Even back in high school, she'd been disappointed in herself, and she'd been the most popular girl in Piney. Head cheerleader and homecoming queen but not valedictorian, she always pointed out.

Hopewell told her she was her own worst enemy. When they were grown and joined the county historical society together, Sammie Jo had come to just one meeting and decided it wasn't for her. Then she'd gone off on her own and formed the Hoity-Toity Society. When asked what they did, she said, "Nothing. We have no purpose, no officers, no dues, and nobody keeps minutes. Once a month we meet at the Dairy Queen and talk about people."

Everybody in South Baldwin County thought she was a hoot and loved her antics. Well, maybe not everybody. A few people thought she ought to behave herself and stop acting out. They were mostly old people who remembered Doc's mother, Louise Wooten, and how sedate and proper the Wooten home place had been when she was alive. Of course, Miz Louise had been dead for years now, and there weren't all that many people who remembered her. She'd had TB and died when Doc was a boy, and he and Big Doc had gone on living in the house, just the two of them, with a housekeeper who lived out back. Mattie cooked and took care of the place until Sammie Jo married into the family and took over. By then, Mattie was old and went to live with her daughter in town.

The Wooten place sat in a pecan grove a few miles west of town on the road to Fairhope. Originally, it had been a twenty-acre section of a big farm that had been in the Wooten family for generations. When Big Doc came home from World War I and married Miz Louise, the pecan grove came to them as a wedding present, and he built the house on the back of the property for her. They both thought it was a fine house, and they expected to raise a big family there and share a long life.

The house was constructed of yellow brick with a green tile roof, not an architect's design, but a bigger and better house at the time than others up and down the road. Compared to the small clapboard houses occupied by tenant farmers, the Wooten house looked both substantial and cheerful.

Big Doc had had enough of war and tromping across Europe through mud, cold, and barren landscapes to last him a lifetime. He'd seen killing and horror and things too awful to mention. When he got home, he'd wanted some happiness.

It hadn't lasted long. The happiness. With him and Miz Louise. She was the girl of his dreams, all right, but, after their boy was born, she took sick and nothing could be done about it. She lingered, in her bed with Mattie looking after her, and finally died when their only child was just beginning to fill out and get his height.

After that, the house had seemed forlorn. That is until years later when Little Doc married Sammie Jo and brought her home. Sammie Jo made all the difference to the place. To Big Doc and Little Doc. By the time Big Doc died, he'd lived long enough to see three of his four grandsons come into this world. That, he thought, made up for a lot in his life, and he blessed Sammie Jo for the new happiness she brought to the yellow house.

Having been meant for a big family, the house had plenty of room. It was a solid structure with a wide front porch, a central hall, double parlors, one of which later was paneled in knotty pine and served as a den, a dining room with a butler's pantry, and a large kitchen. There was a sunroom off the front parlor and a carport off the kitchen. Upstairs, there were three bedrooms, a sewing room, two baths, and a sleeping porch lined with screens on the inside and windows that cranked out. The boys slept there all summer and, in the Lower Alabama heat, well into the fall.

So, the big yellow house had served its purpose—if a generation late—and got filled up the way it was meant to be. Little Wootens all over the place. Boys tearing around. Sammie Jo did her best to keep up with the four of them, and after Big Doc died, Claude himself became Doc and took over the drugstore and made some money.

Sammie Jo knew she'd had a good life. Make no mistake about it, she counted her blessings. And she had wonderful memories, better by far than most, and she carried them around and savored them like pieces of candy tucked in her jaw.

But...still...nevertheless.... Well, there you have it. What was she going to do now with the rest of her life? The next twenty years. She'd recently turned seventy and fully expected to live another twenty. Except for some dizzy spells, there wasn't a thing wrong with her. Well, her cholesterol was a little high, but so was everybody's. That didn't count. Besides, she took the pills.

No, she had another twenty years, give or take a few, to contend with. She needed a plan.

Now Hopewell was saying, "You decided to change your name so, in your old age, people will take you seriously?"

"Yes, but it's not getting the job done. Everything's still the same. I called each of the boys last night and told them. They didn't pay attention. Horton just groaned and said, 'Oh, Mother!' like I'd made a *faux pas* or talked bad at the dinner table."

Sammie Jo pronounced it 'fox pass,' and Hopewell hoped she did this to be funny.

"When I called Garrett, he immediately started composing me a song. 'Sa-man-an-an an-tha. How I love ya, how I love ya, my good ole Samantha-anna-anna-anna blues.' Such nonsense.

"And you know what Derwin said? 'Whatever.' Whatever! As if it wasn't important."

"What did Buddy say?"

"He said, 'That's all right, Mama. Don't worry about it.' He seemed to think I was apologizing for something."

"Buddy's a sweet boy."

"None of them got what I was trying to tell them."

"Now, honey, they all love you. After all, they did give you an anniversary present." Hopewell looked at her sideways, then gave a little whoop.

"Right," Sammie Jo said, and they both burst out laughing.

"It was my own fault," Sammie Jo allowed. "They asked me what I wanted, and I said something that would prop me up and get me ready for old age. I didn't think they'd take me up on it. And a walker wasn't exactly what I had in mind."

She didn't want to think about getting old.

"Well, you get what you ask for, I reckon," Hopewell said.

"I reckon."

"Well, I, for one, enjoyed the party," Hopewell insisted.

"Did you?"

"Sure. Kids all over the place. And all four boys home."

"Yeah. I wish Garrett and Derwin and their kids could have stayed longer. You know, helped clean up some of the mess. Of course, Horton came over the next day and folded up all the chairs we'd borrowed and took them back to the funeral home. That was a big help."

Horton, Sammie Jo's oldest, had followed in his father's footsteps and become a pharmacist. He'd taken over the family drugstore when Doc retired, but then one of the chains had bought them out, and now Horton just worked there and managed the place the way they told him to. Wooten's Drugstore, as such, no longer existed.

"They got lives of their own now, honey," Hopewell said.

"I know."

"They were there for you, sugar. What else do you want?"

Sammie Jo shut her mouth then. Hopewell didn't have any children, and her late husband, Guy Jennings, had shot and killed himself last year, at which time Hopewell, along with everybody else, had discovered he'd gambled away everything they had. Guy had been a successful insurance agent in Piney. Except for a few years away in college and the army, he and Doc had played golf together practically every Saturday morning of their adult lives. The two couples had been best friends forever. Gone to school together, double-dated, and vacationed together every summer for half a century.

Sammie Jo still wanted to wring Guy Jennings's neck. Always would, she reckoned. Hopewell may have forgiven him, but Sammie Jo hadn't.

Hopewell was left with nothing but this little house in Fairhope she'd inherited from her grandmother. It was in pitiful shape and had been rented out for years. Now Hopewell lived here, in the back, and used the front rooms for her shop. She'd gone into linens because she'd always loved them, and the old lady, her grandmother Hopewell, had left her a chest full of them. Selling them had been the first money Hopewell ever earned. Guy had been the center of her life. A right high life it had been too. Off to Las Vegas every chance they got. Then to the casinos in Biloxi when they opened up. Wherever Guy wanted to go.

Now Sammie Jo felt chastised. Complaining about her children, her life. Sometimes though, and she was ashamed to admit it, she felt envious of Hopewell. How simple her life was. How in control. It was just hers, her very own life, to do with whatever she wanted. All neat and organized and contained in this little house. What a relief that would be!

"I didn't mean to sound ungrateful, you know," Sammie Jo said now.

Hopewell nodded. She knew Sammie Jo hadn't meant anything by what she'd said, and Sammie Jo knew Hopewell knew. They had that kind of friendship. Not once had they ever had an argument that amounted to anything, even though Sammie Jo had a life-long tendency to hold Hopewell responsible for her own lapses in judgment. For instance, fifty years ago on the morning of her wedding, Sammie Jo decided to dye her lovely auburn hair, and it had turned out this horrid greenish color, not at all what she had expected and nothing like the picture on the box. She had cried. She had wanted blonde highlights. She looked awful, and, in her frustration, she'd blamed Hopewell. "Why did you let me do that?" she'd demanded.

Hopewell had hugged her and hadn't even pointed out that she'd tried to stop her. She just helped her arrange her veil to cover most of her hair and insisted no one would ever know.

Of course, people had known because, at the reception, Sammie Jo hadn't been able to resist taking off her veil and showing everybody. Everybody had laughed, and Doc had insisted on cutting off a lock and putting it in the wedding album. It was there to this day, bearing witness to Sammie Jo's frivolity.

Oh, she thought now, how young she'd been! She hadn't even been close to a real grown-up. She had just been play-acting, pretending to be an adult who knew her own mind. And the awful truth was she hadn't changed. When was she going to grow up, be her own person, not act like a fool? When in this world if not now?

To this day, she still couldn't imagine how Hopewell—and Doc—walked through life so calm, as if everything was perfectly reasonable and to be expected and all one had to do was just take hold and not get wrought up. Sammie Jo knew everybody wondered how she could ever have gotten through life without them. Sammie Jo wondered herself. They were self-sufficient. In control. Both of them. She and Guy had been the ones out of control. The two couples had been partnered with their opposites. No doubt Guy had needed the stability Hopewell offered, and, no doubt about it at all—not even in Sammie Jo's mind—she needed Doc and his dependability and steadiness and…and his very Doc-ness. Everybody knew that for a fact, and so did she.

What she didn't know—and had never been able to figure out—was what he needed from her. Something, apparently. She kept his world turned upside down. That was for sure, and yet he seemed to tolerate her, even enjoy her. Why? What did she, Sammie Jo Horton Wooten, have to offer Doc Wooten? What had she ever offered him but confusion, chaos, and—she smiled ruefully to herself—good loving, not to mention four handsome sons.

Of course, sex was no longer the driving force it once had been. But oh, Sammie Jo thought, over the years it sure had ironed out the wrinkles—for both of them. Kind of like Hopewell's iron. Always hot.

This thought made Sammie Jo smile.

The kids—and grandkids—knew Doc was reliable, but they never knew about Sammie Jo. Just for the fun of it, at any moment, she might throw you a curve or a monkey wrench. Doc wouldn't do that. He might say no, and Sammie Jo hardly ever did, but he didn't get carried away so that things got—well, out of hand, embarrassing, even, at times, unsafe.

Like the time when Garrett was a baby and she backed down the driveway with him on top of the car. Forgot he was there. Or more recently, when she left Susie Q at the grocery store. Came home without her.

She couldn't even keep track of her own flesh and blood. No wonder they thought she was a dingbat!

Sammie Jo was thinking that now as Hopewell set the sandwiches out on Blue Willow plates and poured glasses of sweet tea.

"It's just that I wish they gave me credit sometimes for all the things that went right. I mean they're all still in one piece, aren't they? I didn't injure any of them or lose anybody permanently, did I?"

She looked at Hopewell in bewilderment. And teared up.

"Ah, honey," Hopewell said and put her arm around her. They sat in silence for a moment. Then Sammie Jo shrugged, and Hopewell sat back and picked up her sandwich.

"Fact of life," Hopewell said. "All offspring find fault with their mothers. Whatever's wrong with them, mothers are to blame."

They gave each other sad smiles. Hopewell was a realist, Sammie Jo a romantic, if not a cock-eyed optimist. Basically, Hopewell believed people never really changed and you had to accept them—and yourself—pretty much as you found them. Sammie Jo, on the other hand, had spent a lifetime working on people, mostly herself, thinking any day now she'd solve the riddle of who she really was and what she really wanted and life would—finally, at long last—be simple and manageable. It was an exhausting theory and one she never gave up on.

"So," Hopewell said, ready to move on, "let's get this straight. Which one are you—Sammie Jo or Samantha?"

"Well, I'm not both," Sammie Jo said. "I'm either one or the other. I can't be Samantha to myself and Sammie Jo to everybody else."

"You can't?"

"No."

"You want people to call you Samantha?"

"Yes."

"At this late date," Hopewell said, "that might be a little hard to arrange."

"Look," Sammie Jo said, "is this so hard to understand? I want to be known as Samantha. Someone with dignity. Sammie Jo sounds so...oh, haphazard. You know? As if you can just call me any old thing and it doesn't matter. Well, if it doesn't appear to matter to me, I guess there's no reason to think it would matter to anybody else. But it does matter to me. Always has."

Names are important, she thought. What people call you is an indication of what they think of you. Like how each of her four sons called her something of his own devising, according, she believed, to how he saw her. Horton said Mother, Garrett Mom, Derwin Ma, and Buddy Mama.

These weren't really names, of course. They were titles. Like Grandma and, God forbid, Mother Wooten, which was what Horton's wife, Ann, called her.

"All right then," Hopewell said, placing both hands flat on the table as if making an announcement, "Samantha it is."

Sealing the deal, they nodded in agreement.

Hopewell was such a good friend. How many pacts, Sammie Jo wondered, had they formed over a lifetime. Secrets kept as little girls, plots hatched as teenagers, miseries and pleasures shared as women. True blue always.

But the rest of the world was not so accepting and reinforcing.

"There's just one problem," Sammie Jo said. "How do I get to be Samantha?"

"Honey, I don't know," Hopewell confessed. "I'm afraid that's up to you."

When she got home, Sammie Jo took a nap and dreamed she was getting dressed for a wedding. Maybe she was the bride. Or a bridesmaid. Or mother of the bride. It was confusing. Sometimes she seemed to be one, then the other, then another altogether. But always she was the one in charge, and the hubbub that was happening was at her house. She was responsible for getting everyone ready to leave for the ceremony. And then they were all gone, and there was no one left to zip up her dress and drive her to the church.

When she woke up, she felt bereft, as if she'd lost something elusive and hard to name. She was reminded of her disappointment about the anniversary. Of course, she had been touched and surprised by Doc's present. She'd never expected a diamond of her own, but the boys' gift had hurt her feelings. They had thought the walker was funny. Actually, she had too, but she didn't enjoy the joke much.

Truth was she was often dizzy and unsteady on her feet, and that embarrassed her. The boys seemed to think this was part of her personality, one of her hilarious quirks, like the way she had of renaming things she couldn't remember the real name for. The way she called the Stop-and-Shop the Get-in-and Get-Out and the TCBY yogurt store the XYZ. And the boys themselves, when she called them first one name and then another and finally gave up and just called them all George for the rest of the day.

What her sons never seemed to understand was that the dizziness often left her sick at her stomach, and an incessant ringing in her right ear became so wearing she sometimes wanted to bang her head against the wall. They just thought their mother was a character—a notion, she thought grimly, that she would like to disabuse them of before she became senile.

Still though, she didn't object completely to their teasing. Just as long as she wasn't reduced to nothing but the butt of their jokes. That, she supposed, was what she feared.

But, Lord, they were funny. She often wondered how the mothers of daughters could stand it. Girls tended to take themselves so seriously and were likely to get their feelings hurt. Like Sammie Jo herself, she supposed. And there was all that pouting and whining. And door slamming. With boys, there was overturned furniture, broken windows, wrestling matches, bloody noses, racket, contests of strength and will, but no pouting and whining. Sammie Jo was glad for that.

And their silly presents over the years. Never the sweater that was just the right color or the replacement piece of china that had to be specially ordered or a weekend at a spa—gifts her friends' daughters gave them.

One year for Christmas, her boys had given her a karaoke machine. It was a joke, of course, because Sammie Jo was a terrible singer who loved to sing. Once, when Garrett, who turned out to be musical, was a baby, barely talking, he'd sat up in her lap and said, "Rock, Mommy, don't sing."

Another time—this had been for a birthday—they'd given her dozens of TV trays because, they said, her mantra, her favorite thing in the world to say, was "Put it on a tray." Every time they made a snack and started to leave the kitchen with it, she shouted that directive from somewhere, even when they thought she wasn't watching.

For Mother's Day one year, they gave her a hundred tulip bulbs. Every spring Sammie Jo longed for a yard full of flowers. Most yards in the area blazed with azaleas, daffodils, and tulips while the pecan grove looked like an athletic field with trees in the way. Baselines had worn paths from tree to tree on one side of the driveway, football scrimmages had left bare spots under the trees on the other, and balls, gloves, bats, helmets, rackets, scooters, bicycles, and motorcycles were scattered everywhere in between.

Of course, Sammie Jo was no gardener. She had only planted four of the bulbs, two on each side of the front steps, and the rest she had placed in a basket beside the mailbox with a sign that said, "Free tulip bulbs. Just plant 'em where I can see 'em and they're all yours." She still drove along the road in the springtime and said, "Oh, look at my beautiful tulips! I'm so glad you boys gave them to me."

Oh, her boys, her boys. The house couldn't hold them, and neither could the yard. They were always everywhere at once. To this day sometimes she could feel them jostling her, pulling at her with sticky hands, stepping on her feet. "You walk on the tops, I'll walk on the bottoms," she used to tell them.

And the noise. Oh Lord, the noise. Shouting, laughter, teasing, fighting, radios, TVs, stereos blaring. Now it was iPods, whatever those were, with kids walking around zoned out and plugged into their own world, but when she was raising her boys, the noise had been right there with her square-dab in the middle of it and nobody hearing a word she said.

"Don't say Mother, Mom, Ma, Mama another time today. Do you hear me? Not one more time. There's nobody here by that name. She's gone for the day. On vacation. Whatever you need her for, you'll have to do yourself."

But, of course, they didn't hear. And she never stopped answering. Not even for a day.

Now, the memory of those years raising boys made her head swim. All those scout meetings and camping trips and ball games. And in and out of the emergency room and the principal's office.

Those were the good times.

Later, with Derwin, in and out of the police station too, though there had never been serious trouble. Speeding mostly. And drinking. And speeding while he was drinking, but Doc had put a stop to that. Now Derwin kept the two separate and, as far as Sammie Jo knew, reserved his speeding for the NASCAR circuit. She wasn't sure where he did his drinking— and didn't want to know.

And the girls. How many girls had she stood holding in her kitchen while first this one and then that one cried because one of her sons had broken her heart? All of her sons were good-looking, not just Derwin who had killer good looks, and they liked the girls, although Buddy, she supposed, was shy.

Now they were all grown up and gone. Except for Buddy, the baby. Doc and Sammie Jo had always pretended the day would come when Buddy could manage on his own, but the truth was, thus far, it hadn't happened, and they were finally of the belief that it never would.

A few years back, Doc decided maybe Buddy just needed a little encouragement, and he suggested he find a place of his own. Buddy himself seemed to think that was a good idea and acted as if he'd just been waiting for someone to propose it to him. He packed up some of his favorite possessions and clothes and moved out.

A few days later Sammie Jo discovered him living out back in the maid's quarters that, years ago, had been built onto a tool shed that housed an old hay rake and Doc's John Deere. Nobody had lived out there for years. Not since Miz Louise died and Mattie left.

When Sammie Jo told Doc Buddy was living there, Doc groaned in despair. "Oh hell, Sam, that makes me feel terrible. Tell him to move back in the house."

"I did," she said, "but he doesn't want to. Says he likes it out there, having a place of his own."

Doc shook his head and gave a tired smile. "Well, he's gonna need an air conditioner when summer comes. That's for sure."

Buddy was forty and a little slow to make transitions, but once he got hold of something, he didn't let go. He'd had the same job at the garden center since he was sixteen. Never married, loved his brothers. Oh yes, and they looked after him, all three of them, in their own way. Horton made sure he was all right and had what he needed. Garrett entertained him, taught him to play the harmonica. And Derwin—well, Derwin fought his battles for him. Anybody who bothered Buddy had Derwin to answer for it.

My family, my boys, Sammie Jo thought. God bless 'em.

"You did no such thing!"

This came from Elmira, Sammie Jo's older sister, who dropped by later that afternoon to pick up the card table she'd loaned Sammie Jo for the party. Elmira couldn't do without her card table more than a couple of days, and she was irritated with Sammie Jo for not returning it herself. Elmira did jigsaw puzzles. Ever since she'd retired as the police dispatcher, she'd given her life over to puzzles. Sammie Jo didn't know how she stood it.

"I'm telling you. Just listen," Sammie Jo said. "I went to the courthouse and changed my name."

"Whatever for?"

"Because I'm tired of being good ole Sammie Jo."

"Oh, for crying out loud, Sammie Jo. You're seventy years old. You're not a teenager. That's the kind of stunt adolescent girls pull to irritate their mothers."

"Well, I probably should have done it then, only it didn't occur to me. I've always wanted a real name, not just a nickname."

"Since when?"

"Since my whole life."

"Well, this is the first I've heard of it."

"You haven't been listening."

"I haven't been listening! Sammie Jo, you haven't listened to anybody since the day you were born, and you're accusing me of not listening. What's gotten into you?"

Sammie Jo didn't know what had gotten into her. Whatever it was, it felt different, new unlike anything that had ever gotten into her before.

"It's always something with you, Sammie Jo. Going off the deep end, this way or that."

"I don't know what you're talking about."

"Sure you do. No impulse control at all. When you take a notion to do something, anything at all, you up and act on it. Anything that crosses your mind with no thought to the consequences. Then later when you find yourself in over your head, you expect the rest of us to pull you out."

"What are you talking about?"

"Why, just the other day, at the party, you were lamenting about having such a big family, like you didn't know where all those babies came from. They came from you, Sammie Jo. Every time you'd get one out of diapers, you'd start longing for another one. Say your arms felt empty. Next thing I'd know you'd be pregnant again. One after the other. Without a thought as to what that meant down the line."

"Oh, that's not true. I never said I wished I hadn't had them. That's putting words in my mouth. I love my children, every one of them."

"I didn't say you don't love them, Sammie Jo. I'm just telling you you've never in your whole life thought ahead."

"Well, I'm thinking ahead now. I don't want to grow old as Sammie Jo. I want to grow old as Samantha."

"Now there's a plan for you." Elmira folded up the legs on the card table and prepared to leave.

Sammie Jo felt a flash of anger so strong she wanted to hit her sister. Actually hit her.

"One impulse after another. Just give in to them. No more impulse control than a child."

"Take your card table and go home," Sammie Jo said between gritted teeth. "You have no idea how much impulse I'm controlling right this minute."

The two sisters glared at each other. They'd squabbled their whole lives. Elmira telling Sammie Jo to straighten up. Sammie Jo telling Elmira to loosen up. Still Sammie Jo had never told Elmira to go home before. And, except in her dreams, she had never in her adult life felt overwhelmed by the urge to hit her.

Now Elmira stood with the card table between them like a shield. "Sammie Jo," she said in a reproving voice as if Sammie Jo was the one out of line, "I certainly will go home now. And let you rest. The party must have worn you out. Take a nap, and we'll all feel better."

"I just had a nap," Sammie Jo shouted after her as Elmira bumped the card table down the steps.

"Well, take another one," Elmira said over her shoulder. She slid the card table into the back seat of her car and drove away.

Sammie Jo went back in the house and stomped up the stairs. She didn't know why she was going upstairs. She just needed to stomp her feet, and stairs were good for stomping. Back when the boys were growing up, Doc used to say to them, "Look out, yore momma's stomping. One of these days she's going to stomp the house down." Well, it might be today, Sammie Jo thought now.

In her and Doc's bedroom, the bed was still unmade. The covers were pushed back, this way and that, the spread part way on the floor. The sight of the messy bedding made her all the more furious.

"You make your own bed," she said angrily, "and then you lie in it. And you lie in it. And you lie in it."

She began ripping the sheets, blankets, and spread off the bed. Gathering them up, she stormed across the room to the open window. She stuffed them through the opening, knocking the screen loose in the process. It banged against the house as it fell and landed, splat, in the yard. The bedding floated down and collapsed on top of it like the witch melting in *The Wizard of Oz* .

Then, as if putting periods at the end of a sentence, Sammie Jo grabbed up both pillows and threw them out too.

When Doc came in from the golf course, he said, "What are the bedclothes doing in the yard?"

"I threw them out the window," Sammie Jo said. She was stretched out on the couch with her arm across her eyes.

"Oh," he said, as if that made perfect sense.

She heard him walk through the den into the kitchen and open the refrigerator. She knew he was standing there trying to talk himself out of a second beer. He would've already had one at the club. She waited, counted to four before she heard the door close and the cap flip off. Sometimes she got to five.

He came back in the den with the bottle and sat in his recliner. He didn't take off his shoes and lounge back. She could feel him looking at her.

"What?" she said without opening her eyes.

"Are you going to leave those things out there?"

"I don't know."

He seemed to think that over.

"Okay," he said and sighed.

Then he removed his shoes and lay back in his chair.

CHAPTER THREE
Thursday, Three Days After Memorial Day

The next morning Sammie Jo began pulling things out of the house and setting them in the front yard. She didn't begin with any sort of plan, but once she started, she couldn't seem to stop.

It began simply enough with the vacuum cleaner. An old recalcitrant Hoover upright that didn't suck worth a damn. It wasn't broken. Sammie Jo knew it well enough to know that. The bag needed replacing. And she knew, after she'd removed the full bag, she'd have to go through God-knows-how-many shelves and closets to locate a new one, which she might or might not be able to find. And then—oh, it wouldn't be over yet—she'd have to get the tongs from the barbecue grill and dig in the opening and pull out months of cat hair, dropped toothpicks, bread bag twisters, paper clips, and God-knows-what-all until she'd unplugged the blooming thing and then...and then she'd be able to vacuum the rug in the front hall, which she despised. It had some sort of Chinese design that frustrated her. A maze that turned in sharp angles, in and out, up and down, and ended nowhere.

She had nobody but herself to blame for the rug. She'd bought it when she was too young to know what she liked. Well, okay, so she still wasn't sure what she liked, but she knew this much—that rug wasn't it.

She was sick to death of it...and the vacuum cleaner.

She took the vacuum out and deposited it under the nearest pecan tree and went back for the rug. She wanted them both out of the house. NOW. But the rug took some doing. Before she could roll it up and drag it out, she had to get the furniture off of it. There wasn't all that much in the hall—an umbrella stand containing two broken umbrellas, a yardstick, three walking canes, and a sprung tennis racket, plus a hall tree with hats and jackets that hung there from one winter to the next, and a teacart holding a silver tea service there wasn't room for in the dining room.

She didn't take the silver service to the yard. She left it on the front porch. It had belonged to Miz Louise, who had actually used the damn thing.

The teacart though, she took all the way, losing a wheel when she pushed it down the front steps. She left it listing in the grass as if it had been shipwrecked and then went back and fetched the wheel and laid it on top where the silver service had been. She was fed up with that wheel. For years now, every time she scooted the teacart so much as a few feet that damn wheel came off. Enough! She wasn't putting it back on ever again.

She slapped her hands up and down. Good riddance.

The hall tree gave her pause. Grandpa Horton had made it in his workshop before she was born. She set it on the front porch beside the tea service. She'd been caretaker of both for as long as she could stand, but they ought to stay in the family. She'd give the tea service to Ann, Horton's wife. Tell her to save it for Olivia. Let them polish it for a couple of generations.

The hall tree she'd pass on to Derwin, who'd never in his life made it all the way to a closet to hang up anything.

The umbrella stand was not a thing of beauty and had been a wedding gift from somebody Sammie Jo couldn't remember.

She pulled out one of the walking canes. It had been handed down in Doc's family, and he valued it. It was an oddity, made of rings of cow horn in graduated sizes and topped with an ivory handle. The story was Doc's great grandfather—or maybe great great grandfather—had won it in a poker game in Biloxi before the Civil War. She'd ask him about it. Doc, not the grandfather. Maybe he'd like to give it to Buddy. Buddy liked things like that.

Once she'd emptied the room, she went back for the rug. She got it rolled up and part way down the front steps before she gave up. It was too heavy to drag any farther. Obstinate old thing. She gave it a good kick.

Well now, she thought, might as well empty the hall closet while she was at it. She found things she hadn't thought about in years. The floor was a clutter of outgrown and abandoned footwear: boots, sneakers, swim fins, football cleats, flip-flops, and seven pairs of bunny slippers still in their boxes. These made her sad. She'd bought them years ago when the first batch of grandchildren were still babies: Horton and Ann's twins, Garrett and Cindy Lou's first two, and Derwin's first baby, Susie Q, with Sissy Winfrey, whom he never married but was considered family anyhow, plus two babies by his first wife. He'd had another by his second wife and was now expecting yet another by his third. Derwin had had too many wives and, as Doc said, "kept on keeping on" where babies were concerned.

Sammie Jo had known, somewhere in the back of her mind, that the bunny slippers were there. They reminded her of what a fool she'd always been. Come Christmas morning that year—and that had been back when everybody still came home for Christmas—she'd gone to get the slippers so she could put them on all those babies and pose them in their little pj's in front of the Christmas tree for Doc to take their picture, and she hadn't been able to find them. The slippers, not the babies. She'd hidden them so nobody could find them, and then she couldn't find them herself. She was so disappointed, she'd cried, and nobody paid the slightest attention to her feelings. They laughed. The boys thought it was hilarious that, once again, she'd hidden gifts from herself. They gave each other high fives, and money changed hands. Apparently, there had been wagers on whose presents she wouldn't be able to find this Christmas. They claimed one year when they were growing up she'd misplaced the electric train Santa Claus was to bring and hadn't found it until after New Year's.

Sammie Jo hoped that wasn't so.

Later, over the years, when she would come across the bunny slippers, she would remember that Christmas, all those barefoot babies, although some of them wore foot-in pajamas, and she would think about what a dingbat she was. Good ole Sammie Jo couldn't keep up with anything.

That afternoon when Doc came home from the golf course and saw the things piled in the front yard, he said, "We having a yard sale?"

This observation caught Sammie Jo off guard. Up to then, she hadn't thought of a yard sale.

"I reckon," she allowed.

"When?"

"Maybe Saturday."

"I'll be gone Saturday. Leaving in the morning."

"Oh yeah, right."

Doc would be gone to Orlando for his golf school, his present from the boys. She knew he was excited about it. She wouldn't dream of asking him to postpone it to help with a yard sale. If that's what she was working up to, and she wasn't sure it was.

Maybe a bonfire, she thought and felt a demonic flash of glee.

"I won't be here to help," he said now.

"That's all right," she said. "I'll get Buddy. Maybe Hopewell too."

"What if it rains between now and then?"

"Rains?"

"You know, Sammie Jo. That wet stuff that falls out of the sky."

"I don't know."

"Sure you do. It's the primary source of water on Earth, which is the planet I live on. What planet do you live on?"

He was sitting in his chair, taking off his golf shoes. She thought maybe he was irritated. Then he looked up with a sly smile. "You in never-never land, babe?" he asked.

She blinked as if she couldn't see clearly. Then, to her humiliation, tears sprang up. She nodded in his direction.

He couldn't stand to see her cry. Anything but that. He patted his lap as though signaling the cat to jump up. "Come here," he said.

She stumbled across the room and sat in his lap. Sammie Jo was plumper than she used to be but still petite. Doc was big with long arms and legs, spare and bony. They were an odd pair and a good fit.

"What's going on?" he asked, pushing her hair back from her forehead.

"I don't know." She shook her head against his shirt. She wasn't sobbing, just leaking around the edges.

"I feel all cluttered up," she said. "I don't seem to want anything we own. I just want to get it all out of here."

"We've spent a lifetime accumulating this stuff."

"I know."

"And now you don't want it anymore?"

"No."

"You want new stuff?"

"No. I want a clean slate."

"I don't know how to give you that."

"I know."

Doc tended to try to come up with solutions for Sammie Jo's problems, but this one appeared to be beyond his capabilities. Maybe it would resolve itself without his getting involved. He hoped she'd leave his stuff alone and just clean out a few closets, then settle down again. Thank God most of his stuff was in the carport and tool shed. And too heavy for her to lift.

She snuggled against him. He felt something stirring. That didn't happen as often as it once did. Doc was seventy-two.

"Honey baby," he said and felt for skin under her sweater.

"H-m-m-m."

"Let's go upstairs."

She didn't move.

"Come on." He nudged her. "I can't carry you."

She kissed his neck and sighed. It would feel good not to worry about the clutter. To let the junk go for a little while. Still, making the effort to climb the stairs seemed impossible.

After a moment, he seemed to think so too and relaxed against her. They rocked a little, back and forth, sank into each other, and gradually drifted off.

Nestled together, they enjoyed a little catnap. After a while, he jostled her and said, "You're going to have to get up. My leg's gone to sleep."

She blinked, stood up, and padded barefoot into the kitchen to see about supper.

He stood slowly, straightening his legs and hobbling about. He was stove up. He limped outside to the driveway, lifted his golf bag out of the trunk of his car, and carried it over to the grass. He turned on the hose and washed the dirt off his clubs.

When they were clean, he dried them, put them back in the bag, returned the bag to the trunk, and went back in the house to his chair. He could hear Sammie Jo stirring pots, moving things around in the kitchen.

He thought perhaps they were in for a storm. At least, a little turbulence. He was relieved to be leaving town.

CHAPTER FOUR
Friday, Four Days After Memorial Day

Early the next morning Doc was up and gone. Still in her pajamas, Sammie Jo kissed him goodbye at the top of the stairs. She was glad to see him off. She felt the urge to make headway. Get things out from underfoot. Just walking to the bathroom, she'd stumbled over the cat, then careened into a stack of magazines. Next she'd bumped into the exercise-cycle or whatever you called the damn thing.

It was time to empty this house of some of its clutter. Get rid of a few things. Maybe everything.

She felt compelled, as if this could not wait another minute. Barefoot and still wearing the oversized T-shirt and pajama bottoms she'd slept in, she picked up the stack of magazines and as many clothes hanging on the exer-cycle thing as she could carry and stumbled down the stairs with them. Out the door, across the porch, and into the yard. She dumped them onto yesterday's castoffs and went back in the house for more. She pretty much just grabbed up anything that got in her way. After her third trip, she turned to go back inside when a pickup truck turned in, drove up the long dirt driveway, and stopped in front of the house.

A big hefty fellow got out, raised his hand and nodded, and walked toward her. She squinted at him, wondered if she knew him. She might. He wore jeans, a plain white T-shirt, work boots, and a bill cap. He was probably forty or so and looked vaguely familiar.

"How you doing?" he said.

"Okay. You?"

"Can't complain."

She waited.

"You having a sale?"

"Maybe. You interested?"

"Depends on what you got."

"I got most everything."

He looked away for a moment, like maybe he was thinking about something else. He had mild blue eyes, a trimmed russet beard, a handsome face.

"You Horace Miller's brother?" she asked.

"No'm." He still didn't look at her. "I'm Horace. Used to be. Go by Hank now."

"Well, I'll be."

Horace Miller had been a classmate and friend of Derwin's until they both dropped out of school. Rode motorcycles together, chased girls, got drunk, got into trouble, got put in jail. Doc had bailed them out once, talked them out another time.

Sammie Jo remembered him as a scrawny teenager who couldn't be trusted. Not anybody good-looking who'd drop by and start a conversation with you.

"You sure have changed," she said.

"Bout time." He looked at her now, shrugged as if embarrassed, and bent down to pick a blade of grass and bit the end off of it.

"You need some help?" He nodded toward the pile of stuff.

"You offering?"

"Sure."

"When?"

"Now, I reckon."

He looked at her and waited.

Since she didn't know what she was doing, Sammie Jo didn't know how to tell him to help. It was one thing just to carry anything out of the house that got in her way or irritated her, but it was something else to tell somebody else how to do that.

"Look, Horace."

"Hank."

"Yeah, well, Hank, I'm just trying to clear a path here. Understand?"

He gave her a funny look, like maybe he was catching on to the fact that she didn't know what she was doing.

"Okay."

"Okay. I'll pay you whatever your going rate is."

He nodded and looked away.

"Well, look, why don't you start by carrying that rug on down the steps while I go in and make coffee."

"Okay."

Before she got all the way in the house, he'd picked up the rug like it was a rag doll and slung it over his shoulder. "Where you want it?" he called after her.

"Under that first pecan tree," she answered. She'd better hurry. This was going to go fast. Whatever this was, it was gathering speed.

They worked until noon. Sammie Jo forgot about breakfast. Never even bothered getting dressed. She was in a frenzy. Now that she had help, she wanted everything out. Some things—the piano, couch, sideboard, beds—were too heavy for the two of them. She couldn't manage her end. Still, they carried out a lot of stuff, and by lunch time the front yard looked like a flea market.

She made ham sandwiches and sweet tea and brought a tray to the front steps. After a few bites, Hank said, "Where you moving?"

"Moving?" The word jarred Sammie Jo. "Who said we were moving?"

"Aren't you?"

"Not that I know of."

"Well, you're not just clearing a path. Looks to me like you're emptying the house out."

"Yeah, well, I guess so."

"How you going to live in an empty house?"

"I don't know."

He looked puzzled but didn't comment.

"How come you changed your name?" she asked.

"Couldn't be Horace no more."

"How come? What was wrong with Horace?"

He gave her a sidelong glance before answering. "Pretty much everything." He shrugged. "You know."

"Well, yeah," she allowed. She did know. "So what happened?"

"You mean to turn me around?"

"Uh-huh."

"Motorcycle wreck."

"Oh Lord."

He didn't seem inclined to go on.

"How long were you in the hospital," she prompted.

"Long enough to get sober."

"You were drunk?"

"Must have been. Only a drunk fool would hit a tree straight on in the middle of the night. Flying down the road. No lights. By the time they found me the next morning, there wasn't much left of Horace."

Sammie Jo didn't know what to say. It could easily have been Derwin.

"Anyway," Hank said, taking a slug of tea, "by the time I got out of the hospital and finished rehab, I was done with motorcycles and drinking. I'm still on probation. Now it's one day at a time."

They sat in silence for a moment.

"You must think I'm acting crazy," she said.

"Miz Wooten, you ain't the one hit a tree going sixty miles an hour in the dark."

"Sammie Jo," she said. "I mean Samantha. I changed my name too. To Samantha."

"That's nice."

"You like it?"

"Sure."

"Then you call me Samantha. Nobody else will."

"Samantha."

She smiled. "You want to know why I changed my name?"

"Sure."

"Because Sammie Jo's about used up. I can't grow old as Sammie Jo. I just can't. In fact, I don't hardly see how I can grow old at all. I just can't face it."

"Ain't no twelve-step program for that."

"Nope. Not that I've heard of."

"On the other hand, the alternative…."

"Yeah, I know."

"Getting older's been good for me," he said, thinking about it.

"Sure. Because you're still young. Getting older's always good. Getting old is what's for the pits."

He didn't have anything to say to that. Nobody did.

By late afternoon, the lawn was littered and the downstairs pretty much emptied of lightweight stuff. The main pieces of furniture though were still in the house, and they hadn't even gotten to the upstairs yet.

"We're going to need some help," Hank said. He seemed to have accepted the idea they were emptying the house, not just cleaning out odds and ends. "Tomorrow I'll bring Brother James."

"Who's Brother James?"

"My partner."

"Partner in what? Crime?"

"Naw. Actually, he preaches on the side. Him and me—we got a booth over at the flea market."

"That how you make a living?"

"Yep. That and lifting and hauling."

"Two Men and a Truck, huh?"

"Right, except we ain't no big company. We really are just two men and a truck. And a few friends who pitch in when we need 'em."

He studied her for a moment as if something was on his mind.

"Samantha?"

The sound of her new name made a shiver run down her arms.

"Yes?"

"I don't want to mind your business or nothing, but it probably ain't a good idea to leave all this stuff setting out here—you know, just strewn around like this—overnight."

"Oh." She hadn't thought of that. But then she hadn't been thinking. She'd been emptying her house.

"No," she allowed. "I guess not. It might rain, huh?"

"Well, yeah, though that ain't too likely given the dry spell we're in. I was thinking more that somebody might run off with a good part of what you own, you know, with it just setting out here for the taking."

"Oh." That hadn't occurred to her, but it sounded all right. Then she wouldn't have to decide what to do with it.

Of course, that was foolishness. She knew that.

"Maybe we ought to cover things up with some tarpaulins and post some signs," he suggested. He pronounced it tar-pole-yuns.

"Signs?"

"Yeah. I know a sign painter. Has some already made up. We could get No Trespassing and Beware Bad Dog and put 'em up."

"Sounds unfriendly. Besides our dog—Rascal, remember him?—he died. Wasn't a bad dog anyhow."

"Well, whatever you want to do."

She didn't respond, and he decided to let the signs go.

"I'll go get some boxes," he said, "in case you want to pack up the dishes instead of just carrying 'em out in your hands."

"Oh yeah, that's a good idea. Let's pack things up. Makes it easier to move them out." She sounded pleased, is if packing was a novel idea.

He wondered if she was all right. What she was doing—whatever it was—didn't seem quite normal. Not any ordinary kind of housecleaning.

He'd noticed, as the afternoon wore on, that she hadn't seemed quite steady on her feet. When she carried an armload out of the house, it was if she had to take aim for the pile of things under the pecan tree in order to get there. And when she arrived, she often dropped things, willy-nilly, before stumbling back to the house.

She wasn't drinking. He felt certain he'd know if that was the case. And she wasn't stoned. Too wired for that. He wondered if she was on something though. Right now she was holding onto the porch railing as if she was afraid it might get away from her.

"Want to ride along?" he asked. He was a little worried about leaving her.

"Sure."

She climbed in his truck and gripped the dashboard like she was going for a ride on The Whip at the state fair. She was being very careful. He wondered if she'd never ridden in a truck before, but hell, everybody in the state of Alabama had ridden in a truck.

"You okay?" he asked.

"Oh yes," she said, but she fumbled with the seat belt until he had to do it for her. He felt like he was looking after a child.

As he drove he watched her closely. Maybe she was sick. Coming down with something. She didn't look feverish, but sort of cold and clammy, and she gave an involuntary shudder.

"You cold?" he asked. They'd been working all day in the heat, and he was soaked through with sweat.

She seemed a bit puzzled by the question and finally nodded her head. He turned off the air conditioning and opened his window.

He wondered if he should call someone. Doc Wooten maybe, but she'd already told him Doc was out of town. Still, maybe Doc should know about this.

On the other hand, Hank told himself, it wasn't any of his business.

Of course, he could stop by the drugstore and mention what was happening to Horton, but he and Horton had never gotten along. Back when they were in high school, Horton had gotten on Hank's case for supplying Derwin with pot. Of course, that had been a long time ago, but, still, Hank didn't have much truck with Horton. Doc Wooten was something else. Mad as he used to get at him and Derwin, he didn't seem to get permanently bent out of shape about things.

But Horton...when he got bent, he stayed bent. Self-righteous son-of-a-gun. Of course, there was no calling Garrett or Derwin. No telling where they were on any given day. Garrett stayed over in Mississippi most of the time. Working at some sort of museum dedicated to preserving the blues, his mom said.

As for Derwin, he was running at Talladega this week. Everybody knew that. Derwin was all the time in the papers, and there was always lots of talk about him. People rooting for the hometown boy. Even those who used to say he'd come to no good. And there were still those who said that.

That left Buddy. Buddy wasn't exactly your go-to kind of guy, but Hank thought maybe, when they got back to the house, he'd hang around until Buddy got home from the garden center. Hadn't seen him in a while. Always liked him. Everybody liked Buddy.

"Who's that singing?" Sammie Jo asked.

They were on the way back to the house with a truck bed of tarps Hank had borrowed from a fellow he knew at a furniture store and cardboard boxes they'd picked up behind the Winn-Dixie.

"Steve Earle," he told her. "You like him?"

"I don't know."

Every morning since he'd gotten the truck, Hank picked out a set of tunes to play that day. His truck had a CD player.

He was proud of his truck. It was almost paid for. He was proud of that too. He'd get her paid off this time. He had some confidence now. One day at a time, he'd get her done. One monthly payment at a time. The truck was his investment in the future.

"That's a wild song," she said. "Where'd he get a song like that?"

"He wrote it."

They listened while ole Steve sang in his lowdown growl about turning left when he should have gone right and going down to Mexico and pretty much throwing his life away for a few days of whooping it up.

"What's the name of it?"

"A Week of Living Dangerously."

"Oh my," she said.

When they got home, a half-dozen cars and trucks were parked under the trees, and Buddy was talking to a cluster of people. Some of them Hank recognized but hadn't seen in a while. Buddy was shaking his head and talking to them. They were looking at the piles of stuff under the pecan trees, speculating, Hank figured, about a yard sale. Hank wondered if that was what they were doing—him and her—getting ready for a sale.

Sammie Jo didn't seem interested in talking to anybody and carried herself unsteadily up the steps and into the house. Hank went over and said how you doing. He made everything sound normal, like it was all planned out, and said, yes, he was helping Miz Wooten get set up for a yard sale. Not sure when, he said. Everybody but Buddy nodded and left. That left the two of them standing there.

Buddy looked pretty much the same, Hank thought, not even much older except for some grey hair that showed beneath his John Deere cap. Buddy would probably always look like a little kid, sort of stuffed into his clothes and with big hands and feet he didn't quite know what to do with.

"You know what's going on?" Hank asked him.

Buddy seemed puzzled by the question, which wasn't unusual. He'd seemed puzzled pretty much his whole life, and Hank had known him since they were kids.

"A yard sale I guess," he said. "That's what you said."

"I know," Hank agreed, "but she doesn't seem to know what she's doing."

"Oh, well," Buddy said, like there was no help for that.

"You reckon Doc knows she's carrying all this stuff out of the house?"

"Probably."

"She says tomorrow she wants to empty everything out."

Buddy looked more puzzled now. "Everything? You mean the beds and the furniture? Things like that?"

"That's what she says."

"That don't sound right."

"I didn't think so. You know how to get in touch with Doc?"

"No. But he always calls in every night when he's gone."

"Maybe he ought to know the extent of this yard sale."

"Maybe, but he's working on his back swing right now."

"That mean we shouldn't bother him?"

"Probably. Besides, I live out back now. I won't be there when he calls unless I eat supper with her, and with all this going on," he gestured in the direction of the piles of stuff, "that don't seem likely."

"Maybe you should mention it to Horton."

"I could do that I reckon."

"All right then. See you."

And, leaving things in Buddy's hands, Hank left.

He didn't know what else to do.

CHAPTER FIVE
Saturday, Five Days After Memorial Day

The next morning Sammie Jo knocked on the door of The Hope Chest early. Barely daylight.

"My God, Sammie Jo, do you know what time it is?" Hopewell said, letting her in and forgetting her vow to call Sammie Jo by her new name. Hopewell, who usually looked put together and dressed with flair, had bed-hair, an unmade face with sleepy eyes, and was wearing an antique satin robe that had seen better days. She looked like a crone in a fairy costume.

"What in the world?" she said as Sammie Jo barreled past her.

"Miz Louise came to see me last night," Sammie Jo said. Her hair was standing out in all directions and she was wearing pajama bottoms and a T-shirt. The T-shirt said "What Happens at Grandma's Stays at Grandma's." She looked worse than Hopewell by a long shot.

Hopewell felt disoriented. What was Sammie Jo talking about? She was beginning to wonder if she should be worried about Sammie Jo.

"Who?" she ventured.

"Miz Louise," Sammie Jo yelled. "My mother-in-law. Who'd you think I was talking about?"

"Honey, Miz Louise is dead. Has been forever." It was too early in the morning for this.

"Of course, she is!" Sammie Jo sounded fit to be tied.

"Let's sit down, honey. I'll make us coffee."

They made their way through the shop toward the kitchen. Sammie Jo was weaving, holding onto display cases and doorways as she passed them, and, what she didn't guide herself around, she bumped into.

Hopewell set the coffee maker to working and sat down at the table beside her friend while the water dripped through. "Tell me about Miz Louise," she said, patting Sammie Jo's hand. "How's she doing?"

Her tone indicated nothing but interest, not even an overly amount of concern or annoyance, both of which she was surely feeling.

"She came in stages," Sammie Jo said.

"How do you mean?"

Sammie Jo closed her eyes. She was trying to remember clearly. The effort was like looking down the wrong end of a telescope. Miz Louise now seemed intent on escaping from Sammie Jo's consciousness, and she had been right there, in the room with her, during the night.

"There was a phone call."

"From Doc?" Hopewell asked.

Sammie Jo waved the suggestion away. "Yes, of course, but that was earlier. Before I went to sleep. This was about three o'clock in the morning. The phone rang a long time before it woke me up enough to answer it. When I picked up the receiver, someone was already talking. After a minute, I realized it was Grandma Horton. I couldn't understand what she was saying, but I knew she was talking to Miz Louise, who was downstairs on the other phone.

"They were friends, you know. Grandma Horton and Miz Louise. A long time ago. They used to talk on the phone a lot. They were confidantes, I think. I remember, after Miz Louise got sick, Grandma took covered dishes over to her. Sat with her. Saw to her."

Sammie Jo paused, thinking this over. "Of course, this was back before either one of 'em passed away."

"I would certainly think so," Hopewell said.

"Well, anyway," Sammie Jo continued, "at some point, I started trying to make heads or tails of what was happening— or maybe I just wanted to put a stop to it. So I say, 'I'm sorry to interrupt, but both of you are dead.' And you know what Miz Louise says? 'Then how come you're talking to us?'

"Well, that was too much to take, if you know what I mean. It's one thing to show up in the middle of the night and use the phone, but it's something else altogether to as good as tell me to mind my own business.

"So I go tearing down the stairs to find her, and, sure enough, there she is, big as life, sitting in the needlepoint chair beside the hall telephone. I say, 'What are you doing here?' and she says, 'I've come back to haunt you.' Then she laughs like it's a joke! 'Besides,' she adds, 'there's no place else to sit. Except for this one, every chair in the house seems to be out in the front yard. Why're you dragging the furniture out of the house?'"

"You're dragging the furniture out of the house?" This was the first Hopewell had heard about this.

"Well, just a few things," Sammie Jo admitted. "You know, cleaning up a bit."

"Oh." Hopewell could tell there was more to this than Sammie Jo was telling. She wondered what.

"Well, you know something, Hopewell?" Sammie Jo continued, caught up in her story. "I didn't like the way Miz Louise was talking. I took exception. It sounded to me like she was saying I didn't have the right to empty my own house. Like it was still her house and her things. As if I ever wanted her house and her things! They were foisted off on me in the first place. They were all part of the package. You know what I mean? Doc—and his father until he died—and the house and everything. She acted all high and mighty and as much as said I'd barged in and taken over.

"So I say, 'I never wanted your things in the first place. Or your house, for that matter! I wanted my own.'

"And guess what she says to that? She says, 'I know exactly what you mean, duckie. Half of the things out there that you think are mine came to me from my mother or my mother in-law. Don't you know a lot of what we have—and who we are—just trickle down from one generation to the next?"

"She called you Duckie?" Hopewell said.

"Yes! Can you believe it?"

"No! What did you say to that?"

"I told her my name was Samantha!"

"And what did she say to that?" Hopewell was more interested in the name calling at the moment than the stuff sitting in the yard.

"She said she and Grandma had talked it over, and they agreed Samantha was indeed my birthright. According to her, Grandma had always wished I'd been given her real name to start with. Said it hadn't been her doing that my mama didn't do a proper job of naming me.

"Well, that was news to me. I'd always assumed Mama didn't give me Grandma's proper name because Grandma objected. Come to find out she wanted me to have it."

"That's nice," Hopewell agreed. "Good to know."

"Yes. Anyway, I tell Miz Louise that I'll thank her to call me Samantha, not Sammie Jo and certainly not Duckie!"

"You said that to her?" Hopewell asked. "Straight out?"

"Yes. Straight out. And you know what she said? She looked me right in the eye and said, 'All right then, Miz Samantha, it's time for you to start living up to your name.'"

Sammie Jo gave a huge sigh and, as the air went out of her, lay her head on the table. She looked totally bewildered. Her eyes didn't quite focus, and she seemed exhausted.

Hopewell put her arm around her and patted her. "You must be very tired," she said.

Sammie Jo's face crumbled and her eyes welled with tears. She pursed her lips, shook her head, and refused to look at her friend.

"I shouldn't have come," she announced. She shrugged Hopewell's arm from around her shoulder and stood. "I have to go," she said.

"Why?"

"I'm cleaning house."

"You need some help?"

"I've hired a fellow to help me. Hank Miller. Used to be Horace."

"I know him."

"Oh, but he's not like he used to be. He's changed."

"I know. He and Brother James have a booth down from mine at the flea market."

"I'll be."

"Sounds as if you're doing a big cleaning." Hopewell tried not to sound like she was probing, even though she was. Something was going on. She was sure of it.

When Sammie Jo didn't respond, she asked, "Does Doc know about this cleaning project?"

"Not exactly. He thinks I'm just having a yard sale. Getting rid of a few things. Some old junk."

"But it's more than that?"

"Maybe. I'd like to start over with a clean slate. I told Doc that, and he said he couldn't help me there."

"I see," Hopewell said, although she really didn't. "I guess he's in for a surprise when he gets home."

"I reckon," Sammie Jo said, ready to leave.

When the door closed behind her, Hopewell fell back in her chair. She felt as if a whirlwind had swept through, followed by a warning rumble of thunder. And, if she knew Sammie Jo—and she did—a storm was not far behind.

Brother James turned out to be a big black man, wide and tall, topping six feet. He wore wire-rim glasses, big loose pants held up by rainbow-striped suspenders, a black shirt that looked as if it might, upon occasion, hold a clerical collar, and a gold cross. Brother James had presence, maybe even, in some people's opinion, an aura. When Sammie Jo got home, he was in the front yard with Hank examining her household goods with a proprietary manner and an acquisitive interest.

"This here's Brother James," Hank said.

"Morning," Brother James said. He had the booming voice of a born-again preacher.

Sammie Jo nodded.

"Hank here says you're disposing of things," Brother James began. "We can provide a full range of estate-sale services—pricing, tagging, selling, hauling. Even cleaning up after it's all over. We'll be happy to put ourselves at your disposal."

Sammie Jo looked at Brother James long and hard. She had the feeling she was about to get run over. "Look here," she said, "we're just emptying the house. Okay? Just setting things out here in the yard."

"That so?" Brother James said and looked at Hank.

"Everything?" Hank asked. With Brother James here, Hank seemed less sure of himself and gave Sammie Jo a look that made her think he felt caught in the middle. "What about the refrigerator and the freezer?"

"Well, not the refrigerator and freezer, I guess," she said. "No need for the food to spoil. Got enough mess as it is.

"And leave the carport and the shed alone," she added. "That's Doc's stuff out there, and not mine to do...to do anything with."

A confrontation with Brother James was pending—and hanging in the balance was who was in charge here. Sammie Jo sensed she could easily lose control of the situation.

"Look, James...," she said.

He frowned at her as if she had deliberately slighted him by not calling him Brother, which, of course, she had.

"We're just emptying the house, that's all. We're not selling anything," she told him. "At least, not yet. I'm just trying to get a good look at things. You understand, spread 'em out and look 'em over. I can hardly see my life all jammed together like it is inside the house."

"We just emptying, huh?" Brother James said and gave Hank a hard look. This was clearly news to him. Disappointing news. Sammie Jo wondered if he was going to turn on his heel and leave.

Hank stepped in. "Look, today we empty the house. Later Samantha here may want us to help dispose of some—maybe even all—the contents."

"Oh." Brother James gave Sammie Jo a disdainful look and gazed past her at some spot on the horizon. "I get it. She don't know what she's doing, and we're here to help her do it."

"Well now," Sammie Jo said. "I wish you hadn't said that."

"Brother James," Hank interceded, "Samantha and I got a deal. We pull things out of the house, and she looks her hand over and decides what she wants done with them. Then, whatever that is, we do it for her. Okay? Either way, we get paid. Okay?"

Shaking his head and looking disgusted, Brother James finally said, "Okay, I reckon, but next time you make a deal like this, you talk to me first."

"Well then," Hank said, looking chagrinned but trying not to show it. "Let's get started." And they did.

On his way to the garden center that morning, Buddy stopped by the drugstore.

"Mama's on a tear," he told Horton.

"What's she doing?"

Horton was standing on the raised platform behind the counter under the pharmacy sign. Buddy had to look up at him, and Horton didn't come down. He stopped pouring pills into a little bottle and regarded his younger brother with dissatisfaction.

"Pulling things out of the house and stacking them in the front yard," Buddy said.

"What kind of things?"

"Everything she can get her hands on."

"She having a yard sale?"

"Looks more like an everything sale."

"Doc know?"

"Don't know. He's gone you know."

"Yeah. You talked to him?"

"No."

"Has she?"

"I reckon. He always calls. She's got Horace Miller helping her."

"Horace? I thought he was in jail."

"Rehab for a long time, but he's out now."

"Oh Lord."

"Reckon we should call Doc?"

"I'll go out to the house at lunchtime," Horton said. "See what's happening. Ask her if she's told him what she's doing."

"Okay."

Buddy went on to the garden center then. He would have stayed for a cup of coffee if the store still had a soda fountain, but it didn't. Since the chain had bought the store, Buddy didn't come here anymore if he could help it.

He wished things were the way they used to be. He often wished that.

Even though it made him feel disloyal, sometimes he went to Mahan's Rexall instead of coming here. Mahan's was what Doc called an anachronism. It was old-timey and didn't keep up with the times. Mahan's still had a soda fountain but not much else. They made good milkshakes though, and these days those were hard to find.

Buddy slumped down inside himself and sighed. He felt like an anachronism himself.

When Horton got to the house at lunchtime, there was a good-sized crowd. School was out, and children were riding their bikes through the pecan grove and hopping off to look at anything that caught their attention. "Hey, look at this," they called out, holding up old toys and pieces of sports equipment that had belonged to Horton and his brothers. "Can I have this?" they asked of any adult who appeared to be listening.

His mother, Horton noticed, wasn't anywhere in sight.

Neighbors from up and down the road were there in full force. Mrs. Bennett who lived in a little house in the pecan grove next door, Lulu Rankin from a double-wide across the road, a couple of snowbirds from up North who'd come for the winter last year and decided to stay and had built a phony Mediterranean villa next to Lula's double-wide, old Mrs. Osborn who hardly ever left her porch, and Old Man Atkins who'd ridden over on his garden tractor from a half-mile away.

A few cars and trucks had stopped too, and people were getting out. Horton recognized some of them, some he didn't.

He nodded to people and weaved among them to find Sammie Jo. Horace and a big black man were carrying a mahogany sideboard out into the yard. It weighed a ton, and they were sweating and struggling so much with the weight of it they didn't notice him. She came behind them, dragging an armload of what appeared to be the dining room draperies down the front steps.

"Mother," he said.

"Hi, hon. What are you doing here?" She kept on going past him. She wasn't even making an effort to keep the draperies up off the ground, just trailing them along behind her. Horton thought they were some kind of expensive fabric, velvet maybe, old, of course, but nice, and the way she was handling them wasn't doing them any good.

He noticed she was wearing pajama bottoms and a T-shirt one of the grandchildren had given her for Mother's Day. And purple Crocs like the ones they sold at the drugstore.

Good Lord.

Trying to scoop up the draperies, he followed her across the yard. She didn't seem to notice he was behind her. She didn't stop until she reached the growing piles of stuff where she dumped the heavy curtains, making no attempt at folding them. When she turned around, she bumped into him. He steadied her on her feet. Her eyes didn't seem to focus.

"Horton," she said. "You still here?"

He looked closely to see if she was teasing him. She didn't seem to be.

"Mother, what's going on?"

She appeared uninterested in the question. "Listen," she said, "as long as you're here, can you give Hank and Brother James a hand. I don't think they can move the piano by themselves."

"Who's Hank? And Brother James?"

"Over there." She gestured vaguely in the direction of the two men.

"That's Horace Miller."

"I know."

"And the rug from the hall. You reckon you could get it in the back of your car? If you can, take it home with you and see if Ann wants it. The Chinese-y-looking one with the maze."

"Mother!" He took her elbow and demanded her attention. "What are you doing?"

"Oh, cleaning up a little. You know."

"No, I don't know. Does Doc know about this?"

"About what? That I'm housecleaning. Now why would he care about that?"

"You're doing a little more than cleaning. Looks like you're emptying out the house."

"Well, yes. High time." She looked at him now, for the first time. She had the annoyed expression she used to get when he and his brothers were kids and she'd had enough of their nonsense, although Horton himself had never been all that nonsensical. Still it was a look he knew well, one she had used on the four of them when she was tired of boys being boys and never good for anything else.

227

"Horton," she said flatly, "if you're not here to help, go on back to the store and get out of the way."

It always irritated him when she treated him like he was one of his brothers. He'd never done anything but what he was supposed to do, and yet sometimes she treated him as if he was a bother. And still a kid at that.

Well, okay, he'd let her have it her way. He'd leave.

And call Doc.

Horton left a message, and Doc called him back that evening. "Hey son what's up?" he said. "Anything wrong?"

Now, upon hearing his father's voice, Horton found himself reluctant to jump into the problem. He never liked to appear to be overreacting to a situation. It didn't look good for a pharmacist to be the sort who jumped to conclusions. He might not be Doc to the whole town like his father, but he wanted people, most of all Doc himself, to know he had a good head on his shoulders.

"What'd you do today?" he asked now.

"Worked on my slice. Then played a practice round," was the answer. Doc was waiting for the reason for the call. He hadn't expected anybody to call him this week.

"How'd you hit?"

"Seventy-eight. Not bad for an old guy." He wondered what Horton wanted.

"You talk to Mother last night?"

"Yep. Why?"

"You know what she's up to then."

"What's she up to?"

"She's dragging stuff out of the house and leaving it all over the yard."

"Yeah, well, she said something about a yard sale."

"This looks like something more than a yard sale. She's even got some of the furniture out there under the trees."

"That right?"

"She's got a couple of fellows helping her. One of them's Horace Miller."

"He out of jail?"

"Rehab, Buddy says. But yeah."

"How's he look?"

"What?"

"Horace. He seem okay?"

"I don't know. But he's Horace, isn't he? No telling what he's up to."

"Probably not."

"What you want me to do?"

"About what?"

"About Mother."

"You want to do something about your mother?"

"Doc, she's creating a mess."

"I understand that, son, but I'd leave well enough alone if I was you. No harm ever comes from staying out of your mother's way."

"When are you coming home?"

"Next week."

"You wouldn't consider coming sooner?"

Doc chuckled. "No. Sounds to me like a good time to be gone."

"Doc, I think you might want to...."

"Good night, Horton."

CHAPTER SIX
Sunday, Six Days After Memorial Day

The next morning Sammie Jo was at The Hope Chest again. Bright and early. "Oh Lordy," she said when Hopewell opened the door, "on top of everything else, now I've got a ghost."

"Where?" Hopewell asked, looking behind her friend as Sammie Jo stumbled into the shop.

"At home, of course" Sammie Jo said, as if everybody knows where ghosts hang out. She moved right past Hopewell, weaving around the racks of linens, and headed for the kitchen in back. When Hopewell caught up with her, Sammie Jo was rocking herself in a straight chair, moaning, her arms around her knees, which were pulled up under her chin.

"Does this ghost have a name?" Hopewell asked. It was Sunday morning, the one morning of the week when she could sleep in. Anybody but Sammie Jo she would have told to take her ghost story and go elsewhere.

"A name?" Sammie Jo said, raising her head and looking alarmed. "Why? Why would she have a name?"

"She?" Hopewell asked. "It's a she? Without a name?"

"Yes. No. I don't know." Sammie Jo stood up and prowled around the room.

"Sit back down, Sammie Jo, and tell me about it—about her—while I make some coffee."

Sammie Jo sat, and Hopewell filled the pot.

"I was asleep," she began. "And I was dreaming. I was walking through the house, from one room to another, and she—the ghost—began beckoning me to follow her. I did, and she said, 'You don't know the half of it!' And I said, 'The half of what?' And she said, 'Of what you have here. Miz Louise tried to tell you, but you didn't listen.'

"And, Hopewell, this is the scary part. She took me into rooms in the house I didn't know existed. Room after room. Big, beautiful, bright, sunny rooms. One after the other.

"When I woke up, I was on the other side of the house on the sleeping porch where the boys used to sleep in the summertime. She was standing there beside me, at least at first, and then she began fading away. I tried to grab her and couldn't. It was as if she was air. I said, 'Wait. Hold on. Who are you? What's your name?'

"And she said, 'You know who I am.' And then she disappeared."

Looking grief-stricken, Sammie Jo put her head in her arms and began to cry.

Hopewell sat down beside her and enfolded her in her arms. She let her cry for a few minutes before she raised Sammie Jo up to look at her and said, "Who was she, Sammie Jo?"

Holding onto Hopewell with both hands, Sammie Jo sobbed and—as if it was being wrung out of her—said, "Samantha. It was Samantha."

"How in the world…?" Hopewell said, holding onto Sammie Jo.

"I dunno. Dunno. Dunno," Sammie Jo cried.

Hopewell, who had known Sammie Jo all her life and seen her through thick and thin—the same Hopewell who was not prone to overreaction on any front, certainly not in regard to Sammie Jo—this Hopewell was alarmed.

Of course, being the Hopewell she was, she did not show her concern.

She said, "Well, now," and fetched the coffee pot. She was still in her robe and hadn't yet had her first cup.

When she poured one for Sammie Jo too, Sammie Jo pushed it away. "Hopewell," she said, "I'm trying so hard to be Samantha, but it's like I can't find her. And when I do, I can't hold onto her. She keeps slipping away."

"Oh, honey, I know, and I'm so sorry. Maybe you're trying too hard. You're wearing yourself out. I hate to see you exhaust yourself this way."

"Hopewell, I'm worn out. May I take a nap in your bed?"

"Of course."

Sammie Jo went to sleep almost as soon as she lay down. Hopewell tiptoed around her and dressed for church. When she returned, Sammie Jo was still asleep, so she went out to lunch. This time when she returned, Sammie Jo was awake but still in bed. She asked for an ice pack for her head. When Hopewell fetched it, Sammie Jo put it on the back of her neck and lay back down. At four that afternoon, she sat up and put on her shoes and said she had to go home. Hopewell said maybe she should drive her, and Sammie Jo seemed too tired to argue with her.

That evening when Doc called home, Sammie Jo sounded so vague and disengaged, he was concerned. He called Hopewell then and said, "What's up?"

Since the four of them—Hopewell and Guy and Sammie Jo and Doc—had been in high school, Doc had occasionally sought Hopewell's advice about Sammie Jo. Usually, Hopewell could offer an explanation that helped him stay on board. He depended on Hopewell for this and relied on her like she was his sister. As for her, she did it out of love for Sammie Jo and Doc both. They were the closest thing she had to family.

"She all right?" he asked now.

"Why? Are you worried about her?" Hopewell replied cautiously.

"She doesn't sound right, Hopewell. And Horton says she's gone off the deep end or something."

"I think she's okay. But she does seem to be walking in her sleep again," she told him.

"That's not good," he said. "Does she know it?"

"I think so." Hopewell decided not to tell him about the ghost. Sleepwalking was enough for now.

"I'm afraid she'll hurt herself. Fall down the stairs or something."

"She never has."

"True. But she might."

"How long has it been?" Hopewell asked. She couldn't remember the last time Sammie Jo had had sleepwalking episodes, but it had been a long time.

"I don't know," he said. Some years. During The Change probably. The worst of it though had been many years ago, back when Buddy was a baby. At the time, the doctor had said it was brought on by fatigue, but Doc doubted he knew.

Of course, she had been tired. Buddy had been a preemie. Sammie Jo had hovered over him for weeks, months, afraid he would die. She'd worn herself out.

"Is she tired?" he asked now.

"Yes."

"That's probably it. Is she crying?"

"Sometimes."

"Oh dear."

"Has she told you what she's doing?" Hopewell asked cautiously.

"Horton tells me she's got stuff scattered all over the yard."

"Yes."

"He thinks she's acting crazy, but then Horton thinks that of most folks."

Hopewell smiled.

"She did say something kind of odd on the phone the other night," Doc went on. "Asked me if I thought a rose by any other name—say, a tulip—smelled just as sweet."

"What did you tell her?"

"I told her yes. You reckon that was the right answer?"

"I don't know."

"Me either."

"She's not dizzy, is she?" Doc always worried about this.

"Yes, but I've kept her car here so she can't drive."

"That's good. Maybe I better come on home."

"I tell you what," Hopewell said. "You stay and finish your clinic. I'll get Buddy to keep an eye on her tonight, and I'll drive over first thing in the morning and see how things are. If there're any problems, I'll call you before you go to the golf course. How's that?"

They talked a few more minutes, and he let himself be persuaded to stay put. Until the clinic was over. Lord knows, he didn't want to go home right now. Especially not to chaos. He was playing too well for that. Of course, he didn't want her to hurt herself, but Hopewell was right. She never had. When she walked in her sleep, he'd just find her roaming around the house and not knowing a thing about it. It always upset him more than it did her.

CHAPTER SEVEN
Monday, Seven Days After Memorial Day

The next morning when Hank and Brother James arrived, the truck was loaded with more packing boxes, a dolly, and a ramp to put down the front steps. They were into heavy-duty furniture moving now. The old piano would be their first order of business today. Sammie Jo would pack up dishes in the kitchen.

They worked diligently, mostly without talking, until lunchtime when Hank went to town and brought back cokes and Big Macs for them. Sammie Jo ate a whole one. And fries with lots of salt. She'd never done that before. Usually she just had a plain hamburger, but she was ravenous and realized she hadn't had anything to eat since early yesterday. Running on adrenalin and steam, she reckoned.

They'd just started back to work when Hi-Test Johnson, who lived down the road and didn't have much to do since his retirement from the filling station, passed by on his way to the fire station where he now hung out and played dominos, and he told the fellows there the Wootens' house had caught fire—an assumption he made because why else would Sammie Jo and all of 'em be dumping things out in the yard in such a hurry. The firemen were obliged—and curious enough—to climb on the truck and turn on the siren and the flashing lights and go wailing out of the fire station. Hi-Test followed them to the Wootens' house, and they picked up a caravan of cars along the way. Some people were on their lunch hour. Plus it was summertime, and there wasn't a whole lot going on. Besides, in a small town, you follow the fire truck whenever you have a chance to. For one thing, it might turn out to be your own house that's on fire and, if it isn't, you at least find out whose is.

When the caravan got there, some folks drove on back to town and spread the news that the Wooten house was burning to the ground, and others parked up and down the road to watch. Some got out and others sat and waited.

Facing the fire chief and a half dozen of his men and surrounded by people straining to hear, Sammie Jo tried to explain, but the effort seemed to frazzle her. The fire chief, Albert Brighton, who'd known her and Doc forever, put his hand on her elbow to steady her, but she still appeared unfocused, and she stammered when she spoke. He wondered what was the matter with her. If the house wasn't on fire—and she insisted it wasn't—then something else must be wrong. Sammie Jo was usually bright and bouncy, and he'd always sort of had a crush on her, not, of course, that he'd ever let on. Today she seemed a bit bewildered.

There was no fire and no need for the fire truck, she insisted. In an effort to keep a tremor out of her voice, she strained to speak up and then wondered if she was talking too loud. She couldn't be sure, her ear was ringing and she couldn't hear much else.

She just wanted to empty the house out and get a good look at everything, she said, as if this made perfect sense and was nobody's business but her own. After all, she said, it was her life, spread out here under the trees, and she could look at it if she wanted to, couldn't she?

"Now, Sammie Jo," Albert said in a conciliatory tone, "we just came to help you out if you needed us, that's all."

One of the bystanders said. "We didn't mean to intrude. We just wanted to know what was going on."

"That's right," others agreed.

Sammie Jo wasn't usually haughty, and she hadn't meant to hurt their feelings.

"I'm just taking stock, you see," she said now in a placating voice. "Of my life, I reckon. My situation—so I can decide how to proceed."

Or, if I want to proceed, she thought but didn't say. Not even Sammie Jo, as it was widely believed, blurted out everything that popped into her head.

"We're just here to see if you need any help," someone else said, which, of course, wasn't the truth but made everybody feel better about their curiosity.

"Sure," several others chimed in. "Want us to give you a hand? We'd be glad to help."

None of them had intended any such thing, but now, eager to think better of themselves, people begin to volunteer. They'd be neighborly and help her out. After all, that was what neighbors were for, although some who came forward didn't actually live close by. They just had nothing else to do and got caught up in the moment. They liked the idea of being neighborly and helpful, and those who turned to leave did so hurriedly to hide their guilt.

The newspaper had sent a young fellow with a camera to follow the fire truck, and when he found out what was going on, he took a picture of Sammie Jo, still in her pajama bottoms and What-Happens-at-Grandma's-Stays-at-Grandma's T-shirt, with Hank and Brother James and some of the volunteers. Everybody was happy to pose, and the picture-taking made the hubbub seem like a social occasion.

Throughout the afternoon, people united in an effort to help Sammie Jo empty out her house, even though they didn't understand why she was doing it. By the time the sun was low in the sky, they were enjoying themselves. Talking back and forth about how everybody ought to help one another out and how people used to do that and didn't anymore. Sammie Jo had Hank drive her to the curb market down the road. She brought back a case of cold beer and some Dr. Peppers, and people gathered under the trees and drank them before heading home.

Sammie Jo enjoyed herself thoroughly, and so did everyone else.

When Hank and Brother James were leaving, Sammie Jo waylaid them. "That sign painter you mentioned...?"

Hank stopped. "Uh-huh?"

"You reckon he could paint me a sign? Not 'No Trespassing' or 'Beware of the Dog.' Something personal."

"Sure."

"Here I wrote it out." She handed him a scrap of paper.

He looked at it and smiled. "Taking a stand, huh?"

"I reckon," she said, although she wasn't sure about what. "And tell him to make it big enough to see from the road. A banner we can hang across the front porch. Easy-to-read lettering in bright colors."

From force of habit, she started to go back in the house, although she didn't know what for. Most everything she and Doc owned was now in the front yard. As an afterthought, she turned back to Hank and said, "And tell him to put a rush on it. I want to put it up as soon as possible."

As Hank and Brother James turned the truck around, she called after them, "Tell him I'll pay extra."

Through the windshield, she saw Brother James shake his head and look at her sadly.

Bone-tired, she went indoors and weaved her way among boxes to the refrigerator to look for something to eat. It was full of food, of course. Sammie Jo's refrigerator was always full of food. Had to be. For years, she'd never known how many people would be there for supper, but a lot, she could count on that. Of course, that was no longer the case. At least, not very often. Hadn't been for some years now, she reckoned. But still, she kept plenty on hand for the times it was needed.

She pulled out salad makings from the vegetable drawer, only to discover she had no knives handy to cut with. She ate a tomato leaning over the sink and a couple of pieces of bread and drank milk directly from the carton. How many times had she told her boys not to do that? Then she ate a handful of Famous Amos cookies and drank some more milk and went up to bed.

The empty bedroom startled her. The bed wasn't there.

She went in the bathroom and washed her hands and face and, when there was no towel on the rack, she dried herself with her T-shirt. She returned to the yard and, in the twilight, managed to find a pillow and a couple of quilts. Back upstairs, she made a nest of them in the bathtub, kicked off her Crocs, and climbed in.

CHAPTER EIGHT
Tuesday, Eight Days After Memorial Day

It was lunchtime, and the waiter came to the table where Doc and his fellow golfers were eating and said Doc had an emergency phone call. Doc left the table with reluctance. Sometimes, he thought, as he followed the waiter through the dining room, Horton took himself too damn seriously.

"We've got a situation here," were the first words out of his first-born's mouth.

"What kind of situation?" Doc asked. Hopewell had gone over early yesterday morning to check on things and had called Doc to tell him Sammie Jo was fine. Still in an uproar but fine.

"A real hullabaloo," Horton said now.

"A hullabaloo, huh? I take it your mother is involved." Doc shook his head and gave a sigh.

"Doc, this is serious. She's put up a sign."

"A sign? What does it say?" He hoped she hadn't put the house up for sale.

"It's a banner across the house. It says 'Sammie Jo Doesn't Live Here Anymore.'"

Now Doc couldn't help laughing.

"You think this is a joke, Doc? It's attracting a crowd. People are driving by just to see what's going on. Coming in the store and asking me what it means. Laughing. Saying what a card she is."

"No wonder they're laughing, son. Your mother's a funny woman."

"What does it mean? Is she leaving? Where's she going?"

"Damned if I know," Doc said. "I'll be home next week, and we'll straighten this out.

"Oh, and by the way, call me if she puts the house up for sale."

That night Sammie Jo slept out in the yard. Under the stars. In her own bed. Which she'd had Hank and Brother James set up out from under the trees so she could see the sky.

The idea of sleeping out under the stars appealed to her, but she could have used mosquito netting.

In fact, she was getting eaten alive. Swat. Swat. Swat. There was no sleeping. She reached under her pillow for the cell phone Hopewell had insisted she keep with her. Hopewell had practically forced it on her. Sammie Jo had never owned one. Thought they were a bloody intrusion on life and civil discourse, which, to her, meant face-to-face conversation with everybody paying attention to the people right before their very own eyes.

But right now there wasn't anybody right before her eyes she could talk to. Nor was there anybody around who would be annoyed if she made a call. And besides, she was miserable out here. Swat. Swat. She had to talk to somebody. But she couldn't talk to Hopewell. She had Hopewell's phone. Well, there was a business phone out in the shop, but Sammie Jo wasn't going to make her get up in the middle of the night to go answer it.

And she'd already talked to Doc that evening. She told him she was fine and how was he? He was fine. And playing well enough to be having fun and learning a lot.

So she called Horton. That took some doing, but she figured it out. She poked a bunch of buttons at random until the damn thing came on, and, when it lit up, she could see which numbers to punch.

She was relieved when he answered instead of Ann. She and Ann never saw eye-to-eye, especially in the middle of the night.

"Mother, what's wrong?" Horton said as soon as he heard her voice.

"Nothing's wrong." She was put off that he immediately assumed something was.

"Where are you?"

"In the yard."

"Why?"

"Because that's where my bed is."

"It's two o'clock in the morning, Mother."

"Oh. Well, listen, Horton, I was wondering—do you like your name?"

"What?"

"Your name. Horton Stanley Wooten. Are you glad I named you that, or have you always wished you were named something else?"

"You woke me up to ask me if I like my name?"

"Do you?"

"I like my name just fine. What I don't like is the way you're behaving."

"Oh well," she said airily, "I know that. Good night, Horton."

Garrett, when she called him, answered on the first ring. On his cell phone. He was up. She could hear music and voices in the background. A harmonica, a piano. Someone singing.

"How you doing, Mom?" he said.

"Fine. Are you glad I named you Garrett?"

"Okay by me. Listen. Can you hear that? We've got the greatest bunch of old guys playing here tonight."

He laid the phone down—to applaud and whistle she surmised—then came back on. "You want anything, Mom?"

"No, that's all."

"Gotta go then. Call you soon. Bye."

Derwin was in a garage somewhere. No surprise there. She could hear motors revving.

"Derwin?"

"Wait a minute. I can't hear you." He went somewhere and shut a door behind him.

"Can you now?"

"Yeah. Ma? What's happening?"

"Do you like your name?"

"Like my name? Well, I reckon it's a little late now if I don't. Hell, I'm all over the papers these days. You see yesterday's sports page?"

"I missed it, honey. I'll try to find it."

"You okay, Ma? It's kind of late."

"Of course."

"How's Doc?"

"Fine. He's down in Orlando. His golf school, you know."

"Oh yeah. That's right. How's he playing?"

"Fine. Fine."

"Shooting his age?"

"I don't know."

"Seventy-two, Ma."

"No, no. I mean I don't know if…."

"Yeah, yeah. I'm teasing you, Ma."

"Okay. You know you were named for my brother who died."

"Sure, I know. Better than being named Junior. I'm making Derwin a name to remember, Ma. You don't have to worry about me."

Sammie Jo wished that was so. "Okay," she said.

"I love you, Ma."

"I love you too."

When she called Buddy, he answered his cell while walking from the tool shed around the house toward her. In the dark, lying on her back looking up at the stars, she didn't see him.

"Buddy, you know you're named for the doctor who delivered you, don't you?"

"Yes, but I don't remember him."

"No, of course not. He died a long time ago. He was a good man, Buddy."

"That's nice."

She looked up as he sat down near her in a rocking chair. "Oh hello."

"Hello Mama."

They continued talking on their phones.

"We could call you by your proper name, David Samuel Wooten. I mean if you would prefer. We don't have to call you Buddy."

"No, I like Buddy fine."

"It's a love name, you know. You were just our best buddy when you came along."

"That's nice, Mama."

"All right then. Bye."

"Bye."

They hung up and looked at each other across the piles of stuff.

"You sleeping out here tonight?" he asked.

"Yes."

"I'll keep you company."

"Okay. What'll you sleep on?"

"I brought my sleeping bag." He pointed to a bedroll beside him.

"Oh. Thank you for coming."

"You're welcome."

Despite the time, Horton called his father.

"She's sleeping in the yard, Doc."

"Why?" Doc had been sound asleep. Now, with the interruption, chances of a good round tomorrow were shot to hell in a hand basket.

"Because that's where the beds are."

"Oh."

"Doc, her picture was in the paper again this afternoon."

"Again?"

"Yeah, first time it was her and Horace and James and a bunch of the neighbors who were helping out when the fire truck came. This time it was just her and her sign."

"The house was on fire?"

"No. Somebody called the fire department because they thought it was, but it wasn't."

Horton wasn't making a whole lot of sense.

"Who's James?" Doc asked now.

"He's helping Horace."

"What does he help Horace do?"

"Move Mother out of the house into the yard, apparently."

"Oh."

"Doc, this is serious."

"No, son, world hunger is serious. And, quite frankly, I'm worried about illegal immigration, global warming, and the Middle East, but this is not serious."

"She's making a public spectacle of herself."

"That doesn't worry me. If she's hurt, sick, or crying—now that worries me." He paused. "She's not crying, is she?"

"No."

"Well, then okay."

"She seems sort of, you know, hyper. Excited."

"Yes, I know. Well, I'll be home in a few days."

They hung up.

Doc lay back and stared at the ceiling of his motel room. He was going to have to go home.

In a few more days.

Let her wear herself out first. Then she'd need him. She'd be exhausted, bone-tired—and crying possibly. They'd climb in bed together and he'd put his arms around her and they'd sleep a really long time. And when they woke up, things would be back to normal.

He knew how it would be. He'd been married to Sammie Jo a long time.

Oh hell! He just remembered. The bed—their bed—was in the front yard.

Of all the damn silliness! Well, he'd just wait the situation out. Stay down here until things returned to normal. Assuming they would.

Oh bloody hell! Maybe he'd better go on home.

CHAPTER NINE
Wednesday, Nine Days After Memorial Day

The next morning, early, Sammie Jo sat in her bed in the front yard and looked at the piles of accumulated living on the lawn. She could hardly believe this is what her life looked like. But when you took it apart and laid it out in the grass, this is what it looked like. Mattresses, pots and pans, chairs, lamps, fruit jars of peaches she'd put up last summer, a dressmaker's dummy from her sewing room, a pool table in need of repair, the kitchen stool she sat on to peel potatoes, a laundry basket of dirty clothes, the living room chairs with their frayed slipcovers. On and on and on. Fifty years of living.

It looked like the most haphazard, disorganized, messy mound of junk Sammie Jo had ever seen. It wasn't at all what she'd had in mind when she started out. Back when she and Doc married. She'd thought they'd have a structured, orderly, picture-perfect life. Honest to God, that's what she'd thought. She had everything planned.

Well, no, not planned exactly but visualized. Daydreamed maybe was more like it. Anyway, it was going to be perfect, she had been sure of that, and once she was Mrs. Doc Wooten, she would know how to organize and run her life so it looked like a picture postcard.

Well, no, not exactly like a picture postcard. More like an MGM 1950s musical. That was it. When she fell in love, she expected automatically at that point to be able to sing and dance. Perfectly. Like Doris Day and Debbie Reynolds. That, she just knew, was how it would be.

The first thing that didn't seem quite in line with what she'd expected was the house. It wasn't a little cottage surrounded by flowers and a sweet picket fence. It was this yellow brick monstrosity that Doc had grown up in. Why in the world had she thought it was temporary? All her life, whatever came along, she thought any decision about any problem or dilemma was temporary. Never had it occurred to her that such a decision might be marking a turning point in her life, that the die was being cast, and that she herself might bear some responsibility for casting it.

"I was just going along and going along," she said now, aloud to herself.

Not that she hadn't liked the yellow brick house. The thing was she had liked it. She'd just never intended it. And Doc, who had been an only child, was so pleased to fill it up with children and living. This, he said, is how he had always wanted it to be when he was growing up here lonesome for brothers and sisters. He'd delighted in just turning the place over to Sammie Jo and the children and the dogs and the cats and the pet rabbits and the entire kit-and-caboodle that went with the chaos and confusion of daily life at the Wooten house.

Every day she'd lived here, for fifty years, Sammie Jo had planned on getting things organized and under control. She realized now she'd had her chance when the kids grew up and left, but that had happened so gradually that she'd never really felt the time was right. And, then, the grandchildren started coming along, and they were in and out and, of course, Buddy had still been there until a few years back and even now was still in the back yard. And, too, Derwin came back for brief periods between his marriages, and Cindy Lou had moved in and out a time or two when Garrett was off somewhere saving the blues from extinction and she'd needed help with the babies. So there never had been an exact, clear-cut right time for getting organized.

Sammie Jo started to cry. Her life was such a mess. She was such a mess.

"I don't understand you," a disgruntled voice said. It was still early in the morning, and, when she turned and looked over her shoulder, she was surprised to see Brother James already there. He was leaning against a chest of drawers under a pecan tree watching her.

Looking disgusted, he walked over to her.

"You got a perfectly good house—a wonderful house— standing empty, and you're out here sleeping in the yard," he said.

Sammie Jo wasn't sure she liked Brother James. From the outset, she hadn't been sure about him, and this morning she wasn't of a mind to listen to criticism from him.

"You got a problem with that?" she said back at him.

"It ain't no way to act. A lady like yourself."

"What's that mean? A lady like myself."

"Hank told me all about you."

"What about me?" This Sammie Jo had to hear.

"How you raised that house full of boys, and Doc Wooten always at the drugstore, pretty much seven days a week, and you making this house the kind of place where all the kids wanted to be all the time, so that Hank and a bunch of others who didn't have the kind of home they wanted to go home to—if you know what I mean—hung out here. Shot hoops, tuned up their motorcycles, brought girls over to meet you. How you were all the time feeding them, listening to them, enjoying them."

"Is that what Hank said? That's how he remembers being here? How he remembers what it was like when they were growing up?"

"Yep. That's what he says. He says all the kids knew you could be counted on. Always there for them."

"You're making this up. I'm the most unreliable person on earth."

"Not to hear him tell it. Now it's true—none of 'em had any idea what you might do or say next, but you were always there. They could count on you."

"I don't understand. I was hanging on by my fingernails."

"Maybe it felt that way to you, but it sounds to me like you were coping."

"Coping, huh? I've never thought of myself as much of a coper. Now, Doc he's a coper. Takes everything in stride. Always has."

"Oh, yeah, Doc Wooten's a mighty fine man. That's for sure. Hank tells me Doc straightened him and Derwin out a time or two. Derwin? He the one that drives the racecars? Yeah, Hank recollects Doc getting the two of them back in line upon occasion."

He laughed. "Yeah, I heard all about that."

He nudged a box of dishes with his toe and kept on laughing. He seemed to be considering something. Sammie Jo wondered what.

"I never kept anybody in line," she said. "I couldn't even get the kids to pick up their socks. They thought I was a joke. Still do, for that matter."

"Oh, no. They think you're right surprising and unpredictable, but everybody in town knows you're the heart and soul of this family."

Sammie Jo looked at him as if he'd lost his mind.

"Now, why don't you act like the queen you are and let us get you reinstated?"

"Reinstated?"

"Yes 'm. This place could use some fixing up. So long as your belongings are here in the yard, might as well refinish the floors and repaint the rooms, don't you think? And I got some members of my congregation that are just the ones to do it. First-rate sanders and painters.

"Then, when we got everything spruced up, we'll move you back in, and you'll be sitting pretty."

"Did Hank really say those nice things about me?"

"Said he did, didn't I?"

"You really a preacher?"

"Didn't you just hear a sermon?"

"I reckon," she said and gave him a challenging look. "What's the name of your church?"

"The Prodigal Sons of Jesus Sanctified in His Holy Blood, Sweat and Tears Tabernacle Mission." He rolled out the words like he was pronouncing a benediction.

"You made that up," she said.

"Me and the Lord," he answered solemnly.

She paused and thought that over, then said, "I only want to move my favorite things back into the house. What are we going to do with the rest of this stuff?"

"Hank and I'll sell it at the flea market and make a big fat profit for you, and you'll give us fifty percent."

"Fifty?"

He shrugged. "Okay, forty. Unless you think the advice is worth another ten percent."

"Forty-five," she agreed, but gave him a grim look. "But if I find out you're lying about...you know...the kids thinking I was something special, I'm not paying you a dime, and I'll sue your ass."

He laughed. "Would I lie to you?" he asked.

"Probably," she said and climbed out of bed.

That evening Horton was back on the phone with Doc.

"Now she's got convicts in the house. I'm telling you, Doc, you've got to come home."

"Convicts?"

"Yep."

"Where'd they come from?"

"You remember that James fellow I mentioned? The one helping Horace with the emptying?"

"Yeah."

"Last name's Gilliam. Big black guy. You know him?"

"Brother James? That's who's helping her?"

"Yeah."

"He's a preacher, son. Nice fella."

"He's also a parole officer."

"That's right."

"Yeah. That's how he got partnered up with Horace. He's Horace's parole officer."

"Okay."

"He's got a bunch of his parolees—six of 'em—in the house painting and refinishing the hardwood floors."

"They any good at it?"

"At what?"

"Painting and refinishing."

"How would I know?"

"Well, I'd just like for the work to be done right."

"Doc, listen. Mother's in there with them. Working along side 'em. She thinks they're members of Brother James's congregation."

"They probably are."

"What are you going to do about it?"

"Brother James there supervising?"

"Yes."

"Good."

"Good?"

"Yep. Sounds like a good way for her to get some work done and leave me out of it. I'm too old to be painting and sanding. I think I'll stay on down here until they get the job done."

Doc hung up. He was relieved. For a while there, he'd been worried Sammie Jo didn't know what she was doing. It had sounded like she was on some kind of rampage that might put her in the hospital. She was just fixing up the house. Going about it in peculiar fashion, but then Sammie Jo hardly ever worked in a straight line. Most things she got done she seemed to back into. Yes sir, he was relieved.

And then Sammie Jo disappeared.

CHAPTER TEN
Thursday, Ten Days After Memorial Day

She was helping to paint the dining room—a rich emerald green with white woodwork—when she began to feel very tired. She could hardly lift her arms, and her head was swimming. She hated to admit it, but she couldn't go on.

You're pitiful, she told herself.

Truth was she'd had more energy for emptying out than for sanding and painting. Making a mess always came easier to her than cleaning up afterwards. She hated herself for that, but there you have it.

Besides, she felt in the way. In her own house. That didn't seem right. But she could see Hank and Brother James and their crew had things well in hand. They knew what they were doing, and she didn't. They worked fast, and she couldn't keep up with them. They were always having to step around her or show her how to mix the paint. Or pry the lids off the cans for her. Once, when she'd done it on her own, she'd spilled paint all over the floor and made a terrible mess. Of course, nobody said anything about it. To her face. But she knew what they thought. Behind her back, she could feel them roll their eyes and shake their heads.

She hated that.

What was she to do with herself? There was no place to just be.

At Brother James's insistence, she took his clipboard and went outside and sat under a pecan tree to make a list of the things she couldn't live without. Things to be moved back into the house when the work was done. She tried real hard, but these were not easy decisions.

Some choices were practical, like the kitchen table, and some were sentimental, like the karaoke machine the boys had given her. A few things like that she couldn't imagine getting rid of. But most things she couldn't make up her mind about. She just didn't know whether she wanted to live with or without them.

Her dressing table, for instance. She never sat at it, but it was where she kept all her perfume bottles on display. She always leaned over the bathroom sink to put her makeup on. That didn't seem like the sort of thing Samantha would do, but then Samantha couldn't see any better than Sammie Jo, and Sammie Jo needed to lean up close to the mirror under the bright bathroom light to put her mascara on, and so would Samantha.

So, it was a dilemma, and not one she had a ready answer for.

She'd always envisioned sitting at the dressing table in a slinky peignoir—is that what you called those sexy bathrobes things?—languidly brushing her hair and powdering her nose, but she'd never actually done such a thing.

And, in her heart of hearts, she knew she never would.

But that didn't mean she was ready to give up the dressing table. Besides, Doc had given her all that perfume. That's what he always gave her for Christmas and birthdays. The prettiest bottles he could find. For Valentines, he always gave her a dozen red roses. And for special occasions, like the big anniversary, he gave her jewelry. Doc was a traditionalist.

If she put it on three times a day, she'd never in her life use up all that perfume, but that didn't mean she was ready to give it up.

Or did it? Fifty years of perfume bottles to dust and work around? What in the world was she holding on to here? And why?

But give them away? To Brother James? Why in this wide world would she do that?

After an hour of sitting under the pecan tree, all she'd written down was the kitchen table and the karaoke machine. That didn't seem right. It certainly wasn't progress. Besides, now that she thought about it, she wasn't even sure about them. Nobody ever really ate at the kitchen table anymore. It was just a place to set things. And then they just accumulated there. So maybe she ought to....

Good Lord, she couldn't even make up her mind about the kitchen table! Never mind the karaoke machine.

When Brother James came out to retrieve his clipboard and see her list, he looked at her in disbelief, shook his head in disgust, and went mildly rigid. That is, he stiffened up, pretty much all over, and wouldn't look at her, but he didn't yell. He just whispered, very deliberately, like he was getting ready to explode, but he controlled himself. With great effort. And disappointment.

"Do you mean to tell me, we have done all this for nothing?"

Hank stepped in then. Sometimes Sammie Jo just loved Hank. One day when she'd ridden in the truck with him to go buy hamburgers for everybody's lunch, he'd played a song by somebody named Guy Clark. A song-writing fellow, not much of a singer, who wrote about a high-speed train going through the little Texas town where he grew up. He called the train "a mad-dog cyclone." Sammie Jo thought that was wonderful. She'd said as much, and Hank had said, "There's more than one kind of 'mad-dog cyclone,' ain't there, Samantha?" And he'd winked at her, and she knew he understood her better than most.

And now, with Brother James about to blow a gasket, Hank took over and calmed him down and pointed out that they were still getting paid for their time. Plus, Sammie Jo added, they could for sure have the old Hoover upright that had started this whole thing, along with the teacart with the broken wheel and the Chinese rug with the maze that went round and round and wound up nowhere which nobody, including Horton and Ann, ever wanted to see again.

Sammie Jo said they could have those things free and clear without paying her any percentage, plus all the kids' old athletic equipment and toys. Anything the grandkids could use, they'd long since taken over. Oh, and the bunny slippers. And the umbrella stand. Brother James could have those too. And the old twenty-two in the carport. She didn't want any more shooting at parties in the future.

So, Brother James said, what were they supposed to do about this yard full of stuff? Just leave it out there under the pecan trees?

Well, for the time being....

That was as much of an answer as Sammie Jo had.

She felt very dizzy. She needed to get away. In the worst way. Right away. She had to lie down and rest. Away from the confusion. Let these fellows sand and paint. She couldn't help it if she couldn't stay to help. Maybe that's just they way things were: some people were starters and others were finishers. Maybe finishing just wasn't her area.

Well, okay, so maybe that didn't speak well of her character, but that's just the way it was. She was a starter, not a finisher.

Oh Lord, that was so sad.

She'd get away and think about that later. After she'd put her head down and the world had stopped spinning. She had to stop the spinning first. Then she'd worry about her character.

She couldn't let Brother James and Hank know she was leaving. She felt they would object. On general principles, not because they didn't want her out of the way because they did, but her intuition was telling her, loud and clear, to get the hell out of Dodge and not tell a soul. That was the only way she could get some rest and stop this whirling, whirling, whirling, spinning, spinning, spinning. As long as she stayed here, everything was going to keep on spinning. She had to go some place where it wasn't. Where things stood still like they were supposed to and she could get some rest and clear her head.

Yes.

If she took it slow, avoided the interstates, stuck to back roads, she thought she could get away. She'd avoid merging. Just the thought of merging made her mouth dry. She'd definitely avoid the interstates. Stay on sensible roads with reasonable intersections and stop signs.

Everybody always fussed so about her driving with the dizzies. The dizzies. That's what Doc called them. Her spells. She'd settle for calling them Mad Dog. Like that song Hank played her. A Mad Dog Cyclone. Sammie Jo's Mad Dog wasn't a train but a whirling dervish. And when he wasn't whirling, he was under the bed or, sometimes behind the chair in the corner, waiting to jump out and grab her. She fought him off with a stick. Most of the time she kept him at bay, sometimes running him off altogether. But every now and then he caught her, and together they went spinning up in a mad-dog cyclone.

She hated the son-of-a-gun.

She was trying to be practical. Reasonable. Operate with a plan. With safety mechanisms. She'd be safe enough if she took it slow, nice and easy, and avoided merging. And traffic. And she had Hopewell's cell phone, didn't she? Where was the damn thing? Well, she'd find it and take it with her.

Then, suddenly, she realized she didn't have her car. It was over at Hopewell's. Oh, hell, she'd forgotten that. Well, she'd just have to get somebody to drive her to Fairhope to get it.

With all that was going on, nobody would miss her for a couple of days. And she didn't want to upset people—Horton, for instance. Good Lord, Horton would have a fit if he thought she was going to drive very far by herself.

Well, she wouldn't tell him.

That meant she couldn't tell Buddy either because Buddy would tell Horton. Buddy had never quite grasped the whole concept of secrets. He didn't think it was fair or right or polite or something to keep anybody in the dark about anything.

Well, that was good. Admirable, of course. Sammie Jo had taught him that herself so she'd always know where he was and wouldn't be worried about him.

And, of course, she didn't want to worry him either. So she wouldn't. She'd tell him she was sleeping over at Hopewell's. That would work.

Of course, it was a lie, and Sammie Jo wasn't accustomed to lying. The truth was she didn't know how. She'd intend to sometimes. Have every intention of sparing somebody's feelings with the polite social fib—"No, no, of course, that dress doesn't make you look fat" or "Oh, I would love to baby-sit this afternoon, but I've already promised so-and-so to do such-and-such"—but then, willy-nilly, the truth would just jump right out before she could stop it. "Well, yes, that dress does make you look broad across the beam, if you know what I mean. No offense." Or, "You know, the last time I kept Susie Q, she gave me a terrible headache, and, thank you very much, but until she gets past this tantrum stage, I don't really want to baby-sit her."

But right now, a little deception, a little sleight of hand, sure would grease the wheels, so to speak. Sammie Jo might not know how to keep her mouth shut, but she thought Samantha might well be capable of sharing information, upon occasion, only on a-need-to-know basis. She thought she might give that a try.

So late that afternoon, at quitting time, when she heard one of Brother James's helpers say he was headed over to the bay for a little fishing, she asked him for a lift to Fairhope. With her offer to buy the gas, he was happy to oblige. She made a point of commenting within range of Hank and Brother James that she thought, while they finished up the sanding and painting, she'd spend a night or two with Hopewell. And would they be so kind as to relay that information to Buddy when he got home from work.

Well, that was easy enough, and she had the extra set of car keys from the pegboard in the carport in her pocket. She was good to go and, with a little luck, she'd be able to make her getaway without encountering Hopewell, who would put her foot down about Sammie Jo driving right now.

But Sammie Jo could drive, slowly and carefully. She knew her limitations.

Once Tyrone—that was the fellow who gave her a lift— dropped her off in Fairhope, she managed to crank up her car and back it out of the alley behind Hopewell's shop without raising any alarm. Hopewell must have been busy because she didn't even look out a window or come to the back door. Sammie Jo was off.

And once she got going, she couldn't seem to stop. She drove down to Gulf Shores, got on the beach road, and headed east. She drove along through the twilight, the stop-and-go traffic of vacationers out to dinner, past Orange Beach, up and over the bridge, into the Florida Panhandle. She didn't think about eating or stopping or anything else. She just drove, paying close attention to the cars around her, making sure not to run into them, trying her best to stay out of their way.

When it got dark, traffic thinned out and she began to relax. She was doing fine. She began to want to go faster, make some time. She drove north to Interstate 10 and had no trouble at all. She merged right on. Nothing was coming. She was swift, cool as a two-dollar bill. She sped up. She went very fast. She looked down. She was going eighty miles an hour.

There was hardly any traffic, so she kept it up until her foot began to grow tired pressed against the accelerator. Then she eased up and went thirty-five for a while. When she had rested, she sped back up.

She supposed she could use speed control—cruise control—whatever you called it, except she couldn't remember how to operate it. Besides, it always alarmed her. Taking off and slowing down on its own, as if she wasn't even there doing her very best to keep everything under control.

She was doing fine on her own.

Who said she couldn't drive on the interstate? Maybe Sammie Jo couldn't, but Samantha was doing fine.

Just to show off, she even exited. Bought herself a candy bar and three packages of nuts, went to the restroom and, as an afterthought, put gas in the car. Then she drove right back up that ramp, shot right on to that interstate without giving it a second thought.

She was free as a bird. Not a care in the world. Maybe she'd play the radio, but she'd have to let go of the steering wheel to fool with the buttons. And she might have to look at them too. All that seemed too complicated. Confusing. She didn't want to let go of the steering wheel. It was what was keeping her anchored. Attached to the world. She didn't think she ought to let go.

She'd sing some songs instead. What was that song Hank played for her? "A Week of Living Dangerously?" That was it. Maybe she'd have a whole month of living dangerously. Going up and down the ramps, on and off the interstate. Whee!

When she got to the cutoff to Interstate 75, she took it. Because she could. She was whizzing along. Just her and a few others and their lights driving across America. And when she came to a fork in the road, she took it. Because it was there.

That made her giggle. The fork in the road was like the mountain. You climbed it—or took it—because it was there.

And you were free. Here you go. Up and over and around the ramp—whee—onto another road to freedom.

Oh, she was moving along.

CHAPTER ELEVEN
Friday, Eleven Days after Memorial Day

Then it got light, gradually at first, but when the sun rose up hot and heavy in the sky, Sammie Jo got sticky and itchy. And nervous. She didn't know how long she could stay on this interstate before it began to eat her alive. Now trucks were barreling down on her, blowing their horns, big, blasting, scary air horns, and they were racing each other to see who could pass her the fastest, and she couldn't tell which lane they were in or which lane they wanted to be in. She was dodging them, trying to get out of their way, but that was impossible, and first one and then another was coming after her, and she was bouncing around among them like she was in a pinball machine.

Being in a pinball machine with all that clatter and bing, bing, bing, hitting her in the head was more than Sammie Jo could stand. She had to get off this interstate. It was more exhausting and confusing than sanders and painters and a yard full of junk and not knowing what your life amounted to. This interstate was desperation itself.

She took the first exit she could find. She just tore down the ramp onto a country road and slid into the first parking lot she saw. She stopped as soon as she could, spraying gravel and fishtailing around, but without hurting anybody. She turned off the motor, lay her head back, and closed her eyes. Whew! She had escaped alive.

She wondered if she could stand up. In a few minutes, she'd give it a try. She opened her eyes and peeped out. Nothing was moving around her. No whirlwinds. That was a relief. Just a slight rockiness. That was all right. She had that a lot. She closed her eyes again. No pinwheels against her eyelids at the moment either. That usually meant she could walk. She'd give it a try.

She tried the car door, and it opened. That was good. She wasn't in the mood for stuck doors right now, and it seemed, half the time in her life, just when she needed a door to open, it didn't. Then she'd be stuck with one of two choices. She'd either have to push and shove and ram her shoulder into it and risk falling on her fanny when it suddenly let go, or she'd have to get help. Either way was a nuisance. Life was much better when doors just opened like they were supposed to.

She wished she could count on them.

Well now, here she was standing up beside the car in sunlight that was too bright and that was blinking on and off. She wished it would stop that. She liked for the sun to be dependable, liked for it to rise and set on schedule, and not blink on and off like it was doing now.

"Stop it!" she said crossly and looked up. There above her, between her and the sun, was a giant sailfish, blue and green, blinking on and off in a series of neon tubes that sent it jumping through the sky. Beneath it, in bright pink, the words SAILFISH MOTEL flashed off and on.

Sammie Jo was stunned. A minute ago she had been gasping for air, hyperventilating, and now, suddenly, she was too awestruck to breathe. This sign was the most beautiful thing she'd ever seen. What did it mean? Coming to her like this—out of the blue. This fish flying through the morning sky in glorious bouncing colors.

She could look at it forever. It was as if she were riding it, flying through the air atop this wonderful fish. She'd always wanted to swim with the dolphins, but this was better. She didn't have to find out where the dolphins were, when they were running, buy a bathing suit, rent scuba-diving equipment (if that's what you had to have), find out if that's what you had to have, learn to scuba dive, if that's how you did it, and find out if that's how you did it, then make the plans, not to mention all the energy it would take to act out the plans once they were made.

Oh no, this was so much better. It was right here. Hers for the asking. The taking. Oh, she was mad about this fish. It was hers, and they were flying away together.

When she finally looked around, she discovered the Sailfish Motel itself was a long, low, slightly dilapidated stucco building. Something out of the past, from oh, maybe forty or fifty years ago. It looked vaguely familiar, although she didn't recall ever being here before. Still, it reminded her of something she hadn't seen, hadn't even thought about, in a very long time, and here it was, just when she needed it.

She headed toward the office, remembered her purse, went back and got it, dropped it, picked it up, squatted and picked up things that had fallen out of it, and weaved her way across the gravel parking lot.

It was hard to keep her balance on the rocky surface. Well, of course, that was what it was—rocks—so naturally it was rocky. Watch yourself there, she cautioned herself, and despite all obstacles, she made her way to the door, which opened outward instead of inward and caused her some confusion but then cooperated, and she found herself in air conditioning.

Well, wasn't this wonderful!

A teenage girl sat watching television behind a desk. It was some sort of reality show than seemed surreal to Sammie Jo, if surreal meant bizarre and too awful to be real, which is what she thought it meant. A mean-looking, hairy man was slouched over and laughing while an ugly fat woman yelled and hit him with her fist. An emcee in a suit kept trying to interrupt them but couldn't, so he looked at the camera and raised his eyebrows, Groucho-like, shrugged, and went to commercial. That's when the teenage girl looked up.

She didn't say anything.

"Hello. I'm...Samantha. I'm on a trip," Sammie Jo told her.

The girl still didn't say anything. She just sat there, looking at Sammie Jo and chewing gum and waiting, as if that was her plan in life—to wait until life came to her. Sammie Jo doubted that was a very good plan, but she chose not to discuss it.

Instead she rented a room for fifty-eight dollars and ninety-four cents and wondered how the girl, or her parents, or whoever owned the motel, came up with that amount, but she didn't ask. Just as well not to know. She gave the girl her credit card and took the key, and the girl advised her that checkout the next day was ten o'clock. Sammie Jo told her she might stay several days, and the girl looked at her like she was out of her mind.

"Why?" she said, showing interest for the first time.

"To rest," Sammie Jo told her. "This looks like a good place to rest. Nice and quiet."

"Yeah," the girl agreed. "Quiet as a tomb. Ain't nothing going on around here."

That sounded fine to Sammie Jo, who left the office and went directly to room four. She didn't bother to move the car, although she noticed that it wasn't properly parked. Oh well, some things couldn't be helped.

When she opened the door—no small feat for her and she almost gave up before she got the key to turn—she found the room dark and hot. Leaving the door ajar so she could see, she immediately went to the window air conditioner and punched buttons until a blast of stark cold air hit her in the face. Then she kicked off her Crocs and lay down facing the torrent of cold air and went to sleep.

When she woke, it was dark outside and she was thirsty. She found some change in her purse and, holding onto the stucco walls along the walkway, made her way to the drink machine outside the office. She bought herself a Coke and stood drinking it and admiring the sailfish sign. It looked even more spectacular in the dark than it had in daylight.

When she finished her Coke, she bought another one to take back to her room. It was blessed quiet and peaceful in the parking lot. Not a soul in sight, very few cars, and no rumbling trucks trying to run her over.

Some fool, she noticed, had left a car door open, and the car's interior light gave off an eerie glow, and Sammie Jo thought, it was 'a lovely light.' Like in the poem…what was it? She couldn't remember. Something about candles burning at both ends and casting 'a lovely light.' Yes, that was it.

Nice. A lovely light.

Back in her room, she ate her packets of salted nuts—one peanut, one cashew, one mixed—and drank her second Coke. She lay back down. The room was spinning ninety miles an hour now. She wasn't riding the sailfish through the sky. Oh, that had been wonderful. No, no, now the whole world was spinning… spinning…Lord God Almighty, like a mad-dog cyclone.

She was going to throw up. She knew it. That awful, sudden rush of saliva, and then here came the heaving.

She couldn't stand. She caught the up-chuck mess in her T-shirt and stripped it off and rolled it into a gooey, smelly bundle and laid it on the floor beside the bed. She dared not move. She was rocketing through space, which was spinning at the speed of light. Oh, God, stop it. Please stop it.

She just held on. There was nothing else to do. Hold on and wait. There was no help for it—for her—until this was over. It would pass. In a while.

It would pass, wouldn't it? She'd never had an attack this severe before. Mostly the Mad Dog just lurked, tilting the floor, imprinting the backs of her eyelids with swirls of color. But this...maybe she was dying. Maybe this was what dying was like. After all, who would know? Who could tell you but the dead themselves, and they were...well, dead. So this was what dying was like, and she would so love to tell someone before she went to the other side.

Maybe she should call 911. Now there's a thought. In case of emergency, dial 911. Everybody knew that. Even Sammie Jo knew that much. Call 911. She should tell someone about this spinning. Maybe they could even stop it.

But they'd take her to the hospital. That would scare everybody to death. Doc in particular. He would act calm, like he wasn't scared, but her going to the hospital in an ambulance would scare him worse than anything else in the world. Worse than him going himself. He could always take care of himself, but when he couldn't take care of her, he was undone.

No, that wouldn't do.

Besides, she peeped through squinted eyes, the phone was on the bedside table out of reach. If she turned on her side and moved her arm, she would turn the bed over. Or the table. Or the floor. She couldn't risk it.

She'd have to wait. And hope.

She waited and hoped for nearly two hours before things slowed down. Then, gradually, as if the energy force that controlled the universe and set it spinning at the highest possible velocity was growing tired of this cyclonic effort, the room, the whole Earth, came back to its senses, and stability returned.

When Sammie Jo peeped out this time, the storm had passed, and calm had returned. She sighed. She was wet and limp. She had a terrible, morning-after taste in her mouth and dried vomit on her face. Slowly, she peeled herself off the damp bedspread and stood.

So far, so good.

She picked up the soiled T-shirt and dropped it in the wastebasket. Holding onto walls and furniture, she made her way to the bathroom. She washed her face, rinsed out her mouth, stripped off the rest of her clothes, and wrapped herself in a bath towel.

Making her way carefully back to the bed, she turned off the lamp and crawled under the covers and, blessedly, slept.

CHAPTER TWELVE
Saturday, Twelve Days After Memorial Day

On this beautiful bright and sunny day on a golf course in Orlando, Florida, Doc Wooten of Piney, Alabama, hit a hole-in-one. He also played the best game of golf of his life with a score of a seventy-six.

The fellows in the pro shop immediately went to work mounting his lucky ball on a plaque, and the other members of his foursome bought him a round in the clubhouse. Then he went back to his motel to clean up before dinner, happy and confident in a day well spent.

That evening after dinner he was sitting in his room basking in his victory and replaying each hole in his head when he received a series of calls. He had just mentally reached the dogleg on the fourth fairway when the phone rang the first time.

Call Number One

"Mother's been kidnapped. I've notified the sheriff."

"Son, I don't understand."

"I'm telling you, Doc, she's disappeared, and the last time she was seen, she was in the car with one of Brother James's convicts headed west."

"West? You mean toward Fairhope?"

"Yes."

"Sounds like she was catching a ride over to Hopewell's to get her car."

"I called Hopewell, and she hasn't seen her, but Mother's car's gone."

"Gone?"

"Yes."

"Well, there you are. She went and got it. She's probably headed home. She must be feeling better."

"Doc, I'm telling you, a convict's got her and stolen her car."

"Slow down, son. I thought you said she left in his car."

"She did, but I figure he forced her into her car so it wouldn't look like a kidnapping. Besides, don't you think he'd prefer her Buick to his rattletrap?"

"He has a rattletrap?"

"Well, he must have. He's a convict, isn't he?"

"He's a parolee, Horton."

"Yeah. Well. So he's an ex-con who has kidnapped Mother."

"We'll see."

Doc hung up and went back to the dogleg on the fourth fairway. He'd just reached the green with a chip shot out of the sand when the phone rang again. As he rose to answer it, he wondered if Valium would help Horton.

But this time it wasn't his first-born but his second.

Call Number Two

"Doc?"

"Yes."

"It's Garrett."

"Hello son. How are you?"

"Fine."

"Garrett, listen, today I hit a hole-in-one."

Garrett didn't even pause. "Have you talked to Horton?"

"Yes."

"He says Mom's been kidnapped."

"He seems to think so."

"You coming home?"

"Well, sure, if she doesn't turn up."

"You don't think she's been kidnapped?"

"Seems unlikely. Where are you, Garrett?"

"In Clarksdale, but I'm headed home."

"Well, if she doesn't turn up in a day or two, I'll head that way myself. I've been lonesome for your mama ever since I've been down here. I hate to think she won't be home when I get there, but I'm sure she'll turn up. She's just out gallivanting somewhere. You tell her to stay put when you find her."

Doc made it all the way to the seventh green before the phone rang a third time.

Call Number Three

"Doc?"

"Hey Derwin. How'd you do? The papers say you had a good pole position."

"Yeah. Well, I didn't run today. I'm in Piney, Doc."

"Horton called you home, huh?"

"Yep. Says Ma's missing and nobody knows where she's gone to."

"So, she didn't show up in Daytona?"

"No. Why would she?"

"I thought maybe she'd gone down there to see you drive."

"You know she can't stand to watch me race."

"Yeah. Well, I thought maybe she'd changed her mind. You mother can be unpredictable."

"I'll say."

"This golf clinic's helping me a lot, son. You all were mighty nice to give it to me."

"So, Doc, you're not worried about her?"

"Course not. She'll be on directly."

And he made it halfway around the back nine before the fourth call came in.

Call Number Four

"Doc?"

"Hello, Buddy."

"We can't find Mama."

"I heard."

"We've looked ever' where."

"She probably just got lonesome for the old man here. I bet she's gone to stay with somebody. A friend somewhere."

"She's not at Hopewell's. We checked."

"What about Elmira's?"

"Nope. Not there either."

"Well, she's somewhere, Buddy. Maybe with one of the Hoity-Toities. Don't you worry now. She'll turn up. She always does."

"Okay. Maybe I should tell the others to settle down."

"Good idea. Keep your big brothers in line."

"Sure. I'll do that, Doc. I'll tell 'em you said no need to worry. She'll turn up."

"That's good, Buddy."

"She will, won't she, Doc?"

"Turn up? Sure, Buddy. Don't you worry now."

"Okay then, Doc. I'll see her when she turns up. You too. I'll see you when you turn up too, Doc."

"That's fine, Buddy. It won't be long now. You take care of yourself. Bye-bye now."

Doc turned out the light and got in bed, but he didn't sleep.

CHAPTER THIRTEEN
Sunday, Thirteen Days After Memorial Day

Sammie Jo was dreaming about her boys. They were little and clean and all lined up in row. And looking at her with fresh, shining faces. All of them, so beautiful and perfect and so much their very own selves. That's what they were saying. In her dream. "I'm me, me, my very own self. I'm me," they chanted, like a song. Beaming at her, pleased with themselves.

"I can fix things," Horton sang, standing up and taking a bow.

"I can make music," Garrett sang, air-strumming a guitar.

"I can drive like the wind," Derwin added, zooming around his brothers and striking a pose.

"And," Buddy sang, jumping up and laughing, "I'm everybody's best bud-dy."

"But," she asked them, "how did you get to be you? Where did you come from? You're nothing like me. None of you. I can't do any of the things you can do. You didn't learn them from me. You didn't get those talents, those abilities from me. How did you get to be you?"

Then, still singing "I'm me, me, my very own self" as sweetly as the choirboys they never were, they floated up into the sky. She drifted after them, swept along on a wafting breeze that sustained her.

Then, quickly, an updraft caught her and flung her through space. Alarmed, she jolted, almost awake, and then, with a great sigh of relief, she folded herself up against the sturdy real-ness of Doc. Spooned in his arms, she snuggled against his Doc-ness, and together they flew the open skies.

And they slept. Oh, they slept.

CHAPTER FOURTEEN
Monday, Fourteen Days after Memorial Day

A loud banging woke her, and she sat up confused. She didn't know where she was or where the noise was coming from. Bright sunlight leaked into the room around the window shades and left the rest of the room swimming in haze.

Doc un-nestled himself from around her and stood up. "Who is it?" he said.

"Sheriff's office. Open up."

Doc pulled on his pants, which had been draped across a chair, and opened the door. A blinding glare flooded the room, and all Sammie Jo could see were large forms in brimmed hats.

"Stand aside," one of the hats said.

Doc, in his undershirt and sock feet, started to object. He was rumpled with his hair standing on end, and he looked annoyed.

But the men were intent on entering the room and, rather than be pushed aside, Doc gave them a nod and moved out of their way.

Sammie Jo pulled the sheet up under her chin and stared.

As they entered the room, both men had their hands on their guns.

"Are you Mrs. Sammie Jo Wooten of Piney, Alabama?" one of them said.

"I am not," Sammie Jo said. "I am Samantha Wooten of Piney, Alabama, and I'll thank you to remember that."

The two men exchanged a quick look, as if to say, "Uh-oh, what have we here?"

"Can you identify this man?" one of them asked, gesturing at Doc.

"Of course, I can. He's Doc Wooten, also of Piney, Alabama, although I have no idea how he got here."

The other one took a breath and started to say something, but Sammie Jo cut him off. "What's the matter with you people? Bursting in here. Scaring us half to death."

"Ma'am, is this man a relation of yours?"

"Of course, he is. He's my husband. Has been for fifty years as of Memorial Day."

Sammie Jo's head was swimming. The men were beginning to warp and bend and twist. She blinked to straighten them out and couldn't. Her right ear was ringing like a damn siren. She punched it with her finger and shook her head.

"Anything wrong, ma'am?"

"I'm tired," she said. "And dizzy, very dizzy. The Mad Dog's got me."

"Mad Dog?" they said together.

"Who's Mad Dog?" one said.

"Is he Mad Dog?" the other said, pointing to Doc.

"Sam," Doc said, "lie back down."

She collapsed against the pillow and put one arm across her eyes.

"Ma'am, do you have a medical condition?" one asked.

Sammie Jo flapped her hand, waving him away.

"Ma'am, are you here of your own free will? Have you been drugged and brought here, across the state line, over your own objections?"

She sat back up, this time forgetting to pull up the sheet with her, and, bare-breasted, turned to Doc in bewilderment and said, "What in tarnation is he talking about?"

Doc tried to say something, but the officer could not be deterred. Raising his hand like a stop sign, he addressed Sammie Jo again. "Just answer the question, ma'am."

"Of course, I'm here of my own free will. I've never done anything in my life against my will, and I'm not about to start now."

Doc picked up his wallet off the nightstand and pulled out his driver's license. He nodded toward the door and said, "If you officers would step outside, I think I can clear this matter up."

With Sammie Jo sitting up like that without anything on, he wanted them out of the room.

Reluctantly, they followed him outside and pulled the door shut. Sammie Jo sighed and lay back down.

Late that afternoon Doc and Sammie Jo headed home. They drove slowly and didn't talk much. Sammie Jo kept her eyes closed and an ice pack behind her head at the base of her neck. Doc stopped twice to make phone calls. Once to ask Derwin to send some of his crew down to fetch Sammie Jo's car. Another time to tell Horton—and, thus, the rest of the family—how things were to be when he got their mother home.

He also called Hopewell.

He and Sammie Jo spent the night in the panhandle near Panama City. She needed to stop, and Doc could tell she'd had enough for one day. And, truth was, so had he. He brought supper back to their room—a Big Mac and coffee for him, fruit and yogurt for her. She was queasy and didn't want much. He thought that was just as well.

CHAPTER FIFTEEN
Tuesday, Fifteen Days after Memorial Day

The next morning they drove Highway 10, which was less hectic than the interstate. They continued to take it slow. Doc stopped at Souvenir City in Fort Walton and bought her clean clothes—white beach pants and a baby blue T-shirt. She'd been wearing a golf shirt of his ever since they left the Sailfish Motel.

They were almost home when Doc said, "Don't you want to know how I found you?"

"Shucks, Doc," she said behind closed eyes, "there ain't any place on the face of the Earth where you wouldn't find me if I needed finding. And, Lord knows, I needed finding."

"That you did," he agreed. And kept on driving.

When they reached Gulf Shores, Sammie Jo announced she couldn't possibly go on home just yet.

Doc gritted his teeth but didn't sigh or roll his eyes. He just said all right. What did she want to do?

She wanted something to eat, and she wanted to walk on the beach.

They went to MacDonald's and got French fries and Cokes. He found a place to park, and they walked between two high-rises onto the sand, through clusters of sunbathers, families under beach umbrellas with picnic baskets and coolers, children building moats and sand castles, Frisbee and volleyball games.

Sammie Jo wobbled, but he held onto her, and they made it to the water's edge.

The sea was quiet, barely moving. It was a glorious, sparkling day.

Heedless of getting wet and sandy, Sammie Jo plopped down close enough for the waves to lap her toes. With nothing to sit on and not wanting to get his pants wet, Doc stood beside her. She sprinkled two packets of salt on her fries and began to eat.

"Sit," she said after a minute. Scowling up at him through hand-shaded eyes.

This time he did sigh and roll his eyes. But he sat. There was nothing else to do. He just wanted to get on home. Get her off the road and into bed.

"I can't hardly think about going home to that mess," she said.

So, that was it. She couldn't face the mess she'd made. And gone off and left. That was understandable. Still, the sooner they got home and got started, the sooner they'd get it cleaned up. At least, get the bed set up so they wouldn't have to sleep in the yard. Doc wasn't about to sleep in the yard.

She ate some fries and drank some Coke and sat very still staring at the waves. Quietly, gently, inevitably, they rolled in and out. She put one hand on each side of her, palms down in the sand, as if balancing herself.

"Uh oh," she said, "here it comes."

Doc looked out, thinking she meant a big wave, but there wasn't one. The ocean was barely rocking.

"What?" he asked.

"The Mad Dog," she said.

He looked around. There was no dog anywhere.

She tried to stand, but her legs seemed badly hinged, folding unpredictably this way and that. She couldn't get a foothold and lurched sideways into the water.

Bounding to his feet and dropping his fries and Coke, Doc tried to catch her, but he couldn't prevent her falling.

Already she was struggling to regain her footing, but again she toppled over, this time headfirst into deeper water. The wave rolled over her and pulled her away from him. He caught a glimpse of her face, sputtering and spewing water, her hair glued to her forehead and plastered onto her neck.

She rose again and reached her hand out to him, but when she took a step toward him, her foot seemed to turn over. This time she fell onto her backside and washed farther ashore.

Several people had turned to stare, thinking she was drunk perhaps. Or being attacked by sharks. Or God knows what.

No telling what they were thinking. Doc didn't know what to think himself. Something was wrong though. Something was badly out-of-kilter.

"Call 911," he said to a young man who'd been running along the water's edge and had stopped to watch. The fellow moved toward him as if to help pull her out of the water.

"No," Doc said. "I'll get her. Go call 911."

"What's the matter with her?" the young man asked.

"I think she's having a seizure," Doc said over his shoulder.

As the fellow ran off to find a phone, Doc thought, "Terrific! I've asked the one person on the beach without a cell phone to call for help!"

As he waded into the surf toward Sammie Jo, gulls circling above them began swooping down to feed on the spilled French fries. Sammie Jo, flopping in the water, seemed to think they were dive-bombing her.

"No, no, no," she cried, waving her arms frantically at them and slipping yet again out of Doc's grasp. "Go away. Go away."

"It's all right, honey. They just want your French fries. It's okay." Doc tried to soothe her.

"No, no. Help! Help!" She looked wildly about as if pleading with some distant source to come to her rescue.

By now, Doc had maneuvered her to the edge of the water, and she simply folded up and dropped onto the sand.

"I can't go on," she said. "He's won."

"Who's won?" Doc asked.

"Mad Dog," she said, clutching Doc's hand. "He's got me."

What was she talking about? Why did she keep raving about a mad dog?

He sat back down in the wet sand beside her. She gagged then and threw up French fries and Coke all over both of them. As if this hadn't happened, Doc wrapped his arms around her and said, "No, he doesn't have you. I've got you, and I won't let him get you."

He sat holding her tight until the rescue squad arrived. Even then he didn't let go of her, and the EMTs put both of them in the van and, with red lights flashing and bleeps from their siren hustling spectators out of the way, drove them across the sand and down the road to the nearest hospital, which was in Piney.

After notifying the boys where they were, Doc spoke with each of his sons as they arrived at the hospital, but he didn't let any of them see their mother. Sammie Jo was in no shape to see anybody.

"I don't understand," Horton kept saying, as if Doc should be able to clarify matters for him. "What was she doing in the water? Why couldn't she stand up? What's the matter with her?"

Garrett took a different tack. He said, "You reckon it would cheer her up if I got some of the musicians to write a special song for her? They could play it for her over the phone."

Derwin, of course, took another approach altogether. He had already dispatched members of his crew to fetch her car. "We're gonna give it a good going-over," he told Doc, as if car trouble was at the root of his mother's problem. "Reline the brakes, check all the belts, make sure the battery'll hold a charge. Fix that old heap so it doesn't leave her stranded again."

"That's fine, son. Good. She'll appreciate it, I'm sure." Doc decided not to point out that Sammie Jo's Buick wasn't but three years old, had less than thirty thousand miles on it, and was the least of her troubles. There wasn't any problem in life that Derwin thought couldn't be solved by a tune-up in a good garage.

Buddy, bless him, just said, "Is she all right, Doc? I don't like it when nobody knows where she is. It don't seem right."

"No, son," Doc agreed. "It don't."

In the ER, Sammie Jo wouldn't stay on the gurney for fear of falling. After Doc had sent the boys off to bring his own car back from the beach, he brought a chair in from the waiting room and settled himself in the cubicle with her. Over the objections of the staff, he sat and held her on his lap while they took her vital signs.

Like a child, Sammie Jo thought. She was embarrassed and disgusted with herself. The Mad Dog turned her into a baby. Sooner or later, one way or the other, she was going to turn on him and send him running.

"Bite him on the ass," she whispered.

Doc wondered if she was delusional.

Surely not. Sammie Jo was not nuts. Just different.

And, at the moment, very different.

He didn't know just how much of this difference was tolerable.

For either one of them.

After two and a half hours of sitting in Doc's lap and from time to time answering questions from a series of young people wearing white coats or green pajamas, Sammie Jo raised up and said she was ready to leave. Nobody, least of all Doc, thought that was a good idea, but she was adamant. The Mad Dog had backed off, she said, and she was no longer whirling. She was just very tired and had to get some sleep, and everybody knew you couldn't sleep in a hospital.

Doc came to some sort of meeting of the minds with the staff. Sammie Jo didn't know what it was, but they wrote things down on slips of paper and gave them to him, and everybody shook hands. Then somebody rolled her outside in a wheelchair. Doc brought his car around to the entrance and helped her in, and they left.

Sammie Jo didn't know—or much care—where they were going. She just wanted to lay her head down and take a nice long nap.

Doc, of course, couldn't take her home. From all accounts— not just Horton's—home was badly dismantled. Before they left the hospital, Doc had phoned the Beach Club out on Fort Morgan Road. It was far enough from home to keep people from dropping in on them, and, Lord knows, Sammie Jo didn't need company right now. And, though it was on the beach, it was removed from the hubbub of downtown Gulf Shores. It had a nice restaurant and a view of the ocean. Besides, he'd been wanting to check out their golf course.

Yep, they'd stay there a few days. Long as it took to get Sammie Jo back on her feet.

And he'd call Hopewell to bring her some clothes. And come talk to her. Doc didn't know how to talk to her right now.

And he'd tell the boys to stop acting like lunatics and leave her alone.

And get that mess in the yard cleaned up and the house sorted out.

No, better not. For now, he'd just tell them to beg, borrow, or steal a tent from an auctioneer or an evangelist or a circus—anybody who has a tent—and move everything under it and batten down the hatches—or the flaps—and secure it as best they can. Then he'd talk to Hopewell about where to go from there.

Well, actually, he needed Hopewell's advice about this whole business. What in hell had happened these past few days since the Memorial Day party? How could everything a person understood and took for granted go down the tubes in such a short time? He goes off to play golf for a few days, and nothing's ever the same again!

God, he didn't know what to do. What if he was losing Sam?

To Alzheimer's.

There! He'd said it. That's what was in the back of his mind. Scaring him to death. What would he do?

Shoulder the load, of course. But not Sammie Jo. Please God, not Sammie Jo. He couldn't get along without her.

No, no. Of course he could if he had to. But—and this was the real question—what would be the point?

He couldn't think of one. Of any reason to go through the motions of life without her.

Now that was crazy. She wasn't dying. Good vital signs. That's what the hospital said.

He'd take her to that ear specialist they'd recommended. Maybe he could be of some help. Inner ear problem, the kids at the hospital speculated. But they were just guessing. None of them was over thirty-five.

Don't borrow trouble, Doc, he told himself. No good comes of that.

CHAPTER SIXTEEN
Wednesday, Sixteen Days After Memorial Day...and Counting

Sammie Jo mostly slept. Between naps, she ate snacks of fruit and Melba toast (the sesame seed kind without salt) and sat at the window high above the gulf and watched the water and the people below on the beach. She and Doc were on the fourteenth floor. She would have enjoyed going on the deck and stretching out on the chaise in the sun, but she would have had to crawl. And then, she wasn't sure how—or if—she could get back inside.

No, best to stay indoors.

She didn't see anybody but Doc and Hopewell and the ear doctor and his office help. A pleasant, sweet-faced girl put her in a sound booth and gave her a hearing test. Sammie Jo found it disorienting, like being in the cockpit of a small airplane, but she was sure she heard all the tones and bells and whistles over the earphones. Sometimes there were long silences in the earphones, and she had to wait for the girl to get her act together. Maybe she was just learning how to operate the equipment, but, Sammie Jo reminded herself, sometimes you have to be patient with the young. They were just learning, not just how to do their jobs but everything. How to live their lives.

Sammie Jo missed a step coming out of the booth. The floor wasn't quite where she thought it was, but the young woman held onto her and didn't let her fall.

That was a good thing about the young—they were strong and had good balance. Sammie Jo just sometimes wished they didn't dart around so fast. She would like to smarten them up and slow them down.

And, while she was at it, she'd like to stand them up straight and get the hair out of their eyes.

And get them off those skateboards. In the parking lot of the ear clinic, a kid who was losing his pants almost ran over them. Doc said he missed them by a mile, but Sammie Jo didn't think so.

She thought there ought to be a law against skateboarding, but Doc said no, no, there were already too many laws on the books. And half of them unenforceable.

Sometimes Sammie Jo wondered how Doc could be so sure of everything. That was the irritating thing about Doc— he was all-fired sure of things.

That and he sometimes picked his teeth with a pocketknife, although, to be fair, she'd never seen him do it in restaurants.

In the parking lot when the asphalt shifted under her feet and she tried to get in the wrong car, Doc kept a firm grip on her. The ground never moved under his feet. Doc always knew where he stood.

Thank God for that, Sammie Jo thought. At least, one of us knows.

Maybe that was enough. Maybe that was what balanced them out. Doc knew how to find solid ground, and Sammie Jo knew where the alligators were.

And the Mad Dog. Sammie Jo knew where he was all right. He was hiding under the bed, ready to jump her again.

At a moment's notice. Sure as shooting.

The ear doctor...Sammie Jo couldn't remember his name. She called him Dr. Hush Puppy. At least, he wasn't a teenager.

He had a soft gray mustache and wore soft gray Hush Puppies shoes and was a sweetheart. He held her hand while she cried. She cried when she told him she couldn't keep track of things and the world was whirling around and, even when it wasn't whirling, it was tilting back and forth and unreliable, and she had become unreliable too.

And, on top of everything else, the Mad Dog was always there, waiting to grab her again. She could feel him lurking in the shadows.

Hush Puppy said he knew some ways to fight off the Mad Dog. But, he agreed with her, the Mad Dog was tricky. It was going to take a tough, ongoing campaign to get the best of him, and, even then, let down your guard, and he might be waiting for you around the corner.

Well, in truth, that's not exactly what Old Hush Puppy said. That was what Sammie Jo got from what he said. Doc always said Sammie Jo got more from a conversation—any conversation—than it dawned on most folks was there to get. What Doc got from a conversation was Information. Data. Facts.

What Sammie Jo got was apt to come in the form of colors, shapes, feelings, hunches, metaphors, old wives' tales, New Age miracles, sweet dreams, nightmares, trips down memory lane, and journeys to far-off places. Sometimes to the moon and back. It was no wonder she couldn't keep her feet on the ground.

Grounded she was not.

Anyway, after they saw the ear doctor, Sammie Jo was geared for battle, and she and Doc knew what to do. Together, they were going after Mad Dog, which Doc said Hush Puppy called Meniere's Disease.

Well, he could call it anything he wanted. Sammie Jo knew a mad dog when she saw one.

First of all came some pills. Sammie Jo knew they were blue. Doc knew the proprietary and generic names for them. And they both knew they were to alleviate fluid in the inner ear.

And—this was important—as little salt as possible. And, they both soon discovered, everything except raw fruits and vegetables seemed to have some salt in it.

No swimming. The water was too disorienting. But walking was good. Somehow when she planted her feet, her brain stabilized. Odd but true.

Lots of rest. Stop and lie down when the Mad Dog so much as growled. That was the new policy.

And avoid the kinds of places that seemed to rile him up—like Wal-Marts and grocery stores and shopping malls. Places with bright lights, noise, aisles full of things, shopping carts that could roll right out from under you.

And parking lots with skateboarders.

And so—with this information, this ammunition—she was grateful for all the things that weren't wrong. She didn't have cancer or heart trouble or Alzheimer's. Nothing serious, as Doc put it, just a management problem.

If it could be managed. They'd take a little time and see.

Over the next few weeks, Sammie Jo dozed and walked and ate her fruits and vegetables and took her pills. Gradually, a step at a time, the Mad Dog slunk off into the corner, turned around three times, lay down, and—finally—went to sleep. He left her hard of hearing in the right ear, and tired, but clear-headed and calm.

She tiptoed around him, not daring to deviate from her regimen lest she rouse him. Best, she'd learned, to let sleeping dogs lie.

And now, at last, she could even venture out onto the deck and take her naps on the chaise in the sun. Such a joy! Such a pleasure!

Hopewell came often, and they lay side by side and talked and talked.

Doc, for his part, played golf, honed his backstroke, and made good use of the tips he'd picked up from the pros down in Orlando.

Sammie Jo was herself again. He could breathe easy.

But she still wasn't ready to go home.

CHAPTER SEVENTEEN
The Fourth of July…and Still Counting

Doc was surprised when Sammie Jo neither wanted to go home for the fourth nor wanted to invite the kids down to watch the fireworks on the beach. She said she'd had enough fireworks to last her a while, maybe a lifetime.

Doc thought that was odd. Sammie Jo loved fireworks like a little kid. They got her excited. Made her ooh and ah and sometimes squeal. He hadn't expected her to ever get enough of fireworks. Or excitement of any kind.

She was still sleeping a lot. He phoned the ear doctor and asked about that, but Hush Puppy said that was to be expected. (Sammie Jo even had Doc calling him Hush Puppy.) Out of frustration, Doc also asked the good doctor if could tell him when—if ever—Sammie Jo was going to be willing to go home again.

Hush Puppy said he didn't know the answer to that question, but—and Doc had to give him credit for this—he was nice about it.

Doc continued to bide his time.

One evening when Doc was exasperated with the whole situation—them just staying on and on, open-ended at the beach when, not twenty miles away, they had a perfectly good empty house—he asked Sammie Jo if she just wanted to give their house to Horton and Ann and be done with it.

He thought that would get a rise out of her. They both knew Sammie Jo didn't like Ann, and he couldn't imagine she'd want her daughter-in-law living in her house.

What Sammie Jo answered gave him a surprise.

"You know, Doc, I've been wondering about that. Whether or not you'd object."

"Me?"

"Well, sure. It's really your house, you know. I mean it was your family's. It's where you grew up. I just moved in when we married. The house was just part of the package. You know what I mean?"

"No, I don't know what you mean. It's our house, Sammie Jo."

"Well, if you say so. All I meant was the house pretty much came with the territory and always has."

He was vexed. What did she mean? The house was his? It was part of the package? It came with the territory? It was their home. A home they'd made together. Home was where Sammie Jo was. Didn't she know that? And that yellow brick house was where she had been practically every day for fifty years until lately.

He jerked up, strode into the kitchenette, turned the light on and off, came back out, and raised himself up and down on his toes.

Then he went out on the balcony and lit a cigar, took a few puffs, put it out, and came back inside.

"Now see here," he began, although he didn't know what he was going to say next.

"I didn't mean to make you mad," she said.

"I'm not mad," he said.

"Oh," she said and smiled.

The smile went all over him. Why did women act this way? Talk in circles. Get your goat. What the hell were they talking about anyhow?

Goddamnit, she'd gone and gotten him confused. Sometimes he thought she did it deliberately. She was good at it. She had honed her skills over the years until she was better at it than anybody else he knew.

If you wanted to know what Sammie Jo was good at, there you had it! She was good at getting his goat.

Nothing more was said about the house for a few days. At least, nothing more was said between Doc and Sammie Jo. There was talk between Doc and Horton, Doc and the bank, Doc and his accountant, and Doc and his attorney, and, eventually, between Doc and Hopewell. He talked to Hopewell in preparation for bringing up the subject again with Sammie Jo. He had to make sure he had his ducks in a row and wasn't going to say everything all wrong and get Sammie Jo riled up again.

"Okay," he began one morning after breakfast, pushing his stool back from the counter and beginning as if he and Sammie Jo were continuing a conversation from the previous moment, not the previous week.

"Here's what I propose."

Sammie Jo perked up. He had her full attention.

"Maybe the time has come for a change. A big change. Instead of waiting until the kids have to cart us off to the nursing home, maybe we should just go ahead and move to a smaller place now. Someplace down here on the beach, if you want. A place of your choosing, Sammie Jo. Whatever you want, just so long as it's not too big.

"We'll turn the home place over to Horton and Ann. They're the only ones still living here who can use it, and we'll stipulate that Buddy lives out back from now on and shares ownership of the property."

Sammie Jo could hardly believe what she was hearing. She was always a little astonished at how thoroughly Doc worked things through in his head before he said anything. Usually, the times when she didn't think he was listening to her at all were when he did this. All of a sudden, she'd find herself presented with the solution to whatever was aggravating her when she doubted Doc had even grasped the situation.

Now, although a little taken aback by how quickly he'd taken charge of the situation and run with it, she said, "Doc, I think that's an inspired idea. Horton and Ann and Oliver and Olivia can live in the house, and we won't have to take care of it anymore, but it'll still be in the family."

"Would you mind terribly?" he asked her gently, as if this was entirely his own idea, which, maybe, he was beginning to think it was.

"I think it's time, Doc. Don't you? I mean we don't need that big house anymore."

"Of course not," he said.

"Maybe get a condo of our own somewhere down here. Close to the water. Big enough to have one of the grandchildren spend the night occasionally. You know, one at a time."

"Play with 'em. Take 'em swimming, maybe fishing. And when we're tired and they're cross and dirty, send 'em home," he elaborated.

"My thinking exactly," she agreed.

They smiled at each other. In cahoots. No longer at odds.

"Can we afford to do that?" she asked now.

"If we're careful, I think we can arrange it. Horton is keen to do it. I told him not to tell Ann yet and get her hopes up. Of course, they'll have to sell their house, and we'll have to work out a financial arrangement that suits everybody. I've already put a pencil to some numbers and talked to the bank. We ought to be able to work it out."

"Doc, I love you."

"Well, my God, Sammie Jo, it's about time you came to your senses."

They smiled and went to take a walk on the beach.

CHAPTER EIGHTEEN
A Few Weeks Later

After that conversation, neither of them spoke of this new plan again. Oh, Doc tried, in a halfhearted way, to work out the details, but he couldn't get excited about the prospects of a move. In fact, he didn't even like to think about it. Nevertheless, feeling obligated as he did, he brought the subject up again with Horton. But, to Doc's surprise, Horton seemed to have lost his initial enthusiasm. He said Ann liked the house they had. She didn't want to move, and she certainly didn't want an old house with cantankerous plumbing and inadequate heating and cooling systems.

And, she'd added, why would anybody want to live several miles out from town in a pecan grove where nothing was going on? Why, she'd run herself ragged just driving back and forth to town all the time!

This attitude, while it might have been understandable had it been presented in an appreciative and gentle manner, hurt Doc's feelings. He'd lived in that yellow house his whole life, and anybody who had any sense thought it was a good house. He and Sammie Jo had raised their kids there, and it had been good enough for them all these years, and now his smart-alecky daughter-in-law was saying it wasn't good enough for her and her kids?

So, Doc thought, now he knew why Sammie Jo didn't like Ann. Truth was she wasn't likable. He'd just been slow in catching on to that. Sammie Jo had him beat all to hell and back in catching on to people.

Well, he said to himself, he'd be damned if he was going to give his house to somebody who didn't want it and wouldn't appreciate what he was doing for them. Hell's bells. He'd be damned if he was going to set 'em up in the home place if they didn't want it. Give it to one of the other kids instead.

Of course, Garrett was over in Mississippi all the time. He'd bought a house over there now, although for a long time he had sort of lived in both places, Piney and Clarksdale. His kids had even started preschool there, and Cindy Lou had finally settled in and gotten used to Clarksdale and had stopped hanging around Piney and moving in and out of the spare bedroom every time she felt overwhelmed and needed Sammie Jo to help her rock and change her babies.

As for Derwin, he couldn't live in the home place. His home was a garage with a house attached over close to Charlotte, where NASCAR was headquartered. When he wasn't there, he was at Talladega or Daytona.

As for Buddy.... Oh hell, Buddy couldn't take care of the shed out back, much less the whole house. Buddy himself needed looking after. He couldn't take on more responsibility.

Well, hell's bells.

Truth was, Doc didn't want to live down here on the coast anyway. He wanted to go home where his chair was. And his bed. And his tractor. Hell, he missed all that. Down here was fine for a few weeks, but enough was enough. He even wanted to cut his own grass. That's what he'd bought the tractor for, wasn't it?

And he wanted to play on his own golf course. Where he was a member and had been since he and his buddies had built the club forty years ago. And his buddies—he missed them. He wanted to play with them in their regular game instead of all the time with people on vacation who were going home next week and whom he'd never see again. Occasionally, that was fine, but if he was home, those guys would recognize how much he'd improved and they'd be impressed to see how the pros down in Orlando had helped him and gotten the hitch out of his swing. Hell, these days he'd win some money off of them.

Okay, so they only played for quarters, but it was the principle of the thing that mattered, not the money.

Oh hell, there wasn't any principle involved in any of this. He just plain wanted to go home.

The problem was how to tell Sammie Jo. Once she got her mind set on something—some itch that had to be scratched— well, usually it was just easier to go ahead and let her have her way. And, if she wanted another house, well, she deserved it. Hell, she deserved anything and everything in the world he could give her.

They'd just have to put the home place on the market. There wasn't any way around it. It didn't seem right. A house like that. Not that it was grand because it wasn't. But still they didn't build 'em like that anymore—with high ceilings and window seats, and sleeping porches.

Oh, Lordy, Lordy. If this is what growing old means, he didn't see how he could stand it.

One afternoon in late August—out of the blue—Sammie Jo said, "I want to go home."

She wasn't looking at him. She was staring out the sliding glass doors, which were closed. It was too damn hot to have them open, and there wasn't a shade tree in sight. Thank God for air conditioning in beach condos, Doc thought.

Her eyes stayed fixed on the coastline below them where families were pursuing the final days of summer before school started.

At first, he didn't think he had heard her right. For lack of anything else to do, he had been polishing his golf shoes when she said it, and, for a long moment, she left him suspended there holding a shoe in one hand and a rag in the other. Well, not a rag actually. You couldn't find a rag in a rented condo, so he'd been using a paper towel, and you couldn't polish shoes properly with a paper towel. Anybody knows that.

What it amounted to was you could stay in a beach condo, but you couldn't live in one.

Lord knows he wanted to go home too.

Had he heard her right? And, if he had, did she mean it?

He didn't know. He didn't care. He was taking her up on it.

"Me too," he said.

She looked at him then. "I don't want Ann living in my house. She doesn't know how to live there," she said.

"And you do."

"And I do," Sammie Jo agreed, and it was Samantha talking, and he heard this in her voice and recognized it as something new.

"I'm glad to hear it," Doc said and laid his shoe and paper towel down and came and sat beside her.

She reached out and gripped his hand and looked back out at the beach. She wasn't crying. She just looked as if she'd had enough. Enough of whatever had been going on. Doc didn't know what that was—or had been—and didn't care. As long as it was over. Physical maladies he understood. He could get a handle on those. They could cope with Meniere's Disease. It was all that went with it—the escapades of the damn Mad Dog—that wore him out and left him bamboozled. He hoped they never encountered the Mad Dog again. Whatever it was, he wanted it gone, and he wanted Sammie Jo free and clear of it once and for all.

She looked squarely at him now, gave a nod and said, "I've got a list to make out. And the time has come to track down Hank and Brother James."

As she headed for the phone, she turned to Doc. "It's not too late?" she asked. "I mean Horton and Ann aren't counting on moving in, are they?"

"She doesn't want to," Doc said.

"She doesn't?"

"Nope."

"Well, I'll be. What's the matter with that girl?"

"Beats me. I think she's kind of uppity."

"Well, she's always leaned that way."

Then, as if to make something clear, Sammie Jo said, "I've just decided to take hold of what's rightfully mine. Do you know what I mean?"

"No. Can't say I do."

"Doc, I'm going to set that house right."

He considered this and wondered what it meant. He hoped it didn't mean the furniture was going to stay in the yard.

"Sammie Jo, just put my bed back in the house."

"Samantha."

"I can't call you Sammie Jo anymore?"

"No."

"How about Sam?"

"Only upon occasion."

"Samantha, huh?"

"Yep."

"For real?"

"Yep."

"All right. Samantha it is. Can we go home now?"
"Yep."
And they did.

SAMANTHA'S TO-DO LIST:

1) Call Brother James and Hank and tell them to move us back into the house.

2) Give them a list of what to move back in and what to take to the flea market.

3) Call Hopewell to meet me at the house to help decide what goes where.

4) Throw away all T-shirts with slogans on them.

5) Buy new plain ones.

6) Also buy a new pants suit and a couple of nice dresses. (Get Hopewell to go to the mall with me.)

7) Ask Buddy if he wants to move back into the house.

8) When he says no, help him fix up his place out back.

9) Write the girl at the Sailfish Motel a thank-you note for finding Hopewell's cell phone in the parking lot where I dropped it and calling the button that says "home," so she could tell Hopewell where I was so Doc could come and get me.

10) Don't tell Doc I know that's how he found me. Let him keep thinking I believe he has magical powers.

11) Save my perfume bottle collection but put it in the china cabinet so I don't have to keep dusting it.

12) Buy a lighted magnified mirror (10×) for the dressing table so I can sit down to put my makeup on.

13) Wear a satin bathrobe (peignoir?) when I do this. (Tell Doc that's what I want for my birthday this year instead of more perfume.)

14) Tell Hopewell to pick it out for him.

15) Put Buddy in charge of the pecan grove. Have him replace the dead trees. And tell him to arrange some harvesting method besides just gathering a few buckets for personal use and leaving the rest for the squirrels.

16) Keep the kitchen table.

17) Get rid of the karaoke machine.

18) Hang Miz Louise's portrait back over the mantle.

19) Plan a party. (A homecoming? A housewarming?) I don't know. Something—without firecrackers and target shooting.

20) Order stationery with my new name.

21) Send a love offering to The Prodigal Sons of Jesus Sanctified in His Holy Blood, Sweat, and Tears Tabernacle Mission.

EPILOGUE
Clipping from the Baldwin County Gazette

Labor Day Celebration

WELCOME HOME, SAMANTHA!

*T*hat's what the latest banner on the Wooten home place read when the clan gathered for a Labor Day celebration. The occasion marked the homecoming of the lord and lady of the manor, Doc and Samantha (formerly known as Sammie Jo), who had spent the summer vacationing at the Beach Club in Gulf Shores while the house underwent renovation.

The new banner dispelled rumors that Sammie Jo had been kidnapped or had run away and was refusing to return home. When questioned about those rumors, Sammie Jo...excuse us...Samantha insisted she didn't know anything about them and couldn't imagine where people got such ideas.

In an effort to dispel further rumors, Doc stated unequivocally that the house is not for sale and that he and Samantha plan to remain in residence indefinitely. As he put it, "We're here to stay as long as we're upright or, I should say, as long as we're right-side-up, seein' as how I'm not sure we've ever been all that upright to start with. Things may have been a bit upside down this summer, but I think we've got 'em straightened out now."

At the party, Hopewell Jennings, chair of the Baldwin County Historical Society, announced the Wooten home place had officially been named a Baldwin County Heritage Pecan Grove and placed a plaque designating it as such on the fence at the entrance to the property. Upon the deaths of Doc and Samantha, the property has been placed in trust to go to the historical society, with Buddy Wooten to be given a lifetime position as live-in overseer and caretaker of the property.

Buddy said that was very nice and he accepted the appointment on the condition that he could continue to work at the Blooms Galore Garden Center during the week and handle his duties at the pecan grove on weekends. Buddy, as everyone knows, has been employed at the garden center for 24 years and is a fixture of the place.

Hopewell said she felt confident the society would find that arrangement congenial.

The first official event at the Wooten Historical Pecan Grove will be a harvest festival this fall when children will be invited to come and gather as many pecans as they can pick up. Prizes will be given for the heaviest sacks, and refreshments will be served. Proceeds from the sale of these choice holiday nuts will benefit area schools.

Fireworks, guns, and skateboards will be strictly prohibited.

ELVIS'S EYES

Book Three

"Do not seek the because—in love there is no because, no reason, no explanation, no solutions."

—Anais Nin

CHAPTER ONE

Elmira Horton was a jigsaw aficionado. She had been for years, but upon her retirement as police dispatcher for the City of Piney, Alabama, she became a fanatic. She was the best at putting together one-thousand-piece puzzles of famous people, places, and paintings of anybody she knew, and she knew almost everybody in Piney and a lot of people in surrounding areas. You had to when you were police dispatcher. Otherwise, you'd be sending patrolmen off on a lot of wild goose chases.

Elmira did not believe in wild goose chases, for herself or anybody else. As far as she was concerned, when you headed out somewhere, you needed to know where you were going. If you didn't, how were you going to know when you got there? Right? This kind of thinking and intentionality had kept her on the mark as a dispatcher, and she was widely known and respected for sending the police, down to the very last man—woman, too, once they'd taken to wearing the uniform—to the exact locations where they were needed without any detours caused by misdirections.

Elmira herself took pride in that. After all, it wasn't everybody who could single-handedly dispatch a whole police force in the right direction day in and day out. Of course, the night shift was likely to receive more emergency calls than she did on the day shift, but the day shift had its share of excitement too. Someday, Elmira always thought, she'd write a book about her experiences as a dispatcher. She'd seen some things in her time. Well, if not seen them, she'd been right there on the radio through some mighty hair-raising episodes.

Of course, that was in the past now that she was retired, and retirement gave her pretty much full time for her jigsaws. Her goal was to do every five-hundred-piece-and-up puzzle for sale at the Hobby Lobby. That, she figured, would be quite an accomplishment and very nearly cover all the walls in her house. You see, when she was done with a puzzle, she varnished it with this spray can of special finish that held the pieces together and gave them a nice shine too. Then, once they dried, she glued them on the wall. She'd filled up the walls in the living room and was now starting on the dining room. Puzzles were her decorating theme, and a good one, too, she had reason to believe. Everybody who came in her house was drawn to them right away and seemed pretty much awestruck. They all said they'd never seen anything like them. And they hadn't, that was for sure. Elmira hadn't either.

It was not that Elmira set out to seem odd. She didn't. She didn't seek to stand out in any direction. It was just that she liked to exhibit her competence. Let people know up-front who they were dealing with, and that was somebody who got things done, down to the very last letter—or, in this case, down to the very last piece—and had something to show for her efforts when all was said and done.

Elmira was all business that way and somebody who could be counted on. She was like that old coffee commercial—good to the last drop, and that drop was good too.

Sometimes she wished she was still the chief's and everybody else's right hand down at the police station. She pretty near ran the place for forty years. Saw dozens of patrolmen come and go and broke in three chiefs and no telling now many night dispatchers over the years. Being in charge came naturally to Elmira and made life easier on the various chiefs and kept things running smoothly. They still called her in when the new dispatcher was out sick, and sometimes she dropped by and lent a hand just to help out when she knew things were apt to be especially busy. Like during spring break when half the state came streaming through town on their way to the beach, and speeding tickets were handed out like door prizes to the first hundred speeders every day for a week. Or right after the Christmas holidays when the snowbirds from up North came through on their annual pilgrimage in search of sunshine and warm weather for the rest of the winter. Then you'd have your broke-down RVs and runaway trailers to deal with it, and extra dispatching to do.

Elmira knew how to make herself useful. Useful and competent—that's what she was, and she wouldn't have tolerated being any other way.

Elmira had majored in math in school, first at the local high school and then at Faulkner Junior College. She liked math because there was always one right answer. Unlike literature or psychology, for instance, where there were multiple interpretations and ways of looking at things, any one of which might be right. Who knew? One answer was as good as another. She could never understand why anyone would bother. She herself didn't read fiction. Novels never seemed to have any point, regardless of how "socially relevant" they were made out to be. As far as she could tell, most of what the schools were teaching kids today amounted to subjects without disciplines. And half the kids coming through couldn't make change on their own without a computerized cash register, much less say their multiplication tables.

Take Susie Q, her illegitimate great-niece who lived behind her. Susie Q was a grandchild of Elmira's sister Sammie Jo, and Sammie Jo couldn't do a thing with her. And neither could Sissy, Susie Q's mother, not that Sissy made the effort.

Anyhow, Susie Q went off to school every day happy as a lark and played on her computer and came home quoting useless bits of information—and misinformation—such as whales are as smart as we are only we don't understand them, and the same is true of the aborigines in Australia and people with autism. And the more Susie Q learned about how equal everybody was, the greater sense of superiority she seemed to have. The school system was more concerned with enhancing children's self-esteem than with teaching them anything. Susie Q now had so much self-esteem Elmira was worn out with her, but there was no getting away from the child.

With her inflated sense of importance, Susie Q felt entitled to everything the world had to offer, including Elmira's time and space and even the juice in her refrigerator and the cookies in her cookie jar. And when she locked the door, Susie Q found the key under the flowerpot and came on in anyway.

If they weren't going to teach kids arithmetic in school, couldn't they at least teach them manners? But, of course, that was Sissy's job, and don't even get Elmira started on Sissy, who had no business having a child in the first place. Sissy hadn't been but sixteen when Derwin, Sammie Jo's wildest boy, got her pregnant and immediately took off to go on the NASCAR circuit. As member of a pit crew first, then later as a driver himself. Sissy brought Susie Q into this world as if she was a baby doll to play with while they both tried to grow up together.

No good, Elmira always said, ever comes of children having children. Why, look at Sammie Jo. One baby after another, and she was brought up to know better. And married to a good man. She didn't have to behave that way. It wasn't as if they were Catholic, for crying out loud! They were brought up Baptist, although Elmira had transferred over to the Methodists where the music was more interesting and more apt to be on key.

Oh, Elmira was full of opinions, all right. Once, when they were children, Sammie Jo had said in great vexation, "Elmira, your opinions just fill up a room." Elmira knew a compliment when she heard one and took that as one of the best she'd ever received. Even as a child, she had her principles and believed in standing up for them.

In the spring of the year when Elmira's greatest tribulations came, she had planned on taking a trip out West. She wanted to see the Grand Canyon. She'd just finished a one-thousand-piece puzzle of it, and that started her to wanting to see it in person. She thought she'd drive, and she was even thinking of taking Susie Q with her. Not that she enjoyed the child's company. Lord knows, she didn't, but she thought it might be good for Susie Q to see something that much bigger and more significant than herself. The Grand Canyon might be the very way to put things in perspective for Little Miss Know-It-All.

Besides, if she went off without her, Elmira didn't know who'd keep her out of the street and make sure she had regular meals. Sissy had never quite caught on to motherhood, and Elmira wasn't sure she had the knack for it. Not that Sissy didn't love Susie Q. She did. Elmira gave her that much. But, let's face it, Sissy's talent was nails, and there wasn't room in that blonde head of hers for much more. Once she finished trimming and filing, buffing and polishing, and gluing false nails on the females of Piney, it was all Sissy could do to find her way home at night—and she didn't always manage to do that.

People loved Sissy. She was the most popular manicurist in Baldwin County. Just ask anybody. She was sunny and affectionate, and she petted everybody and called them honey and sugar. Men and women, black and white, large and small. Sissy was egalitarian. She loved everybody. Why, she even called Elmira sweetheart.

Anyway, that's how it was. Sissy trotted around all over town in her tight pants and backless high-heel shoes, and Susie Q ran loose without a care in the world. Sometimes Elmira called Sammie Jo and told her younger sister, "You've got to come over here and do something about your granddaughter," and Sammie Jo would come and take Susie Q home with her for a few days. Especially if Sissy had a new boyfriend, which she often did, so as to—in Sammie Jo's words—"give the poor girl a little privacy," as if that was what Sissy needed.

In Elmira's opinion, that was the last thing Sissy needed, and what Susie Q needed was a strong hand and a stable home.

Well, anyway, those were the plans, but they fell apart, and Elmira and Susie Q never made it to the Grand Canyon that year. That was because in the spring a tornado blew through Piney, and a tree fell on Elmira's house and knocked a hole in the roof. One limb tore all the way through the attic and left a gap in the bedroom ceiling big enough for Elmira to lie on her bed and look straight up and see the sky. She couldn't go off and leave it.

Of course, for some weeks, she couldn't get it fixed either. Every carpenter up and down the Gulf Coast was busy repairing roofs and rebuilding whole houses and condos that had blown away in a recent hurricane. By comparison, the tornado damage in Piney, which was ten miles north of the beach, was piddling. They'd get to it when they could. In the meantime, she was advised to get the tree off the house the best way she could, tack plastic sheeting over the hole, and hope for good weather.

Susie Q was delighted with the hole in Elmira's roof and took credit for it herself. She pointed out that the tree that had fallen was actually on her mother's property, not that Sissy owned the lot her doublewide sat on. She was a renter and— Elmira felt certain—always would be. But Susie Q didn't know the difference between renting and owning. As far as she was concerned, it was her tree that had fallen, and, thus, the hole in Elmira's bedroom ceiling was her hole. And she loved it. She pitched a fit when Elmira called Buddy, Sammie Jo's youngest, and asked him to bring a chain saw and cut the tree away and patch some plastic over the opening.

"Oh, no," she wailed. "Elmira, why are you covering it up? Now you won't be able to see the sky when you go to bed. I wish I had a hole in my ceiling so I could see the sky at night. If I did, I sure wouldn't cover it up."

"You'd just lie there and get rained on?" Elmira said. Sometimes Susie Q really wore her out.

"It's not raining now. Wait until it rains. Then cover it up."

"Susie Q, why don't you go home?"

"Nobody's there. Besides my tree is here at your house, and that's my hole in your roof, and I plan to stay as long as I want to and look at it."

"Why in the world?"

"Holes are my favorite things, next to peanut brittle. Do you have any peanut brittle?"

"No."

"I have twenty-two holes. I'm collecting them."

"Twenty-two?"

"Yes ma'am," she said with certainty. "Twenty-two."

Elmira could tell she'd pulled the number out of the blue. "And where do you keep these holes?" she asked her. "In the ground?"

"Some of them. You don't have to be snotty about it."

"Susie Q, don't talk to me that way."

"Well, you're acting like you don't believe me."

"I don't."

"That's not fair."

"Life's not fair. If life was fair, your tree would have fallen through your roof. Not mine."

"Elmira, you don't know everything."

"I don't?"

"No. Come over to my house, and I'll show you my holes. I have more holes than you've ever even seen in your whole life."

Elmira went. She didn't want to, but sometimes she felt sorry for the child. Counting holes like they were blessings! Besides, every now and then it was expedient to go over and check on things. Make sure there was food and somebody was taking out the trash. Elmira didn't like it, but it fell to her to keep an eye on things.

Susie Q made an officious tour guide, which did not surprise Elmira. First they walked through the weedy, unkempt yard, where Susie Q presented a number of chipmunk and squirrel holes for Elmira's inspection. Some of them, Elmira suspected, Susie Q herself was discovering for the first time. She was determined to produce twenty-two holes.

After circling the yard and finding twelve holes, two of which were in trees and one of which was in the rusty mailbox, Susie Q took Elmira into the mobile home, where she pointed out eight more. A few were legitimate. That is, necessary. Keyholes, for instance, and the drain in the kitchen sink. Others made Elmira sad. The holes in Susie Q's shoes and socks, the hole in the couch where someone had once dropped a cigarette, the holes in the wallboard that had never been patched, and one in the screen door.

For a moment, Susie Q looked downhearted. She had only come up with twenty. Then she remembered the pierced holes in her ears, which, as far as Elmira was concerned, only made the girl's ears more noticeable and they already stuck out more than they should. Susie Q was not a pretty child. She was skinny, all arms and legs, and covered with freckles, her colorless hair straight as straw. Nevertheless, she did have twenty-two holes to be proud of.

Twenty-three, she pointed out, claiming bragging rights to the one now in Elmira's bedroom ceiling.

They went back to Elmira's house and lay on the bed together and looked up at it. Susie Q out of pride in ownership, Elmira because she was tired.

"Watch the clouds move past it," Susie Q said. "Aren't they beautiful?"

"Is that why you like holes? You think they're beautiful?" Elmira had closed her eyes. She wanted a little nap.

"Elmira, why are you always making fun of me?" Susie Q sounded hurt.

Elmira looked at her with one eye. "Well, is it?"

"Of course not! Some are just plain ugly. Take gopher holes. You think they're pretty? I saw one once, and it was full of mud."

"So, why do you like holes?" Elmira asked. She was tired, but she might as well ask. Susie Q was going to tell her anyway.

"I like to poke my fingers in 'em. I make a round every day and poke my finger in six—no, seven—holes," she said, counting up. "Plus you can hide things in 'em, like the one in the oak tree. That's where I keep my secret supplies."

"Supplies for what?"

"Oh, you know. Candy. Magic markers. Hair ribbons. Things Sissy might take if she knew where they were. Things that are mine alone."

Susie Q called her mother Sissy. Elmira wondered when the child would realize how appropriate—and pathetic—that was.

"I see," Elmira said, drifting off.

"Of course, the best holes are the ones you can see through. Like into another—what do you call it? Inter-de-mention? Like the peephole I can see through into Sissy's room."

Elmira's easy breathing halted. She waited, but Susie Q didn't elaborate. Thank goodness. No telling what went on in Sissy's bedroom.

"Elmira," Susie Q went on, "are you listening? I'm telling you this hole here in your ceiling is the best of all. It's my favorite. Twenty-three must be my lucky number."

Elmira snored softly.

Susie Q poked her. "Do you have a lucky number?" she asked.

"One," Elmira mumbled sleepily.

"Why?"

"Because if there was just one of us here I could take my nap."

Soon after this discussion of holes, pieces began to disappear from Elmira's puzzles.

CHAPTER TWO

The puzzle pieces didn't disappear all at once. They went missing over a period of weeks. The first one to vanish was out of the Grand Canyon thousand-piecer, just finished and still on the card table. One morning, on her way to the kitchen to make coffee, Elmira stopped to admire it and discovered it was no longer a perfectly executed rendition of this Wonder of the World, her proudest achievement to date, but now a flawed nine-hundred-and-ninety-nine-piecer with a hole right in the middle where the Colorado River went roaring through. The missing piece had been the focal point of the whole puzzle—a single white-water rafter braving the rapids. Now somebody had gone and ruined the effect. The river was empty, and the grandeur of the mightiest canyon on earth was spoiled.

Nobody had been in the house for weeks but Susie Q and Elmira herself.

Susie Q came and went as she pleased. Day and night. Upon occasion Elmira even woke up and found the child in bed with her! So Susie Q had to be the culprit.

"I never," was Susie Q's response when Elmira accused her.

This child, Elmira realized, was not only a master thief but also a pretty good liar. No surprises there, she supposed.

Elmira phoned her sister. Well, something had to be done, and Susie Q was not—by anybody's standards—Elmira's responsibility. When she told Sammie Jo what had happened, Sammie Jo immediately got defensive, as if Elmira had accused her of something.

"Well, I'm sure I don't know where the piece to your puzzle went," she said. Sammie Jo was a few years younger than Elmira and often assumed, perhaps with cause, that Elmira was taking her to task for something.

"I didn't say you did," Elmira explained patiently. "I know where it went. Your precious granddaughter took it."

"You're accusing Susie Q?"

"Certainly."

"Why? Did she say she took it?"

"Nope. Denied it flat-out."

"Then why...?"

"Because I know she took it."

"Elmira, I hate to tell you, but I don't think anybody on God's green earth would steal a piece of your stupid puzzle, let alone lie about it. Not even Susie Q, who is...."

"Your beloved grandbaby, who can do no wrong," Elmira finished for her.

Actually, that hadn't been what Sammie Jo was going to say. She was going to say, "Not even Susie Q, who's apt to tell fibs when it suits her." But, feeling put upon and not wanting to argue with her sister, she sighed loudly and said instead, "I hate to say this, Elmira, but I'm afraid all those years of dealing with crooks and ne'er-do-wells down at the police station have made you paranoid."

"Sammie Jo, I wish you'd stop telling me things you hate to tell me."

"Then stop calling me up and telling me things I don't want to hear."

"Susie Q's your grandchild, not mine."

That comment seemed to knock the wind out of Sammie Jo. There was a long pause. Then, in a resigned voice, she said, "What do you expect me to do about her?"

"Take her home with you and keep her there. Once and for all, get her out of my hair. She's not my responsibility."

Elmira had gone too far. Dead air hung heavily between them. Sammie Jo couldn't take Susie Q home with her and keep her. There were at least two reasons too obvious to discuss.

For one, Sissy wouldn't let her. Dire as the situation might be, Sissy didn't see it as dire and often congratulated herself on what a good mother she was.

Besides, Sammie Jo couldn't take care of a child these days. She had spells. Couldn't stand up sometimes. And ever since she'd changed her name to Samantha—at age seventy, of all things—she'd pretty much resigned from taking on more than she could handle, which had been her life-long mode of operating until that time.

Even though Elmira was glad to see her sister settle down and stop making a fool of herself—why, once they even had to send the sheriff down to Florida to bring her home, although, thank goodness, Doc, her husband, found her first—she still wished Sammie Jo realized Susie Q was getting out of hand.

Maybe she did and just wasn't able to do anything about it.

They were at an impasse—Elmira and Sammie Jo—and neither of them had a solution for what to do about Susie Q.

Slowly, one at a time over several weeks, pieces began disappearing out of the finished puzzles that hung on the walls. The varnish that held them together didn't keep you-know-who from prying pieces out of them. The first one desecrated was the Lord's Supper by Michelangelo. A piece gone smack-dab out of the middle of Jesus' face.

Elmira was furious! When Susie Q came over that afternoon in hopes of an after-school snack, Elmira met her at the door. "You little scamp," she said.

Susie Q smiled sweetly and said, "Hey Elmira. You got any peanut brittle?"

"I do not."

"Oreos?"

"No!"

"What's the matter with you?" Susie Q asked, all nonchalant.

"You know full well what's the matter with me," Elmira retaliated.

"Nope." She paused and then gave Elmira a knowing look. "Oh," she said, "that time of the month, huh? Better lay down, and I'll make you a cup of tea. Where do you keep the Midol?"

Elmira was fit to be tied. She called the beauty shop and told Sissy to come home at once. "We have a situation here that needs your immediate attention."

Sissy came flying home. She thought Susie Q was either badly hurt or had done something really awful. Either she'd been hit by a car or set the house on fire.

When she got there and found neither blood nor flames, she was irritated with Elmira for scaring her half to death. Elmira explained the problem, and Sissy gave both Elmira and Susie Q a menacing look, as if she'd like to wring both their necks. She neither doubted Elmira's version of what happened nor asked Susie Q for hers. Instead, she turned on her daughter and demanded, "Why'd you take a piece out of Elmira's puzzle?"

Susie Q rolled her eyes. "What would I want a piece of her stupid puzzle for?"

At this, Sissy rolled her eyes, went back downtown, and left Elmira with the situation.

A few days later Mount Rushmore was vandalized. George Washington's nose disappeared.

Next it was American Gothic by Grant Wood. Two pieces gone this time, the farmer's nose and his wife's.

Next a cow disappeared from a Grandma Moses' farm, and then a Currier & Ives couple ice-skating on a pond lost a top hat and a fur muff.

The straw that broke the camel's back though was Elvis's eyes. Plucked right out of his face! Elmira was stunned. She couldn't believe it. She closed her closet door and leaned against it to catch her breath. Then she opened it again slowly and looked at The King's handsome portrait hanging on the inside of the door. He had been blinded.

This was more than she could bear. And more by a long shot than she was willing to tolerate.

She didn't know what to do. The little brat had her over a barrel. No one—but no one—was ever to know about Elmira and Elvis. Elvis was Elmira's and hers alone. How dare Susie Q intrude on this...this private life of Elmira's! No one had the right to do this. No one!

Elmira had been invaded. Some things in a person's life were sacred and not to be shared with others. And Elvis was one of those things—the only thing—in Elmira's entire life that was hers alone. She had spent her life in public service to the community. Not once in her forty-two years as police dispatcher had she ever faltered in her duties or betrayed the public trust. She'd never even taken sick days without running a fever, and the chief had to get after her every year to take a vacation.

And now this! And from family! Elmira had specifically told Susie Q to stay out of her closet, that it was private, but privacy wasn't anything Miss Smarty Pants understood. She knew no boundaries herself, and respect for other people's was beyond her. But—ill mannered, untrained, and illegitimate as she was—Susie Q was still Elmira's great niece. She was stuck with her, and she'd never turn on or abandon a family member. Elmira was the one they all relied on in times of need and distress. She was the responsible one, the one to be counted on in an emergency. She was the one who had taken hold when Grandma Horton died. Probated the will. Seen to things.

And this was the thanks she got!

She sat down on the floor and rocked herself.

CHAPTER THREE

Elmira's life with Elvis began when she was a teenager, nearly fifteen but still so tiny she looked no more than ten or eleven. She'd never forget the day she first saw him. Evening actually. A Sunday night. She was wearing saddle oxfords and a skirt and sweater and a locket without a picture in it. She was sitting on the couch in Grandma and Grandpa Horton's living room doing her homework. Grandpa was sitting in his chair reading the paper, and Grandma was in the kitchen drying the dishes and putting them away. Sammie Jo was outside playing and so was their little cousin Mavis, and Elmira was glad. Once she saw Elvis she knew right then that she would never, ever in her lifetime, share him with anybody else, living or dead.

Ed Sullivan introduced him, and when Elvis began to sing, the audience, mostly teenage girls, began to clamor and shriek. Then he turned to the camera and began to sing directly to Elmira. To her alone. Like there was no one else in the world. Just Elmira and Elvis. Those dark eyes looked deep into her own and then, with that lock of hair falling down over his forehead, he smiled. Right at her. He drew her right to him.

Elmira dropped her books and stared.

And then, oh then, be began to move. Rocking his hips and laughing, oh, so tenderly. At that moment, Elmira knew the two of them shared a secret that no one else knew or ever would know, and it was hers and his alone.

She rocked gently with him, and, smiling to herself, she began to hum. Then she swayed and sang along. She felt tingly and happy and knew something wonderful was happening.

That's when Grandpa got up in a huff and turned off the TV. He glared at her and said, "What are you staring at, girl?"

Confused, she looked around the room in an effort to locate the source of his fury. Where had it come from and why was it aimed at her? He was acting as if she'd done something unforgivable—and done it to him.

She knew he was often angry, but she didn't know why. That was just the way he was, mean-spirited, although she didn't have a name for his anger then. He was just plain mean, and you stayed out of his way when you could and when you couldn't, you watched out.

They all knew that. Everybody in the household: Grandma, little Mavis and her mother, Aunt Tootsie, until Aunt Tootsie ran off with a traveling salesman, and Elmira and Sammie Jo and their parents, although their father was seldom there. He worked on oil tankers out of Mobile and was gone practically all the time. When he was home, he was only there for a few days at a time, during which he mostly slept. And ate. He loved Grandma's cooking, and Elmira and Sammie Jo's mother said that was the only reason he ever came home. Not that their mother was there all that much herself. She worked at the Merchants and Farmers Bank and sometimes went home to her own mama, who lived in the country north of Summerton.

This was how home was—everybody was drawn to Grandma, who was love itself, and they all tiptoed around Grandpa. All her life Elmira had known not to irritate him, and she had succeeded better than most. Until now.

Now, without knowing she was doing anything wrong, she had brought his wrath down on her head.

He came and stood over her and said, "Don't you know indecency when you see it?"

With that, he jerked her up off the sofa by the arm. She felt it pull apart from her shoulder, and they both heard it pop. He said, "Git out of my sight and don't ever let me see you acting common again."

He curled his lip and glared at her. She fled up the stairs.

The next morning she skipped school and went to the bus station downtown and bought a ticket to Memphis. She was sitting on a bench outside the station when Grandpa pulled up in his car. He flung the passenger door open.

"Git in," he said.

She did.

Neither of them spoke. When they got home, he marched her into the house and said to her mother, "Ida, take care of your daughter. She's yours."

That afternoon her mother took her to the doctor, and he put her arm back in the shoulder socket, but he couldn't secure it in place. Eventually it stopped hurting, but it never fit properly again, and the rest of her life, one of Elmira's shoulders rode higher than the other.

Elmira never interacted directly with Grandpa again. When she made straight A's, he left a silver dollar on the table beside her plate. Neither of them mentioned it. When speaking was required, she limited it to "Yes sir" and "No sir" without looking at him. Anytime she felt him looking at her, she left the room.

She knew, on that evening of the Ed Sullivan Show, she had experienced the distilled essence of both love and hate, and she never let go of either one. Her love for Elvis and her hatred of Grandpa were the poles she danced between to this day, and they were both secrets she hoarded. She always knew she must not reveal either one, or her life, her very being, would be exposed.

By the time of Elvis's appearance on Ed Sullivan, Grandpa had already run off Aunt Tootsie, his only daughter, and later he would run off Mavis, Tootsie's only child, too. Grandma stood fast, although Elmira never knew how she did it with the old man always angry about something. Righteous indignation he had, like a cancer. It poisoned him, and when he died, Elmira consoled Grandma and never once said she was glad the old tyrant was dead, but she was. Oh Lord, she was.

Elvis and Grandpa were Elmira's two secrets—her true love and her pure hate. And nobody was going to take them away from her.

Elmira didn't tell Susie Q she knew she had blinded Elvis. She had accused the child straight-out about the other puzzles, as soon as she noticed the missing pieces, but not this time. In some weird way she herself didn't understand, to acknowledge Elvis's closeted presence in her life was more than she could bear. She felt she had lost something precious that she had nurtured and kept alive for sixty years. Something no one else was ever to know.

When Susie Q came over, Elmira didn't let on. Not that day or any thereafter. Susie Q kept coming and Elmira kept not mentioning Elvis's missing eyes until, over several weeks, a strained silence developed between them. Each of them knew a secret about the other, and each knew the other knew, and it was becoming clear that each also knew the other was never going to mention it. The longer this impasse lasted, the bigger it became until it hung between them, ominous like a pending disaster. A dark, vacant hole they each walked around, peered into, and dreaded.

They circled each other, sniffing, waiting for the other to break the silence. Neither of them was willing to speak of Elvis, blind or sighted, in Elmira's closet. He was supposed to have remained unseen, and Elmira felt certain Susie Q knew that. Knew it in the same uncanny way she knew other things, had always known things, about how to manipulate people and have her way. She was now having her way with Elmira, holding an unspoken threat over her head. Be nice to me, was the silent message, or I'll tell.

Elmira was sure that was what was going on.

Then, when she found the note in the refrigerator and the words on the bathroom mirror, she knew she was right. Susie Q was holding her hostage to emotional blackmail. The note in the refrigerator said, "Elmira loves Elvis." The words written in soap on the mirror said "Elmira + Elvis" encircled in a heart.

The messages sounded innocuous enough. Except for who they were about. This wasn't grade school, and they cut into Elmira's steadfast secret of more than half a century.

And they ate at her heart.

CHAPTER FOUR

Elmira went and talked to her preacher. Not about Elvis. Of course not. About Susie Q. Her secretiveness, her surreptitiousness.

"You reckon," she asked the minister, "this child is a congenital liar? Can't help herself?"

"Tell me about her," Charlie Fisher said. He was a pleasant young man, not long out of seminary. He had sandy hair and blue eyes and tended to wear short-sleeved sport shirts and no jacket. Even in his vestments on Sunday morning, he exhibited a sunny nature, as if Christianity was basically a happy business and not something to worry about. At church socials, he was apt to tell jokes about religion. He seemed to want people to know he could see the funny side of his profession.

Still, Elmira thought this young man might be helpful. Primarily because he wasn't pious and stuffy like some preachers, nor did he have tattoos and ride a motorcycle like the fellows Sissy typically brought home. Maybe this young minister could provide some insight into what was going on with the youth of today. Elmira decided to ask him whether Susie Q sounded normal or if she was right to be worried.

Of course, she wouldn't let him know Susie Q made her furious and fit to be tied.

They sat in his study at the church. Elmira had asked for a few minutes of his time after Tuesday morning Bible study, which was attended only by women, most of whom Elmira thought had too much time on their hands. But then she was a woman too, and now, since her retirement, most people probably thought she had too much time on her hands too. Unlike the others though, she didn't waste her time. She wanted people to understand that. Why, this very minute she was trying to decide whether the Bible class was a time waster. For the most part, she already knew the Bible better than the rest of them, but Charlie, as everybody called him, surprised her sometimes with how much he knew. Maybe a seminary education was still worth something.

So after they'd settled themselves in facing chairs—in an effort to seem accessible, she guessed, he didn't sit behind his desk—she told him something had to be done about Susie Q, and he was probably the one who was going to have to do it.

"She takes anything she wants, regardless of who it belongs to," Elmira explained.

"What kind of things?"

Elmira told him about the missing puzzle pieces—except for Elvis's eyes, of course.

"You have these puzzles on the wall?" he asked. He'd never been to her house. Ministers used to make house calls, but maybe, like doctors, they didn't do that anymore. Just as well, she thought. She didn't need him coming to see her as if she was a shut-in who needed company. Elmira wasn't crazy about company. Still, she wondered, since when had it ceased to be a pastor's duty to call on the members of his church?

When he expressed interest in her puzzles though, she decided to overlook his shortcomings and explained that puzzles formed the decorating theme throughout her house, although, thus far, she had only completely covered the walls in the living room. She'd made a good start on the dining room though, and others were scattered throughout the rest of the house. She assured him she was working diligently at filling in the gaps. And, she told him, trying to make a little joke so he wouldn't consider her all work and no play, if the Hobby Lobby had more puzzles than she had walls, well, she guessed she'd just have to build on.

He suddenly was overwhelmed by a coughing fit and, asking to be excused, left the office. He was gone for several minutes, and she could hear him down the hall making strangling noises as if he were choking. When he returned, he looked sober and was drying his eyes.

"You might want to have that cough looked at," she told him.

With a backhanded wave, he dismissed the suggestion. "Elmira," he said—he called everybody by his or her first name, regardless of age or station—"Elmira, do you think it's possible this child—Susie Q—just wants attention?"

Elmira sighed. She realized he didn't fully grasp the problem. He thought she was talking about some irritating prank by a normal child. Not a kleptomaniac. Who might well be developing sadistic tendencies.

"She holds it over me," she tried to explain.

"I don't understand," he said.

"She's daring me to do something about it."

"She is?"

"Yes."

"How is she daring you?"

"She taunts me."

"How?"

"She...." Elmira could not finish the sentence. She couldn't tell him about the messages in the refrigerator and on the mirror.

There was an extended silence between them. Finally he said, "Elmira, how do you think you might help this little girl?"

"Help her! She's not my child. She's not my responsibility. That's what I'm trying to tell you. I just want her to stop trooping in and out of my house and taking whatever she wants."

"So you want the problem to go away?"

"Of course, I want it to go away." This was ridiculous. What kind of minister was he?

"And the problem is Susie Q, and you want her to go away?"

Elmira glared at him. Was the man deaf?

"Then," he said carefully, "why don't you lock her out. Don't leave the key where she can find it. Get an alarm system if you have to."

"What in tarnation are you talking about? An alarm system? Treat the child like a burglar? A criminal?"

"Why not? You want her to go away. What do you care what happens to her?"

"I don't care. This is not personal. I'm just trying to be a good citizen, an upstanding member of the community. A Christian, if you will!" She was rigid and livid.

"Oh," he said. "I thought you didn't care about this girl."

Neither of them spoke for a few minutes.

Then, gently, he said, "What can I do to help, Elmira?"

"Talk to her," she said. "Make her see she's doing wrong."

"Have you spoken to her mother about this?"

"Of course. She doesn't care what Susie Q does."

"But you do?"

"This isn't about me! Once and for all, can't I get this through your head—the child is not my responsibility!"

Neither of them spoke. He kept looking at her, as if waiting for her to come around. She refused to look at him. She stood up. She'd had enough of this. They were going in circles, and she saw no reason to continue the conversation. She wished she hadn't come.

"Thank you, Pastor," she said sarcastically and picked up her pocketbook. "I'll be going now and leave you to your duties."

She was furious. Wasn't he supposed to be a spiritual counselor? What kind of double talk was this? She was of a good mind to stop coming to church altogether. Go back to the Baptist church.

But she couldn't face the music. There or elsewhere.

CHAPTER FIVE

Buddy Wooten came to pull the tree off the roof and nail plastic sheeting over the hole. He was Elmira's nephew, Sammie Jo's youngest, and could be counted on for odd jobs. Plus he had a chain saw. He spent most of the morning cutting off limbs and lowering them to the ground with a rope. The chain saw made a terrible racket, and Elmira went to the town library to get a way from it.

That afternoon when Susie Q got home from school, Buddy was still on the roof. Having cleared the debris, he was now attempting to spread out and nail down a sheet of blue plastic. She got a pocketful of Fig Newtons out of Elmira's cookie jar and climbed up the ladder to watch. Straddling the gable, she began eating her cookies. Fig Newtons were not her favorite, but they would have to do. She pretended she was high on a mountaintop and offered to share her picnic with Buddy.

Buddy didn't think she ought to be on the roof but didn't know how to make her get down. He wasn't even sure he ought to be up there, but he didn't know how to tell Aunt Elmira no. Nobody knew how to tell her no.

So the two of them were up there together, Buddy being very careful, and Susie Q eating her cookies and looking around grandly, as if she was surveying her kingdom from on high.

"Watch yourself there," Buddy said.

"H-m-m-m," Susie Q said, brushing crumbs airily from the front of her shirt and not holding on to anything.

"Have you ever climbed an Alp?" she asked.

"No," Buddy told her. "I went up on Mount Cheaha once. That was high enough for me."

"Where's that?"

"North of here. Close to Birmingham."

"The Alps are in Switzerland."

"That right?"

"Yep. You know how I know?"

"Nope."

"I read it in a book I got off Elmira's shelf."

"You did?"

"Yep. She's got a bunch of old books I bet she's had her whole life. She has this one about a girl name Heidi who lives on an Alp. I wish I lived on an Alp."

Then Susie Q let out a loud squall, and Buddy jumped so suddenly he almost lost his balance and fell. He did let go of his hammer, which he watched with dismay as it slid down the roof and lodged in the gutter.

"Gosh darn," he mumbled.

"That's what you call yodeling," Susie Q informed him, letting out another squall. "That's a kind of singing you do when you live on an Alp.

"But you know something else?" she went on, licking her fingers and paying no attention to the height or the dropped hammer. "Heidi's pretty boring compared to Harry Potter. She's no wizard, that's for sure, but she does have some goats. I'd like a goat. You ever had one?"

"No," Buddy said, trying to figure out how to retrieve the hammer. Reckon he could ease down the roof and get it without falling? Or was he going to have go down the ladder, move it, climb back up and fetch the hammer out of the gutter, then move the ladder again to climb back on the roof? This was not the sort of dilemma Buddy was good at solving.

Out of the blue now, Susie Q said, "You like Elvis?"

"Sure," Buddy said, turning to look at her, glad to ignore the hammer problem for the moment. "Everybody likes Elvis."

"Do you have a picture of him in your closet?"

"No. Do you?"

"No, but Elmira does."

"She does?" This didn't sound like Elmira to him.

"Yep."

"You sure?"

"Yep. It's one of her dopey puzzles."

"It is?"

"Yep."

"I'll be," Buddy said. He was often amazed at the things people did and never said a word about. His own mother, for instance. You never knew from one day to the next what she was going to do. Once she set all the furniture in the house out in the yard for no reason at all except she wanted to.

"How do you know Elmira keeps Elvis in the closet?" he asked now. "You been snooping around?"

"Oh yeah," Susie Q said casually. "Big time."

She sighed. She was getting restless. "Listen, Buddy, I'll give you Elvis's eyes if you'll let the hole go and not cover it up."

"Elvis's eyes?"

"Sure."

"You stole Elvis's eyes?"

"Yep."

"How?"

"I just pried 'em loose."

"Out of the puzzle?"

"Sure. You didn't think I had his real eyes, did you?" Susie Q began to giggle. This made him even more nervous. He was afraid she might have a laughing fit and fall.

"Stop that," he said. He wished one of his big brothers was here. They'd know what to do about Susie Q and the hammer. She was waving her arms around and talking away like she wasn't thirty feet up in the air.

"I got 'em right here in my pocket," she said.

"Got what?"

"Elvis's eyes. I'll give 'em to you if you'll leave the hole alone."

"I dunno." Buddy didn't want Elvis's eyes, but he was beginning to want down off this roof and away from Susie Q in the worst way. Humoring her—although he didn't know what he'd do with Elvis's, or anybody else's, eyes—seemed the quickest way down.

"Okay," he said, "if you'll get the hammer and then get off the roof."

"Where is it?" she asked.

"Down there." He pointed to the gutter.

"I see it," she said, dusting off her hands and eying the hammer.

She stood full upright then and stretched, casually, as if she were a cat getting out of bed. Then, holding her arms out like a tightrope walker, she took baby steps in bare feet down the steep slope of roof all the way to the edge, bent from the waist like a ballerina, and picked up the hammer. Then, just as precisely and nonchalantly, she tippy-toed back up to him.

"Here's your hammer," she said, smiling sweetly and handing it to him. "And here are Elvis's eyes."

Sometimes Susie Q knocked the breath right out of him.

Later that afternoon when Elmira came home from the library, she climbed on the roof herself and tacked down the plastic sheet. She was disgusted with Buddy for leaving without covering up the hole. What did he think he was doing—just walking off like that and leaving a gaping hole so the rain could get in? She considered calling Sammie Jo and complaining, but decided not to bother. Buddy was a sweetie and did the best he could. He couldn't help it if he was a little slow.

CHAPTER SIX

Three days later, Elmira woke up on the floor just inside the front door and didn't know where she was. Such a thing had never happened to her before, and she was frightened. At first, all she could see was a yellow glow surrounded by blackness. A spotlight at the end of a tunnel. Gradually, it dawned on her she was seeing the daffodils she'd picked from the yard. They were scattered on her face and over her eyes.

Slowly, her vision and her grasp of the situation expanded until she saw she was on the living room floor. She had no idea how she got there. The last thing she remembered was coming into the house with the flowers.

The back of her head hurt, and something was wrong with her left foot. It lay at an odd angle beneath her ankle. When she tried to move it, she couldn't.

"I've fallen and broken my foot," she said aloud, and the acknowledgment brought tears to her eyes. Not so much tears of anguish—the pain hadn't started yet—as tears of humiliation. How could she do such a thing? Her of all people. She wasn't some crazy old fool who fell down and knocked herself out. Why, just the other day, she'd climbed on the roof. Now, here she was sprawled in the floor. She was as bad as Sammie Jo.

Maybe it was only a severe sprain, but she suspected her ankle was broken. She needed ice for it, she knew, but she couldn't get it. She couldn't stand.

She dragged herself across the living room rug, through the hall, to the bedroom. When she pulled herself up on the bed, her foot dangled at an alarming angle, and she felt blackness descend. Here I go again, she thought.

But the blackness subsided and, when she could see again, she put a pillow under her foot and waited for the pain. She knew it was on its way. She needed to get to the phone, only it wasn't within reach. She had only one, and it was on the wall in the kitchen. Dumb of her, she thought now, to put it there instead of beside the bed, but she never liked to have her sleep interrupted and made a practice of never answering the phone after nine at night. There was no one she wanted to talk to that late and nothing anybody might have to say that couldn't wait until morning.

Obviously, Elmira didn't have children—or a husband either for that matter. Mothers and wives didn't feel that way. They believed they always had to be available.

All those years of working at the police station had taught Elmira to compartmentalize her availability. That was how she'd maintained her sanity, and Elmira was a staunch believer in sanity.

She had to figure something out. Susie Q was her only frequent visitor, but she was at school. The clock on the bedside table said it was twenty minutes to two, another couple of hours before Susie Q would come looking for her after-school snack.

Elmira closed her eyes. She'd have to wait it out. Nothing else to do.

She lost track of time, maybe even went back under for a while. When she heard a noise on the roof, she didn't know how long she had been lying there. At first, she thought the noise was squirrels. Then she realized it was footsteps, and she muttered, "That blooming Susie Q." She listened to the plastic being pulled back and reluctantly opened first one eye and then the other.

But it was not Susie Q she saw. The eyes looking down at her weren't blue and childlike but dark and hooded. And they were smiling and strangely familiar.

"Yoo-hoo," he said, gazing deep into her eyes. "That you down there?"

"Yes," she answered, scarcely able to breathe. "It's me. And it's you, isn't it?"

"Yep, I reckon it is."

He smiled then, and she knew him for sure. She would have recognized him anywhere.

"You Miss Horton?" he asked.

"Elmira," she said.

"Well, Miss Elmira, I come to fix your roof."

"Oh?"

"Mind if I come in? Need to look at the ceiling 'fore I start up here. See how bad you're tore up."

"Come on in," she said. "I've been waiting for you."

She heard him come down off the roof and walk across the porch. She'd left the front door standing wide open.

"Yoo-hoo," he called again.

"I'm in here," she answered. "Come on back."

When he stood in the bedroom door, she saw he was long and scrawny and old. Good Lord, he was older than she was. He'd aged over the years just as she had. He still had a thick head of hair combed back in ducktails, but it was silver now, no longer black. And his face was weathered and creased. When he nodded and smiled, she saw he was missing two front teeth. In the last pictures she'd seen of him, he still had all his teeth, but he'd put on weight. Now he was down right skinny, muscular but gnarled. She always remembered him as young, but, of course, he wasn't. He was showing his age. And he no longer wore a spangled suit but work boots, faded jeans, and a sleeveless T-shirt that might once have been red.

"Ma'am?" he said, puzzled. He hadn't expected to find her still lying there.

When she didn't answer, he raised his eyebrows and scratched the back of his neck. "Ma'am," he said again. "If you could just excuse me. I'm gonna need to come in here and check your ceiling and...you know...look things over."

"Yes," she agreed. "Assess the damage."

"That's it," he concurred, relieved she understood the situation.

Except she made no move to get up.

She put fingers to her forehead, sighed, and closed her eyes. Oh Lord, she hated this. She was going to have to tell him.

She opened her eyes and looked at him. He was waiting, apprehensive but patient.

Finally, she said, "I can't get up."

For an instant, he looked confused, then nodded as if this was understandable. "You're crippled." He stated this as a fact.

"Not usually," she told him.

They both waited a few seconds before speaking again. Trying to get their bearings. She knew it was up to her. He couldn't think of a single move he could make.

"You can get a good look at the damage from here on the bed," she said at last.

"I 'spect you can," he agreed.

"You got a drop cloth?" she asked.

He looked at her dumbly. He wasn't tracking.

"In your truck?" she said. "A drop cloth?"

"Yes'm."

"Go get it."

He went.

When he returned with a paint-smeared cloth, she said, "Spread it over the other side of the bed and lie down here beside me."

"You gonna get up?"

"Can't."

"Oh."

He walked around the bed and began spreading the stiff cloth carefully, folding the edges so they didn't intrude on her. He patted it about a bit, as if he making a bed for a dog or a cat. When he was finished with his nesting touches, he stood mute and still, waiting for what might come.

"Lie down," she instructed.

He did. Gingerly and stiffly. Keeping well to his side of the bed.

"Look up."

He did.

"What do you see?"

"A hole," he replied.

"Can you fix it?"

"Yep. You want me to?"

"Yep," she replied. She closed her eyes. At the foot of the bed, her ankle was beginning to throb like a giant beast.

He started to get up.

"Not yet," she told him

He lay still.

Throbbing with pain and unable to move, she lay beside him.

After a few minutes, she put her hand over his and bore down on it with the pulsating rhythm of the pain.

Eyes wide open, he stared at the hole in the ceiling and dared not move.

Neither said a word for a long time.

Finally, he said, "Lady...."

"Elmira," she reminded him.

"Well, look, Miss Elmira, I got to go."

"Take me with you."

"Where to?"

The possibilities seemed endless to her. She considered many destinations where she had followed him in her dreams—the Caribbean, Hawaii, Acapulco—but didn't voice them.

"To Doctor Bingham's office," she finally answered with resignation. "Around the corner, then three blocks south."

Her answer was disappointing, perhaps to them both, but it was something. And it was do-able.

CHAPTER SEVEN

Elmira was small enough to be picked up and carried about like a pet, but no one ever dared. In fact—except for Susie Q, who was unconcerned with Elmira's dignity—people rarely touched Elmira. Even as a child, she hadn't invited demonstrative affection from family or friends, and she had never had a boyfriend, although several had tried. Unmarried, she had lived alone all her adult life. She always washed and cut her own hair, trimmed and filed her own nails, and seldom, almost never, went to the doctor, so there was no touching by hardly anyone. She might, upon occasion, feel obliged to shake someone's hand, but that was it. Nobody was foolish enough to hug her—and those who tried never did it but once.

Although he had never seen her before in his life, this man, the roofer—whoever he was—sensed that Elmira's request for help was out of character for her. Thus, he proceeded with caution. Carefully, he helped her up and tried to stand her on her feet, which did not work. She couldn't put her left foot down, and when she stood, she appeared woozy. He considered the situation and, with some trepidation, said, "I'm gonna have to pick you up."

She looked at him like he was speaking a foreign language.

"Put your arm around my neck."

She did, and he lifted her gingerly, as if she was a package labeled Handle with Care.

Tenderly, she thought, remembering his song. "Love me tender, love me true" echoed in her head.

My, my, she thought. He's carrying me right out of here. No one's ever picked me up before. Maybe when I was a baby, if I ever was one.

She sighed, and he felt her grow still lighter in his arms.

In all her born days, it had never occurred to her that he might come and swoop her up in his arms and carry her out of the house. But that's what he did.

When they reached his truck, she saw it was a camper. A very old, dilapidated camper that had seen better days.

"Will it run?" she asked.

"Yep," he replied. "She's on her third engine, and I keep her oiled. Hold on now so I can open the door."

She did, and he deposited her gently on the seat. Inside, the camper was bare bones without seatbelts. Masking tape covered a crack in the windshield.

"How do you pass inspection?" she asked.

He considered the question and replied, "I go slow and do good work."

"That'll get you by," she agreed.

She closed her eyes and focused on the pain. Best not to let her mind wander. She told herself to pay attention to what was at stake here.

And what was that? She couldn't remember. Something different, new to her, something that had come at her from outside herself.

She looked at him and knew he was carrying her away. Up, up, and away.

CHAPTER EIGHT

W hat's your name?"

Susie Q peeked over the top of the ladder and asked the question. The roofer inspected his interrogator. He figured she was eight or ten. Her face was covered with freckles, way too many to be pretty, he thought, and her hair hung in thin strands over protruding ears. She had intense eyes that nailed you and made it hard to consider her a child.

"Jerome."

She seemed dissatisfied with his answer. "I didn't think that was your name," she said.

"You didn't? What did you think my name was?"

"I thought it was Elvis."

"Nope."

"You look like your picture, only you're old. Are you here to fix the roof?"

"Yep."

"I wish you wouldn't."

He didn't reply to that. He was trying to figure in his head how much lumber and roofing material he was going to need for the job.

"I saw you carry Elmira off," the girl said. This sounded like an accusation, and she looked at him hard as if waiting for an explanation.

He lost his place with his figuring and looked at her. "You did, huh?"

"I know where you took her."

"You do?"

"Yes. You took her to your house in Memphis."

"That right?"

"Yes. I bet she called you to come and get her."

"Why would she do that?"

"She's been waiting for you."

"For me?"

"Yep."

"How come?"

"She's been waiting for you her whole life."

"That ain't likely."

"It's the truth."

"Elvis is dead, you know."

"No, that's just a...what do you call it? A hoax."

She pronounced it in two syllables—ho-ax—as if she'd seen the word but never heard it. "I read about it in a newspaper at the grocery store," she continued. "Elvis isn't dead. He just left the building."

Jerome couldn't think of a comeback to that.

"You know what building that was? Graceland. Your house in Memphis."

"That so?" He didn't know what else to say.

"We're gonna have to go up there and get Elmira."

"That right?"

"Yes."

"Well, I can't drive all the way to Memphis today. I got work to do."

"Then I reckon I'll have to go myself." She said that as if it was a threat, but even Susie Q couldn't imagine how she would get there on her own. She didn't even know where Memphis was.

"Well, if you see Elvis," he said, "give him my regards."

"Your regards?"

"Yeah. Tell him I said hi-dy."

She thought this over and gave him a long look.

"You're pulling my leg," she said at last.

"Who's pulling whose leg?" he said back.

She wasn't sure that's what she was doing, but she liked the idea that he thought she was putting him on. It made her feel grown-up—that he thought she was doing the same thing to him that he was doing to her.

They spent the rest of the afternoon together, him measuring and clearing out ripped shingles and splintered wood and her telling him things. Mostly about Elmira. She seemed intent on him knowing all about her great aunt, whom she referred to as Elvis's long lost love.

After a while, having grown comfortable with him, she said, "You have to tell me where you took her."

He played along. "I thought you knew. You said I took her to Memphis."

"Well, did you?"

"What do you think?"

"How far is Memphis?" she asked.

"Well, it's farther than around the corner. You can't just run up there and back in, say, an hour and get back here in time to start working on a torn-up roof before it gets dark."

"You can't?"

"Nope."

"So where'd you take her?"

"To the doctor."

"Why?"

"She broke her foot."

"How?"

"I dunno."

"Is she still there?"

"Nope. They sent her on to the emergency room in an ambulance."

"To the hospital?" Her eyes grew big.

"Yep."

"Why, we can't just leave her there!"

"She said she'd call her sister when she was ready to come home."

"Grandma lives halfway to Fairhope."

"She does?"

"What kind of boyfriend, are you?" she demanded of him now. "To just go off and leave Elmira that way?"

He squinted up at her. "Boyfriend?" he said.

"Well, ain't you?"

"Where'd you get that idea?"

"She loves you. She's got your picture hanging up. And has had ever since I've known her, and I've known her my whole life. She's been waiting for you all this time."

"She doesn't even know me! I never saw the woman until a few hours ago."

"What'd she do when she saw you?"

"She...she...." He laid a crowbar aside and considered what had taken place. He was reluctant to talk about it. He didn't know himself exactly what had happened between him and the lady in question, but whatever it was, it was private and didn't bear discussing.

"I bet she told you she'd been waiting for you," Susie Q said knowingly. "Didn't she?"

"Yes," he agreed. "Yes, she did say that."

"There! You see."

"But that was because I told her I'd come to fix the roof."

He didn't dare tell the child that the lady had told him to lie down with her in the bed. He didn't think he'd ever tell anybody about that.

"Nope," Susie Q insisted. "She was waiting for you and, even after all this time, she knew you as soon as she saw you."

"Look here," he said, wanting to get things straight once and for all, "you do know, don't you, that I am not Elvis?"

She considered this. "Maybe," she allowed, clearly not convinced.

"And," he added with finality in his voice, "I'm sure your Aunt Elmira knows that."

"No, she doesn't," Susie Q, insisted.

He considered her. And the situation, and didn't know what to do about either. He wondered if it was possible the lady did think he was somebody he was not. She certainly didn't seem like the kind of person who would ask a total stranger to climb in bed with her. And yet she had.

Jerome and Susie Q sat in silence for a moment, each mulling over the situation and trying to decide what to make of it.

When he stood up, she did too and followed him down the ladder.

"You going to get her?" she asked hopefully.

"Yeah," he said.

He couldn't see any way around it. He couldn't just leave somebody with a broken leg at the hospital without a convenient ride home. Besides, if the lady was in love with him, well then, he was obliged, wasn't he.

"I'm coming with you," Susie Q said, and she climbed in the camper beside him.

CHAPTER NINE

Whed they got Elmira home, Susie Q said to Jerome, "You can't leave her. She can't walk."

That was true. Elmira's leg was in a cast, and she was on crutches. Also—and this wasn't like Elmira—she wasn't handling the situation well. Her hands and arms were flailing about, and—worst of all—she seemed furious.

"I made a career out of handling emergencies and accidents," she said. "Now, I wish you'd look at me! How could I be so stupid as to fall down and end up...this helpless?"

At this, her lower lip quivered, and Jerome thought, oh my God, she's gonna cry.

But she didn't. She swung her crutch through the air and knocked a lamp off a table.

Susie Q turned to Jerome and said, "You have to stay."

Of course, there was no law that said he couldn't leave. And this child saying he couldn't didn't make it so. This child—this Susie Q—had some notions, and he didn't know where she got them.

Besides, Jerome told himself, none of this was his responsibility. He was a roofer. An itinerant roofer. He followed storms and went wherever roofs got blown away, and when there wasn't roof damage from bad weather, he went where there was new construction. He liked his life, such as it was. No ties, which meant no people to tie him down. There had been some ties once, a long time ago, but they weren't the binding kind, and they weren't the happy kind either. A mean woman and a baby that wasn't right. From birth. Never had been right and never could be. And when the baby died, he had left.

But that had been decades ago.

He got his satisfaction now out of living in a camper, roofing and roaming. He'd been up and down the Gulf Coast—Florida, Alabama, Mississippi—and into Louisiana and part of Texas. Someday he had a mind to go way on out West. Right now he just wanted to fix the hole in this woman's roof, get paid, and be on his way.

The three of them—Jerome, Elmira, and Susie Q—were in Elmira's living room, which he noticed for the first time appeared to be wallpapered with jigsaw puzzles. He'd never seen the like, but he thought it was a good way to fix up a house. Elmira had her cast propped up on a stool and, at the moment, reminded him of a bantam hen with ruffled feathers. She wasn't bigger than a minute, spry with black snapping eyes and black hair touched with gray and cut in a bob like a child's. I bet, he thought, she cuts her hair herself, and I bet she could cut mine.

He needed a haircut.

Susie Q looked from one adult to the other, waiting to see what they were going to do.

Finally, Jerome said to her, "You better get Miss Elmira some supper."

Susie Q went to the kitchen and came back immediately with a jar of peanut butter with a knife stuck in it. "She's out of bread," she reported.

They were both talking around and over Elmira like she wasn't sitting there.

"Go to the store and get some," he said, pulling his wallet out.

"There's no loaf bread," Elmira said between clenched teeth, "because I was going to make cornbread."

"Oh well," he said, as if that cleared everything up, "I know how to make cornbread. What you got to go with it?"

"Meat loaf," she said, "and string beans. Left over from last night."

He went to the kitchen and, rummaging around, fixed some supper. Including cornbread, which—it turned out—was better than most folks knew how to make.

Susie Q helped Elmira to the bathroom and back, and then they all sat down together and ate.

That's how it started.

That night Jerome slept in the camper in Elmira's front yard. It didn't feel right to drive away and leave, even though he usually parked down close to the beach where he could hear the ocean. That was something he liked to do, and usually there wasn't anything or anybody to keep him from doing what he liked to do.

Susie Q slept in the house with Elmira, which wasn't all that unusual, and the next morning he cooked bacon and eggs for the three of them. They sat around the kitchen table, eating and talking about the roof.

The talk sounded casual, but it was careful, and all kinds of alarms were going off in Jerome's head. This scene, he thought, is downright homey and—if I'm not careful—might go on a long time.

The coffee was hot, the sun was up, and he felt good.

Oh Lord, he thought, what have I got myself into.

But he poured himself another cup of coffee.

Susie Q announced she wasn't going to school. She said she needed to stay and nurse Elmira.

Elmira told her to get on out of there and not show her face again until after school that afternoon. Susie Q went—complaining as she slammed out of the house.

During the day company came and went—Sissy, who struck Jerome as a prissy thing in clothes too tight for her own good, and Miss Elmira's sister, who introduced herself as Samantha and whom Elmira called Sammie Jo. They both brought food—Sissy hamburgers from Wendy's for lunch and Samantha a casserole for supper.

Jerome said howdy to each of them from the roof. Sissy was in a hurry and waved and went on. Samantha was talkative and thanked him as if he'd done her a personal favor. She asked how long he'd be around.

A while, he told her. The roof would take a while.

At lunchtime, he and Elmira sat on the screened-in back porch, where she'd stretched out on a glider, and ate the hamburgers. They didn't talk a whole lot. She seemed to be a woman of few words, and, Lord knows, he never had much to say.

In due time, he got around to telling her that, besides the storm damage to her roof, he'd found rotten wood where some shingles seemed to have been missing around the chimney from some time back.

She said she hadn't realized that.

They were quiet for a while, each of them thinking that over and deciding what it might mean.

Yes, he said, once he'd got the damage cleared away, he realized this was more that just a simple patching job.

She said h-m-m-m.

Of course, he continued, he could just patch the hole and go on. That's what some roofers would do. But that wouldn't be right. That would be asking for trouble down the line.

Yes, she said, she could see how that might be.

He liked to do a job right, so there wouldn't be problems later.

Well, of course, she said.

Yes ma'am, that rotten spot needed fixing, along with the hole where the tree fell. No point in fixing one without the other.

She thought he was probably right about that.

He couldn't say for sure how long it would take—a while—but he would give her an estimate.

That would be fine, she said.

That was the way the conversation went. He knew how to ease people along, and she was patient with being eased. He'd been working up and down the coast for a long time, and this was where she lived, and they both knew how things got done. They were enjoying themselves.

And they both knew this was the start of something and fixing the roof might take some time. It might even take as long as was needed.

CHAPTER TEN

The following week Charlie Fisher sat in Elmira's living room and looked around. He was rather overcome by the puzzles and felt as if he might be visiting a grotto in a foreign land. He had never seen anything like this room and the adjoining dining room. He wondered if archaeologists felt a similar sense of awe when they came upon a caveman's drawings deep inside the earth.

"Nice of you to come," Elmira told him, not adding that she thought it was too bad you had to fall and break your leg these days before your pastor paid you a house call. Not that she'd wanted his company, then or now. She wasn't the sort of person who craved attention. And she had bristled when she saw her name in the church bulletin listed under "shut-ins."

"I'm not sick, you know," she told him. "I just can't get out and about right now."

"I know," Charlie said. He believed in agreeing with members of his flock whenever possible. He was always looking for common ground, especially with the likes of Elmira, whom he experienced as more prickly than most.

He walked around and examined the puzzles on the walls.

"You will note," she said, "that the missing pieces are still missing."

"Yes," he agreed. "I see they are." Indeed, there were gaps like missing teeth in each of the puzzles, and there were dozens. And dozens.

"Ruins the effect, don't you think?" she said. There was a plaintive tone in her voice.

Uncertain what effect she was aiming for, Charlie chose not to respond to that. Instead, he asked if she would like for him to schedule Meals-On-Wheels for her.

She found the suggestion offensive. How would they know what she wanted to eat, and why would she want strangers trooping in and out of her house? It was bad enough just having friends and family underfoot. Sammie Jo had come every day or two with a casserole until Elmira put a stop to it. Sissy brought in fast food constantly until Elmira told her enough was enough. And people from the police station and neighbors had brought in enough food to feed an indigent foreign country.

No thank you. She'd had enough charity. "Besides," she said, "Jerome knows how to cook, and Susie Q can help around the house and run errands."

"Who's Jerome?" Charlie asked.

"The roofer. Happened by the day I fell. Been here ever since. On the job. Fixing the roof."

"I see. Well, that's good. So you have the help you need. That's what matters."

"Of course, it is."

"How are you getting along with Susie Q?"

"Fine, fine," Elmira assured him with a wave of dismissal. Given how wrought up she'd been about the child the last time they had talked, he was surprised at her cavalier attitude now. Maybe Susie Q was behaving better. Or, more likely, maybe Elmira just needed her now. And knew it.

"Maybe she'd like to go to church camp this summer," he said. He had been trying to come up with some way to engage the girl ever since Elmira told him about her.

"Maybe," Elmira said.

She didn't appear eager to pursue this.

"Elmira," he ventured, "is there anything at all I can do for you?"

Or, he thought, do you just want me to go away.

"You can tell me something," she said abruptly.

"What?"

"You're a man who deals with the...," she paused here, as if uncertain how to continue. Charlie had no idea what was coming and was curious to hear what it was Elmira thought he dealt with.

"The supernatural," she concluded. "Right?"

"Well, your spiritual well-being is of great concern to me."

"Okay, okay," she said, shaking her head and waving off this response as if it was unimportant. "Just tell me, have you ever received a visitation?"

"You mean experienced a vision?"

"Yes."

"Well, no, I can't say I have. I have, however, experienced a conversion. Is that what you mean?"

"No, it isn't. I mean have you ever seen something you knew was there—just knew—even if it didn't seem likely? Or reasonable? Or even possible?"

There was a long silence.

"Elmira," he said at last, "have you had a vision?"

"Yes," she said. She closed her eyes. For a moment, he thought she might not continue.

Elmira was the last person on earth he would have expected to confess visions to him. He wasn't even sure he believed in them. Not in this day and age. Moses on the mountain, sure. Or Jesus in the desert. He himself would probably have visions if he wandered off and fasted for forty days and nights. But Elmira? It hardly seemed possible under any circumstances.

"Did this happen when you fell?" he asked. She must have knocked herself coo-coo.

"Afterwards," she said.

He waited.

When she didn't continue, he said, "What did you see?"

"Eyes," she said.

"Whose eyes?" he asked.

"Elvis's," she said.

"Elvis's?" he said, unable to suppress a smile. "The King himself?"

"You heard me," she said sharply.

Oh Lord. There, for an instant, he had assumed she was entertaining him, but he should have known better. She had been serious, and he had offended her. Always on thin ice with Elmira, he had lost ground yet again.

The silence sounded loud in both their ears and lasted much too long.

Finally he said, "Do you want to tell me about it?"

"No," she said abruptly. "I've said too much already. Would you like some coffee, or do you want to leave and get on with your duties?"

Given the choice, he left. And got on with his duties.

"What was I supposed to say," he said that evening to his young wife, Leslie, who had a master's degree in psychology and on whose advice he relied in matters of counseling. "What was the appropriate response? In seminary, they didn't teach me how to deal with Elvis visions."

Leslie said she didn't know. They hadn't taught her that in graduate school either.

"When Elmira refused to say more, I just left and went back to the church and met with the committee on lethargy.

Excuse me," he corrected himself. "The committee on liturgy. The only visions they have are of new choir robes for Easter."

Neither Charlie nor Leslie knew whether to laugh or cry. His conversation with Elmira, they agreed, was disturbing. Or might be. On the other hand, how could you take visions of Elvis seriously?

And so they laughed. They held each other and laughed— and cried a little because life was funny and hard and they couldn't fix it. For Elmira or anybody, and they were beginning to realize that.

CHAPTER ELEVEN

Jerome watched Elmira closely. For clues as to whether this was a woman in love or just a woman with a broke foot. It was hard to tell. He felt some obligation toward her either way, but helping somebody out who couldn't get around was one kind of obligation. Having a woman in love with you was another. He was accustomed to helping people out. He was unaccustomed to love.

"My name is Jerome. Jerome Tooley," he told her one day on the back porch. She was on the glider; he was in the rocking chair. They were drinking iced tea.

She looked at him skeptically.

"I am not Elvis," he told her, straight-out. He wanted to make this clear. If not to Susie Q, at least to her. Susie Q had all kinds of things to learn, most of which were life lessons she was sorely in need of. Elmira was a different matter. In spite of himself, he was concerned about her.

At the moment, she looked flustered, and he was willing to bet that was unusual. For her, it might well be unprecedented.

It made her look kind of innocent. Girlish. Not that that was anything she was going for.

"Well, I know you're not Elvis," she said sternly, summoning back her dignity. "Who would ever have thought otherwise?"

He nodded, as if giving her the benefit of the doubt. "Well, Susie Q said...," he began.

"Oh, well, Susie Q." She waved any mention of Susie Q aside.

"Oh yeah, well," he agreed.

There didn't seem to be anything else to say. He hoped he had cleared the matter up and, once and for all, set things straight.

He finished his tea and was on his way out when he turned and said, "You like cherry so-dy pop?"

"Why, yes," she said. "I do."

"I'll bring you some," he said,

"I'd like that," she said.

"Tomorrow," he added.

She smiled and nodded.

Okay, he thought.

CHAPTER TWELVE

He's still here?"

This question came from Sammie Jo. (Elmira couldn't and wouldn't call her sister Samantha regardless of how many times she was asked to. She'd called her Sammie Jo all her life and, at this late date, she wasn't about to give in to a silly whim and start calling her something else.)

Sammie Jo had come in with a sack of groceries, which she set on the kitchen table. She began moving about the kitchen, putting things in the refrigerator and the cupboard. Elmira sat watching her, crutches beside her chair. Overhead they could hear hammering.

"He's fixing the roof," she said.

"How long is it going to take? He's been here going on two weeks."

"Well, there's repair work around the chimney that has to be done too."

"So...?"

"So, yesterday, he said while he was at it, he might just as well go ahead and reroof the whole house."

Sammie Jo turned around and studied her older sister. "Does it need it?"

"Well, of course, it needs it. I wouldn't let him do it if it didn't need it."

"No, I guess not," Sammie Jo acquiesced and turned back to the cupboard.

Each afternoon after school, Susie Q visited Jerome up on the roof. She would settle in astride the gable while she ate her snack. One day, while licking the filling out of an Oreo cookie, she said, "There are pieces missing out of every one of Elmira's puzzles."

"Uh-huh," he said around a roofing nail he held in his mouth. He'd noticed. "Why's that?"

"I stole 'em."

"How come?"

"To aggravate her."

"It work?"

"Oh yeah. Big time."

"What'd you want to go and do that for?"

"I dunno."

"I dunno either. Miss Elmira don't deserve aggravation."

Susie Q ate the cookie part of her Oreo then and thought that over. What people might deserve and not deserve was a new way of thinking for her.

"What do you think Elmira deserves?" she asked.

"A lady like her deserves better than she gets, if you ask me," Jerome said. He hammered in a nail to his satisfaction and reached for another shingle. "As far as I can tell, she's done everything for herself her whole life."

"Well, why wouldn't she?"

"Most folks have somebody to help 'em."

"You don't."

"Well, that's so."

"I know something you can do for her."

"What?"

"Take her to Memphis."

"Susie Q, haven't we already had this conversation?"

"Well...but she wants to go."

"How do you know?"

"I can just tell."

"You can, can you?"

"Yes."

"I'll tell you something I can tell. At least, something I suspect."

"What?"

"That she knows it was you who swiped the pieces out of her puzzles, and she'd be much obliged if you put them back."

Susie Q tried to hold the hard look he was sending her way, but she couldn't. Something about him made her want to measure up in his eyes, even if it meant owning up to aggravating Elmira. Aggravating Elmira was supposed to be fun, but when he put it to her the way he just did, it didn't feel like fun anymore. It felt mean and childish, and she wanted Jerome to treat her like a grown-up, which he did most of the time. More often than anybody else did anyway. For instance, he never told her to get off the roof or to be careful because she might fall. He never even told her to go away and stop bothering him. And when he went somewhere, he'd say, "Wanna go?"

Yes sir, she liked Jerome a lot, even though he had covered up the hole in the roof. Just having him around was worth it. She wished he'd stay on and on. The only time he'd ever told her no was the day she asked if he would go to school with her for show-and-tell. He'd asked what was that, and, when she told him how it worked, he said flat-out NO in no uncertain terms.

"I am not some kind of curiosity for you to parade around and show off," he said, and she realized then, for the first time, that he had feelings and she had hurt them. She felt ashamed of herself, and that left her not knowing how to act.

While he was mad at her, he'd added, "And I'm not now, nor have I ever been, Elvis. So, once and for all, just get that through your head."

Then she felt even more shame because maybe he had guessed—and guessed right—that she'd been going around telling her classmates Elvis wasn't dead and she'd bring him to school and prove it.

Now she wasn't going to get to show him off, and she'd made him mad to boot.

"Hand me that shingle," he said to her, and she did, and they went on then as if nothing had happened, and she was relieved.

For the next few days, every time Susie Q caught Elmira out of the house or with her back turned, she wedged a missing puzzle piece back into its place. If Elmira noticed the return of the pieces, she didn't mention it, and neither did Susie Q, of course. Or Jerome for that matter.

After Susie Q had put back all the pieces, with the exception of Elvis's eyes, she phoned Buddy. "I got to have those eyes back," she told him.

"Aw, Susie Q," he said, "I don't know about that."

"I'll give you my baseball cards for 'em," she told him.

"No, no, I don't want nothing for 'em. It's just that I don't know where they went to."

"What do you mean? Did you lose 'em?"

"No, you know I didn't need 'em for anything, so I traded 'em to a boy down at the garden center for some pretty rocks. One of 'em is a real fossil. You can tell cause it's got ridges on it."

"Buddy, I don't know what I'm gonna do without them eyes."

"I sure am sorry to hear that, Susie Q. Could you use a fossil?"

"No. Buddy, listen, who is this boy you traded the eyes to?"

"Oh, that I don't know. They were passing through—him and his folks—on their way to the beach. His mother bought a pot of frilly petunias to take to somebody they were visiting. They were real pretty, two-toned, purple and white, on sale this week."

"Oh great," Susie Q said.

"Well, they made a nice present."

"Good-bye, Buddy."

"Good-bye, Susie Q. Just let me know if there's ever anything I can do for you."

"You bet," she said and hung up. She sat on her hands and squeezed her eyes shut. What was she going to do now? Elvis's eyes were gone for good, and it was all her fault.

CHAPTER THIRTEEN

A day short of Jerome finishing the roof, Elmira asked him if he ever did any painting. Well, yes, he allowed, sometime ago he'd done a right smart of painting and wouldn't mind getting back into it over the summer when roofing was such hot work.

"Why?" he asked, smiling at her like a gnome, then ducking his head in embarrassment. "You lookin' for a painter?"

"My house needs painting. Don't you think?"

"Yep. It could use it. That's for sure."

"I was thinking of painting it blue."

"Blue?"

That surprised him. The house was white now, but he found Elmira full of surprises. He liked that about her. When she opened her mouth, he never knew what she was going to say.

"Gray blue," she said now.

"That'd look nice," he said. "Reckon I could drop by the paint store and pick up some chips for you to look at."

"I'd be much obliged," she told him.

They'd been sitting on the back porch eating pimento cheese sandwiches. As he left, she said, "Take your time. There's no hurry. A good, careful job's what I want. Nothing slap-dab that's done in a hurry."

"Yes'm," he said, nodding thoughtfully as if he'd just received a gift.

Well, the painting took a while. The rest of the spring and on into summer. There was no need for Jerome to sleep in his camper all the time. It stayed full of roofing materials and now buckets of paint too. He took Elmira up on her invitation to sleep on the glider on the back porch. Because it was screened in, there was no problem with mosquitoes. After a night or two out there, Jerome installed a ceiling fan, which kept the breeze stirring. He told Elmira he got it for free from a fellow down at the hardware store. Actually, he'd traded him an old jackhammer he had no use for and two pocketknives.

Besides painting the house, he drove her wherever she needed to go. During the week he chauffeured her to the doctor's office and the drugstore. On Saturdays he took her grocery shopping and carried the bags in for her. On Sundays he drove her to church and waited in the parking lot to drive her home.

After these outings, they usually sat on the glider under the ceiling fan and drank iced tea or the cherry soda he bought. He smoked and, out here on the porch, she didn't mind and fetched him a saucer for an ashtray, which he always emptied before getting back to his painting.

They began to talk. Neither one of them had ever talked much before. Now she told him about police dispatching—about runaway children, family feuds, traffic accidents, hold-ups, an overturned truck loaded with chickens, and a bank robber who forgot where he parked his get-away car.

He told her about roofing and roaming—about hurricane damage in Mississippi, broken levies in New Orleans, people he'd met all up and down the Gulf Coast and how they were pretty much the same everywhere you went but different in their own way too, how most of them treated you fair and square if you treated them that way and, those that didn't, well, no need to let them into your life. He told her how once he'd had pneumonia and spent the winter in a veterans' hospital in Gulfport and how another time he'd fallen off a roof and been laid up in Galveston.

They spent hours talking about their lives, gliding in the glider, and drinking iced tea or cherry soda, depending on the preference of the day.

When she joined them, Susie Q always chose cherry soda. She often sat cross-legged on the floor, picking scabs off her knees and listening. Once she said, "I like to listen to y'all talk. I never heard folks talk as much as y'all do."

Elmira watched her in wonderment. Susie Q's learning a new skill, she thought. She's learning to listen. I never thought I'd see the day.

As for Elmira, maybe she was learning to share herself, although she didn't think that way. She was just enjoying herself and the company she was keeping. That was enough. A gracious plenty by anybody's standards, and Elmira's standards for the company she kept had always been so high as to exclude most everybody she knew.

CHAPTER FOURTEEN

The next time Sammie Jo came by, she asked Elmira how long Jerome was there for. Elmira didn't like the tone of the question and started to tell her sister it was none of her business, but that might have sounded like Elmira herself was guilty of something. What people nowadays called being defensive. Elmira wasn't up for sounding defensive. Or feeling guilty either. So, she simply said she didn't know. When he finished painting, she reckoned.

"Well," Sammie Jo demanded, "how long is that gonna take?"

"It'll take as long as it takes," Elmira said and shut the door on her. That, she realized, didn't seem so much defensive as just plain mad, which she was.

A few days later Sammie Jo's husband, Doc Wooten, dropped by.

"Doc," Elmira said, meeting him on crutches at the door and not initially grasping the reason for his visit. "What brings you by?"

"Elmira." He nodded politely on the other side of the screen. "Mind if I come in?"

She let him in. She couldn't recall Doc ever paying her a visit alone before. Even dropping by with Sammie Jo was a rarity for him. Usually she saw Doc at family gatherings at his and Sammie Jo's big house out from town. Then there'd be a crowd. She figured he'd come with bad news—Sammie Jo must've died. If she was just in the hospital, he would have called. And if someone else in the family had died, Sammie Jo would have come herself.

"How you gettin' along?" Doc said uncomfortably.

"Fine." Elmira gave him a peculiar look. If something needed saying—if bad news had to be delivered—Doc wasn't the sort to beat around the bush.

"You want to sit down?" she asked.

"Yes, I reckon," he said.

"You want some tea? A glass of water?"

"No, no," he said.

She was relieved. Fetching drinks on crutches would have posed a problem. She sat down across from him and waited.

"I see you got your roof fixed," he began cautiously.

"Yes."

He looked at the puzzle-covered walls. They took him aback every time he saw them. He'd forget about them, and then he'd walk in and there they'd be again.

He could see Elmira was waiting for him to state his business. He'd better get on with it. "That same fella—Jerome? I see he's painting your house now," Doc said carefully.

"Yes. You see correctly."

"He's not overcharging you, is he?"

"No."

"Well, that's good. He live around here?"

"Around and about," she replied. She was beginning to catch on. Doc hadn't come with bad news. He'd been sent to check things out. Now, Elmira liked and admired Doc. Most everybody did and for good reason. He was, she supposed, the patriarch of the extended family and believed in looking after his own. That apparently included her, although looking after his sister-in-law wasn't anything he'd ever felt obliged to do in the past.

Attempting to do so now made Doc terribly uncomfortable. If Sammie Jo hadn't insisted he come and see for himself, he wouldn't be here. She said this fellow was not only taking Elmira's money for more work than needed to be done but that he had taken to living here. Doc found that hard to believe—that any man would live with Elmira—so he had agreed to pay her a visit and see for himself.

"Elmira," he now said earnestly, leaning forward in his chair with his hands on his knees, "I don't mean to butt in, but what do you know about this man? Nobody I've asked about him seems to know who he is."

"His name's Jerome Tooley. He's a good roofer and a pretty good painter."

"Yeah, well, I guess that's what matters. I just wanted to make sure he wasn't taking advantage of the situation."

"What situation is that, Doc?"

"Well, you know, a woman alone. With a nest egg." He was too embarrassed to look her in the eye.

"A pension," he added lamely.

"And a broken leg," she concluded for him.

"I just want to make sure this fella's not looking to...."

"Take advantage of an old fool."

"Elmira, don't go putting words in my mouth."

"Doc, since when did I become an old fool?"

"Now let's don't go gettin' our feathers ruffled. Anybody can get taken in by a smooth talker."

"Doc, I worked at the police station for forty years and saw all kinds and never once got taken in by anybody."

"That's true."

They looked each other in the eye now. Him feeling awkward and sorry he'd come, and her feeling angry with her sister for sending him.

"Doc," Elmira said wearily, "go home. And tell Sammie Jo to mind her own business."

"I think I'll do that, Elmira. I just dropped by, you know, to see if you needed anything."

"I know," she said and watched him get up and leave.

She let him show himself out.

CHAPTER FIFTEEN

Though a bit amused by Sammie Jo and Doc's concern, Elmira was also affronted that anyone would think she was someone a wandering stranger could take advantage of. Who did they think she was—Katharine Hepburn in *The Rainmaker*? A poor old spinster at the mercy of the fast-talking Burt Lancaster? Hardly!

And if Elmira was no Kate—and she certainly wasn't—Jerome was no Burt Lancaster. Or Cary Grant in *The Philadelphia Story* or Spencer Tracy in *Pat and Mike* and the rest of those movies the two of them did together. Jerome wasn't even Humphrey Bogart in *The African Queen*, although he was sort of ugly in an appealing way like Bogie was.

His eyes though were pure Elvis.

Of course, he wasn't Elvis either. Everybody knew that—except Susie Q.

Elmira had been thinking about old movies lately because she and Jerome had moved the television set out to the back porch and now spent their evenings watching some of their favorite oldies together. Whatever was on the classic movie channel. Elmira preferred crime dramas—what they called film noir—and Jerome liked westerns. Every now and then they'd get lucky and catch a Marx Brothers, Charlie Chaplin, or Buster Keaton festival. Those were the best.

One evening when they were watching *A Night at the Opera*, they got to laughing so hard they woke Susie Q up next door, and she came over in her pajamas and curled up between the two of them, and they all watched together. It was the longest Elmira had ever seen Susie Q sit still.

After that, she asked every day if Elmira and Jerome were going to be watching the Marx Brothers that night. She'd never heard of the Marx Brothers until now, and she immediately developed an imitation of Harpo. When she'd start rolling her eyes, Jerome would do a funny low kind of walk, stretching his legs way out and tapping an imaginary cigar like Groucho. Nothing would do then but for Elmira to try to make faces like Chico, and soon they would be howling with laughter. Elmira couldn't remember when she'd laughed so much.

It was pleasant, sitting out there in the dark with the night sounds all around, watching old movies, and drinking cherry soda. That's what they did—she and Jerome and sometimes she and Jerome and Susie Q—and there was no harm to it. Elmira would thank busybodies to mind their own business.

One night Susie Q fell asleep between the two of them. They had been watching *Shane*, and it had gone on too long for her. Instead of waking her and sending her home to the trailer, Elmira told Jerome to carry her into the house and put her in her bed. She'd let Susie Q sleep with her.

They tiptoed through the dark kitchen, Elmira first, Jerome behind her, edging sideways through the doorway to avoid bumping Susie Q's dangling legs. They crossed the hall into Elmira's room, where she turned on a little bedside lamp. Jerome laid the child in Elmira's bed, and she stirred but didn't wake.

The two of them stood looking down at her. Asleep in the soft light, Susie Q took on a tranquil sweetness not visible in her waking hours.

"I had a baby girl once," Jerome said suddenly, his voice startling them both.

The words reverberated in the stillness. For a moment, Elmira didn't absorb their meaning. She was remembering the first time—the only other time—Jerome had been in her bedroom. The day he had carried her out in his arms. Gradually, the meaning of the words he'd just spoken seeped into her consciousness.

"What happened to her?" she whispered, although she didn't really want to know. She just wanted to go on standing beside him in this room for a long time.

"She died," he said.

"How?"

"Never knew. One morning she didn't wake up."

"How old...?"

"Not yet a year."

After a pause, he added, "Never even learned to walk," as if therein lay his greatest sadness.

"What was her name?"

"Justine."

Elmira turned to him. If she hadn't been on crutches, she might have touched his face. As it was, his eyes searched hers for a long time as if in hopes of finding the answer to some question he didn't know how to ask.

Then, holding her by the shoulders, he kissed her. It was a kiss filled with longing and regret.

"Ain't neither one of us thirty," he said, "and we won't ever be again."

He studied her a moment longer, then turned and left the room.

"Jerome," she said in the silence, but he didn't answer.

That night he slept in the camper.

In the house next to the sleeping child, she lay awake. She had been wondering something she now knew—how he tasted. Like cigarettes and cherry soda—that was it.

"Cherry so-dy pop," she said aloud.

CHAPTER SIXTEEN

The next visitor to warn Elmira off Jerome was Charlie Fisher from the church. His admonition to be on the lookout for scam artists surprised Elmira. Jerome seems like a nice fella, Charlie said, but what did he really have to offer Elmira? Elmira was stunned by the comment. Charlie talked like she was getting ready to marry Jerome and turn over her bank account. She had thought Methodists were more enlightened than that. Charlie almost sounded like a Baptist the way he went on.

She supposed she was especially rankled because—it was true—just the day before she'd given Jerome a five hundred dollar advance on the house painting. She'd already paid him for the roof. Enough for sure, but he hadn't taken a thing from her she hadn't offered.

She was of a good mind to stop going to the Methodist Church. Maybe she'd try the Presbyterians for a while.

A few days after Charlie's visit, Nick Hawthorne, the chief of police, paid Elmira a call. Elmira had taught Nick just about everything he knew—which was plenty and sufficient for the responsible job he held. He was a good chief, and common sense told Elmira she had no choice but to listen to what he had to say.

Nick was embarrassed. Hat in hand, staring down at his polished shoes and looking too young to be wearing a badge and carrying a gun, Nick clearly hated the task at hand. But Doc Wooten and several others had asked him to check out Jerome Tooley, just to be on the safe side. Nick had, and, to his dismay, he had found an outstanding warrant for the man.

Elmira sat numbly on the living room sofa and looked at the same spot on the carpet that Nick was looking at. Together they stared such a hole in the carpet that Elmira half-expected it to start smoking. Neither she nor Nick wanted to look at anything else. Certainly not at each other. He was embarrassed, and she was mortified.

The warrant was for desertion of a woman who claimed to be his wife and for emptying a joint bank account in both their names of eight hundred dollars and for theft of her brother's new camper truck. Of course, Nick said, all this had happened a long time in the past—nearly forty years ago—but, according to authorities in Texas, Jerome had been dodging the law ever since and the woman was still after him, although the brother-in-law was now deceased.

"I see," Elmira said. "He did mention being in Texas once."

Sneaking a glimpse of her face, Chief Nick could see she was stricken. He saw his news working on her around the eyes, and her mouth twitched. She covered it with her hand.

Behind her fingers, she said, "Go on back to the station, Nick. I'll bring him down myself. I don't want the neighbors seeing him carried off in a police car."

The chief hesitated, and then said all right. He didn't want to embarrass her further.

"I'll have to impound the camper," he said.

"Of course," Elmira replied, still not meeting his eye. "Send the tow truck on to get it."

"Don't be long," he said at the door, holding his hat in his hand.

"No," she said. "We'll be on down shortly."

When he was gone, Elmira went in the bathroom, closed and locked the door behind her, and shook all over like a wet dog. She sat on the edge of the tub, trembling and gulping air, until there was a knock on the door.

She unlocked the door, opened it, and looked at Susie Q, whose expression was a mixture of curiosity and anxiety.

"Susie Q," Elmira said.

"Why was the po-lice here? I saw his car. What's wrong?" she asked.

"The chief came to talk to me."

"What about?"

Elmira bit her lip. There was never any point in being evasive with Susie Q. It just made her more relentless. "Jerome," she said.

Immediately Susie Q said, "They're gonna take him away, aren't they?"

How she knew this Elmira couldn't fathom, but then Susie Q had always known things she wasn't supposed to know. And now she didn't ask why, perhaps because, to her way of thinking, there could be no justifiable reason for such an awful deed.

She began to cry. "I knew it was too good to be true," she said.

"What was too good to be true?" Elmira asked.

"Having him here. When something's too good to be true—like having a daddy or a special friend—it's always...." She choked on a sob before she continued. "Too good to be true."

"Hush," Elmira said, "Go pack. We're taking a trip."

"Where're we going?" Susie Q said. "We can't just go off and let 'em take Jerome to jail."

"We're taking him with us," Elmira said briskly. "Now go get your things."

"We're going on the lam?" Susie Q said, wide-eyed now and rising up on her toes. The excitement of the idea nearly knocked the breath out of her.

"Breathe," Elmira instructed, "and go get your things. Hurry."

Susie Q ran home. Sissy was at work, so she didn't have to deal with interference. She put a cap pistol, sixteen baseball cards, three pieces of bubble gum, and a turtle shell in a pillowcase and ran back to Elmira's.

Elmira said, "Did you get your toothbrush and pajamas?"

"No."

"Well, go back and get them. I'll meet you in the car."

CHAPTER SEVENTEEN

When Elmira had collected her own essentials in a tote bag, she hobbled around the house to where Jerome was—or had been—painting. He was nowhere in sight. His ladder was propped against the house, and an open bucket of paint and brush were beside it, but no Jerome. She called, but there was no answer.

She went back around the house to where the camper had been parked. It was gone.

She climbed in her car, where Susie Q was waiting, and said, "He's gone."

"Maybe he's gone to the paint store," Susie Q said. Her voice quavered.

"No," Elmira said. "I think he saw the chief's car and knew the jig was up."

"What's a jig?"

"A hoax."

"Hoax? You mean a ho-ax? Like in Elvis is dead?"

Elmira couldn't answer. She sank, empty as a sack against the steering wheel. Her shoulders shook, and she hid her face.

Her collapse frightened Susie Q, who was already in tears. "Elmira, Elmira," she crooned.

When Elmira didn't respond, Susie Q put her arms around her old aunt and leaned her head against her shoulder. Elmira heard sobs and realized, from a distance, they came from inside her. She had heard weeping, seen it, but never before in her whole life felt it. At the police station, she had witnessed diverse displays of rage and anguish, but she could not remember ever hearing herself cry. Now she experienced a wracking, ungodly noise from the inside out, and it consumed her. Her body was tight as a torque. Her face burned; her cheeks and forehead ached. She moaned with pain. Hot tears scalded her skin and stuffed her nose closed. She gasped for air.

Finally her sobbing eased, and she hiccupped and sat up. She looked at Susie Q and, seeing that the child was terrified, put her arm around her.

"It's just you and me now, kiddo," she said, and her mouth moved in an odd way she couldn't control. She wasn't sure she'd ever have full control again.

"Where'd he go?" Susie Q said softly.

"I don't know," Elmira said, as if it was an old story she'd heard many times before.

"He's gone for good?" Susie Q whispered and shook her head. She didn't believe it. "Let's go find him," she said.

"No," Elmira said. "He doesn't want us to find him, and I don't want to."

Susie Q didn't have anything to say to that. For once in her life, she'd encountered something she knew she didn't comprehend, something that was beyond her.

The two of them remained huddled together until the heat got them. Their skin and clothes had sealed together, and they had to pull themselves apart. Neither of them knew what to do now.

"Elmira," Susie Q said tentatively, "how far can you drive?"

"Oh, pretty far I guess. You know it's my left foot that's broken. Jerome just drove me around because...." Her voice trailed off. She didn't know how to finish the sentence.

"Could you drive all the way to Memphis?"

"I reckon. Why? Do you want to go to Memphis?"

"I thought...you know, since we're all packed and ready to go, we might as well take a trip. You know...somewhere."

"You did, did you?"

"I mean just if you want to."

"Dear heart," Elmira said, giving her a little hug, "I think a trip might be timely."

Susie Q could hardly believe her ears. Was this Elmira she was talking to or somebody who looked like Elmira but was a totally different person?

"Let's ask you mother's permission," Elmira said.

Now Susie Q knew for sure this was somebody new. The old Elmira never asked Sissy's—or anybody else's—permission for anything.

CHAPTER EIGHTEEN

The drive to Memphis was slow and quiet. Elmira had to stop and stretch her leg often, but Susie Q didn't seem impatient. They ate turkey sandwiches at a place reputed to raise its own turkeys, and Susie Q thought that was interesting and asked to see the turkeys but didn't complain when she was told they weren't nearby.

When they passed a water tank shaped like a giant peach, all she said was, "Elmira, look at that."

Elmira let the child be and found no cause to correct her or give her instructions. The two of them seemed to have reached the kind of consensus that comes out of a shared loss. They were alone, but together, in a place that could not be shared with others.

When they drove through Birmingham, Elmira thought about taking Susie Q to meet Cousin Mavis, but she didn't. This wasn't the trip for meeting long-lost relatives.

When they drove by the Vulcan statue atop Red Mountain, Susie Q asked, "Who's that?"

"Vulcan," Elmira told her. "What do you think of him?"

"I dunno," Susie Q said.

Elmira thought that was an adequate answer. She didn't know what she thought of him either.

They didn't stop to see him up close and kept on toward Memphis.

When they reached the outskirts of the big river town, Elmira stopped at a filling station and asked directions to the Peabody Hotel. She had heard of it, and she needed to rest. If Susie Q was disappointed they weren't going directly to Graceland—and she was—she kept the dissatisfaction to herself. Now, she understood, was no time to aggravate Elmira. In fact, she didn't think she would ever want to aggravate Elmira again. And she didn't want anybody else to aggravate her either. Elmira was sad, and right now Susie Q thought she needed looking after.

Not that Susie Q had ever looked after anybody but herself before. Until recently, Elmira had never seemed to need help—from her or anybody else. But now…well, now, Susie Q thought things were different. She didn't quite understand the difference, but she felt responsible for Elmira. Now that Jerome was gone, who was going to take care of her?

Susie Q sat in the lobby of the Peabody Hotel and watched ducks swim round and round in a little pond. She didn't know what ducks were doing in a hotel, but then she had never been in hotel before. Maybe it wasn't all that unusual. Like aquariums in seafood restaurants down on the coast. Maybe ducks just went with hotels out of some sort of tradition like fish tanks went with restaurants. Of course, the fish were usually tropical and beautiful unless it was the sort of restaurant where you ate the fish in the tank. These ducks were just ordinary ducks, and Susie Q hoped nobody was going to eat them.

She went up the elevator and found Elmira in a bed with too many pillows and a heavy spread. She wasn't crying. Susie Q didn't think she could bear for Elmira to cry anymore. There was a brightly lit bathroom next to the darkened bedroom, and Susie Q went in and closed the door. She turned on the water in the tub and climbed in, and while the water gushed out, she emptied little plastic bottles of lotion, shampoo, and bath gel—whatever that was—under the stream of water and watched them foam up. The mixture smelled flowery and felt soft on her skin.

She played with the bubbles and turned over on her stomach and pretended to swim. She didn't turn the water off until it was almost overflowing.

She stayed in the tub until the water cooled, and when she got out, she wrapped herself in a white towel almost as big as a blanket.

Elmira was asleep, and Susie Q curled up beside her and slept too.

CHAPTER NINETEEN

At Graceland the next day, everybody seemed to think Elvis was dead. The tour guides said he was still alive through his music, but Susie Q could tell they knew he was really dead and just didn't want to talk about it.

Of all the things in the house, she thought she liked the peacock windows the best. And the staircase. The staircase was huge, bigger than the one in *Gone with the Wind*. Susie Q could imagine Elvis sweeping Elmira up in his arms and carrying her up the steps.

Elmira, for her part, could imagine nothing of the sort. Her left leg hurt, and being on her feet had caused it to swell. She went outside and found a wrought-iron bench under a tree and sat down.

Truth was she didn't care about Graceland. It didn't seem to have anything to do with her private relationship with Elvis. That had always been between him and her and not something public and open to tourists. She'd let Susie Q satisfy her curiosity, and then they'd go home. Face the music there. Maybe she could ask the chief not to mention Jerome's outstanding warrant to anybody. She didn't think she could bear for folks to think she was an old fool. To realize she was an old fool, for surely that's what she was.

She surprised herself by smiling. Elmira Horton, of all people, an old fool! Well, what do you know? Life was full of surprises. She didn't know if she could live it down, but she sure had learned something—that everybody has a vulnerable spot, even her. She had always considered herself the one person in the world who was inherently sensible. The one person nobody could make a fool of. Now here she was, and the joke was on her. Maybe she was the biggest fool of all.

No, probably not. She knew for a fact there were bigger fools out there. She'd known some. But, she thought with an odd sense of relief, no one was immune from foolishness, including her. Perhaps no one was immune from love either because, after all, wasn't it love that, sooner or later, made fools of us all?

At least, she thought, of the lucky ones. Like me.

Somewhere deep inside herself—maybe in her heart—she felt a strange satisfaction. For the second time in her life, she had encountered a stirring kind of love. And this time in real life, not just in her dreams. Oh, she had always known the kind of love that comes with family ties and that, upon occasion, prompts not only a sense of responsibility but its own sort of sentiment. But what she felt for Jerome was unprecedented in her actual experience. She had loved that old, loose-jointed, shabby, toothless, rambling roofer with a longing that made her heart ache and left her shaking her head in wonder.

How about that? As a naïve teenager, she had been willing to believe she and Elvis had something special between them—or would have if she ever met him in the flesh. But with Jerome, she had experienced something special—romance such as it was—in real life.

Romance—that was it! She, Elmira Horton, had had a little romance! All right! Let people think what they would of that. Nobody ever understands anybody else's romances anyway. Why should they understand hers?

Of course, the object of her affection had apparently been married to somebody else and had a warrant out against him. Well, so be it. There was a good explanation for that, she felt sure.

When she realized she was making excuses for him, she laughed out loud. Oh ho, she thought, Elmira, you had it bad. Still do probably because you miss him and, admit it, you wish he was here right now. With him, this trip would have been fun. You and Susie Q would have had a fine time. Jerome knew how to make us happy.

And we made him happy too, she thought, and was reassured by the memory.

Of course, she had paid him in advance, and he hadn't finished painting the house. Still she knew he hadn't taken advantage of her. He hadn't tried to get anything from her that she didn't offer.

There was no way she could be angry with him. She was embarrassed—yes. Unlike Sammie Jo, Elmira cared what people thought of her. Or, at least, she always had. Maybe it was time to rethink that. After all, the people she knew who were happiest didn't seem to care a whit what others thought of them. Like Sammie Jo and Sissy for instance. Elmira had always thought both of them needed to be reined in a bit. But maybe they knew something she didn't. Maybe she could learn from them.

That was an odd thought. Good gracious, here she was so old and wise she'd just realized she didn't know everything. Sitting here at Graceland like a star-struck tourist—which, of course, was what she looked like—finally grasping what had always been missing in her life. Foolishness, that was it! When all was said and done, that was what made people happy.

She had never thought about being happy before. That had always seemed irrelevant. Childish. And now, here she sat realizing that in recent weeks she had been happy. She, Elmira Horton, had known the pleasure of shared happiness.

Was it gone? With Jerome? Had he brought it and now taken it away? She didn't know. Certainly she had learned something from him, and she'd always sensed that he cared for her. She wondered if he had learned anything from her. That was another odd thought, and she rather doubted it. Maybe she didn't have as much to teach others as they had to teach her.

But he had liked her! He had enjoyed being with her. And he had appreciated her. She gave a rueful shake of her head—and he had loved her too. She was sure of it.

When Susie Q came out of the house and found her aunt, she sank down on the grass beside Elmira's bench and leaned her head against her leg. "Tired?" Elmira asked.

Susie Q shook her head and ducked her chin. "He isn't here," she said, and Elmira realized she was crying. "I looked everywhere, even behind the doors and under the beds until the tour guide made me get back in line, and he wasn't anywhere to be found."

"No," Elmira agreed. "He isn't here. Neither one of them is here."

Before they left town, they went to see the Mississippi River. They sat high on the bank and watched Old Muddy flow past below them. Across the way was Arkansas and, beyond the Ozarks, the Great American West. Elmira had never been there. Someday she would go and take Susie Q with her. They'd see the Grand Canyon then. Maybe go all the way to California and see the Pacific Ocean. Hm-m-m. Maybe she would buy a camper, and they'd go in that.

But no, she thought. She might be an old fool, but she was not a sentimental old fool. Nobody in their right mind would stay cooped up in a camper truck with Susie Q, even if she was on her best behavior, for days at a time. No, they'd go in Elmira's comfortable car and stay in motels where she could get some rest. And they would eat in restaurants. Next spring they'd do that. On Susie Q's Easter vacation. Before it got too hot.

"I want to go home now," Susie Q said.

"Me too," Elmira said and took her hand.

CHAPTER TWENTY

When they got home, Elmira let Susie Q out at the house and went directly to the police station. Without speaking or letting anyone catch her eye, she walked through the squad room into the chief's office and closed the door.

"Elmira," Nick said from behind his desk. She couldn't read his expression.

"Chief," she said and sat down across from him. "Am I interrupting you?"

"No." He folded his hands atop his desk. "I hear you've been on a trip out of state. Sissy told me."

"Well, yes," she said and took a deep breath.

For a long moment, neither of them spoke.

Elmira broke the silence. "I know what this looks like, Nick, and if you feel you have to charge me, go ahead. I've come to turn myself in. But for the record, I...."

"And what would I charge you with, Elmira?"

"Well, aiding and abetting a fugitive, I assume, but for the record...."

"Elmira, he was gone 'fore I ever left your house."

"He was?"

"Yep. I was still standing on your front steps when I saw him turn the corner. I know you didn't warn him off. I followed him a ways on out of town."

"You catch him?"

"No."

"How come? That old camper won't go over fifty."

"I figured I'd leave well enough alone. An old warrant like that from out of state. Besides, if you didn't see no harm in him, that was good enough for me. You were always a good judge of character."

He shrugged.

She didn't know what to say. Finally she asked, "Who else knows there was a warrant out for him?"

"Nobody, and I plan to keep it that way. As far as I'm concerned, that's nobody's business but yours and mine."

"Thank you, Nick."

"Don't thank me. Just doing my job. No sense in chasing after somebody who's not causing trouble."

When Elmira got home, she went around to the side of the house where Jerome had been working when he left. He'd finished the other three sides, but this side remained part white and part blue. His ladder was still propped there where he had left it. She sealed the paint can he had left open on the ground.

Maybe I'll just leave things this way, she thought. She couldn't stand to think about somebody else finishing his job. Her house had been his to paint.

Inside, she found Susie Q on the living room couch. She was curled into herself like a wounded animal. "Elmira," she said, sitting up. "I need to tell you something, and I've got to say it even if it kills me."

"What in the world?"

"I took Elvis's eyes."

"I know."

"Yeah, but I can't get 'em back. I tried, but I can't. They're gone." And she told about giving them to Buddy and how Buddy traded them to someone passing through and how they were now gone forever.

Elmira didn't speak but studied the child's troubled face with such sympathetic eyes Susie Q began to squirm. She'd never been looked at this way before, and Elmira's expression alarmed her, and she began to cry.

"Elmira, please don't...," and that was as far as she got.

"Come with me," Elmira said and held out her hand.

She led Susie Q into her bedroom and opened the closet door. "There," she said, standing before the puzzle with her hands on Susie Q's shoulders. "See, no harm done. There's Elvis still smiling at us with his wonderful eyes. Nobody can ever take those away from us."

"But Elmira," Susie Q said, looking up at her and starting to protest.

"Hush," Elmira said. "For once in your life, be still and hush."

And, for once in her life, Susie Q did just that. She stood still and didn't say anything and, not knowing what to think, she didn't think anything either. She closed her eyes and listened to the rhythm of her own breathing and to the beating of Elmira's heart. They leaned into each other and rested together inside their shared space.

When Susie Q opened her eyes, she looked into Elvis's eyes, and he smiled.

"He's smiling at us," she whispered.

"Always," Elmira said.

Then the two of them lay down in Elmira's bed and took a nap.

EPILOGUE

One day in early December the three Horton girls reunite at the Galleria Shopping Mall in Hoover, about ten miles south of Birmingham. The occasion that brings them together is a meeting of the Alabama Pharmacists Association, of which Doc is past president. At a banquet at the Winfrey Hotel the previous evening, the organization gave him a plaque. This morning he has gone off to play golf with three cronies he hasn't seen for a while, so Sammie Jo and Elmira (who has accompanied Doc and Sammie Jo on this trip) have asked Mavis to meet them for lunch. When Mavis invited them to her house instead, they declined. After all, Elmira pointed out, the last time they were at their cousin's house, she went off and left them drinking coffee in her living room while she sneaked out the back door and drove away. So, no thank you. This time they'd let Mavis come to them.

They meet in the hotel lobby, which opens into the mall. Perhaps, even from an objective point of view, all three look better than they did the last time they met. Mavis keeps her hair tinted now, and she looks downright fashionable in a knit dress, matching stole, and heels. Of course, she is a few years younger than the other two. Still, they're holding their own. Since Sammie Jo has become Samantha, she's stopped wearing T-shirts with slogans on them, and today she's dolled up in an aqua pants suit. Never much concerned about her appearance, Elmira wears a plaid skirt, navy cardigan, and orthopedic shoes, but her hair is neat and she stands up straight as she can.

After greeting and inspecting one another, the trio makes their way around a group of photographers taking pictures of a plump elderly woman in a wheelchair. The woman's face is wrinkled, her hair is set in tight white curls, and she's wearing a voluminous lace pageant dress, a rhinestone tiara, and a banner across her sagging bosom that says Ms. Alabama Nursing Home. She smiles placidly into flashing cameras and accepts a gigantic bouquet of red roses as if it is her due.

As the Horton girls walk through the mall to the Ruby Tuesdays, they pass other aging beauties bedecked in similar garb. First comes an ancient black woman whose wizened face is partially masked by thick smudged glasses. She wears a peach satin dress, a tiara, and a banner that says Ms. Bessemer Rest Home. Pushed in her wheelchair by a weary-looking man who may be her son, she scowls straight ahead, looking neither left nor right.

Next comes a petite little lady in a burgundy lace dress, tiara, and silver shoes. She concentrates on walking carefully between two nursing attendants who support her by the elbows. Her banner says Ms. Shoals Crest Retirement Village.

Then they pass a sleeping fat woman outfitted in a brilliant blue caftan and tiara and a banner that says Ms. Southside Nursing Center. Her mouth is open, and her head slumps down into rolls of flesh. A pimply-faced orderly intent on getting her through the strolling shoppers pushes her with noticeable effort.

As each contestant approaches, the Horton girls stand aside. Each time Sammie Jo says, "My, aren't you pretty!" Mavis smiles politely, and Elmira looks up at the mall's glass-domed ceiling.

After settling themselves in a booth at the restaurant and placing their orders, they look from one to the other, not knowing what to say. It has been a long time since they have been together, and the parade of beauty queens has left them somewhat unnerved. No one knows what to say.

"Oh Lord, deliver us," Mavis finally remarks with a shake of her head.

"There but for the grace of God...," Elmira echoes her sentiment.

They smile sadly at each other.

"Oh, I don't know," Sammie Jo says cheerfully. "It might be sort of fun to dress up in a costume and be wheeled about."

"Didn't you get enough of that when you were homecoming queen?" Elmira asks.

"Well, yes, I suppose I did," Sammie Jo concedes, remembering that she is Samantha now and no longer needs the kind of attention beauty queens receive.

"I wonder where we'll be a few years down the road. When we're that old, maybe senile and disabled?" Mavis asks.

"Oh, I have it all planned," Sammie Jo says with confidence.

"You do?" Elmira asks. This is news to her.

"Yes, if Doc dies before I do, heaven help me...."

"Heaven help us all," Elmira says, rolling her eyes.

Ignoring her sister, Sammie Jo continues, "I'm going to check into the Grand Hotel over on the bay and invite Hopewell over. And the two of us will sit on the veranda and rock and talk and laugh our heads off."

"Oh my god," Elmira mutters, holding her head. "Better Hopewell than me." She doesn't know what she will do if she has to tend Sammie Jo through senility.

But, happy with her plan, Sammie Jo turns to her cousin and says, "How about you, Mavis? Are you going to a nursing home?"

"Lordy, Lordy," Mavis says. "I'm looking for alternatives. When I was on a cruise a while back, I met an old woman—she must have been in her nineties—who books one cruise after another. She says a cruise ship is the ideal retirement home. Nice accommodations with good food, and they wait on you hand and foot. The scenery changes constantly, and you meet new people all the time. Plus you have beauty shops, saunas, message therapists, all on board, and—best of all—excellent health care. What more could you want?"

Elmira studies Mavis in silence and wonders about her stability these days, but Sammie Jo responds to her cousin's plan as if it's a reasonable possibility.

"That does sound nice," she agrees, "but personally I can't tolerate boats. The Mad Dog gets me."

"The Mad Dog?" Mavis raises her eyebrows.

"Meniere's Disease," Elmira explains.

"Too bad," Mavis says. She doesn't know what Meniere's disease is and hopes they are not going to tell her. Everywhere she goes these days, aches, pains, and ailments are all so-called "seniors" talk about. "What about you?" she asks Elmira to change the subject. "Have you picked out a nursing home?"

The suggestion offends Elmira, but she bites her tongue. "Well now," she says, "you two have some pretty fancy plans. Not too practical though, given what they'd cost. I, for one, can't afford a fancy resort or cruise ships."

Feeling reprimanded, Mavis and Sammie Jo busy themselves with their salads. They were being frivolous, of course, but don't like having it pointed out. Neither of them wants to think about being incapacitated.

"I have another plan," Elmira tells them with authority. "I'm going to print up a batch of counterfeit bills, which I'll run through the washer and dryer a few times so they'll look old.

Then I'm going to go around Piney handing out homemade twenties to pay for my groceries, gas, and necessities. You know, whatever I need."

She takes a bite of noodles in cream sauce and wipes her mouth with a napkin.

With forks paused in midair, Mavis and Sammie Jo stare at her.

Elmira is enjoying herself. "Of course," she continues, "I won't get away with it, and Chief Nick will be obliged to call in the feds because passing counterfeit currency is a federal offense. So I'll have to go to trial, where I will confess, and I'll be sentenced to ten to twenty years and sent to the women's federal penitentiary.

"Speaking of excellent health care. You can't beat what they'd give a little old lady with a sterling reputation and a sweet disposition in the federal pen."

With that pronouncement, Elmira takes another bite of pasta and washes it down with iced tea.

For a moment, there is dead silence at the table. Then, in unison, the three of them begin to chuckle and then to howl with laughter.

"Talk about a sensible plan, there you have it!" Sammie Jo says, delighted with Elmira's whimsy.

Mavis says, "Lordy, Lordy!" and shakes her hands in the air, unable to breathe.

Elmira grins, pleased with herself.

After a quiet moment, Sammie Jo says, "Heaven only knows where we'll all end up. But, in the meantime, we have some time. Sweet blessed time."

Holding that thought, the three look at one another as if memorizing the moment.

After lunch, before Mavis departs, Sammie Jo says to her, "Now don't send me any set-abouts for Christmas. I've cleaned out my house, and I want it to stay that way."

Taken aback, Mavis is at a loss how to respond. The three of them have not exchanged presents in years. But, she thinks, maybe she will send them gifts this year. They are her only living relatives—the only ones worth counting anyway. Besides, the three of them seem on a different footing now. Today something in their relationship has shifted. No longer is anyone keeping score or taking offense or bringing up past resentments. It has been a good lunch.

So, she says to Sammie Jo, "What would you like?"

"What would I like?" Sammie Jo asks uncertainly. She hadn't meant to be asking for a present and now doesn't know what to say. She'd only said that about no set-abouts to brag on her recent housecleaning. And for something to say.

"Well," she concedes, "I don't know. I can't think of a thing. I have pretty much everything I want."

"Me too," Mavis agrees. "It's taken a long time, but I feel well supplied and perfectly satisfied. How about you, Elmira?"

"Oh, I don't need a thing."

"Yes, but is there anything you want?"

Elmira considers this. "Maybe a six pack of cherry soda," she allows. "Maybe even a whole case."

Somewhat surprised, Mavis says, "I'll put that on my list."

Then, in turn, the sisters embrace their cousin. Even Elmira gives her a big enveloping hug. All three stand speechless for a moment, then Mavis walks away. When she reaches the exit to the parking lot, she turns and calls back to them, "I'll come to see you on visitors' day."

"I'll count on it," Elmira replies.

Made in the USA
Lexington, KY
17 November 2010